The Goddess of Atvatabar

Map of the Interior World.

The Goddess of
Atvatabar

William R. Bradshaw

LEONAUR

The Goddess of Atvatabar
by William R. Bradshaw

Leonaur is an imprint of Oakpast Ltd

Material original to this edition and
presentation of text in this form
copyright © 2010 Oakpast Ltd

ISBN: 978-0-85706-290-1 (hardcover)
ISBN: 978-0-85706-289-5 (softcover)

http://www.leonaur.com

Publisher's Notes

The views expressed in this book are not necessarily
those of the publisher.

Introduction

It is proper that some explanation be made as to the position occupied by the following story in the realm of fiction, and that a brief estimate should be made of its literary value.

Literature may be roughly classified under two heads—the creative and the critical. The former is characteristic of the imaginative temperament, while the latter is analytical in its nature, and does not rise above the level of the actual. Rightly pursued, these two ways of searching out truth should supplement each other. The poet finds in God the source of matter; the man of science traces matter up to God. Science is poetry inverted: the latter sees in the former confirmation of its airiest flight; it is synthetic and creative, whereas science dissects and analyzes. Obviously, the most spiritual conceptions should always maintain a basis in the world of fact, and the greatest works of literary art, while taking their stand upon the solid earth, have not feared to lift their heads to heaven. The highest art is the union of both methods, but in recent times realism in an extreme form, led by Zola and Tolstoi, and followed with willing though infirm footsteps by certain American writers, has attained a marked prominence in literature, while romantic writers have suffered a corresponding obscuration. It must be admitted that the influence of the realists is not entirely detrimental; on the contrary, they have imported into literature a nicety of observation, a heedfulness of workmanship, a mastery of technique, which have been greatly to its advantage. Nevertheless, the novel of hard facts has failed to prove its claim to infallibility. Facts in themselves are impotent to account for life. Every material fact is but the representative on the plane of sense of a corresponding truth on the spiritual plane. Spirit is the substance; fact the shadow only, and its whole claim to existence lies in its relation to spirit. Bulwer declares in one of his early productions that the *ideal* is the only true *real*.

In the nature of things a reaction from the depression of the realistic school must take place. Indeed, it has already set in, even at the moment of the realists' apogee. A dozen years ago the author of *John Inglesant*, in a work of the finest art and most delicate spirituality, showed that the spell of the ideal had not lost its efficacy, and the books that he has written since then have confirmed and emphasized the impression produced by it. Meanwhile, Robert Louis Stevenson and Rider Haggard have cultivated with striking success the romantic vein of fiction, and the former, at least, has acquired a mastery of technical detail which the realists themselves may envy. It is a little more than a year, too, since Rudyard Kipling startled the reading public with a series of tales of wonderful force and vividness; and whatever criticism may be applied to his work, it incontestably shows the dominance of a spiritual and romantic motive. The realists, on the other hand, have added no notable recruits to their standard, and the leaders of the movement are losing rather than gaining in popularity. The spirit of the new age seems to be with the other party, and we may expect to see them enjoy a constantly widening vogue and influence.

The first practical problem which confronts the intending historian of an ideal, social, or political community is to determine the locality in which it shall be placed. It may have no geographical limitations, like Plato's *Republic*, or Sir Philip Sidney's *Arcadia*. Swift, in his *Gulliver's Travels*, appropriated the islands of the then unknown seas, and the late Mr. Percy Greg boldly steered into space and located a brilliant romance on the planet Mars. Mr. Haggard has placed the scene of his romance "She" in the unexplored interior of Africa. After all, if imagination be our fellow-traveller, we might well discover El Dorados within easy reach of our own townships.

Other writers, like Ignatius Donnelly and Edward Bellamy, have solved the problem by anticipating the future. Anything will do, so that it be well done. The real question is as to the writer's ability to interest his readers with supposed experiences that may develop mind and heart almost as well as if real.

The Goddess of Atvatabar, like the works already mentioned, is a production of imagination and sentiment, the scene of action being laid in the interior of the earth. It is true that the notion has heretofore existed that the earth might be a hollow sphere. The early geologists had a theory that the earth was a hollow globe, the shell being no thicker in proportion to its size than that of an egg. This idea was revived by Captain Symmes, with the addition of polar openings. Jules Verne takes his readers, in one of his romances, to the interior of a volcano, and Bulwer, in his "Coming Race," has constructed a world of underground caverns. Mr. Bradshaw, however, has swept aside each and all of these preliminary explorations, and has kindled the fires of an interior sun, revealing an interior world of striking magnificence. In view of the fact that we live on an exterior world, lit by an exterior sun, he has supposed the possibility of similar interior conditions, and the crudity of all former conceptions of a hollow earth will be made vividly apparent to the reader of the present volume. *The Goddess of Atvatabar* paints a picture of a new world, and the author must be credited with an original conception. He has written out of his own heart and brain, without reference to or dependence upon the imaginings of others, and it is within the truth to say that in boldness of design, in wealth and ingenuity of detail, and in lofty purpose, he has not fallen below the highest standard that has been erected by previous writers.

Mr. Bradshaw, in his capacity of idealist, has not only created a new world, but has decorated it with the skill and conscientiousness of the realist, and has achieved a work of art which may rightfully be termed great. Jules Verne, in composing a similar story, would stop short with a description of mere physical adventure, but in the present work Mr. Bradshaw goes beyond the physical, and has created in conjunction therewith an interior world of the soul, illuminated with the still more dazzling sun of ideal love in all its passion and beauty. The story is refreshingly independent both in conception and method, and the insinuation, "*Beati qui ante nos nostra dixerunt*," cannot be quoted against him. He has imagined and worked out the whole thing for himself, and he merits the full credit that belongs to a discoverer.

The Goddess of Atvatabar is full of marvellous adventures on land and sea and in the aerial regions as well. It is not my purpose at

7

present to enumerate the surprising array of novel conceptions that will charm the reader. The author, by the condition of his undertaking, has given *carte blanche* to his imagination. He has created a complete society, with a complete environment suited to it. The broadest generalization, no less than the minutest particulars, have received careful attention, and the story is based upon a profound understanding of the essential qualities of human nature, and is calculated to attain deserved celebrity. Among the subjects dear to the idealist's heart, perhaps none finds greater favour than that which involves the conception of a new social and political order, and our author has elaborated this subject on fresh lines of thought, making his material world enclose a realm of spiritual tenderness, even as the body is the continent and sensible manifestation of the soul.

The forces, arts, and aspirations of the human soul are wrought into a symmetrical fabric, exhibiting its ideal tendencies. The evident purpose of the writer is to stimulate the mind, by presenting to its contemplation things that are marvellous, noble, and magnificent. He has not hesitated to portray his own emotions as expressed by the characters in the book, and is evidently in hearty sympathy with everything that will produce elevation of the intellectual and emotional ideals.

The style in which the story is told is worthy of remark. In the beginning, when events are occurring within the realm of things already known or conceived of, he speaks in the matter-of-fact, honest tone of the modern explorer; so far as the language goes we might be reading the reports of an arctic voyage as recounted in the daily newspaper; there is the same unpretentiousness and directness of phrase, the same attention to apparently commonplace detail, and the same candid portrayal of wonder, hope, and fear. But when the stupendous descent into the interior world has been made, and we have been carried through the intermediary occurrences into the presence of the beautiful goddess herself, the style rises to the level of the lofty theme and becomes harmoniously imaginative and poetic. The change takes place so naturally and insensibly that no jarring contrast is perceived; and a subdued sense of humour, making itself felt at the proper moment, redeems the most daring flights of the work from the reproach of extravagance.

Mr. Bradshaw is especially to be commended for having the

courage of his imagination. He wastes no undue time on explanations, but proceeds promptly and fearlessly to set forth the point at issue. When, for example, it becomes necessary to introduce the new language spoken by the inhabitants of the interior world, we are brought in half a dozen paragraphs to an understanding of its characteristic features, and proceed to the use of it without more ado. A more timid writer would have misspent labour and ingenuity in dwelling upon a matter which Mr. Bradshaw rightly perceived to be of no essential importance; and we should have been wearied and delayed in arriving at the really interesting scenes.

The philosophy of the book is worthy of more serious notice. The religion of the new race is based upon the worship of the human soul, whose powers have been developed to a height unthought of by our section of mankind, although on lines the commencement of which are already within our view. The magical achievements of theosophy and occultism, as well as the ultimate achievements of orthodox science, are revealed in their most amazing manifestations, and with a sobriety and minuteness of treatment that fully satisfies what may be called the transcendental reader. The whole philosophic and religious situation is made to appear admirably plausible: but we are gradually brought to perceive that there is a futility and a rottenness inherent in it all, and that for the Goddess of Atvatabar, lofty, wise, and immaculate though she be, there is, nevertheless, a loftier and sublimer experience in store. The finest art of the book is shown here: a deep is revealed underneath the deep, and the final outcome is in accord with the simplest as well as the profoundest religious perception.

But it would be useless to attempt longer to withhold the reader from the marvellous journey that awaits him. A word of congratulation, however, is due in regard to the illustrations. They reach a level of excellence rare even at this day; the artists have evidently been in thorough sympathy with the author, and have given to the eye what the latter has presented to the understanding. A more lovable divinity than that which confronts us on the golden throne it has seldom been our fortune to behold; and the designs of animal-plants are as remarkable as anything in modern illustrative art: they are entirely unique, and possess a value quite apart from their artistic grace.

The chief complaint I find to urge against the book is that it stops long before my curiosity regarding the contents of the interior world is satisfied. There are several continents and islands yet to be heard from. But I am reassured by the termination of the story that there is nothing to prevent the hero from continuing his explorations; and I shall welcome the volume which contains the further points of his extraordinary and commendable enterprise.

Julian Hawthorne

CHAPTER 1

A Polar Catastrophe

I had been asleep when a terrific noise awoke me. I rose up on my couch in the cabin and gazed wildly around, dazed with the feeling that something extraordinary had happened. By degrees becoming conscious of my surroundings, I saw Captain Wallace, Dr. Merryferry, Astronomer Starbottle, and Master-at-Arms Flathootly beside me.

"Commander White," said the captain, "did you hear that roar?"

"What roar?" I replied. "Where are we?"

"Why, you must have been asleep," said he, "and yet the roar was enough to raise the dead. It seemed as if both earth and heaven were split open."

"What is that hissing sound I hear?" I inquired.

"That, sir," said the doctor, "is the sound of millions of flying sea-fowl frightened by the awful noise. The midnight sun is darkened with the flight of so many birds. Surely, sir, you must have heard that dreadful shriek. It froze the blood in our veins with horror."

I began to understand that the *Polar King* was safe, and that we were all still alive and well. But what could my officers mean by the terrible noise they talked about?

I jumped out of bed saying, "Gentlemen, I must investigate this whole business. You say the *Polar King* is safe?"

"Shure, sorr," said Flathootly, the master-at-arms, "the ship lies still anchored to the ice-fut where we put her this afthernoon. She's all right."

I at once went on deck. Sure enough the ship was as safe as if in harbour. Birds flew about in myriads, at times obscuring the sun, and now and then we heard growling reverberations from distant icebergs, answering back the fearful roar that had roused them from their polar sleep.

The sea, that is to say the enormous ice-pack in which we lay, heaved and fell like an earthquake. It was evident that a catastrophe of no common character had happened.

What was the cause that startled the polar midnight with such unwonted commotion?

Sailors are very superstitious; with them every unknown sound is a cry of disaster. It was necessary to discover what had happened, lest the courage of my men should give way and involve the whole expedition in ruin.

The captain, although alarmed, was as brave as a lion, and as for Flathootly, he would follow me through fire and water like the brave Irishman that he was. The scientific staff were gentlemen of education, and could be relied upon to show an example of bravery that would keep the crew in good spirits.

"Do you remember the creek in the ice-foot we passed this morning," said the captain, "the place where we shot the polar bear?"

"Quite well," I said.

"Well, the roar that frightened us came from that locality. You remember all day we heard strange squealing sounds issuing from the ice, as though it was being rent or split open by some subterranean force."

The entire events of the day came to my mind in all their clearness. I did remember the strange sounds the captain referred to. I thought then that perhaps they had been caused by Professor Rackiron's shell of *terrorite* which he had fired at the southern face of the vast range of ice mountains that formed an impenetrable barrier to the pole. The men were in need of a change of diet, and we thought the surest way of getting the sea-fowl was to explode a shell among them. The face of the ice cliffs was the home of innumerable birds peculiar to the Arctic zone. There myriads of gulls, kittiwakes, murres, guillemots, and such like creatures, made the ice alive with feathered forms.

The *terrorite* gun was fired with ordinary powder, and although we could approach no nearer the cliffs than five miles, on account of the solid ice-foot, yet our chief gun was good for that distance.

The shell was fired and exploded high up on the face of the crags. The effect was startling. The explosion brought down tons of the frosty marble. The debris fell like blocks of iron that rang with a piercing cry on the ice-bound breast of the ocean. Millions of sea-fowl of every conceivable variety darkened the air. Their rushing wings sounded like the hissing of a tornado. Thousands were killed by the shock. A detachment of sailors under First Officer Renwick brought in heavy loads of dead fowl for a change of diet. The food, however, proved indigestible, and made the men ill.

We resolved, as soon as the sun had mounted the heavens from his midnight declension, to retrace our course somewhat and discover the cause of the terrible outcry of the night. We had been sailing for weeks along the southern ice-foot that belonged to the interminable ice hills which formed an effectual barrier to the pole. Day after day the *Polar King* had forced its way through a gigantic floe of piled-up ice blocks, floating cakes of ice, and along ridges of frozen enormity, cracked, broken, and piled together in endless confusion. We were in quest of a northward passage out of the terrible ice prison that surrounded us, but failed to discover the slightest opening. It had become a question of abandoning our enterprise of discovering the North Pole and returning home again or abandoning the ship, and, taking our dogs and sledges, brave the nameless terrors of the icy hills. Of course in such case the ship would be our base of supplies and of action in whatever expedition might be set on foot for polar discovery.

About six o'clock in the morning of the 20th of July we began to work the ship around, to partially retrace our voyage. All hands were on the lookout for any sign of such a catastrophe as might have caused the midnight commotion. After travelling about ten miles we reached the creek where the bear had been killed the day before. The man on the lookout on the top-mast sung out:

"Creek bigger than yesterday!"

Before we had time to examine the creek with our glasses he sung out:

"Mountains split in two!"

Sure enough, a dark blue gash ran up the hills to their very summit, and as soon as the ship came abreast of the creek we saw that the range of frozen precipices had been riven apart, and a streak of dark blue water lay between, on which the ship might possibly reach the polar sea beyond.

Dare we venture into that inviting gulf?

The officers crowded around me. "Well, gentlemen," said I, "what do you say, shall we try the passage?"

"We only measure fifty feet on the beam, while the fissure is at least one hundred feet wide; so we have plenty of room to work the ship," said the captain.

"But, captain," said I, "if we find the width only fifty feet a few miles from here, what then?"

"Then we must come back," said he, "that's all."

"Suppose we cannot come back—suppose the walls of ice should begin to close up again?" I said.

"I don't believe they will," said Professor Goldrock, who was our naturalist and was well informed in geology.

"Why not?" I inquired.

"Well," said he, "to our certain knowledge this range of ice hills extends five hundred miles east and west of us. The sea is here over one hundred and fifty fathoms deep. This barrier is simply a congregation of icebergs, frozen into a continuous solid mass. It is quite certain that the mass is anchored to the bottom, so that it is not free to come asunder and then simply close up again. My theory is this: Right underneath us there is a range of submarine rocks or hills running north and south. Last night an earthquake lifted this submarine range, say, fifty feet above its former level. The enormous upward pressure split open the range of ice resting thereon, and, unless the mountains beneath us subside to their former level, these rent walls of ice will never come together again. The passage will become filled up with fresh ice in a few hours, so that in any case there is no danger of the precipices crushing the ship."

"Your opinion looks feasible," I replied.

"Look," said he; "you will see that the top of the crevasse is wider than it is at the level of the water, one proof at least that my theory is correct."

The professor was right; there was a perceptible increase in the width of the opening at the top.

To make ourselves still more sure we took soundings for a mile east and west of the chasm, and found the professor's theory of a sub-

I SIGNALLED THE ENGINEER FULL SPEED AHEAD, AND IN A SHORT TIME WE
CROSSED THE ICE-FOOT AND ENTERED THE CHASM.

marine range of hills correct. The water was shallowest right under the gap, and was very much deeper only a short distance on either side. I said to the officers and sailors: "My men, are you willing to enter this gap with a view of getting beyond the barrier for the sake of science and fortune and the glory of the United States?"

They gave a shout of assent that robbed the gulf of its terrors. I signalled the engineer full speed ahead, and in a short time we crossed the ice-foot and entered the chasm.

It could be nothing else but an upheaval of nature that caused the rent, as the distance was uniform between the walls however irregular the windings made. And such walls! For a distance of twenty miles we sailed between smooth glistening precipices of *palaeocrystic* ice rising two hundred feet above the water. The opening remained perceptibly wider at the top than below.

After a distance of twenty miles the height gradually decreased until within a distance of another fifty miles the ice sank to the level of the water.

The sailors gave a shout of triumph which was echoed from the ramparts of ice. To our astonishment we found we had reached a mighty field of loose pack ice, while on the distant horizon were glimpses of blue sea!

CHAPTER 2

The Cause of the Expedition

The *Polar King*, in lat. 84', long. 151' 14", had entered an ocean covered with enormous ice-floes. What surprised us most was the fact that we could make any headway whatever, and that the ice wasn't frozen into one solid mass as every one expected. On the contrary, leads of open water reached in all directions, and up those leading nearest due north we joyfully sailed.

May the 10th was a memorable day in our voyage. On that day we celebrated the double event of having reached the furthest north and of having discovered an open polar sea.

Seated in the luxurious cabin of the ship, I mused on the origin of this extraordinary expedition. It was certain, if my father were alive he would fully approve of the use I was making of the wealth he had left me. He was a man utterly without romance, a hard-headed man of facts, which quality doubtless was the cause of his amassing so many millions of dollars.

My father could appreciate the importance of theories, of enthusiastic ideals, but he preferred others to act upon them. As for himself he would say, "I see no money in it for me." He believed that many enthusiastic theories were the germs of great fortunes, but he always said with a knowing smile, "You know it is never safe to be a pioneer in anything. The pioneer usually gets killed in creating an inheritance for his successors." It was a selfish policy which arose from his financial experiences, that in proportion as a man was selfish he was successful.

I was always of a totally different temperament to my father. I was romantic, idealistic. I loved the marvellous, the magnificent, the miraculous and the mysterious, qualities that I inherited from my mother. I used to dream of exploring tropic islands, of visiting the lands of Europe and the Orient, and of haunting temples and tombs, palaces and pagodas. I wished to discover all that was weird and wonderful on the earth, so that my experiences would be a description of earth's girdle of gold, bringing within reach of the enslaved multitudes of all nations ideas and experiences of surpassing novelty and grandeur that would refresh their parched souls. I longed to whisper in the ear of the labourer at the wheel that the world was not wholly a blasted place, but that here and there oases made green its barrenness. If he could not actually in person mingle with its joys, his soul, that neither despot nor monopolist could chain, might spread its wings and feast on such delights as my journeyings might furnish.

How seldom do we realize our fondest desires! Just at the time of my father's death the entire world was shocked with the news of the failure of another Arctic expedition, sent out by the United States, to discover, if possible, the North Pole. The expedition leaving their ship frozen up in Smith's Sound essayed to reach the pole by means of a monster balloon and a favouring wind. The experiment might possibly have succeeded had it not happened that the car of the balloon struck the crest of an iceberg and dashed its occupants into a fearful crevasse in the ice, where they miserably perished. This calamity brought to recollection the ill-fated Sir John Franklin and *Jeanette* expeditions; but, strange to say, in my mind at least, such disasters produced no deterrent effect against the setting forth of still another enterprise in Arctic research.

From the time the expedition I refer to sailed from New York until the news of its dreadful fate reached the country, I had been reading almost every narrative of polar discovery. The consequence was I had awakened in my mind an enthusiasm to penetrate the sublime secret of the pole. I longed to stand, as it were, on the roof of the world and see beneath me the great globe revolve on its axis. There, where there is neither north, nor south, nor east, nor west, I could survey the frozen realms of death. I would dare to stand on the very pole itself with my few hardy companions, monarch of an empire of ice, on a spot that never feels the life-sustaining revolutions of the earth. I knew that on the equator, where all is light, life, and movement, continents and seas flash through space at the rate of one thousand miles an hour, but on the pole the wheeling of the earth is as dead as the desolation that surrounds it.

I had conversed with Arctic navigators both in England and the United States. Some believed the pole would never be discovered. Others, again, declared their belief in an open polar sea. It was generally conceded that the Smith's Sound route was impracticable, and that the only possible way to approach the pole was by the Behring Strait route, that is, by following the 170th degree of west longitude north of Alaska.

I thought it a strange fact that modern sailors, armed with all the resources of science and with the experience of numerous Arctic voyages to guide them, could get only three degrees nearer the pole than Henry Hudson did nearly three hundred years ago. That redoubtable seaman possessed neither the ships nor men of later voyagers nor the many appliances of his successors to mitigate the intense cold, yet his record in view of the facts of the case remains triumphant.

It was at this time that my father died. He left me the bulk of his property under the following clause in his will:

"I hereby bequeath to my dear son, Lexington White, the real estate, stocks, bonds, shares, title-deeds, mortgages, and other securities that I die possessed of, amounting at present market prices to over five million dollars. I desire that my said son use this property for some beneficent purpose, of use to his fellow-men, excepting what money may be necessary for his personal wants as a gentleman."

I could scarcely believe my father was so wealthy as to be able to leave me so large a fortune, but his natural secretiveness kept him from mentioning the amount of his gains, even to his own family. No sooner did I realize the extent of my wealth than I resolved to devote it to fitting out a private expedition with no less an object than to discover the North Pole myself. Of course I knew the undertaking was extremely hazardous and doubtful of success. It could hardly be possible that any private individual, however wealthy and daring, could hope to succeed where all the resources of mighty nations had failed.

Still, these same difficulties had a tremendous power of attracting fresh exploits on that fatal field. Who could say that even I alone might not stumble upon success? In a word, I had made up my mind to set forth in a vessel strong and swift and manned by sailors experienced in Arctic voyages, under my direct command. The expedition would be kept a profound secret; I would leave New York ostensibly for Australia, then, doubling Cape Horn, would make direct for Behring Sea. If I failed, none would be the wiser; if I succeeded, what fame would be mine!

CHAPTER 3

Beginning the Voyage

I determined to build a vessel of such strength and equipment as could not fail, with ordinary good fortune, to carry us through the greatest dangers in Arctic navigation. Short of being absolutely frozen in the ice, I hoped to reach the pole itself, if there should be sufficient water to float us. The vessel, which I named the *Polar King*, although small in size was very strong and compact. Her length was 150 feet and her width amidships 50 feet. Her frames and planking were made of well-seasoned oak. The outer planking was sheathed in steel plates from four to six inches in thickness. This would protect us from the edges of the ancient ice that might otherwise cut into the planking and so destroy the vessel.

The ship was armed as follows: A colossal *terrorite* gun that stood in the centre of the deck, whose 250-pound shell of explosive *terrorite* was fired by a charge of gunpowder without exploding the *terrorite* while leaving the gun. This was to destroy icebergs and heavy pack-ice. A battery of twelve 100-pounder *terrorite* guns, with shells also fired with powder. All shells would explode by percussion in striking the object aimed at. A battery of six guns of the Gatling type, to repel boarding parties in case we reached a hostile country. There was also an armoury of magazine rifles, revolvers, cutlasses, etc., as well as 50 tons of gunpowder, *terrorite*, and revolver-rifle cartridges.

The ship was driven by steam, the triple-expansion engine being 500-horse power and the rate of speed twenty-five miles an hour. By an important improvement on the steam engine, invented by myself, one ton of coal did the work of 50 tons without such improvement. The bunkers held 250 tons of coal, which was thus equal to 12,500 tons in any other vessel. There was also an auxiliary engine for working the pumps, electric dynamo, cargo, anchors, etc. One of the most useful fittings was the apparatus that both heated the ship and condensed the sea water for consumption on board ship, and for feeding the boilers.

The ship's company was as follows:

Officers
Lexington White, Commander of the Expedition
Captain, William Wallace
First Officer Renwick, Navigating Lieutenant
Second Officer Austin, Captain of the *terrorite* gun
Third Officer Haddock, Captain of the main deck battery
Scientific Staff
Professor Rackiron, Electrician and Inventor
Professor Starbottle, Astronomer
Professor Goldrock, Naturalist
Doctor Merryferry, Ship's Physician
Petty Officers
Master-at-Arms Flathootly
First Engineer Douglass
Second Engineer Anthoney
Pilot Rowe
Carpenter Martin
Painter Hereward
Boatswain Dunbar
Others
95 able-bodied seamen, including mechanics, gunners,
cooks, tailors, stokers, etc.
Total of ship's company   110 souls

Believing in the absolute certainty of discovering the pole and our consequent fame, I had included in the ship's stores a special triumphal outfit for both officers and sailors. This consisted of a Viking helmet of polished brass surmounted by the figure of a silver-plated polar bear, to be worn by both officers and sailors. For the officers a uniform of navy-blue cloth was provided, consisting of frock coat embroidered with a profusion of gold striping on shoulders and sleeves, and gold-striped pantaloons. For each sailor there was provided a uniform consisting of outer navy-blue cloth jacket, with inner blue serge jacket, having the figure of a globe embroidered in gold on the breast of the latter, surmounted by the figure of a polar bear in silver. Each officer and sailor was armed with a cutlass having the figure of a polar bear in silver-plated brass surmounting the hilt. This was the gala dress, but for every-day use the entire company was supplied with the usual Arctic outfit to withstand the terrible climate of high latitudes.

Foreseeing the necessity of pure air and freedom from damp surroundings, I had the men's berths built on the spar deck, contrary to the usual custom. The spar deck was entirely covered by a hurricane deck, thus giving complete protection from cold and the stormy weather we would be sure to encounter on the voyage.

Our only cargo consisted of provisions, ship's stores, ammunition, coal, and a large stock of chemical batteries and a dynamo for furnishing electricity to light the ship. We also shipped largely of materials to manufacture shells for the *terrorite* guns.

The list of stores included an ample supply of tea, coffee, canned milk, butter, pickles, canned meats, flour, beans, peas, pork, molasses, corn, onions, potatoes, cheese, prunes, pemmican, rice, canned fowl, fish, pears, peaches, sugar, carrots, etc. The refrigerator contained a large quantity of fresh beef, mutton, veal, etc. We brought no luxuries except a few barrels of rum for special occasion or accidents. Exposure and hard work will make the plainest food seem a banquet. Thus fully equipped, the *Polar King* quietly left the Atlantic Basin in Brooklyn, N. Y., ostensibly on a voyage to Australia. The newspapers contained brief notices to the effect that Lexington White, a gentleman of fortune, had left New York for a voyage to Australia and the Southern Ocean, via Cape Horn, and would be gone for two years.

We left on New Year's Day, and had our first experience of a polar pack in New York Bay, which was thickly covered with crowded ice. Gaining the open water, we soon left the ice behind, and, after a month's steady steaming, entered the Straits of Magellan, having touched at Monte Video for supplies and water.

Leaving the Straits we entered the Pacific Ocean, steering north. Touching at Valparaiso, we sailed on without a break until we arrived at Sitka, Alaska, on the 1st of March.

Receiving our final stores at Sitka, the vessel at once put to sea again, and in a week reached Behring Strait and entered the Arctic Ocean. I ordered the entire company to put on their Arctic clothing, consisting of double suits of underclothing, three pairs of socks, ordinary wool suits, over which were heavy furs, fur helmets, moccasins and Labrador boots.

All through the Straits we had encountered ice, and after we had sailed two days in the Arctic Sea, a hurricane from the northwest smote us, driving us eastward over the 165th parallel, north of Alaska. We were surrounded with whirlwinds of snow frozen as hard as hail. We experienced the benefit of having our decks covered with a steel shell. There was plenty of room for the men to exercise on deck shielded from the pitiless storm that drove the snow like a storm of gravel before it. Exposure to such a blizzard meant frost-bite, perhaps death. The outside temperature was 40 below zero, the inside temperature 40 above zero, cold enough to make the men digest an Arctic diet.

We kept the prow of the ship to the storm, and every wave that washed over us made thicker our cuirass of ice. It was gratifying to note the contrast between our comfortable quarters and the howling desolation around us.

While waiting for the storm to subside we had leisure to speculate on the chances of success in discovering the pole.

Captain Wallace had caused to be put up in each of our four cabins the following tables of Arctic progress made since Hudson's voyage in 1607:

Record of Highest Latitudes Reached

Hudson 80' 23" in 1607	Phipps 80' 48" in 1773
Scoresby 81' 12" in 1806	Payer 82' 07" in 1872
Meyer 82' 09" in 1871	Parry 82' 45" in 1827
Aldrich 83' 07" in 1876	Markham 83' 20" in 1876
Lockwood 83' 24" in 1883	

"Does it not seem strange," said I, "that nearly three hundred years of naval progress and inventive skill can produce no better record in polar discovery than this? With all our skill and experience we have only distanced the heroic Hudson three degrees; that is one degree for every hundred years. At this rate of progress the pole may be discovered in the year 2600."

"It is a record of naval imbecility," said the captain; "there is no reason why our expedition cannot at least touch the 85th degree. That would be doing the work of two hundred years in as many days."

"Why not do the work of the next 700 years while we are at it?" said Professor Rackiron. "Let us take the ship as far as we can go and then bundle our dogs and a few of the best men into the balloon and finish a job that the biggest governments on earth are unable to do."

"That's precisely what we've come here for," said I, "but we must have prudence as well as boldness, so as not to throw away our lives unnecessarily. In any case we will beat the record ere we return."

CHAPTER 4

Our Adventures in the Polar Sea

The storm lasted four days. On its subsidence we discovered ourselves completely surrounded with ice. We were beset by a veritable polar pack, brought down by the violence of the gale. The ice was covered deeply with snow, which made a dazzling scene when lit by the brilliant sun. We seemed transported to a new world. Far as the eye could see huge masses of ice interposed with floe bergs of vast dimensions. The captain allowed the sailors to exercise themselves on the solidly frozen snow. It was impossible to get any fresh meat, as the pack, being of a temporary nature, had not yet become the home of bear, walrus, or seal.

We saw a water sky in the north, showing that there was open water in that direction, but meantime we could do nothing but drift in the embrace of the ice in an easterly direction. In about a week the pack began to open and water lanes to appear. A more or less open channel appearing in a north-easterly direction, we got the ship warped around, and, getting up steam, drew slowly out of the pack.

Birds began to appear and flocks of ducks and geese flew across our track, taking a westerly course. We were now in the latitude of Wrangel Island, but in west longitude 165. We had the good fortune to see a large bear floating on an isolated floe toward which we steered. I drew blood at the first shot, but Flathootly's rifle killed him. The sailors had fresh meat that day for dinner.

The day following we brought down some geese and elder ducks that sailed too near the ship. We followed the main leads in preference to forcing a passage due north, and when in lat. 78' long. 150' the watch cried out "Land ahead!" On the eastern horizon rose several peaks of mountains, and on approaching nearer we discovered a large island extending some thirty miles north and south. The ice-foot surrounding the land was several miles in width, and bringing the ship alongside, three-fourths of the sailors, accompanied by the entire dogs and sledges, started for the land on a hunting expedition.

It was a fortunate thing that we discovered the island, for, with our slow progress and monotonous confinement, the men were getting tired of their captivity and anxious for active exertion.

The sailors did not return until long after midnight, encouraged to stay out by the fact that it was the first night the sun remained entirely above the horizon.

It was the 10th of April, or rather the morning of the 11th, when the sailors returned with three of the five sledges laden with the spoils of the chase. They had bagged a musk ox, a bear, an Arctic wolf, and six hares—a good day's work. Grog was served all around in honour of the midnight sun and the capture of fresh meat. We dressed the ox and bear, giving the offal as well as the wolf to the dogs, and revelled for the next few days in the luxury of fresh meat.

The island not being marked on our charts, we took credit to ourselves as its discoverers, and took possession of the same in the name of the United States.

The captain proposed to the sailors to call it Lexington Island in honour of their commander, and the men replied to his proposition with such a rousing cheer that I felt obliged to accept the distinction.

Flathootly reported that there was a drove of musk oxen on the island, and before finally leaving it we organized a grand hunting expedition for the benefit of all concerned.

Leaving but five men, including the first officer and engineer, on board to take care of the ship, I took charge of the hunt. After a rough-and-tumble scramble over the chaotic ice-foot, we reached the mainland in good shape, save that a dog broke its leg in the ice and had to be shot. Its companions very feelingly gave it a decent burial in their stomachs.

Mounting an ice-covered hillock, we saw, two miles to the southeast in a valley where grass and moss were visible, half a

A SEMICIRCLE OF RIFLES WAS DISCHARGED AT THE UNHAPPY BRUTES, AND TWO FELL DEAD IN THEIR TRACKS.

dozen musk oxen, doubtless the entire herd. We adopted the plan of surrounding the herd, drawing as near the animals as possible without alarming them. Sniffing danger in the south-easterly wind, the herd broke away to the northwest. The sailors jumped up and yelled, making the animals swerve to the north. A semi-circle of rifles was discharged at the unhappy brutes. Two fell dead in their tracks and the remaining four, badly wounded, wheeled and made off in the opposite direction. The other wing of the sailors now had their innings as we fell flat and heard bullets fly over us. Three more animals fell, mortally wounded. A bull calf, the only remnant of the herd on its legs, looked in wonder at the sailor who despatched it with his revolver. The dogs held high carnival for an hour or more on the slaughtered oxen. We packed the sledges with a carcass on each, and in due time regained the ship, pleased with our day's work.

Leaving Lexington Island we steered almost due north through a vast open pack. On the 1st of May we arrived in lat. 78' 30" west long. 155' 50", our course having been determined by the lead of the lanes in the enormous drifts of ice. Here another storm overtook us, travelling due east. We were once more beset, and drifted helplessly for three days before the storm subsided. We found ourselves in long. 150' again, in danger of being nipped. The wind, suddenly drifting to the east, reopened the pack for us to our intense relief.

Taking advantage of some fine leads and favourable winds, we passed through leagues of ice, piled-up floes and floe bergs, forming scenes of Arctic desolation beyond imagination to conceive. At last we arrived at a place beyond which it was impossible to proceed. We had struck against the gigantic barrier of what appeared to be an immense continent of ice, for a range of ice-clad hills lay only a few miles north of the *Polar King*. At last the sceptre of the Ice King waved over us with the command, "Thus far and no further."

CHAPTER 5

We Enter the Polar Gulf

How the *Polar King* penetrated what appeared an insurmountable obstacle, and the joyful proof that the hills did not belong to a polar continent, but were a continuous congregation of icebergs, frozen in one solid mass, are already known to the reader.

The gallant ship continued to make rapid progress toward the open water lying ahead of us. Mid-day found us in 84' 10" north latitude and 150' west longitude. The sun remained in the sky as usual to add his splendour to our day of deliverance and exultation.

We felt what it was to be wholly cut off from the outer world. The chances were that the passage in the ice would be frozen up solid again soon after we had passed through it. Even with our dogs and sledges the chances were against our retreat southward.

The throbbing of the engine was the only sound that broke the stillness of the silent sea. The laugh of the sailors sounded hollow and strange, and seemed a reminder that with all our freedom we were prisoners of the ice, sailing where no ship had ever sailed nor human eye gazed on such a sea of terror and beauty.

Happily we were not the only beings that peopled the solitudes of the pole. Flocks of gulls, geese, ptarmigan, and other Arctic fowls wheeled round us. They seemed almost human in their movements, and were the links that bound us to the beating hearts far enough off then to be regretted by us. Every man on board the vessel was absorbed in thought concerning our strange position. The beyond? That was the momentous question that lay like a load on every soul. While thinking of these things, Professor Starbottle inquired, if with such open water as we sailed in, how soon I expected to reach the pole.

"Well," said I, "we ought to be at the 85th parallel by this time. Five more degrees, or 300 miles, will reach it. The *Polar King* will cover that distance easily in twenty hours. It is now 6 P.M.; at 2 p.m. tomorrow, the 12th of May, we will reach the pole."

Professor Starbottle shook his head deprecatingly. "I am afraid, commander," said he, "we will never reach the pole."

His look, his voice, his manner, filled me with the idea that something dreadful was going to happen. My lips grew dry with a sudden excitement, as I hastily inquired why he felt so sure we would never reach the object of our search.

"What time is it, commander?" said he.

I pulled forth my chronometer; it was just six o'clock.

"Well, then," said he, "look at the sun. The sun has swung round to the west, but hasn't fallen any."

I looked at the sun, which, sure enough, stood as high as at mid-day. I was paralyzed with a nameless dread. I stood rooted to the deck in anticipation of some dreadful horror.

"Good heavens!" I gasped, "what—what do you mean?"

"I mean," said he, "the sun is not going to fall again on this course. It's we who are going to fall."

"The sun will fall to its usual position at midnight," I stammered; "wait—wait till midnight."

"The sun won't fall at midnight," said the professor. "I am afraid to tell you why," he added.

"In God's name," I shouted, "tell me the meaning of this!"

I will never forget the feeling that crazed me as the professor said: "I fear, commander, we are falling into the interior of the earth!"

"You are mad, sir!" I shouted. "It cannot be—we are sailing to the North Pole."

"Wait till midnight, commander," said he, shaking my hand.

I took his hand and echoed his words—"Wait till midnight." After a pause I inquired if he had mentioned his extraordinary fears to any one else.

"Not a soul," he replied.

"Then," said I, "say nothing to anybody until midnight."

"Ay, ay, sir," said he, and disappeared.

The sailors evidently expected that something was going to happen on account of the sun standing still in the heavens. They were gathered in groups on deck discussing the situation with bated breath. I noticed them looking at me with wild eyes, like sheep cornered for execution. The officers avoided calling my attention to the unusual sight, possibly divining I was already fully excited by it.

Never was midnight looked for so eagerly by any mortal on earth as I awaited the dreadful hour that would either confirm or dispel my fears.

Midnight came and the sun had not fallen in the sky! There he stood as high as at noonday, at least five degrees higher than his position twenty-four hours before.

Professor Starbottle, approaching me, said: "Commander, my prognostication was correct; you see the sun's elevation is unchanged since mid-day. Now one of two things has happened—either the axis of the earth has approached five degrees nearer the plane of its orbit since mid-day or we are sailing down into a subterranean gulf! That the former is impossible, mid-day today will disprove. If my theory of a subterranean sea is correct, the sun will fall below the horizon at mid-day, and our only light will be the earth-light of the opposite mouth of the gulf into which we are rapidly sinking."

"Professor," said I, "tell the officers and the scientific staff to meet me at once in the cabin. This is a tremendous crisis!"

Ere I could leave the deck the captain, officers, doctor, naturalist, Professor Rackiron, and many of the crew surrounded me, all in a state of the greatest consternation.

CHAPTER 6

Day Becomes Night and Night Day

"Commander," said Captain Wallace, "I beg to report that the pole star has suddenly fallen five degrees south from its position overhead, and the sun has risen to his mid-day position in the sky! I fear we are sailing into a vast polar depression something greater than the description given in our geographies, that the earth is flattened at the poles."

"Do you really think, captain," I inquired, "that we are sailing into a hollow place around the pole?"

"Why, I am sure of it," said he. "Nothing else can explain the sudden movement of the heavenly bodies. Remember, we have only passed the 85th parallel but a few miles and ought to have the pole star right overhead."

"Professor Starbottle has a theory," I said, "that may account for the strange phenomena we witness. Let these gentlemen hear your theory, professor."

The professor stated very deliberately what he had already communicated to me, *viz.*: that we were really descending to the interior of the earth, that the bows of the ship were gradually pointing to its centre, and that if the voyage were continued we would find ourselves swallowed up in a vast polar gulf leading to God knows what infernal regions.

The terror inspired by the professor's words was plainly visible on every face.

"Let us turn back!" shouted some of the sailors.

"My opinion," said the captain, "is that we have entered a polar depression; it is impossible to think that the earth is a hollow shell into which we may sail so easily as this."

"If I might venture a remark," said Pilot Rowe, "I think Professor Starbottle is right. If the earth is a hollow shell having a subterranean ocean, we can sail thereon bottom upward and masts downward, just as easily as we sail on the surface of the ocean here."

"I believe an interior ocean an impossibility," said the captain.

"You're right, sorr," said the master-at-arms, "for what would keep the ship sticking to the wather upside down?"

"I don't say that the earth is absolutely a hollow sphere," said the professor, "but I do say this, we are now sailing into a polar abyss, and if the sun disappears at noon today it will be because we have sailed far enough into the gulf to put the ocean over which we have sailed between us and that luminary. If the sun disappears at noon, depend upon it we will never reach the pole, which will forever remain only the ideal axis of the earth."

"Do you mean to say," I inquired, "that what men have called the pole is only the mouth of an enormous cavern, perhaps the vestibule of a subterranean world?"

"That is precisely the theory I advance to account for this strange ending of our voyage," said the professor.

The murmurs of excitement among the men again broke out into wild cries of "Turn back the ship!"

I encouraged the men to calm themselves. "As long as the ship is in no immediate danger," said I, "we can wait till noonday and see if the professor's opinion is supported by the behaviour of the sun. If so, we will then hold a council of all hands and decide on what course to follow. Depart to your respective posts of duty until mid-day, when we will decide on such action as will be for the good of all."

The men, terribly frightened, dispersed, leaving Captain Wallace, First Officer Renwick, Professors Starbottle, Goldrock, and Rackiron, the doctor and myself together.

Dreadful as was the thought of quietly sinking into a polar gulf from which possibly there might be no escape, yet the bare possibility of returning to tell the world of our tremendous discovery created a desire to explore still further the abyss into which we had entered. I confess that my first feeling of terror was rapidly giving way to a passion for discovery. What fearful secrets might not be held in the darkness toward which we undoubtedly travelled!

THE TERROR INSPIRED BY THE PROFESSOR'S WORDS WAS PLAINLY
VISIBLE ON EVERY FACE.

Would it be our fortune to pierce the darkness and silence of a polar cavern? When I thought of the natural terror of the sailors, I dared not think of our sailing further than mid-day, in case we had really entered an abyss.

"Commander," said Professor Starbottle, "this is the most important day, or rather night, of the voyage. I propose we stay on deck and enjoy the sunlight as long as we can."

One glance at the sun sufficed to tell us the truth; he was rapidly falling from the sky. At midnight he was 20 degrees and at 1 A.M. only 18 degrees above the waste of waters.

This proved we were as rapidly taking leave of the glorious orb, on an expedition fraught with the greatest peril and unknown possibilities of science, conquest, and commerce.

By a tacit consent we turned our attention to the scene around us. The water was very free from ice, only here and there icebergs floated. The diminished radiation of light produced a weird effect, growing more spectral as the sun sank in the heavens.

Professor Goldrock pointed out a flock of geese actually flying ahead of us into the gulf, if gulf indeed it were. We considered this a good omen and took heart accordingly.

The captain pointed out a strange apparition in the north, but which was really south of the pole, and discoverable with the glass. It appeared to be the limb of some rising planet between us and the sun that seemed faintly illuminated by moonlight. Professor Starbottle said it was the opposite edge of the polar gulf that was about to envelop us. It was illuminated by the earth-light reflected from the same ocean on which the *Polar King* floated.

The sun, as he swung round to the south, fell rapidly to the horizon, and at eight o'clock disappeared below the water. Was there ever a day in human experience as portentous as that? When did the sun set at 8 A.M. in the Arctic summer, leaving the earth in darkness? We knew then that Professor Starbottle's theory of a polar gulf was a truth beyond question. It was a fearful fact!

But the grandest spectacle we had yet seen now lay before us. The opposite rapidly rising limb of the polar gulf, 500 miles away, was brilliantly illuminated by the sun's rays far overhead, and its splendid earth-light, twenty times brighter than moonlight, falling upon us, compensated for the sudden obliteration of the daylight.

It was mid-day, and our only light was the earth-light of the gulf. There stood over us the still rising circular rim of the ocean, sparkling like an enormous jewel. It was a bewildering experience. In the light of that distant ocean I assembled the men on deck and thus addressed them:

"My men, when we started on the present expedition you stipulated for a voyage of discovery to the North Pole (if possible) and return to New York again. The first part of the voyage is happily accomplished. We alone of all the explorers who have essayed polar discovery have been rewarded with a sight of the pole. The mystery of the earth's axis is no longer a secret. Here before your eyes is the axis on which the earth performs its daily revolution. The North Pole is an immense gulf 500 miles in diameter and of unknown depth. Within this gulf lies our ship, at least a hundred miles below the level of the outer ocean!

"The question we are now called upon to decide is this: Are we to remain satisfied with our present achievement, turn back the ship, and go home without attempting to discover whither leads this enormous gulf? As far as the officers of the ship and the scientific staff are concerned, as far as I myself am concerned, I am satisfied if we were once back in New York again, our first thought would be to return hither, and, taking up the thread of our journey, endeavour to explore the farthest recesses of the gulf."

I was here interrupted by loud applause from the entire officers and many of the men.

"This being so, why should we waste a journey to New York and back again for nothing? Why not, with our good ship well armed and provisioned, that has in safety carried us so far, why not, I say, proceed further, taking advantage of the only opportunity the ages of time have ever offered to man to explore earth's profoundest secrets?

"Who knows what oceans, what continents, what nations, it may be of men like ourselves, may not exist in a subterranean world? Who knows what gold, what silver, what precious stones are there piled perhaps mountains high? Are we to tamely throw aside the possibility of such glory on account of base fears, and, returning home, allow others to snatch from our grasp the golden prize?

"My men, I cannot think you will do this. Our future lies entirely in your hands. We cannot proceed further on our voyage without your assistance. I will not compel a single man to go further against his will. I call for volunteers for the interior world! I am willing to lead you on; who will follow me?"

We Discover the Interior World

The officers and sailors responded to my speech with ringing cheers. Every man of them volunteered to stay by the ship and continue our voyage down the gulf. Whatever malcontents there may have been among the sailors, those, influenced by the prevailing enthusiasm, were afraid to exhibit any cowardice, and all were unanimous for further exploration.

I signalled our resolution by a discharge of three guns, which created the most thrilling reverberations in the mysterious abyss.

Starting the engine again, the prow of the *Polar King* was pointed directly toward the darkness before us, toward the centre of the earth. We were determined to explore the hollow ocean to its further confines, if our provisions held out until such a work would be accomplished.

We hoped at midnight to obtain our last look at the sun, as we would then be brought into the position of the opposite side of the watery crater down which we sailed. At eleven o'clock the sun rose above the limb of the gulf, which was now veiled in darkness. We were gladdened with two hours of sunlight, the sun promptly setting at 1 A.M. of the new day.

We continued our voyage in the semi-darkness, the prow of the vessel still pointed to the centre of the earth, while the polar star shone in the outer heavens on the horizon directly over the rail of the vessel's stern.

It did not appear to us that we were dropping straight down into the interior of the earth; on the contrary, we always seemed to float on a horizontal sea, and the earth seemed to turn up toward us and the polar cavern to gradually engulf us. The sight we beheld that day was inexpressibly magnificent. Five hundred miles above us rose the crest of the circular polar sea. Its upper hemisphere glowed with the light of the unseen sun. We were surrounded by fifteen hundred miles of perpendicular ocean, crowned with a diadem of icebergs!

Glorious as was the sight, the sailors were terribly apprehensive of nameless disasters in such monstrous surroundings. It was impossible for them to understand how the ocean roof could remain suspended above us like the vault of heaven. The idea of being able to sail down a tubular ocean, the antechamber of some infernal world, was incomprehensible. We were traversing sea-built corridors, whose oscillating floors and roof remained providentially apart to permit us to explore the mystery beyond.

Mid-day on the 13th of May brought no sight of the sun, but only a deepening twilight, the dim reflection of the bright sky we had left behind. The further we sailed into the gulf the less its diameter grew. When we had penetrated the vast aperture some two hundred and fifty miles, we found the aerial diameter was reduced to about fifty miles, thus forming a conical abyss. We were clearly sailing down a gigantic vortex or gulf of water, and we began to feel a diminishing gravity the further we approached the central abyss.

The cavernous sea was subject to enormous undulations, or tidal waves, either the result of storms in the interior of the earth or mighty adjustments of gravity between the interior and exterior oceans. As we were lifted up upon the crest of an immense tidal wave several of the sailors, as well as the lookout, declared they had seen a flash of light, in the direction of the centre of the earth!

We were all terribly excited at the news, and as the ship was lifted on the crest of the next wave, we saw clearly an orb of flame that lighted up the circling undulations of water with the flush of dawn! We were now between two spectral lights—the faint twilight of the outer sun and the intermittent dawn of some strange source of light in the interior of the earth.

The sailors crowded to the top of both masts and stood upon cross-trees and rigging, wildly anxious to discover the meaning of the strange light and whatever the view from the next crest of waters would reveal.

AT THIS MOMENT A WILD CRY AROSE FROM THE SAILORS. WITH
ONE VOICE THEY SHOUTED, "THE SUN! THE SUN!"

"What do you think is the source of this strange illumination," I inquired of the captain, "unless it is the radiance of fires in the centre of the earth?"

"It comes from some definite element of fire," said the professor, "the nature of which we will soon discover. It certainly does not belong to the sun, nor can I attribute it to an aurora dependent on solar agency."

"Possibly," said Professor Rackiron, "we are on the threshold of if not the infernal regions at least a supplementary edition of the same. We may be yet presented at court—the court of Mephistopheles."

"You speak idle words, professor," said I. "On the eve of confronting unknown and perhaps terrible consequences you walk blindfold into the desperate chances of our journey with a jest on your lips."

"Pardon me, commander," said he, "I do not jest. Have not the ablest theologians concurred in the statement that hell lies in the centre of the earth, and that the lake of fire and brimstone there sends up its smoke of torment? For aught we know this lurid light is the reflection of the infernal fires."

At this moment a wild cry arose from the sailors. With one voice they shouted:

"The sun! The sun! The sun!"

The *Polar King* had gained at last the highest horizon or vortex of water, and there, before us, a splendid orb of light hung in the centre of the earth, the source of the rosy flame that welcomed us through the sublime portal of the pole!

As soon as the astonishment consequent on discovering a sun in the interior of the earth had somewhat subsided, we further discovered that the earth was indeed a hollow sphere. It was now as far to the interior as to the exterior surface, thus showing the shell of the earth to be at the pole at least 500 miles in thickness. We were half way to the interior sphere.

Professor Starbottle, who had been investigating the new world with his glass, cried out: "Commander, we are to be particularly congratulated; the whole interior planet is covered with continents and oceans just like the outer sphere!"

"We have discovered an El Dorado," said the captain, with enthusiasm; "if we discover nothing else I will die happy."

"The heaviest elements fall to the centre of all spheres," said Professor Goldrock. "I am certain we shall discover mountains of gold ere we return."

"I think we ought to salute our glorious discovery," said Professor Rackiron. "You see the infernal world isn't nearly so bad a place as we thought it was."

I ordered a salute of one hundred *terrorite* guns to be given in honour of our discovery, and the firing at once began. The echoed roaring of the guns was indescribably grand. The trumpet-shaped caverns of water, both before and behind us, multiplied the heavy reverberations until the air of the gulf was rent with their thunder. The last explosion was followed by long-drawn echoes of triumph that marked our introduction to the interior world.

Strange to say that on the very threshold of success there are men who suddenly take fright at the new conditions that confront them. It appeared that Boatswain Dunbar and eleven sailors who had unwillingly sailed thus far refused to proceed further with the ship, being terrified at the discovery we had made. I could have obliged them to have remained with us, but their reason being possibly affected, I saw that their presence as malcontents might in time cause a mutiny, or at all events an ever-present, source of trouble. They were wildly anxious to leave the ship and return home; consequently I gave them liberty to depart. The largest boat was lowered, together with a mast and sails. I gave the command to Dunbar, and furnished the boat with ample stores and plenty of clothing. I also gave them one-half of the dogs and two sledges for crossing the ice. When the men were finally seated Dunbar cast off the rope and steered for the outer sea. We gave them a parting salute by firing a gun, and in a short time they were lost in the darkness of the gulf.

CHAPTER 8

Extraordinary Loss of Weight

The first thought that occurred to us after the excitement of discovery had somewhat subsided was that the interior of the earth was in all probability a habitable planet, possessing as it did a life-giving luminary of its own, and our one object was to get into the planet as quickly as possible. A continual breeze from the interior ocean of air passed out of the gulf. Its temperature was much higher than that of the sea on which we sailed, and it was only now that we began to think of laying off our Arctic furs.

A closer observation of the interior sun revealed the knowledge that it was a very luminous orb, producing a climate similar to that of the tropics or nearly so. As we entered the interior sphere the sun rose higher and higher above us, until at last he stood vertically above our heads at a height of about 3,500 miles. We saw at once what novel conditions of life might exist under an earth-surrounded sun, casting everywhere perpendicular shadow, and neither rising nor setting, but standing high in heaven, the lord of eternal day. We seemed to sail the bottom of a huge bowl or spherical gulf, surrounded by oceans, continents, islands, and seas.

A peculiar circumstance, first noticed immediately after arriving at the centre of the gulf, was that each of us possessed a sense of physical buoyancy, hitherto unfelt.

Flathootly told me he felt like jumping over the mast in his newly-found vigour of action, and the sailors began a series of antics quite foreign to their late stolid behaviour. I felt myself possessed of a very elastic step and a similar desire to jump overboard and leap miles out to sea. I felt that I could easily jump a distance of several miles.

Professor Starbottle explained this phenomenal activity by stating that on the outer surface of the earth a man who weighs one hundred and fifty pounds, would weigh practically nothing on the interior surface of an earth shell of any equal thickness throughout. But the fact that we did weigh something, and that the ship and ocean itself remained on the under surface of the world, proved that the shell of the earth, naturally made thicker at the equator by reason of centrifugal gravity than at the poles, has sufficient equatorial attraction to keep open the polar gulf. Besides this centrifugal gravity confers a certain degree of weight on all objects in the interior sphere.

"I'll get a pair of scales," said Flathootly, "an' see how light I am in weight."

"Don't mind scales," said the professor, "for the weights themselves have lost weight."

"Well, I'm one hundred and seventy-five pounds to a feather," said Flathootly, "an' I'll soon see if the weights are right or not."

"The weights are right enough," said the professor, "and yet they are wrong."

"An' how can a thing be roight and wrang at the same time, I'd loike to know? We'll thry the weights anyway," said the Irishman.

So saying, Flathootly got a little weighing machine on deck, and, standing thereon, a sailor piled on the weights on the opposite side.

He shouted out: "There now, do you see that? I'm wan hundred and siventy-siven pounds, jist what I always was."

"My dear sir," said the professor, "you don't seem to understand this matter; the weights have lost weight equally with yourself, hence they still appear to you as weighing one hundred and seventy-seven pounds."

"Excuse me, sorr," said Flathootly. "If the weights have lost weight, the chap that stole it was cute enough to put it back again before I weighed meself. Don't you see wid yer two eyes I'm still as heavy as iver I was?"

"You will require ocular demonstration that what I say is correct. Here, sir, let me weigh you with this instrument," said the professor.

The instrument referred to was a huge spring-balance with which it was proposed to weigh Flathootly. One end of it was fastened to the mast, and to the hook hanging from the other end the master-at-arms secured himself. The hand on the dial plate moved a certain distance and stopped at seventeen pounds. The expression on the Irishman's face was something awful to behold.

"Does this machine tell the thruth?" he inquired in a tearful voice.

We assured him it was absolutely correct. He only weighed seventeen pounds.

"Oh, howly Mother of Mercy!" yelled Flathootly. "Consumption has me by the back of the neck. I've lost a hundred and sixty pounds in three days. Oh, sir, for the love of heaven, take me back to me mother. I'm kilt entoirely."

It was some time before Flathootly could understand that his lightness of weight was due to the lesser-sized world he was continually arriving upon, together with centrifugal gravity, and that we all suffered from his affliction of being each "less than half a man" as he termed it. The weighing of the weights wherewith he had weighed himself proved conclusively that the depreciation in gravity applied equally to everything around us.

The extreme lightness of our bodies, and the fact that our muscles had been used to move about ten times our then weight, was the cause of our wonderful buoyancy.

The sailors began leaping from the ship to a large rock that rose out of the water about half a mile off. Their agility was marvellous, and Flathootly covered himself with glory in leaping over the ship hundreds of feet in the air and alighting on the same spot on deck again.

Their officers and scientific staff remained on deck as became their dignity, although tempted to try their agility like the sailors.

Flathootly surprised us by leaping on a yardarm and exclaiming: "Gintlemen, I tell ye what it is, I'm no weight at all."

"How do you make that out?" said the professor.

"Well, Oi've been thinking," said he, "that, as you say, we're in the middle of the two wurrlds. Now it stands to sense that the wan wurrld, I mane the sun up there, is pullin' us up an' the t'other wurrld is pullin' us down, an' as both wurrlds is pulling aqually, why av corse we don't amount to no weight at all. How could I turn fifteen summersaults at wance if I was any weight? That shows yer weighing machine is all wrang again."

"How can you stand on the deck if you are no weight?" inquired the professor.

"Why, I'm only pressing me feet on the boards," said the Irishman; "look here!" So saying, he leaped from the yard and revolved in the air at least twenty times before alighting on the deck.

"Now," said the professor, "I'll explain why you only weigh seventeen pounds as indicated by the spring-balance. We have sailed, down the gulf 500 miles, haven't we?"

"Yis, sorr."

"And here we are sailing upside down on the inside roof of the world—"

"Sailin' upside down? Indeed, sorr, an' ye can't make me believe that, for shure I'm shtandin' on me feet like yourself, head uppermost."

"Well, whether you believe it or not, we are sailing upside down, just as ships going to Australia sail upside down as compared with ships sailing the North Atlantic. But the point of gravity is this: Here we are surrounded on all sides by the shell of the earth, which attracts equally in all directions. Hence all objects in the interior world have no weight as regards whatever thickness of the earth's shell surrounds them. You see, weight is caused by an object having the world on one side of it. Thus both the world and the object attract each other according to the density and distance apart. What we call a pound weight is a mass of matter attracted by the earth on its surface with a force equal to the weight of sixteen ounces. A pound weight on the surface of the earth weighs sixteen ounces, and all the mighty volume of our planet, with all its mountains, continents and seas, weighs only sixteen ounces on the surface of a pound weight. The earth may still weigh many millions of tons as regards the sun, but as regards a pound weight it only weighs sixteen ounces."

"That is an illustration of Flathootly's mental calibre," said Captain Wallace. "He only believes what his brain can accommodate in the way of knowledge."

"God bless the captain," said Flathootly, "I'm shure his brain is as big as mine any day in the week."

"Now," continued the astronomer, "it seems to me that the substances of the earth, rocks, metals, and water, have, under the influence of centrifugal gravity, massed themselves very thickly at the equator or point of greatest motion, and stretch toward the poles in a gradually-lessening mass until the polar gulfs are reached. Thus the earth's shell resembles a musk-melon with the inside cleaned out."

"It makes me mouth wather to think of it," said Flathootly.

"Now, listen," said the astronomer; "we are also under the influence of the earth's centrifugal motion, and wherever we are on the interior surface we swing round our circle of latitude in twenty-four hours, and thus men, ship, and ocean are held up against the interior vault like a boy being able to hold water in a vertical position at the bottom of the pail he swings round him at the end of a cord."

"Don't you think, professor," I inquired, "we will become heavier as we approach the region of greatest motion under the equator?"

"I don't think so," he replied, "for the ocean around the poles has naturally gravitated to the internal as well as to the external equator, to restore the equilibrium of gravity. The reason why a man does not weigh less on the external equator than at the poles, although flying around at the rate of a thousand miles an hour, is that the deeper ocean, that is, the extra twenty-six miles that the earth is thicker on the equator, counterbalances by its attraction the loss of weight due to the rapid centrifugal motion, and so preserves in all objects on the earth a uniform weight."

"The whole thing," said Flathootly, "is as clear as mud. I'm glad to know, sorr, I haven't lost me entire constitution at all evints, an' if I can only carry home what weight I've got lift I'll make a fortune in a dime museum."

CHAPTER 9

Afloat on the Interior Ocean

As the *Polar King* sped southward over the interior sea the wonders of the strange world we had discovered began to dawn upon us. The colossal vault rose more and more above us and the sun threw his mild and vertical rays directly upon ship and sea, producing a most delightful climate. The ocean had a temperature of 75 degrees Fahr. and the air 85 degrees. We were absolutely sailing upside down to an inhabitant of the outer sphere, yet we seemed to ourselves to be sailing naturally erect on the sea with the sun above us.

Our first experience in the internal sphere was that of a sudden storm. The sun grew dark and appeared like a disc of sombre gold. The ocean was lashed by a furious hurricane into incredible mountains of water. Every crest of the waves seemed a mass of yellow flame. The internal heavens were rent open with gulfs of sulphur-coloured fire, while the thunder reverberated with terrible concussions. The ship would spin upon the water as though every wave were a whirlpool. A golden-yellow phosphorescence covered the ocean. The water boiled in maddening eddies of lemon-coloured seas, while from the hurricane decks streamed cataracts of saffron fire. The lightning, like streaks of molten gold, hurled its burning darts into the sea. Everything bore the glow of amber-coloured fire. The sailors congratulated themselves on the shelter provided by the deck overhead. The motion of the ship exceeded all former experiences, for it leaped and plunged in a terrific manner. It was a question whether we would survive the storm or not, so violent was the shaking up both ship and men received. Fortunately, the loss of weight in everything, which was the cause of the rapid motion, permitted no more damage than would be caused by a lesser storm on heavier objects.

The professor stated that he believed the tempest was occasioned by a polar tidal wave of air rushing into the interior sphere, to supply the exhaustion caused by outgoing warm currents, owing perhaps to a periodical overheating of the air by the internal sun. When a certain volume of the air was expelled, so that it could no longer resist external pressure, then the external air rushed down the polar gulf, creating by meeting warm outward-flowing currents cyclones such as we were then experiencing.

By degrees the storm abated, the sea grew calm, the heavens above us became clearer, and the sun assumed the rose-colour he first presented to our gaze, standing right in the zenith.

The only damage done to the crew was a few broken limbs and some severe bruises. The ship had lost several spars, and one of her boats was blown out of its lashings on deck and was lost.

It was a week since we had left the outer world, and what a change had occurred in that short space of time! The excitement had been so intense that not a man of us had slept during that period, and as for meals, we had forgotten about them altogether.

A general order was given the cooks to prepare a banquet to duly inaugurate our discovery of the new world. Both officers and men, including myself, sat down at the same table, where we satisfied the cravings of a week's hunger.

I expressed my heartfelt pleasure in the safety of the crew and ship so far in making so tremendous a discovery. I relied on the courage and loyalty of the crew for still further explorations in the strange and mysterious planet we had discovered. I declared that those who shared the dangers of the expedition would also share in whatever reward fortune might bestow upon us.

It is needless to say such sentiments were enthusiastically applauded.

I praised my able coadjutor, Captain Wallace, without whose skilful seamanship not a soul of us could ever have reached that secret world. "It was he," said I, "who has guided us without a chart through five hundred miles of polar cavern to the realms of Pluto, to Plutusia, the interior world. On him again we must depend for a safe exit when our explorations are ended."

Flathootly attempted to make a speech, but, like the rest of the company, fell asleep, and in less than half an hour afterward not a soul remained awake, excepting Professor Starbottle and myself.

We both struggled against sleep long enough to take a survey of the internal sphere. The *Polar King* floated on the wide bosom of the sea underneath the perpendicular sun that lit all Plutusia with its beams. With our telescopes we discovered oceans, continents, mountain ranges, lakes, cities, railroads, ships, and buildings of all kinds spread like an immense map on the concave vault of the earth overhead. It was a sight that alone amply repaid us for the discovery of so sublime a sphere.

We thought what a cry of joy would electrify both planets when through our instrumentality they first knew of each other's existence. We alone possessed the tremendous secret! Then, what possibilities of commerce! What keen and glorious revelations of art! What unfolding of the secrets of nature each world would find in the other! What inventions rival nations would discover in either world, and here for the outer world what possible mountains of gold, what quarries of jewels! What means of empire and joy and love! But such thoughts were too vast for wearied souls. We were stunned by such conceptions, and, yielding to nature, sank into a dreamless sleep.

CHAPTER 10

A Visit From the
Inhabitants of Plutusia

How long we slept it is impossible to say. We must have remained in slumber at least three days after the great excitement of our voyage so far. The direct cause of my awaking was a loud noise on deck, and on coming up to learn the cause, I saw Flathootly shaking his fist at two strange flying men who hovered over the ship.

"Bad luck to ye," shouted Flathootly, "if iver I get a grip of ye again you won't sail away so swately after jabbin' me in the neck like that."

"Flathootly!" I cried, "what's the meaning of this? Were those men on board ship? Had you hold of them?"

"Begorra, sorr," he replied, holding his hand over a slight wound in his neck, "I was slaping as swately as a child when I felt something tickling me nose. I got up to see what was the matther wid me, and sure enough found thim two rascals prowlin' about the deck. Whin they saw me making a move they jumped back and roosted on the rail. I wanted to catch howlt of wan of thim as a curiosity and I goes up to the short fellow, an' says I, quite honey like: 'Good-marnin', sorr! Could you give me a match to loight me pipe?' an' before the fellow had time to know where he was I had howlt of him, wings an' all. Why, he was as weak as wather, and I was knocking his head on the deck to kape him quiet, whin the other fellow let fly and stuck his spear in me neck, and whin I was trying to catch the second fellow the first fellow got away. Be jabers, the next time I get the grip on either of thim his mutton's cooked."

"I fear, Flathootly," said I, "you will never catch either of them again. Don't you see they have got wings and can fly wherever they like beyond reach?"

The two men that flew around the ship were strange beings. Their complexions were bright yellow and their hair black. They were not above five and a half feet in height, but possessed athletic frames. Their wings were long polished blades of metal of a gleaming white, like gigantic oars, which were moved by some powerful force (possibly electricity) quite independent of the body. Their aerial blades flashed and whirled in the sunlight with blinding rapidity. Their attire consisted of what appeared to be leather tights covering the legs, of a pale yellow tint with crimson metallic embroidery. The dynamo and wings were fastened to a crimson jacket of unique shape that supported the body in flight. Their heads were protected by white metal helmets, and they wore tightly-fitting metal boots, reaching half way up to the knee, the metal being arranged in overlapping scales. Each flying man was armed with a spear and shields. The *tout ensemble* was a picture of agility and grace.

The sailors, now thoroughly awake, gave expression to loud exclamations of surprise at the sight of the two strange flying men wheeling around the ship overhead. Professor Starbottle thought that the strangers must belong to some wealthy and civilized country, for men in a savage state would be incapable of inventing such powers of flight and presenting so ornate an appearance.

"They are soldiers," said Professor Rackiron; "see the spears and shields they wear."

"They're bloody pirates!" said Flathootly. "It was the long fellow that stabbed me."

"You're all right," said the doctor to Flathootly. "Thank your stars the spear wasn't poisoned, or you would be a dead man."

"Be the powers, I'll have that fellow yet," said the master-at-arms. "I'm going to take a jump, and, be me sowl, wan of thim fellows'll get left."

The strangers were now flying quite close to the ship, and Flathootly unexpectedly gave a tremendous spring into the air. He would have caught one of the aerial men for certain, but they, having wings, foiled him by simply moving out of the line of the Irishman's flight.

ONE OF THE FLYING MEN CAUGHT FLATHOOTLY BY THE HAIR OF
THE HEAD, AND LIFTED HIM OUT OF THE WATER.

Flathootly dropped into the sea about a quarter of a mile away, and would probably have been drowned had it not been for the generosity of the strangers themselves. One of the flying men, hastening to the rescue, caught him by the hair of the head and lifted him out of the water. Flathootly caught the stranger by one of his legs and held on like grim death. The flying man brought his burden right over the ship and attempted to drop Flathootly on deck, who shouted, "I hev him, boys! I hev him! Catch howlt of us, some of you!" Immediately a dozen sailors leaped up, and, grasping the winged man and his burden, brought both successfully down to the deck.

Seeing himself overpowered, the stranger submitted to his captivity with as good a grace as possible. We removed his shield and spear, and, merely tying a rope to his leg to secure our prize, gave him the freedom of the ship.

He sulked for a long time, and maintained an animated conversation with his free companion in a language whose meaning none of us understood. He finally condescended to eat some of the food we set before him, and his companion came near enough to take a glass of wine from his captive brother and drink it with evident relish.

Flathootly was so far friendly disposed to his assailant as to offer him a glass of ship's rum. The stranger to our surprise did not refuse it, but, putting the glass to his lips, quaffed its contents at a single draught. When he became more accustomed to his surroundings we ventured to examine his curious equipment.

Upon examination we found that the wings of our captive were simply large aerial oars, about four and a half feet in length and three feet wide at the widest part, tapering down to a few inches wide at the dynamo that moved them. Such small extent of surface evidently required an enormous force to propel a man in rapid flight. We found the dynamo to consist of a central wheel made to revolve by the attraction of a vast occult force evolved from the contact of two metals, one being of a vermilion colour and the other of a bright green tint, that constituted the cell of the apparatus. No acid was required, nor did the contact of the metal produce any wasting of their substance. A colossal current of mysterious magnetism made the wheel revolve, the current being guided in its work by an automatic insulation of one hemisphere of the wheel.

I put one hand on the dynamo and made a gesture of inquiry with the other, whereupon our strange friend said, "*Nojmesedi!*" Was this the name of the new force we had discovered, or the name of the flying apparatus as a whole? Before we could settle the point our friend became communicative, and, smiting his breast, said:

"*Plothoy, wayleal ar Atvatabar!*"

With the right hand he pointed to a continent rising above us, its mighty features being clearly visible to the naked eye.

CHAPTER 11

We Learn Atvatabarese

This exclamation was a very puzzling phrase to us.

Professor Starbottle said: "It appears to me, gentlemen, before we can make any use of our prisoner we must first learn his language."

Again the stranger smote his breast, exclaiming: *"Plothoy, wayleal ar Atvatabar."*

"Well, of all the lingoes I iver heard," said Flathootly, "this is the worst case yet. It bates Irish, which is the toughest langwidge to larn undher the sun. What langwidge do you call that, sorr?"

Professor Goldrock, besides being a naturalist, was an adept in language. He stated that our captive appeared to be either a soldier or courier or coast-guard of his country, which was evidently indicated by the last word, Atvatabar. "Let us take for granted," said he, "that 'Plothoy' is his name and 'Atvatabar' his country. We have left the two words '*wayleal* ar.' Now the pronunciation and grouping of the letters leads me to think that the words resemble the English language more nearly than any other tongue. The word '*wayleal*' has the same number of letters as 'soldier' and 'courier,' and I note that the fourth and last letters are identical in both 'courier' and '*wayleal*.' On the supposition that both words are identical we might compare them thus:

$$c=w \quad o=a \quad u=y \quad r=l$$
$$i=e \quad e=i \text{ or } a \quad r=l$$

The word '*wayleil*' or '*wayleal*' means to us *leal* or *strong*—by the way, a very good name for a soldier."

At this moment our mysterious friend yelled out:

"Plothoy, wayleal ar Atvatabar, em Bilbimtesirol!"

"Kape quiet, me boy," said Flathootly, "and we'll soon find out all about you."

"Rather let him talk away," said the professor, "and we'll find out who he is much quicker. You see he has given us two new words this time, the words *'em Bilbimtesirol.'* Now an idea strikes me—let us transpose the biggest word thus:

b=p	i=e	l=r	b=p
i=e	m=n	t=d	e=i
s=c	i=u	r=l	o=a
l=r			

Here we have the word 'perpendicular.' What does *'Bilbimtesirol'* as 'perpendicular' mean? It may mean that the interior planet is lit by a perpendicular sun, and that we are in a land of perpendicular light and shadow. See how the shadow, of every man surrounds his boots! Now, granting *'wayleal'* means 'courier' and *'Bilbimtesirol'* 'perpendicular,' we have a clue to the language of Atvatabar. It seems to me to be a miraculous transposition of the English language thus:

a=o	b=p	c=s or k	d=t
e=i or a	f=f or v	g=j	h=oh
i=e	j=g	k=c	l=r
m=n	n=m	o=a	p=b
q=v	r=l	s=c or s	t=d
u=ij	v=qu	w=y c or s	x=z
y=u or i	z=x		

According to this transposition our friend means, *'Plothoy courier of Atvatabar, in Bilbimtesirol.'* Let us see if we can so understand him." So saying, the professor approached and said:

"Ec wayl moni Plothoy?" (Is your name Plothoy?)

"Wic cel, ni moni ec Plothoy" (Yes, sir, my name is Plothoy), promptly replied the stranger.

"Good!" said the professor; "that's glorious! We understand each other now."

I congratulated the professor on his brilliant discovery. It was magnificent! We could now converse with our prisoner on any subject we desired.

We had the key in our hands that would unlock the wonders of Plutusia, or rather Bilbimtesirol, the interior world.

Flathootly turned a dozen summersaults in the air to express his delight. The sailors spun upon the deck, and threw each other into the air like jugglers playing with balls, in pure excitement.

"*Ec Atvatabar dofi moni ar wail saimtle?*" (Is Atvatabar the name of your country?) inquired the professor of Plothoy.

"*E on o wayleal ar Fec Nogicdi, Cemj Aldemegry Bhoolmakar ar Atvatabar*" (I am a *wayleal* of his majesty King Aldemegry Bhoolmakar of Atvatabar), said Plothoy.

Atvatabar, then, was a kingdom. We should go there certainly and see King Bhoolmakar and his people. But where was this mysterious country?

"*Yohili ec Atvatabar?*" we asked of Plothoy.

"*Dohili!*" he replied, pointing to a continent in the southwest. The southwest in the interior world, it should be stated, corresponds to the southeast on the outer earth. Atvatabar, then, lay underneath the Atlantic Ocean.

"*Yohod ec dohi moni ar dohi miolicd gliod sedi?*" (What is the name of the nearest great city?) we asked.

"*Kioram,*" replied Plothoy. "*Dohili ed ec fequi ohymtlit neric tyi caydoh docd.*" (There it is, five hundred miles due southeast.)

We looked in the direction indicated with our glasses and plainly saw the white marble buildings of a large city not three degrees above the plane of our position. Further off, in the haze of distance, a mighty continent unrolled its landscapes, until it was merged in the brightness of the sunlight above us.

All this time Plothoy's companion circumnavigated the ship on his swift wings. We inquired his name.

"*Lecholt,*" said Plothoy, "*omt ohi orca ec o wayleal.*" (And he also is a *wayleal*.)

"What is the name of the sun above us?" we inquired.

"*Swang,*" said Plothoy.

Good! we would sail direct to Kioram, the principal port of Atvatabar.

I assured Plothoy that as long as he was detained by us he would receive the greatest consideration at our hands. We would do him no injury, but, on the contrary, amply reward him for his services. He could understand that, being strangers in an unknown world, it was absolutely necessary for us to have a pilot, or guide, not merely to advise how to direct the ship, but to inform us regarding the laws, manners, and customs of the people we proposed visiting, that we might accommodate ourselves to such novel experiences as we were certain to undergo. We told him we had come to Bilbimtesirol as pioneers of the outer planet, as heralds of the intercourse that would undoubtedly take place between two worlds separated for ages until now. We assured Plothoy how indebted we were to him for the information he had already given, and his great importance to us in a voyage that would affect the interests of thousands of millions of men ought to reconcile him to his brief captivity. We could not afford to lose him, and therefore asked him to remain with us for the remainder of the voyage, and on reaching Kioram we would give him his liberty.

These words, with the treatment he was receiving, completely reconciled Plothoy, who called Lecholt to come down on deck beside him. His companion obeyed, and presently the two strangers sat on the rail of the vessel engaged in earnest conversation.

Presently Plothoy said that his companion Lecholt would go forward in advance of the ship to inform the king of our coming, that due preparations be made for our reception. This was an admirable suggestion, and accordingly we despatched Lecholt with a message of profound respect for King Aldemegry Bhoolmakar, saying that the commander of the *Polar King* with his officers and retinue would do themselves the honour of visiting his majesty and people as soon as the *Polar King* would reach Atvatabar.

Poising himself for a moment on his wings, Lecholt saluted us with his sword and immediately swept away in the direction of Atvatabar.

CHAPTER 12

We Arrive at Kioram

Between the time of departure of Lecholt and our arrival at Kioram we kept Plothoy as busy as possible answering our questions.

We found that all the soldiers of the king were known as *wayleals*, and that all were equipped with magnetic wings. The wings were worked by a little dynamo supplied by *magnicity*. A single cell, six cubic inches in size, produced a current both enormously powerful and constant. I could recollect no cell in the outer world of the same size so powerful, hence here was an inventive discovery of the first importance. The cell was composed of two metals, *terrelium*, a vermilion metal found only in Atvatabar, and *aquelium*, a bright green metal elaborated from the waters of the internal ocean, which metals simply placed in contact, without the addition of an acid or alkaline salt, generated a powerful current. Both cell and dynamo were strapped to the back by a strong leathern jacket, which also supported the soldier in flight. The weight of a man being only fifteen pounds on the surface of the interior earth, and no weight at all fifty miles above it, prevented any fatigue being experienced from flight. It was the easiest of all methods of locomotion, and eminently suited to the inhabitants of such a world as Bilbimtesirol.

Plothoy informed us that the government of Atvatabar was an elective monarchy. The king and nobles were elected for life and no title was hereditary. There was a legislative assembly founded on the popular will called the Borodemy. The king's palace and Borodemy were situated in Calnogor, the capital city of the realm, which lay five hundred miles inland and communicated with Kioram by a sacred railroad, as well as by aerial ship.

The largest building in Calnogor was the Bormidophia, or pantheon, where the worship of the gods was held. The only living object of worship was the Lady Lyone, the Supreme Goddess of Atvatabar. There were different kinds of golden gods worshipped, or symbols that represented the inventive forces, art, and spiritual power.

The king was head of the army and navy and the people were divided into several classes of nobles and common people. The Atvatabarese were very wealthy, gold being as common as iron in the outer world. They were a peaceful people, and Atvatabar being itself an immense island continent, lying far from any other land, there had been no wars with any external nation, nor even civil war, for over a hundred years.

There were plenty of newspapers, and the most wonderful inventions had been in use for ages. Railroads, pneumatic tubes, telegraphs, telephones, phonographs, electric lights, rain makers, seaboots, marine railroads, flying machines, megaphones, velocipedes without wheels, *aerophers*, etc., were quite common, not to speak of such inventions as sowing, reaping, sewing, boot-blacking and knitting machines. Of course printing, weaving, and such like machines had been in use since the dawn of history. Strange to say they had no steam engines, and *terrorite* and gunpowder were unknown. Their great source of power was *magnicity*, generated by the two powerful metals *terrelium* and *aquelium*, and compressed air their explosive force.

As we approached this wonderful country we noticed a number of splendid ships coming to meet us. Plated with gold and fully rigged, they presented a beautiful appearance. They were each propelled by *magnicity*. Plothoy said they were the fleet of Atvatabar coming to welcome us. The royal navy was in command of Admiral Jolar, who had never yet seen active service, but was a worthy representative of the king.

Our rapid steaming in the direction of the fleet, which as rapidly approached us, soon brought the *Polar King* within range of their guns. Plothoy was set free, as we then knew all about Atvatabar necessary to know prior to seeing the admiral, who could give us more definite information.

A roar of guns saluted us from at least one hundred vessels. There was no smoke, the guns being discharged by compressed air.

Each vessel bore the flag of Atvatabar, a pink-coloured disc surrounded by a circle of green on a violet field. The disc represented the sun above us, the green circle Atvatabar, and the violet field the surrounding sea. From the peak of the *Polar King* the American flag floated, the first flag of the outer sphere that was ever unrolled in the air of the interior world.

The ships approached us in double column and presented an appearance of the utmost grandeur. It was evident we were the discoverers of a powerful and opulent country, and not a barbarous land. Here were civilization and courtesy, and, not to be outdone in these qualities, I ordered a salute from our *terrorite* guns. The explosive shells discharged by gunpowder into the sea sent up columns of water and foam all around us to an astonishing height, and it took a considerable time for the sea to subside, the gravity of the water being only one-tenth that of the external ocean.

The Atvatabarese must have been greatly astonished at the explosions, as Plothoy informed us that no such weapon as ours formed part of the armament of the Atvatabar navy.

The fleet ceased firing, and presently a gaily-decorated *magnic* launch shot off from the flagship, bearing two officers in brilliant uniforms. Plothoy, as the boat approached us, said the officers were Admiral Jolar of the fleet and Koshnili, Grand Minister of the government. The boat came alongside the *Polar King*, and, lowering a gangway, the illustrious visitors came on board.

Admiral Jolar was arrayed in an olive-green coat, decorated with overlapping scales of gold embroidery, and olive-green trousers with an outer stripe similarly decorated. The uniform of Koshnili, the Grand Minister, was of electric-blue cloth covered with serpentine bands of gold embroidery, radiating downward. A small but brilliant retinue accompanied each official. As the distinguished visitors stepped on deck, the entire fleet saluted us with a second roar of guns. Plothoy announced their names and dignities. Being able to greet their excellencies in their own language greatly astonished them.

I learned from the admiral that the Grand Minister Koshnili was sent by his majesty, King Aldemegry Bhoolmakar, as a special envoy to bid us welcome in the name of the king and people of Atvatabar. The story told by Lecholt had been proclaimed by royal authority throughout the country, and the day of our arrival in Calnogor, the metropolis, was to be observed as a national holiday.

A brilliant programme of entertainment had been devised, calculated to do us infinite honour. I conferred on Admiral Jolar the title of Honourary Commander of the *Polar King*, and on Koshnili that of Honourary Captain.

The admiral said that both he and Koshnili would remain on our ship until we arrived in the city of Kioram.

The admiral, by signalling from the *Polar King*, put his navy into a series of brilliant evolutions. A curious feature was the fact that each sailor possessed wings, was in fact a *wayleal*, like Plothoy. The sailors, wing-jackets or *fletyemings*, as they were called, of one vessel, would rise like a swarm of bees and settle on another vessel. The evolutions made in this way were both majestic and surprising.

The entire *fletyemings* of each squadron on either side of us were drawn up in battle array in the space between the ships and fought each other in mock battle with spears, while the ships discharged their guns at each other.

We reached the harbour of Kioram, in which the royal navy anchored in double column. The *Polar King* sailed slowly down the imperial avenue of ships amid the thunder of guns and the cheers of *fletyemings*.

The sun shone gloriously as we stepped from the deck of the ship upon the white marble city wharf. Everything was new, strange, and splendid. We were received by Governor Lapalme, of Kioram, the commandant of the fort, and his staff, Captains Pra and Nototherboc. Beyond the notables a vast crowd of Atvatabarese cheered us vociferously, while the guns of the fort, on a commanding height, roared their welcome.

CHAPTER 13

Marching in Triumph

There was a blaze of excitement in the streets of Kioram when our procession appeared on the grand boulevard leading from the harbour to the fortress, some four miles in length. We presented a strange appearance not only to the people of the city, but to ourselves as well.

Prior to our appearance before the people we were obliged to adjust ourselves to the motion of an immense walking machine, the product of the inventive skill of Atvatabar.

Governor Lapalme explained that the cavalry of Atvatabar were mounted on such locomotive machines, built on the plan of immense ostriches, called *bockhockids*. They were forty feet in height from toe to head, the saddle being thirty feet from the ground. The iron muscles of legs and body, moved by a powerful *magnic* motor inside the body of the monster, acted on bones of hollow steel. Each machine was operated by the dynamo in the body, which was adjusted to act or remain inert, as required, when riding the structure. A switch in front of the saddle set the *bockhockid* in motion or brought it to rest again. It was simply a gigantic velocipede without wheels. "We'll ride the bastes," said Flathootly, with suppressed excitement.

"Do you think you can accommodate yourselves to ride such a machine?" said the governor. "You will find it, after a little practice, an imposing method of travel."

We were assembled in a spacious court that surrounded the private dock of the king. Into this dock the *Polar King* had been brought for greater safety and also to facilitate popular inspection. I determined that both officers and sailors should equally take part in the honours of our reception, and I informed the governor that we would like to see first how the machines were worked.

At a signal from the governor, Captains Pra and Nototherboc disappeared and presently returned to the court-yard mounted on two gigantic *bockhockids*, on which they curvetted and swept around in gallant style.

We were both astonished and delighted at the performance. It was marvellous to see such agility and obedience to the wish of the rider on such ungainly monsters. The sailors were only too anxious to mount such helter-skelters as the machine ostriches of Atvatabar. The stride made by each bird was over forty feet, and nothing on earth could overtake such coursers in full flight.

The governor, proud of his two-legged horses, as he called them, grew eloquent in their behalf.

"Consider an army of men," said he, "mounted on such machines. How swift! How formidable! What a terrible combat when two such armies meet, armed with their *magnic* spears! What display of prodigious agility! What breathless swerving to and fro! What fearful fleetness of pursuer and pursued! Aided as we are by the almost total absence of gravity, our inventors have produced a means of locomotion for individual men second only to the flying motor. We possess, also, flying *bockhockids* who are our cavalry in aerial warfare."

The enraptured sailors were only too anxious to mount the enormous birds and sally forth to electrify the city. Ninety-eight *bockhockids* were required to mount the entire company. This number was brought into the court-yard by a detachment of soldiers who nimbly unseated themselves and slid down the smooth legs of the birds to the ground.

"I say, yer honour," said Flathootly to the governor, "have you any insurance companies in this counthry?"

"Why, certainly," replied the governor.

"Then I want to inshure my loife if I have to mount a baste loike that."

"Oh, I'll see that you are amply compensated for any injuries you may sustain by falling off the machine," said the governor.

"Sorr, is yer word as good as yer bond?" inquired Flathootly.

"Certainly," replied the governor.

"Well thin, sorr, gimme yer bond," said Flathootly.

The governor duly put his signature to a statement that Flathootly should be compensated for any injuries received in consequence of his riding the *bockhockid*. Flathootly carefully deposited the document in a little satchel he carried in his breast, and thereupon, sailor fashion, climbed up the leg of the machine and seated himself on the gold-embroidered saddle-cloth.

In like manner the sailors got seated on their machines, the entire company forming an imposing phalanx. I found it quite easy to balance myself on the two-legged monsters in consequence of the large base given each leg by the outspreading toes.

While the sailors were getting seated a military band, composed of fifty musicians, each mounted on a *bockhockid*, played the March of Atvatabar in soul-stirring strains.

The word of command being given, the great doors of the court-yard were flung open and forth issued the musicians with banners flying. Then followed the seamen of the *Polar King*, led by the governor, Koshnili and myself.

The excited populace cheered a hearty welcome. A brigade of five thousand *bockhockids* fell into line as an escort of honour. The ever-shining sun lent a brilliant effect to the pageant. Our complexions were lighter than those of the Atvatabarese, who were universally of a golden-yellow tint, and it was surprising to see how fair the people appeared, considering that they lived in a land where the sun never sets. None had a complexion darker than a rich chocolate-brown colour. This was accounted for by the fact that the light of Swang was not half as intense as that of the outer sun in the tropics. The diminutive size of the luminary counterbalanced its proximity to the surrounding planet. The light that fell upon Atvatabar was warm, genial, glowing, and rosy, imparting to life a delightful sensation. As the procession advanced we saw splendid emporiums of trade chiselled of white marble, crowded roof and window with dense masses of people. On either side of the fine boulevard leading to the palace the people were jammed into an immovable mass and were wild with enthusiasm. The roadway was lined with trees that seemed like magnolias, oranges, and oleanders.

"Now this is something loike a recipshon," said Flathootly. "I'm well plazed wid it."

"I am delighted to know that your honour thinks so highly of our efforts to please you," said the governor.

Flathootly turned round and shouted to the sailors, "Remimber, me bhoys, we will hev a grand feast at the ind of the performance." As he spoke, he unfortunately touched the switch starting the *bockhockid* into a gallop, and in a moment the machine dashed furiously forward, running into the musicians, knocking down some of the other *bockhockids*, scattering others in all directions, and then flying ahead amid the roars of the people. Flathootly was thrown off his seat, but in falling to the ground managed to get hold of the *bockhockid*'s leg at the knee-joint, to which he clung with the energy of despair. A squad of police, who also rode *bockhockids*, dashed after the flying Flathootly, and one of them got hold of the switch on the back of the machine and so brought it to a standstill.

Flathootly was terrified, but uninjured. His first concern was to see if his "insurance" was safe. He found the document still in his breast, and this being so, was induced to remount his steed. "I hope your honour has met with no accident?" said the governor, riding up.

"As long as I've yer honour's handwritin' I'm all right," said Flathootly. "If I break me leg what odds, so long as I'm insured?"

The scattered musicians were assembled in order again and the procession continued its way toward the palace. There were on all sides evidences of wealth, culture, and refinement. Every building was constructed of chiselled marble.

The fortress and palace of Kioram stood in a large square, occupying the most commanding position in the city. From the fort could be seen the white shores and surrounding sea of Atvatabar. The harbour was surrounded with white stone piers lined with the commerce of the kingdom. The charm of the scene was largely lost on Flathootly and the sailors, who cared more for the material benefit of their reception than for its ideal beauty.

The procession arrived at a pillared archway leading underneath the solid walls of the fortress. These walls were fully one hundred feet in height and fifty feet in thickness. The top of the walls consisted of a level circular roadway, whereon a guard of *bockhockids* constantly swept around with amazing swiftness.

It was a sight grotesque in the extreme. The flying *wayleals*

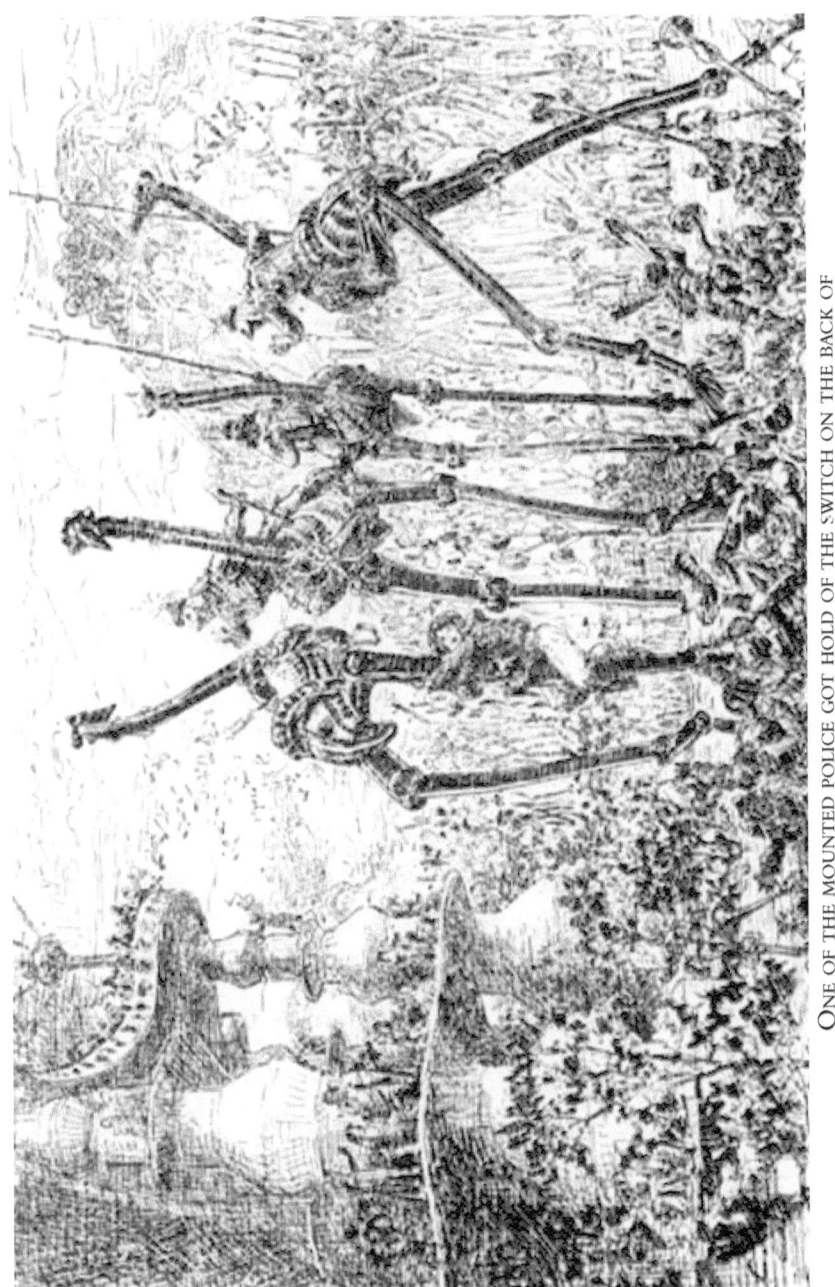

One of the mounted police got hold of the switch on the back of the *bockhockid*, and brought it to a standstill.

looked like a race between enormous ostriches with a wild confusion of legs on the lofty ramparts.

"Flying divils let loose," was the subdued remark of Flathootly.

There was a gay time in the banqueting hall of the palace. We were royally feasted, and for wine we drank *squang*, the choicest wine of Atvatabar.

The governor informed us that our appearance in the interior world had been heralded all over the country, and strange speculations had been made as to what world or country we belonged to. "We know, of course," said he, "that you do not belong to any race of men in our sphere, and this makes public curiosity all the greater concerning you. What country do you come from?" said he, addressing Flathootly.

"Oi'm from the United States, the foinest counthry on the outside of the world; but I was born in Tipperary," said Flathootly.

"Ah," said the governor, "I should be delighted to visit your country."

"You might be gettin' frightened, sorr, at the dark ivery noight," said Flathootly.

"What is the night?" said the governor.

"Och, and have ye lived to be a gray-haired man and don't know that it's dark at noight whin the sun jumps round to the other soide of the wurrld?"

"But it's never dark here," said the governor.

"Thrue for you, but it ought to be. How can a Christian slape wid the sun shinin' all the toime?" rejoined the Irishman.

"Oh, you can sleep here in the sunshine," said the governor, "as well as inside the house."

"Does it iver rain here?" said Flathootly.

"But little," replied the governor; "not more than six inches of rain falls in a year."

"Bedad, you ought to be in Oireland to see it rain. There you'd git soaked to your heart's content. An' tell me how do you grow your cabbages without rain?" he continued.

"Well," said the governor, "rain is produced by firing into the air balls of solid gas so intensely cold that in turning to the gaseous form they condense in rain the invisible vapour in the air."

"Bedad, that's what they do in our country," said Flathootly, "only they explode shells of dynamite in the air. Can you tell me," he added, "have you got tides in the say here?"

"We have never been able to discover what force it is that lifts the sea so regularly," said the governor. "We call it the breathing of the ocean."

"Shure any schoolboy knows it's the moon that does it," replied Flathootly.

"The moon?" queried the governor.

"Why, of coorse it's the moon on the other side of the wurrld that lifts up the wather both inside and out. Ye're wake in geography not to know that," said Flathootly.

The governor looked at me for verification of this astonishing story. "Where is that wonderful moon," he inquired, "that I hear of? Where is the surface of the earth that slopes away out of sight?" Just then the bell sounded its message that called the people to rest, and the banqueting came to an end. We were forthwith shown to the private apartments allotted to us in the palace.

Chapter 14

The Journey to Calnogor

There was in Kioram a temple dedicated to the god Raka-madeva, or Sacred Locomotive, which was one of the many gods worshipped by the Atvatabarese. It belonged to the gods embraced in the category of "gods of invention," and its motive power was *magnicity*, the same force that propelled the flying men. It was a powerful structure built of solid gold, platinum, *terrelium*, *aquelium*, and *plutulium*, and alloys of the most precious and heaviest of metals, and was both car and locomotive, and was hung over a single elevated rail that supported it, the weight resting on six wheels in front and six behind, all concealed by the body of the car.

The battery consisted of one hundred cells of *terrelium* and *aquelium* that developed a gigantic force. The six driving wheels at either end of the car were of immense size, and the tires were hollowed out with a semi-circular groove that fitted upon the high rounded rail. On this rail rested the entire weight of the car, which oscillated as it rushed. The end of each projecting head was inlaid with an enormous ruby, and the framework of the god was enriched in numerous places with precious stones. The sacred locomotive had as attendants twenty-four priests, clad in flowing vestures of orange and aloe-green silk (the royal colours), arranged in alternate stripes of great width, typical of a green earth and golden sky.

Royal and privileged travellers were alone permitted to harness the god, and by command of the king we were to enter Calnogor by means of the sacred courier.

The route to the temple led through a different part of the city than that traversed by us when going to the governor's palace. We had leisure to observe more particularly the architecture and the appearance of the streets through which we passed. The roadway everywhere was one solid block of white marble, and emporiums and dwellings were built of the same material.

"You seem to have sculptured the city out of a mountain of white marble," I said to the governor, who rode his *bockhockid* alongside mine.

"That is, indeed, the fact," replied the governor. "The entire city has been laboriously hewn from an immense mountain."

"Then in building your houses, you laid the foundation with the roof, and built them downward until you arrived at the level of the street," I said.

"That is precisely so," said he. "Our streets are simply ornamental chasms cut in the solid rock. Both roadway and building are composed of the same stone. One stone has built the entire city."

I was surprised at the idea of the stupendous labour involved in carving a city containing half a million of inhabitants, but, considering that a man could easily lift a block of stone weighing half a ton in the outer sphere, I saw that even so prodigious a task as chiselling Kioram might well be accomplished. It was a new sensation to bound on a *bockhockid* over the smoothly carved pavement, where once stood the mighty heart of a mountain of stone. All the buildings along the route were wonderfully sculptured. There seemed no end to the floriated mouldings, pillars and other decorations in relief, wrought in a strange order of art that was most captivating.

As for ourselves, we must have presented an interesting procession. Our Viking helmets of polished brass gleamed in the sunlight like gold. The emblazoned bear thereon was a symbol to the Atvatabarese of a species of divinity that protected us as beings of another world.

We arrived at the temple of the sacred locomotive, and were received by the winged priests in charge. Dismounting amid the sound of music, a procession was formed, the priests leading the way along a wide hallway that terminated in the temple of the god.

The god Rakamadeva was a glorious sight. On a causeway of marble flanked with steps on either side stood that object of *magnic* life and beauty in a blaze of metals and jewels worthy the praise of the priests, in itself a royal palace.

This automobile car in shape seemed a compound of the back of a turtle and a Siamese temple, and was of extraordinary magnificence. Both front and rear tapered down to the solid platinum framework of the wheels, that extended beyond the car at both ends, the projections simulating the heads of monsters that held each between their jaws one hundred cells of triple metal, which developed a tremendous force.

The priests chanted the following ode to the sacred locomotive:

Glorious annihilator of time and space, lord of distance, imperial courier.
Hail, swift and sublime man-created god, hail colossal and bright wheel!
Thy wheels adamant, thy frame platinum, thy cells terrelium, aquelium!
Thou art lightning shivering on the metals, thy breathless flights
affright Atvatabar!
The affluence of life animates thy form, that flashes through valleys
and on mountains high!
The forests roar as thou goest past, the gorge echoes thy thunder!
Thy savage wheels ravage space. Convulsed with life, thy tireless
form devours the heights of heaven!
Labour and glory and terror leap as thy thundering feet go by; thy
axles burn with the steady sweep, till on wings of fire they fly!

The four-and-twenty priests formed a guard of honour as we reverentially entered the car. On our side of the god were seated Governor Lapalme, Admiral Jolar and staff, myself and officers of the *Polar King*, including the scientific staff. The other side contained the sailors under command of Flathootly, master-at-arms, escorted by Captains Pra and Nototherboc.

The priests were distributed around the outside of the car, holding on to golden hand-rails. A priest seated on a throne in front moved a switch, and, with a roar of music, the god leaped upon the metals. The wonderful lightness of the car allowed us to attain a tremendous speed. The mightiest curves were taken at a single breath. The silken robes of the priests flashed in the wind.

The car vibrated with a thousand tremors. In the wide windows of thick glass were framed rapid phantasmagoria of landscapes, as the flying panorama unrolled itself. There were visions of interminable prairies, over which we swept, a blinding flash, leaving a low, spreading cloud of dust on the rails to mark our flight.

We plunged into tunnels of darkness, where the warm air roared

THE SACRED LOCOMOTIVE STORMED THE MOUNTAIN HEIGHTS
WITH ITS AUDACIOUS TREAD.

with the echoes of the delirious wheels. The cry of the caverns saluted us like the shouts of unknown monsters dwelling in the heart of the mountains.

The sacred locomotive was an element of life, as it shot from the tunnels and bounded up curving mountain heights through pastures of delightful flowers. With wheels prevailed upon by the tension of the invincible fluid, the monster swerved not before the proudest precipice. It stormed the heights with its audacious tread, flinging itself on the mountain pass, a marvel of power and intrepidity, and known as the devourer of distance.

In five hours we had traversed five hundred miles, the distance from Kioram to Calnogor.

CHAPTER 15

Our Reception by the King

The sacred locomotive swept through a noble archway into a palace garden, a part of the king's palace in Calnogor. The railway terminal was a wide marble platform, or causeway, surrounded by a sea of tropical flowers. The priests had already alighted, and stood in double file to receive us. Through a sculptured archway a herald approached us, blowing a trumpet and announcing the coming of his royal majesty, King Aldemegry Bhoolmakar of Atvatabar.

We alighted, and I had the sailors drawn up in an imposing column on the platform, every man grasping his sword. Even the remotest walls of the garden were lined with *wayleals*, and military music added to the splendour of the scene.

Presently a stately figure approached us. It was his majesty accompanied by her majesty, Queen Toplissy. Koshnili whispered that it was a special honour that the king and queen should greet us even before we entered the palace. The king was tall and erect in bearing and his complexion was the colour of old gold. His hair, as well as his closely-trimmed beard and moustache, were of a serpent-green tint. He wore a dome-shaped crown of gold, surmounted by a blazing ruby. His dress was a cloth of gold, light as gossamer, that swathed his form after the manner of our Eastern potentates. His boots of gold-lacquered leather were covered with emeralds and curiously turned up at the toes. Queen Toplissy was a handsome lady, rather heavy in physique, of an orange-yellow complexion, with bright copper-bronze hair, and her unclad arms wore a profusion of bracelets and armlets of various metals. Her crown was also of gold surmounted by a blazing sapphire. Her robes were of white silk embroidered with broad bands of orange and arranged in innumerable folds. Her boots were incrusted with sapphires. All this I saw at a momentary glance as Koshnili led me forward to his majesty. I was announced as "His Excellency, Lexington White, commander of the *Polar King*, the discoverer of the Polar Gulf, and the first inhabitant of the outer world who had ever reached Bilbimtesirol and Atvatabar."

The king embraced me and I kissed the hand of her majesty. The officers and sailors received their due share of royal attention. We were the objects of unbounded curiosity on the part of the royal retinue.

Amid a salute of guns and music we passed through the archway that formed the boundary between the palace gardens and the court of the holy locomotive, and saw the palace of King Aldemegry Bhoolmakar before us.

It was a high, conical building, twenty stories in height. Each story was surrounded by a row of windows decorated with pillars. Colossal lions of gold stood on the entrance towers, their claws formed of straps of gold running down the walls and riveted to the lower tiers of stone, giving the impression that they held together the whole structure beneath. The style of architecture was an absolutely new order. It was neither Hindu, Egyptian, Greek, nor Gothic, but there was a flavour of all four styles in the weirdly-carved circular walls and roofs. The palace was surrounded by a spacious court, enclosed by cloistered walls. Flowers bloomed in immense square-shaped vases of stone supported on diminutive square pillars. A tank of crystal water, on each side of which broad wide steps led down into the cool wave, lay in the centre of the court. The tank was fed by a wide rivulet of rippling water that ran along a chiselled bed in the marble floor of the court.

The entire scene was a picture of glorious and blessed repose. The sculptor had covered the base and frieze of the walls with a profusion of ornament in high relief. Imagination and art had produced scenes that created a profound impression. A dramatic calmness held lion and elephant, serpent and eagle, *wayleal* and *bockhockid*, youth and maiden, in glorious embrace.

The banquet given by the king in our honour in the topmost story of the palace was both delicious and satisfying. All the fertility of Atvatabar ministered to our delight. Strange meats and fruits were music to the body, as art and music were meats and wine to the soul.

I sat beside his majesty at the feast, while Koshnili sat at my right hand. Admiral Jolar sat beside the queen, and on her majesty's right sat Captain Wallace. The professors and other officers, as well as a number of noblemen and state officers, also sat at the royal table. At another table sat the sailors, accompanied by the officers of the king's household.

We had again an opportunity of tasting the *squang* of Atvatabar, which was of a finer brand than that served at the table of Governor Lapalme. It added a new joy to life to taste such royal wine.

His majesty, seated on his throne at the feast, raised a glass of *squang* and said: "I drink in welcome to our illustrious guest, His Excellency, Lexington White, commander of the *Polar King* and discoverer of Atvatabar."

The company rising, shouted, "Welcome to His Excellency, Lexington White, commander of the *Polar King*," and drank of their glasses in my honour.

In acknowledgment of this great compliment I rose and proposed the healths of the king and queen. I said: "I drink to the healths of their royal majesties, King Aldemegry Bhoolmakar and Queen Toplissy of Atvatabar, to whom be lifelong peace and prosperity."

The company honoured this sentiment by acclamation and drinking goblets of wine. This constituted the preliminaries of our interview.

"Now," said his majesty, "we are extremely anxious to learn all about the manners and customs of the people of the outer world. Tell us of these people, their laws, religions, and modes of government."

In obedience to the king's request I spoke of America and its nations founded on the idea of self-sovereignty, and of Europe with its sovereigns and subjects. I spoke of Egypt and India as types of a colossal past, of the United States and Great Britain as types of a colossal present, and of Africa the continent of the colossal future. I informed the king that the genius of Asia, of the Eastern world, ran to poetry and art without science, while that of the Western world developed science and invention without poetry and art.

"Ah!" cried the king, who was intensely interested. "Atvatabar has both science and art, invention and poetry. Our wise rulers

THE KING EMBRACED ME, AND I KISSED THE HAND OF HER MAJESTY.

have been ever mindful of the equal charms of science and sentiment in educating our people."

I assured his majesty that we were no less anxious to learn all about the institutions of Atvatabar than he was regarding the external sphere.

"Atvatabar," said the king, "is a monarchy formed on the will of the people. While the throne is inalienably secured to the king for life, the government is vested in a legislative chamber, called Borodemy. This legislative assembly is also our house of nobles, consisting of one thousand members divided into three classes. To be once elected to the Borodemy entitles the representative to receive the title of *boiroon* for life only; at the expiration of five years, the term of each assembly, a member, if again elected, receives the title of *jangoon*; if again elected the highest title is *goiloor*. No one can be elected more than three times, and *goiloor* is a title which but few attain, owing to the limited number of legislators who are three times elected to the Borodemy. The president of the assembly is always a *goiloor*, as only a member of the highest caste is nominated for the presidency. He is also chief minister of state. His council, which is the government, includes the chief officer of each branch of government, as well as a royal representative. Thus Atvatabar is an absolute democracy, ornamented and ruled by those men whom a generous nation loves to honour for distinguished merit employed in the public service."

CHAPTER 16

The King Unfolds the Grandeur of Atvatabar

"Your majesty," I said, "informs us that Atvatabar possesses science and art, invention and poetry. These matters interest us quite as much as your civil and military constitution. We will feel grateful if your majesty will inform us more particularly regarding the condition of those great forces for the development of the soul."

"You are right," said the king; "the government and the protection of society, although matters of the utmost importance, are always much inferior to the glory they defend. Mere police duties can never rank with the sovereignty of mind over matter."

"In other words," said I, "the barricade is ever inferior to the palace, and the treasure house to the heaps of gold within it. But, your majesty, in what way does mind triumph over matter in your realm?"

"Well," said the king, "we worship the human soul under a thousand forms, arranged in three great circles of deities. The first circle contains the gods of invention, that is, the practical forms by which ideas rule the physical world, and also the composite forms of the inventors themselves. The second circle contains the gods of art, and the third circle the spiritual gods of sorcery, magic and love. What gods do you people of the outer world worship?"

"In my own country," I replied, "a great many people worship one God, the Creator of the universe. Many of these only nominally worship God, but in reality worship gold, while a still greater number worship gold without pretence of worshipping anything else."

"Then," said the king, "gold is your god. Our god is the aggregated universal human soul worshipped under its various manifestations, both real and ideal. This universal human soul forms the one supreme god Harikar, whom we worship in the person of a living woman, the Supreme Goddess Lyone. The great generic symbol of our faith is the golden throne of the gods in the Bormidophia, whereon sits Lyone, the supreme goddess, the representative of Harikar."

"Harikar is then your supreme deity?" I remarked.

"Greatest, for he embraces all other gods," said the king. "But the greatest individual god is the Supreme Goddess, the symbol of the Holy Soul."

I felt a strange desire to learn everything about so singular a divinity as Lyone. It was a weird, awful, yet terribly entrancing thought, that amid a thousand gods of dead and silent gold one only should be alive, and that one a beautiful woman. Was it possible that a live goddess could exist, and be both young and handsome? I was anxious to ask a thousand questions concerning this mysterious being, but it seemed a sacrilege to ask them. Was it possible for her to continue worthy of worship, a human being, intoxicated, as she must be, by the ceaseless adoration of millions? In other words, can a woman be a veritable goddess and live? These ideas rushed through my soul like quicksilver. My brain reeled with this discovery of the secret of Atvatabar! What to me were its never-setting sun, its want of gravity, its flying *wayleals* and *bockhockids*, its sculptured cities, its sacred locomotive, its miracles of mechanism and art, compared to a real live goddess with warm blood and a beating heart! No wonder the discovery thrilled me! I felt like embracing his majesty for the information, so simply given, that filled me with delight!

My companions were also greatly excited at the story of the king, and it was with difficulty I could appear interested in the further information he so graciously imparted to us. What were mines of gold to this? But I strove outwardly to appear calm. I felt I must listen further to the story of Atvatabar.

"Our other deities," continued the king, "are the ideal inventors and their inventions. These give man empire over nature. All those who have given man power of flight, who multiply his power to run, those who multiply the power of the eye to see, the hand to labour or to smite, the voice or pen to transmit ideas to great distances and to great multitudes, stand in the pantheon in ideal grandeur. There are the lords of labour, the deities of space and time. They are those gods that breathe the breath of life into unborn ideas, and lo! from brain and hand spring the creatures of their will."

The officers and sailors were listening to the discourse of the king with rapt attention. We were anxious to learn as much as possible about this strange religion of Atvatabar.

"We also worship art and ideal artists," continued the king, "the soul-developers, who work for noble and humane ideas expressed in their most beautiful garb; the builders of earthly palaces for the soul in literature, music, manners, painting, dancing, sculpture, decoration, tapestry and architecture which are represented by ideal statues composed from groups of living artists. These in their ideal or collective perfection are the gods who counteract the evils of an arid and mechanical civilization by arousing feeling, imagination, truth, beauty, tenderness, patriotism and faith in the souls of their fellows.

"The spiritual forces are typified by a goddess, the incarnation of spirit power, of romantic, ideal, hopeless love. Her ministers are the priests of sorcery, necromancy, magic, theosophy, mesmerism, spiritualism and other kindred spiritual powers. These perform miracles, create matter, and impart life to dead bodies. The souls of her priests and priestesses have the power to leave the body at will, and to achieve a present Nirvana of one hundred years."

CHAPTER 17

Gnaphisthasia

The day following our arrival in Calnogor his majesty the king had projected for us a journey to the palace of art at Gnaphisthasia, which stood on the slope of a mountain in a rich valley lying one hundred miles southwest of Calnogor. The palace itself was surrounded by high walls of massive porcelain, beautifully adorned with sculpture mouldings, and midway on each side massive gateways, each formed of rounded cones, rising to a great height and covered with sculptured forms, between which the porcelain wall was pierced with fretted arabesque, running high above the arched opening beneath. Once within the gorgeous gateway, the porcelain walls of Gnaphisthasia stood before the enraptured eyes more than a mile in length and half a mile in depth, a many-coloured dream of imposing magnificence covered with the work of sculptors. The principal part of the wall was of a greenish-white vitrification, finely diversified by horizontal friezes, with arabesques in red and green, purple and yellow, lavender, sea-green, blue and silver and pale rose and deep gray, all separated by wide bands of greenish-white stone.

In the centre of the buildings stood a semi-circle of massive conical towers, gleaming like enormous jewels and connected by sculptured walls. The four corners of the palace were also groups of towers, all the various groups being connected with the rectangular walls that were decorated with arcades and balconies.

Here in this splendid abode were poets and painters, musicians, sculptors and architects, dancers, weavers of fabrics, ceramists, jewellers, engravers, enamellers, artists in lacquer, carvers, designers and workers in glass and metal, pearl and ivory and the precious stones.

In an immense chamber of the palace a fête was being held. On

A PROCESSION OF PRIESTS AND PRIESTESSES PASSED DOWN THE
LIVING AISLES, BEARING TROPHIES OF ART.

either side a double range of massive porcelain pillars supported the roof, which covered this grand sanctuary of art like an immense vitrified jewel. The floor of the court was formed of polished wood of a deep rose colour that emitted a rich, heavy perfume. Wood of a brilliant green, with interlacing arabesques of red, formed the border of the floor. At the further end of the court stood three thrones, being composed, respectively, of *terrelium*, *aquelium*, and *plutulium*, the three most precious metals. On the threefold throne sat Yermoul, lord of art, his majesty the king, and myself. In ample recesses amid the pillars stood the devotees of art, while the centre of the court was filled with the musicians. A procession of priests and priestesses passed down the living aisles, clad in the most gorgeous fabrics of silk spun by gigantic spiders, and they bore singly trophies of art, or moved in groups, supporting golden litters carrying piled-up treasures of dazzling splendour.

First came a band of priestesses bearing fan-like ensigns of carved wood and fretwork, and panels filled with silks, rare brocades and embroideries. Then came priests bearing heavy vases and urns of gold, *terrelium*, *aquelium*, *plutulium*, silver, and alloys of precious bronze. Then followed others bearing litters piled with vases and figures carved from solid pearl, or fashioned in precious metals. Cups, plates, vases in endless shapes, designs and colours went past, piled high on golden litters, looking like gardens of tropic flowers. Rare laces made of threads spun from the precious metals of Atvatabar, mosaics, ivories, art forgings, costly enamels, decorative bas-reliefs, implements of war, agriculture and commerce, *magnic* spears and daggers, with shaft and handle encrusted with grotesque carvings in metallic alloys. These alloys took the forms of figures, animals and emblems, having the strangest colourings, like the hilts and scabbards of Japanese swords carved in *shakudo* and *shibuichi*. There were exhibited vases of cinnabar, vases wondrously carved from tea-rose, coral-red, pearl-gray, ashes-of-roses, mustard-yellow, apple-green, pistache and crushed-strawberry coloured metals. There were also splendid crowns, flowers, animals, birds, and fishes, carved from precious *kragon*, an imperial stone harder than the diamond and of a pale rose-pink colour. Every object was as perfect as though modelled in wax.

Through all this decorative movement there was something

more than decoration understood as mere ornamentation—there was the keenest evidence of soul movement on the part of the artist. The music gloriously celebrated the passions of love, ambition and triumph that had filled the souls of the artists when engaged in their incomparable labours, and pealed forth that serene life of the spirit as symbolized in the perfect works of art exhibited, wherein were sealed in eternal magnificence fragments of the souls that had created them.

Between the pauses of the music an organ-megaphone shouted forth in musically-stentorian tones the words that had been impressed on its cylinders in praise of art. The five thousand priests and priestesses of art had simultaneously shouted their art ritual down five thousand tubes, which were all focussed into a single tube of large calibre. The multitudinous sound of their voices had been indelibly impressed on this phonograph-megaphone that now yielded up the sentiments impressed upon it, its tones being that of a vast multitude, reinforced by the vibrating music of an organ, which was a part of the megaphone. These were the passages repeated by the instrument with a startling splendour of sound:

The Message of the Megaphone.

I. To define art is to define life.

II. Art is a language that describes the souls of things.

III. Art in nature is the expression of life; in art it is life itself.

IV. Art is too subtle a quality to be defined by the formula of the critic. It is greater than all of the definitions that have tried to grasp it.

V. Art is the glowing focus from which radiate thought, imagination and feeling, gifted with the power of utterance.

VI. True art is generous, passionate, earnest, vivid, enthusiastic. So also is the true artist.

VII. To satisfy the far-reaching longing of the spirit, art makes things more glorious than they are. It is the perfect expression of a perfect environment.

VIII. To mould his symbols with the same life that fills his conception of the idea is the supreme effort of the artist.

IX. As nature from the coarse soil produces flowers, so also the artist from every-day life produces the subtle sweets of art.

X. Art that is simply utility is not sufficiently decorative to delight every nerve of feeling in the soul. To feed these, many flavours of form and colour are necessary, and hence the necessity of art.

XI. Where do emotion and imagination begin in art? Where do spirit and flesh unite in a living creature?

XII. The artist is a creator. He breathes into dull matter the breath of art, and it thenceforth contains a living soul.

XIII. Poetry and art make life splendid without science, which is the cold investigation of that which was once thrilled with the passion of life. Invention makes life splendid without poetry and art. By whom will the glorious union of art and science be consummated?

XIV. What is the world we live in? It is for the most part a collection of souls hidebound with treachery and selfishness; of souls covered with a slag from which have departed the fires of love and passion and delight. Such incinerated aliases of their former selves are your judges, oh, artists!

XV. Art is a green oasis in an arid and mechanical civilization. It creates an earthly home for the soul, for those wounded by the riot of trade, the weariness of labour, the fierce struggle for gold, and the deadly environment of rushing travel, blasted pavements and the withering disappointments of life.

XVI. Where is that artist that can sway imagination, create emotion, lift the banner of a high ideal, give the soul a keener appreciation of beauty, add to the mind, strength and grace, cause the brain to develop new nerves of feeling and newer cells of thought, that we may salute him as genius?

XVII. Art is the emotion within made splendid by imagination that clothes everything with perfection. Like colour it dwells only in the soul, but the cause of the sensation is without. In all art, the artist seeks to reproduce the cause of his ecstasy, that he may communicate to others a similar delight. He is like a god, he always gives but never receives, for fame, not money, is his recompense.

XVIII. Given a soul that can feel sublimely, that can respond to beauty and feel thrilled with the joy of existence, that can feel the burden of anguish, that can appreciate the humours and absurdities of life, and given the power to adequately represent the knowledge, truth, understanding and conviction of these impressions in fitting symbols, vitalized by imagination and emotion, then have we both poet and artist.

XIX. The soul in such inspired moments takes the form of sculptured arabesques, or flowers, or resembles the refluent sea, full of incredible shapes and symbols. It accompanies the march of thought, the profusive swell of emotion, is capable of pain and ecstasy, and seeks to be fed with those delightful symbols of its life which we call art, the most priceless of earthly possessions.

XX. Four things are necessary for art, *viz.*: idea, sentiment, imagination and manipulative skill. After these comes prestige, or the applause of the world, to crown the work.

XXI. The art decorator is a type of all art workmen. See him about to manipulate a plastic ornament on the wall. The plaster resembles his idea; its plastic qualities his sentiment, or emotion; the style of ornament into which it is to be moulded resembles his imagination, and the power of the artist to successfully and triumphantly embody in the finished ornament the living, breathing idea that fills him is his manipulative skill. Any work of art, if perfect in itself, still remains unfinished until the world comes along and applauds.

XXII. The age wants the artist. It wants imagination, originality, inspiration, ideality. It requires fertile, dreaming souls, to create ideal breadth.

It requires an earthly Nirvana wherein one may escape a selfish, barbarous, pitiless world. There is a great dearth of the coinage of the soul. We want artists to explain the souls of things, not their mechanical construction, but the unseen secret of their purposes, their unspeakable existence. We want heart-expanding triumphs to counteract the withering influences of life. If a soul is entranced with man or nature, we also want to feel his fascination, to be penetrated with his rapture.

****

The megaphone ceased its musical vociferation, which formed a spiritual exercise for the souls assembled before us. I felt entranced and lifted up to a plane of splendid life hitherto unknown in my experience. I began to understand that art, after all, is the one thing in our terrestrial life worth striving for, in fact our only possession.

For is it not the transmission of the soul to outer matter, whose savagery may be thus charmed and subdued to become a satisfactory spiritual environment?

Following the procession of artists came beautiful, wondrously-arrayed dancers, whose evolutions made the brain dizzy with delight. Fair priests and priestesses of art formed upon the floor of the palace decorative arabesques of scrolls and interlacements of living bodies, the colour of their garments mingling in perfectly harmonious hues, beautiful beyond comparison. Their ceaseless evolutions were made to the measure of perfect music. Panels and bands of living decorations were framed and transformed like the magical changes of the kaleidoscope. At last Yermoul, the Lord of Art, waved his wand, and the dancers stood transfixed, a garden of ecstatic colour like a Persian carpet, wonderfully designed and vividly emblazoned. It was a scene of royal magnificence. These priests and priestesses were the art workers of Gnaphisthasia, who had so finely exhibited their treasures.

Following the rhythmic movements of the art workers came poets, painters, sculptors, whose works lifted the soul to higher planes of being. These in their trophies of art recited or exhibited gave the soul imagination and sentiment, lifting it almost to the enraptured height of worship, adoration and love.

At the close of the ceremonies we were entertained by Yermoul, Lord of Art, at a banquet, at which music and song and the dancing of voluptuous priestesses made hearts thrill with delight. Bidding farewell at last to the Lord of Art and his priests and priestesses, his majesty, myself and our company returned by the sacred locomotive to Calnogor.

CHAPTER 18

The Journey to the Bormidophia

The palace bell announced the beginning of a new day in Calnogor. I had not slept during the hours of rest, excited as I was by our visit to Gnaphisthasia and the strange customs of Atvatabar.

Koshnili arrived soon after the bell had sounded to inform me that the king had commanded his royal army to be assembled in the great square beyond the palace walls to escort us to the Bormidophia, where a solemn act of worship would be performed before the throne of the gods. This was a most delightful message, as nothing on earth could please me better than to witness the glories of the Bormidophia.

The army under the command of Prince Coltonobory, the brother of the king, commander-in-chief, consisted of 250,000 *wayleals*, or flying soldiers, and 50,000 *bockhockids*, or flying cavalry. There was also a detachment of 10,000 *fletyemings*, or sailors of the royal navy. These were drawn up in review in a vast square before the royal palace.

Superb *bockhockids* conveyed us the four miles to the Bormidophia in the centre of the city.

The king and queen, both of whom wore crowns blazing with jewels, sat with Koshnili and myself in the first palanquin of *bockhockids*. The high officers of the government and nobles of the Borodemy, together with the officers and sailors of the *Polar King*, were distributed among the other stately litters.

The route to the pantheon was lined with palaces. An immense population thronged either side of the roadway. A review of the army took place *en route*. The *wayleals* first rose into an enormous flying column, which subsided into whirling domes and afterward broke up into a dozen living globes, that appeared to roll one after another on the ground. These were dissolved into a solid army marching on foot for a time. Then as if by magic the entire mass of men rose into spiral columns which dissolved into vast rings inextricably involved with each other. It was a sight unique and bewildering.

Behind the *wayleals*, fifty thousand *bockhockids* kept up their steady march. The people shouted with enthusiasm.

A mimic battle took place in the air above us. Ten thousand *wayleals* fought on either side, brilliant in many-coloured uniforms. Finally, a rainbow arch of flying men spanned the entrance to the great square of the Bormidophia, or pantheon. Amid the thunder of guns and music, the entire company alighted at the doors of the pantheon, which consisted of an immense circular pile of buildings over a mile in circumference. The interior revealed a scene of surpassing magnificence. Endless tiers of seats were arranged in terraces that, rising above each other, traversed the wide sweep of the amphitheatre. The entire pantheon with its adjacent palaces and colonnades was sculptured out of a hill of green marble. The exterior walls, rising 200 feet, were crowned with a lofty dome of enamelled glass, through which the light of the sun streamed in myriad colours on the sea of worshippers beneath. The walls of the pantheon, both exteriorly and interiorly, were sculptured with immense reliefs, the trophies of invention and art, as well as the magical symbols of spiritual forces.

The lowest circle of the amphitheatre reached down one hundred feet below the level of the outer pavement, and the royal seat was on a level with the ground and fifty feet below the top of the far-famed golden throne of the gods, that stood in the centre of the immense building.

Our entrance was the signal for welcoming music and a suppressed murmur of excitement from the myriads of worshippers that sat both above and below us. The amphitheatre contained not less than 50,000 people. The moment their majesties were seated, a roar of artillery shook the earth. The forthcoming grand act of worship was evidently instituted in our honour, for we were the observed of all eyes in that vast concourse of people.

A dozen choirs, possessed of all kinds of beautiful instruments,

On the throne sat the supreme goddess, Lyone, the representative of Harikar, the Holy Soul.

caressed the ear with their melodious songs. There was no dim religious light; everything was open-eyed beneath that splendid dome. Suddenly a cloud of flying priests and priestesses seated themselves on a pyramid formed of terraces of solid silver fifty feet in height that supported the miraculous throne. They at once began to sing with such force and pathos as to dissolve the multitude into a hush of breathless silence.

Then an immense bell of bronze filled the pantheon with a sonorous moan. Twelve thrilling tones made souls tremble and heads bow down. With the last vibration there rose from the crown of the throne of the gods a living woman, nude to the waist, having a broad belt of gold studded with gems clasping her figure, from which fell to her feet a garment of *aquelium* lace wrought with magical symbols.

She was a girl of peerless development; her arms were long and softly moulded, her breasts firm and splendid. The colour of her complexion and flesh was of soft mat gold, like that of golden fruit, and a perceptible flush warmed her cheeks. Her profile was perfect, being both proud and tender in outline. Her hair was a heavy glossy mass, of a pale sapphire-blue colour, that fell in a waving cloud around her shoulders. Her whole figure bore an infinitely gracious expression, the result of possessing a tender and sympathetic soul.

On her head was a tiara of *terrelium*, the vermilion metal, studded with gems, on her neck she wore a necklace of emerald-green sapphires, while on either wrist were broad gold bracelets, having a magnificent blue sapphire on each.

She was Lyone, the Supreme Goddess of Atvatabar, the representative of Harikar, the Holy Soul; Queen of Magicians; Mother of Sorcerers, and Princess of Arjeels.

Standing erect for a moment, as if to assure the vast congregation of her presence, she then slowly sat down on a broad divan of aloe-green silk velvet, holding in her right hand the *terrelium* sceptre of spiritual sovereignty, whose head bore two hearts formed of flaming rubies.

I was entranced with the appearance of the divine girl, the object of the adoration of Atvatabar. Every feature of her face was carved with a full and ripe roundness, exhibiting repose and power.

Her eyes, large and blue and lustrous, were sorcery itself. There was in them an unutterable tenderness, a divine hospitality, the result of vast pride and still vaster sympathy.

All at once she gazed at me! I felt filled with a fever of delicious delight, of intoxicating adoration. I could then understand the devotion of Atvatabar, of hearts slain by eyes that were conquering swords.

CHAPTER 19

The Throne of the Gods, Calnogor

The throne of the gods was the most famous institution in At-vatabar. It was the cynosure of every eye, the object of all adoration, the tabernacle of all that was splendid in art, science and spiritual perfection. The great institutions of Egyplosis, the college of ten thousand soul-worshippers, the palace of Gnaphisthasia, with its five thousand poets, artists, musicians, dancers, architects, and weavers of glorious cloths, and the establishments for training the youth of the country in mechanical skill, were but the outlying powers that lent glory to the throne itself. It was the standard of virtue, of soul, of genius, skill and art. It was the triune symbol of body, mind and spirit. It was the undying voice of Atvatabar proclaiming the grandeur of soul development; that pleasure, rightly guarded, may be virtue. The religion of Harikar in a word was this, that the Nirvana, or blessedness promised the followers of the supernatural creeds of the outer world, after death was to be enjoyed in the body in earthly life without the trouble of dying to gain it. This was a comfortable state of things, if only possible of accomplishment, and such a creed of necessity included the doctrine that the physical death of the body was the end of all individuality, the soul thereafter losing all personality in the great ocean of existence.

The throne of the gods was a cone of solid gold one hundred feet in height, divided into three parts for the various castes of gods, or symbols of science, art and spirituality. The structure was a circular solid cone of gold, shaped somewhat in the form of a heart. It was indeed the golden heart of Atvatabar, proclaiming that sentiment and science should go hand in hand; that in all affairs of life the heart should be an important factor. The lower section, or scientific pantheon, possessed bas-reliefs of models or symbols of the more important inventions. This section was forty feet in height and seventy-two feet in diameter.

The images of the gods themselves surmounting the lowest part of the throne were in reality composite man-gods, that is to say, each figure was a statue, life size, of the resultant of the statues of all the important developers of each invention and was thus obtained:

As soon as any prominent inventor or developer of an invention died, the government secured a plaster cast of his body, if such had not been made prior to death, and this was preserved for years in a special museum. When twenty or more casts of various developers of any one invention had been accumulated these were placed on a horizontal wheel, which revolved in front of a photographic camera, and thus the composite outline of the future god was obtained. As many outlines were procured as there were eighths of inches in the circumference of the largest cast, and from the collective pictures the ideal cast was made by the sculptor. The cast once perfected, and afterward draped, was reproduced in solid gold and placed with appropriate ceremonies on a pedestal on the throne itself. In like manner the gods of the arts, poetry, painting, etc., were created, as also the priests of Harikar, the Holy Soul.

The reliefs, or symbols of mechanical art, were originally cast on the throne itself. These included the electric engine and locomotive, electric healer, telephone, telegraph, the electric ship, elevator, printing press, cotton gin, weaving loom, typesetting machine, well-boring apparatus, telescope, flying machines (individual and collective), *bockhockid*, sewing machine, photographic camera, reaping machine, paper-making and wall-paper printing machine, phonograph, etc., etc.

This department of the throne being the largest, was significant of the material supremacy of the mechanical arts in the nation. Science itself was a god named Triporus, fashioned like a winged snake, so called because it was said he could worm his way through the pores of matter so as to discover the secrets therein. This god seemed a compound of our ancient Sphinx, or science, and Daedalus, or mechanical skill, but with an entirely new meaning added to both.

THE THRONE OF THE GODS WAS INDEED THE GOLDEN HEART OF
ATVATABAR, THE TRIUNE SYMBOL OF BODY, MIND AND SPIRIT.

The second or intermediate section of the throne was devoted to the gods of art and their attributes. It was sixty feet in its largest diameter, and twenty-four feet in height. It possessed also two sections, the upper containing the statues of Aidblis, or Poetry; Dimborne, or Painting; Brecdil, or Sculpture; Swengé, or Music; Tilono, or Drama; Timpango, or Dancing; Olshodesdil, or Architecture, etc., etc. In the lower section there were tableaux cast in high relief illustrating the qualities of the soul developed by art, *viz.*: Omodrilon, or Imagination; Diandarn, or Emotion; Samadoan, or Conscience; Voedli, or Faith; Lentilmid, or Tenderness; Delidoa, or Truth, etc.

The final section or tapering apex of the throne was thirty feet in greatest width and thirty-six feet in height. It contained a throne and three divisions. The lowest division contained the gods Hielano, or Magic; Bishano, or Sorcery; Nidialano, or Astrology; Padomano, or Soothsaying, etc.

The intermediate division contained the gods Niano, or Witchcraft; Redohano, or Wizardry; Oxemano, or Diablerie; Biccano, or the Oracle; Amano, or Seership; Kielano, or Augury; Tocderano, or Prophecy; Jiracano, or Geomancy; Jocdilano, or Necromancy, etc.

The third division contained the gods Orphitano, or Conjuration; Orielano, or Divination; Pridano, or Clairvoyance; Cideshano, or Electro-biology; Omdohlopano, or Theosophy; Bischanamano, or Spiritualism, etc.

The climax of all was the throne of the goddess. It was a seat of aloe-green velvet that, revolving slowly in the centre of the supporting throne, presented the goddess to every section of the vast audience. Thus seated, the goddess radiated an Orient splendour, herself a blaze of beauty and the focus of every eye. The music of an introductory opera warbled its soft strains with breathless execution. It seemed the carolling of a thousand nightingales, mingling with the musical crying of silver trumpets and the clear electric chiming of golden bells.

CHAPTER 20

The Worship of Lyone, Supreme Goddess

The worship of the goddess began with the appearance on a revolving stage between the nearest worshippers and the base of the throne itself of a veritable forest of trees about one hundred feet in width. There were trees like magnolias, oaks, elms and others splendid in foliage, and amid these there was an undergrowth of beds of the most brilliant flowers.

It was the work of the magicians and sorcerers!

There were thickets of camellias and rhododendrons, amid which bloomed flowers like scarlet geraniums, primroses, violets and poppies. What appeared to be apple, peach, cherry and hawthorn trees, all in full bloom, tossed their white and pink foam of flowers.

They were real trees and flowers, made to exist for a time by the sorcery of the masters of spirit power. They had never before known the outer air. The priests of Harikar had made them, and would dissipate them as living bodies are dissipated by death.

A sacred opera was chanted by the priests of invention, art, and spirituality, on their terraces of silver above the trees and flowers. As the music continued, groups of singers would at times sweep forth on wings and float in wheeling circles around the throne. Their delightful choruses swelling upward were like draughts of rich wine, keen and intoxicating. The priests and spiritual powers marching beneath filled the vast building with broad recitatives, full of vividly descriptive passages and finely contrasted measures, until the soul seemed melted in a sea of bliss.

The throne was bathed and caressed by a blue vapour of incense, while from the great dome above, filled with figures formed of enamelled glass, there streamed lights of all mysterious colours, that illuminated its gleaming sides and lit up the amphitheatre with ineffable effects.

A warm, rosy beam, falling perpendicularly, enveloped the goddess like a robe of transparent tissue. She sat, a living statue, the joy of every heart, the embodiment of a hopeless love that kept the worshipper in a fever of delicious unrest. Wherever the eye wandered, it always came back to the goddess; whatever the soul thought, its last thought was of her.

Amid a tempest of music and the thundering song of two hundred thousand voices repeating a litany of love, the throne itself began to revolve upon the silver cone that supported it. A fresh rapture took possession of the multitude.

In the soul of the goddess what must have been the joy of being surrounded by such an ocean of adoring love?

As I mused on the scene, I thought of the Coliseum at Rome raised to the glory of barbaric force, of empire founded on the blood of its victims, and, being such, has necessarily passed away, becoming a heap of ruins. Here, thought I, is a temple founded on a nobler idea, the glory of the human soul, its ingenuity, art, and spiritual forces.

Many in the outer world would say it was an idolatrous attempt on the part of the creature to usurp the throne of its Creator. Yet it was strangely like the religion of such people themselves. There, as here, I thought, is the same worship of gold, the same dependence on the material products of man's invention, the same worship of art, the same idolatry of each other's souls between the sexes. There is this difference, however: in the outer world men pretend that they worship something else other than such objects; here they have the honesty to say what they do actually worship.

Apart from the idea of attempting to realize a friendship that can only exist in a realm that knows neither interest, fortune, time, ambition, temper, nor sensual love, their idolatry had one splendid truth to unfold, *viz.*, the necessity of a soul for an arid and mechanical civilization. "Every intellect shall enfold a soul" was their motto, and there was this sanity in their creed that sentiment was the breath of its life. Science abhors sentiment; it is the cold investigation of that which once thrilled with the passion of life.

While the singing continued, a band of neophytes of occult

force performed marvellous feats of magic, led by the Grand Sorcerer, Charka, chief of the magicians of Harikar. The people sat enraptured as miracle after miracle was performed. At the waving of fans by the adepts, plants issued from the hands of every god of gold, clothing the throne in one endless wreath of brilliant crimson blossoms and green foliage. The fans again waved and that crimson mass of flowers turned to a pale green, while again the green foliage changed to a vermilion colour. The throne appeared like one enormous Bougainvillea *glabra*, whose leaves are flowers.

Again the fans were waved and the flowers changed to bloom all snowy-white, while the foliage became blue.

The adepts disappeared at a given signal and thereupon entered another band of beautiful girl adepts, who seated themselves, each body in a crouched mass with flowing drapery, around the base of the throne. These priestesses were in a state of catalepsy. The ego, or soul, in each case had been separated from the body, which floated in a state of apparent death. They had so developed their will by thinking enormous thoughts, yearning for spiritual power, that they could suspend the functions of the body and give all their existence to the soul. Thus hypnotized, it was stated their souls were floating freely in the dome above, in blessed converse, and that their reincarnation would afterward take place.

The organ rolled a blessed monotone, with variations exquisitely sweet. The light in the dome faded perceptibly by the magical shadowing of its windows until the rapt audience sat in complete darkness. A circle of electric lights burned around the goddess on the top of the throne, illuminating her figure. The lights faintly lit up the dome, and presently appeared as nude spectres the fifty souls of the priestesses who crouched beneath.

The organ, re-enforced with the wailing of a hundred violins, produced a storm of the most delirious music, while the souls flashed with a strange phosphorescence like a circle of fire. They wheeled with their arms extended horizontally, each aura lying at an angle of forty-five degrees with the horizon. Then, with hands clasping each other's feet, they became a vertical circle like the wheel of fortune, and thus went round and round. Again, they revolved in a circle faces downward, with arms and hands stretched in an attitude of worship, forming for the goddess a wreath of souls. Presently each soul sought its own body floating beneath. The bodies expanding themselves absorbed each its own soul. With the returning light of the outer sun the forest beneath the throne had disappeared and the circular stage was occupied by a band of sorcerers—each having balls of jelly of various colours floating before him. At the command of the grand sorcerer the balls would transform themselves into strange animals resembling cats, dogs, monkeys, serpents, geese, wolves, and eagles. This was a tableau representing man's supremacy over inferior life.

A company of twin souls of the greatest beauty and splendour of raiment took possession of the circular platform beneath the throne and thereupon danced in rhythmic circles wonderfully entrancing and involved, chanting, in harmony with the movement of their bodies, the following hymn to Lyone:

To Lyone

Oh goddess, oh deity glorious,
With golden wan face, and the bloom
Of spirit and figure victorious!
Oh jewel that lighteneth gloom,
Men call thee the soul of a lover,
Invested with purest of clay,
A chrysalis, eager to hover
And fly from thy prison away!

A nautilus, blown on the tide-lave;
So naked a pearl and so pure,
Or coral, that sucks from the sea wave
Those marbles that ever endure!
Thus float on the ocean of being,
Or fathom its deep-flowing sea,
That feeling, believing, and seeing
Thy glory, will worshipped be!

With sense of the body made captive,
While that of the soul is complete.
For love of pure being, receptive,
So blessed, extravagant, sweet.
Oh victim, thy joys are Meresa's,
Who died on the bosom Divine.
Her madness of rapture appeases
The hunger of soul that is thine!

Inflammable impulse of beauty,
The breath of whose ardour is grief;
The God, in fulfilment of duty,
Hath stamped thee in highest relief!
From pots of auriferous metal,
Made pure by the torment of flame,
He pressed thee in fearful begettal,
A coinage too perfect for shame.

He made thee, most splendid, a flower,
A heavy sweet rose, to unfold
Some petals immortal, and shower
Their fragrance on earth frozen cold.
Oh golden-hued rose, in such fashion,
By the love of the world thou art sought
Thus flushed with the triumph of passion
Or pale with the splendour of thought!

Oh soul, that inhales from the blossom
Delight in the rapture of breath,
A goddess aflame with her passion,
Ere beauty is wedded to death!
Oh virginal soul of the fountain,
Alive with the water of Youth,
All these, on the golden high mountain,
Thou dwellest, the image of Truth!

What followed was an intoxicating medley of dancing, song
and magic. Circles of the fairest girls, arrayed in the most ravishing
costumes, made the brain whirl with their gyrations. The oblation
to the dancing gods wound up the performance, and the chorus of
a thousand voices blended with the triumph of drums and explosions from musical artillery.

The incomparable girl goddess then rose to her feet and waved
the blessing of Harikar over the multitude. The girdle of gold that
clung to her figure blazed with a thousand jewels. Her tiara sparkled with enormous diamonds that were blue as sapphires, amber
as topazes, green as emeralds and red as rubies. Accompanied by
the wailing of music, the chant of megaphones, and the song of the
enraptured people, she sank into the heart of the throne, glorious
as she rose, herself its most precious jewel.

CHAPTER 21

An Audience With the
Supreme Goddess

The palace of Tanje, situated about fifty miles from Calnogor, was the metropolitan palace of the supreme goddess. It was sculptured out of a hill of white marble, as were also its walls, enclosing a garden a square mile in extent.

In conformity with the programme prepared by his majesty, King Aldemegry Bhoolmakar, we were to be received by her holiness Lyone in her palace at Tanje. The thought of meeting the adorable figure that crowned the throne of the gods filled me with keenest delight.

I seemed about to visit, not a human being like myself, but a veritable deity. What honour, what pleasure, it would be to speak to her face to face, heart to heart. Disguise it as I might, a feeling for the goddess was being awakened in my soul. Was it the adoration of the worshipper, or was it the dawn of a sacrilegious passion?

It seemed a monstrous idea for any one to love in the ordinary meaning of the term a being so high and holy. I could only worship her afar off, like any adoring citizen of Atvatabar.

His majesty the king, together with Chief Minister Koshnili, Commander-in-Chief Coltonobory, Admiral Jolar and other dignitaries of the kingdom, did us the honour to escort us to Tanje.

The method of travel between Calnogor and Tanje was by means of the pneumatic tube, also a deity of invention. This consisted of a smooth tube six feet in diameter that curved over the country in a sinuous line, being supported on pillars at a height of twenty feet above the ground. A decorative car of gold ornamented in enamelled colours rode the crest of the tube, being connected with the piston inside. The car was steadied between rails on either side and swept over the earth with inconceivable rapidity. The distance from Calnogor to Tanje was traversed in thirty minutes.

A feeling of awe overcame the sailors as we approached the abode of the living symbol of the Holy Soul.

The palace was a noble pile of masonry as it glittered in the perpendicular sunlight. It stood two stories in height and was sur-mounted by a flattened central dome of coloured glass, the ribs of the dome being of solid gold. The lower story was surrounded by a colonnade of pillars carved in the most grotesque shapes im-aginable. The grand entrance on the north side was constructed of alternating pillars of platinum and gold, all three feet in thickness. From the towers brilliant banners, emblazoned with the figure of the throne of the gods, floated on the wind.

The apartments of the grand chamberlain were on the north side of the palace, where the pneumatic car was provided with a depot for the use of travellers.

Cleperelyum, the grand chamberlain, clad in white robes like an Arab chief, received us in the name of the goddess with marked deference and courtesy.

A guard of honour consisting of a thousand *wayleals* was drawn up around the palace. The audience chamber was a rectangular court in the centre of the building, whose ceiling was the roof of the palace itself, surmounted by the dome peculiar to the palaces of Atvatabar.

The hall leading to the presence chamber was lined with the priests and priestesses from Egyplosis in attendance on the goddess.

Led by the grand chamberlain, we arrived at the golden doors of the audience chamber, which were opened by the servitors of the palace. With trembling exultation I saw at the further end of the spacious apartment a royal seat of violet velvet whereon sat Lyone, the supreme goddess of Atvatabar.

As my eyes rested upon the goddess she appeared still more divine than before. It seemed an unhallowed act that rough sailors should venture into such spiritual precincts. We were awe-struck with the presence before us. As the grand chamberlain called out our names, we bowed low to that majestic spirit that seemed much more a deity than human flesh.

HER HOLINESS OFFERED BOTH HIS MAJESTY THE KING AND
MYSELF HER HAND TO KISS.

Her holiness greeted us with marked favour and offered both his majesty the king and myself her hand to kiss. The high officials and my officers and sailors were obliged to remain standing during the audience, according to the etiquette of the holy palace. His majesty the king and myself were allowed to seat ourselves on an elevated dais before the goddess. When thus seated, I had leisure to observe that she was arrayed in a single garment of quivering pale green silk, that caressed every curve of her matchless figure and spread in myriad folds about her limbs and feet. On her head she wore a model of the *jarcal*, or bird of yearning, fashioned in precious *terrelium*. She wore also a jewelled belt of gold. The breast was embroidered with a golden emblem of the throne of the gods, the sacred ensign of Atvatabar. On her neck were circles of rich rose pearls whose light gleamed soft on the green lustre of her attire. On her head was the tiara of the goddess, the triple crown of Harikar.

Her holiness had an air of girlish frankness combined with royal dignity. She was so youthful that she could not have been more than twenty years old. She possessed a charming presence and a clear and musical voice. Her eyes were large and blue, and her finely-formed lips, like blood-red anemones, contrasted finely with the pale golden hue of her complexion.

Her features combined the witchery of a *houri* with the strength of intellect. They were sculptured and illuminated by a grandly-developed soul.

The odour of a high and steadfast virtue surrounded her. It was not the virtue of the ascetic, but rather that strength of soul that could triumph over temptation, that loved fair lights, fine raiment, sweet colours, and all the gladness and beauty of life.

In her soft right hand she bore a rod of divination, the spiritual sceptre of Atvatabar. On either side of her stood a twin soul in fond embrace as a guard of love.

The audience chamber was in itself a dream of grandeur and beauty. From the rose-tinted glass of the dome overhead a light soft and warm bathed all beneath with a peculiar sweetness. The lower part of the walls resembled the cloisters of a mosque. Behind pillars of solid silver a corridor ran all around the chamber. Here an artistic group of singers, clad in classic robes in soft colours, perambulated, singing as they went a refrain of penetrating sweetness.

The audience listened with the deepest respect to the singing and to our conversation with the goddess. In the assembly were all the notables of the kingdom, poets, artists, musicians, inventors, sculptors, etc., as well as royal and sacerdotal officers.

The singing of the choir, that moved like an apparition of spirits in the dim cloisters, seemed to embody our thoughts and feelings. For myself the divine song was a draught of joy. It was a breath of verdure, of flowers and fruits, of a warm and serene atmosphere made perfect by the presence of a peerless incarnation of man's universal soul.

The Goddess Learns the Story of the Outer World

Her holiness was pleased to say how honoured she was by receiving us. Our advent in Atvatabar had created a profound impression upon the people, and she was no less curious to see us and learn from our own lips the story of the outer world. She was greatly interested in comparing the stalwart figures of our sailors with the less vigorous frames of the Atvatabarese. It could not be expected that men who handled objects and carried themselves in a land where gravity was reduced to a minimum could be so vigorous as men who belonged to a land of enormous gravity, whose resistance to human activity developed great strength of bone and muscle.

I informed her holiness regarding the geography, climate and peoples of the outer sphere. I gave her an account of the chief nations of the world from Japan to the United States. I spoke of Africa, Australia, and the Pacific islands. I spoke of Adam and Eve, of the Deluge, of Assyria and Egypt. Then I described the glory of Greece and the grandeur of Rome. I spoke of Caesar and Hannibal, Cleopatra and Antony. I spoke of Columbus, Galileo, Michelangelo, Faraday, Dante, and Shakespeare. I described how art reigned in one kingdom or country and invention in another, and that the soul or spiritual nature was as yet a rare development.

"You tell me," said the goddess, "that Greece could chisel a statue, but could not invent a *magnic* engine, and that your own country, rich in machinery, is barren in art. This tells me the outer world is yet in a state of chaos and has not yet reached the development of Atvatabar. We have passed through all those stages. At first we were barbarous, then, as time produced order, art began to flourish. The artist, in his desire to glorify the few, lost sight of the misery of the many. Then came the reign of invention, of science, giving power to the meanest citizen. As democracy triumphed art was despised, and a ribald press jeered at the sacred names of poet and priest. By degrees, as the pride and power of the wealthy few were curbed and the condition of the masses raised to a more uniform and juster level, universal prosperity, growing rapidly richer, produced a fusion of art and progress. The physical man made powerful by science and the soul developed by art naturally produced the result of spiritual freedom. The enfranchised soul became free to explore the mysteries of nature and obtain a mastery over the occult forces residing therein."

"In the outer sphere," I informed the goddess, "there has also existed in all ages an ardent longing for spiritual power over matter. But this power, which in many periods of history was really obtained, had been purchased by putting in practice the severest austerities of the body. Force of soul was the price of subjugation of passion and the various appetites of the body. The *fakirs*, *yogis*, jugglers, and adepts of India; the magicians, sorcerers and astrologers of Mesopotamia and Egypt; the alchemists, cabalists, and wizards of the middle ages, and the theosophists, spiritualists, clairvoyants, and mesmerists of the present time, were members of the same fraternity who have obtained their psychological powers from a study and practice of mystic philosophy or magic."

"You say that the outer-world magicians derived their powers of soul from abnegation of the body," said the goddess. "Now the soul priests of Atvatabar can do quite as wonderful things, I dare say, as your magicians, and they have never practised austerities, but, on the contrary, have developed the body as well as the soul. In the worship of the gods of science and invention, art and spirituality, both body, mind, and soul are exercised to their utmost capability. In all stages there is exultance, exercise, development. But I am deeply interested in your remarks. Tell me just what the principles of the worshippers of your Harikar are!"

"Spiritual culture in the outer world," I explained, "is obtained by a variety of religious beliefs, but the belief that most nearly resembles that of Atvatabar is that of the soul-worshippers, who deny the existence of any power beyond the human soul, teaching that it is only by our own inward light that we can rise to higher planes and reach at last to Nirvana, or passive blessedness. This inward light can only be truly followed by self-obliteration, fastings, penances, and repression of desires and appetites of all kinds, carried on through an endless series of reincarnations. The final blessedness is a beatific absorption into the ocean of existence which pervades the universe."

"That is a different creed to that of Harikar in Atvatabar," said the goddess, "which is worship of body, mind, and soul. We believe with your Greeks in perfection of body and also with your Hindus in perfection of soul. We re-enforce the powers of body and mind by science and invention, and the soul powers by art and spiritual love. We believe in magic and sorcery. Our religion is a state of ecstatic joy, chiefly found in the cultured friendship of counterpart souls, who form complete circles with each other. Enduring youth is the consummate flower of civilization. With us it lasts one hundred years, beginning with our twentieth birthday. There is no long and crucial stage of bodily abstinence from the good things of life; there is only abstinence from evil, from vice, selfishness, and unholy desire. Our religion is the trinity of body, mind, and spirit, in their utmost development. Such is the faith of Atvatabar."

"And such a faith," I replied, "with such a deity as your holiness, must profoundly sway the hearts of your people."

The goddess was a woman of intuition. Almost before I was aware of it myself she evidently discovered a sentiment underlying my words. She paused a moment, and before I could question her further regarding the peculiar creed of Atvatabar, said: "We will discuss these things more fully hereafter."

At a signal from the goddess the trumpets rang a blast announcing the audience at an end. With the summons music uttered a divine throbbing throughout the chamber, while the singers marched and sang gloriously in the cloisters.

As I sat, my soul swimming in a sea of ecstasy born of the blessed environment, I felt possessed of splendours and powers hitherto unknown and unfelt. A thrill of joy made hearts tremble beneath the crystal dome. It was a new lesson in art's mysterious peace.

The Garden of Tanje

A series of banquets and other entertainments followed each other during our stay at the palace of Tanje. The goddess had held frequent interviews with the professors and myself regarding the external sphere, and had examined our maps and charts with the greatest curiosity.

His majesty did not take nearly so much interest in our revelations as the goddess, being inert   and prosaic in character.

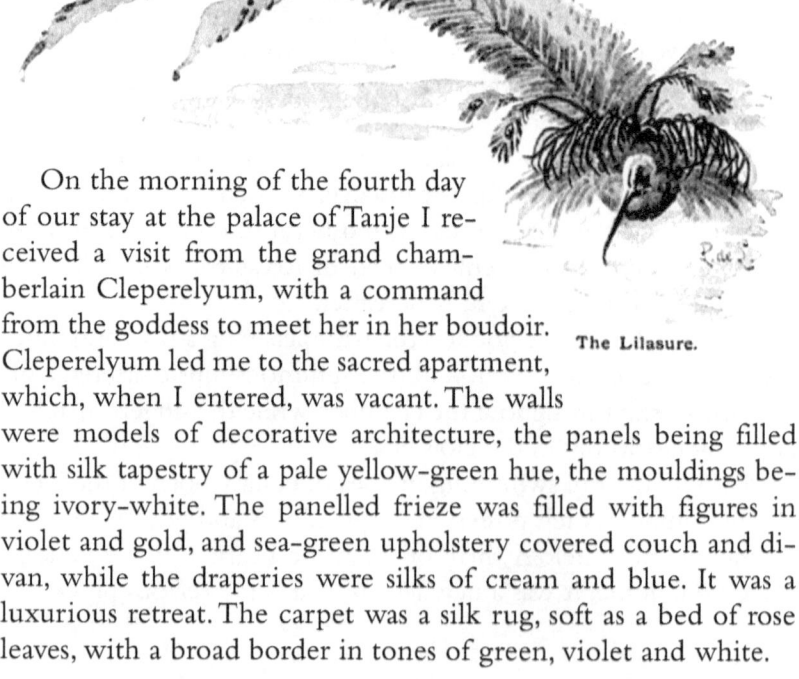

On the morning of the fourth day of our stay at the palace of Tanje I received a visit from the grand chamberlain Cleperelyum, with a command from the goddess to meet her in her boudoir. Cleperelyum led me to the sacred apartment, which, when I entered, was vacant. The walls

The Lilasure.

were models of decorative architecture, the panels being filled with silk tapestry of a pale yellow-green hue, the mouldings being ivory-white. The panelled frieze was filled with figures in violet and gold, and sea-green upholstery covered couch and divan, while the draperies were silks of cream and blue. It was a luxurious retreat. The carpet was a silk rug, soft as a bed of rose leaves, with a broad border in tones of green, violet and white.

Presently the goddess entered with a winning smile on her features. She was arrayed in a dress of soft violet silk, that, apparently, had no other garment beneath, so perfect was the revelation of her figure. Beneath the figure it fell to the ground in a thousand folds, like a wave of smooth water bursting into foaming rapids. Round her neck was a garland of lustrous yellow pearls. On her head she wore a tiara of much smaller dimensions than that worn on public occasions. Her pose was upright as an arrow.

I rose and bowed profoundly, and the goddess also bowing, requested me to be seated.

"I have sent for you," said she, "to learn more about your country and to talk with you about ours. I am consumed with curiosity regarding the external world." "Your holiness," I replied, "permit me to say that your graceful condescension exceeds, if possible, your splendour. I am truly bewildered at the vastness of my good fortune in discovering a country ruled by so glorious a goddess."

The Laburnul

"And I also," said the goddess, "have learned that Bilbimtesirol is not the universe, but a very small portion thereof indeed. I am intensely interested in your accounts of the outer world. I am overpowered with the thought that the exterior surface of the planet is peopled with beings like ourselves, and that civilization, government, religion, art, manufacture, and social life are so

The Green Cazzle of
Glockett Gozzle.

greatly developed beneath a still more glorious sun than ours."

"Did it never occur to your astronomers," I inquired, "that human activity might also pervade the outer sphere?"

"Our astronomers," said the goddess, "have long since decided that the conditions of climate on the exterior planet were too severe to allow human life to exist. They are aware that a great luminary gave the outer earth light by day, for our most daring aerial voyagers have frequently caught a glimpse of its light seen through the polar gulf. They argued that the equatorial regions were too hot, and the polar regions too cold, to support life, consequently the outer earth was a barren waste as desolate and uninhabited as your own satellite."

"Would your holiness like to visit the exterior earth?" I boldly inquired.

"If duty did not prevent me," she replied, "I would love to visit those far-off strange lands and peoples and see your sun and moon and all the stars!"

From the goddess I first learned the precise location of Atvatabar. Lying exactly underneath the Atlantic Ocean it stretched east and west some two thousand miles, surrounded by the interior sea. There were other continents in Bilbimtesirol which we had already dimly seen spread upon the concave walls of the world around us.

"You must come to see both Egyplosis and Arjeels," said her holiness, "but before you leave Tanje you must see my garden."

"It must be a little paradise!" I exclaimed.

"Let us go and see it now," she said, and, so saying, arose with a gracious gesture and led me out of the apartment.

I accompanied her holiness down the terrace leading to the lovely retreat. Curving walks led between banks of flowers of all hues. There were avenues of tall shrubs not unlike rhododendrons, with the same magnificent bloom. Other plants, such as the firesweet, displayed a blinding wealth of yellow flowers.

The goddess led the way to the conservatory in the garden wherein were treasured strange and beautiful flowers and *zoophytes* illustrative of the gradual evolution of animals from plants, a scientific faith that held sway in Atvatabar. The goddess showed me a beautiful plant with large fan-shaped leaves from whose edges hung a fringe of heavy roses; long trailing garlands of clustering star-shaped flowers sprang from the same roots. The plant was a perfect bower of bliss, and while called the *laburnul*, might with greater propriety be styled the rose of paradise.

Jeerloons.

Another fern-like plant was in reality a bird flower, called the *lilasure*. It had the head and breast of a bird, from whose back grew roots and four small feathers resembling those of the peacock. Its tail resembled two large fronds of a fern, which served the animal for wings, for by their aid it flew through the air.

There was also a flock of strange green-feathered creatures, resembling buzzards, called green *gazzles*, on whose heads grew sunflowers. On either side, beneath their wings, were the plant roots by means of which they still sucked nourishment from the soil, as their bills were not yet perfectly developed. They belonged to a locality on the south coast of Atvatabar known as Glock-ett Gozzle.

The *lillipoutum* was another wonderful crea-ture, half-plant half-bird. It represented the animal al-most entirely evolved from the plant stage. A wreath of root-lets adorned the neck, but the most conspicuous features were the stork-like legs that terminated in roots with radiations like *encrinital* stems. The bird fed itself like a plant by simply thrusting its root-legs into the soft ooze of lake bottoms and slimy banks of rivers. Its tail was also a root possessing great ab-sorptive powers. In shape the bird resembled a flamingo, and its feathers were of an old-rose colour, mottled with lichen-green. A beard-like radiation of roots decorated its head, and its bill was extremely delicate.

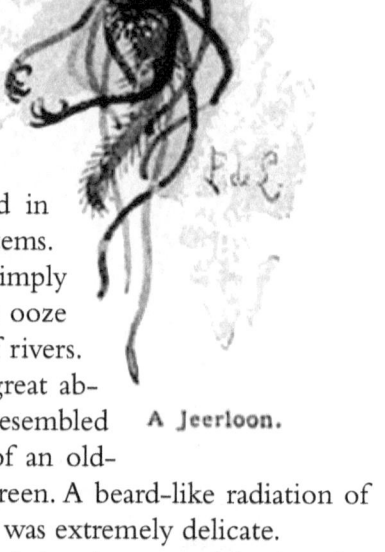

A Jeerloon.

Such wonders as these intensified the glamour of the interior world. I was fast becoming bewildered with the intoxication of an environment of strange, abnormal creatures—unlike anything I had ever seen before.

The goddess regarded her pets with the greatest interest, and was pleased at being the first to acquaint me with such living won-ders of Atvatabar.

"Your holiness," I said, "these creatures are so wonderful that un-less I had actually seen them it would be impossible for me to believe in their existence." As I spoke, two strange bat-like forms flew toward us; they were flying orchids, known as *jeerloons*, with heart-shaped faces and arms terminating in wire-like claws. Their wing projec-tions were bristling with suckers like the rays of a starfish. Altogether they were weird, uncanny creatures. The goddess caught one of them in her hands, and laughed at my excitement. "They will haunt you in your dreams," she exclaimed, "poor, pretty things!"

"But now," she added, "let me show you a plant that is fast becoming a brood of animals, both root and flower. It is the *jugdul*. Still rooted in the soil, strange faces are swelling in the mould, while the flower is a leaf surmounted by a weird, small head, the nasal organ of which is a ponderous proboscis. We do not know as yet what kind of animal life will evolve from the plant, but the botanists and physiologists of Atvatabar are agreed that at least two new species of animals will be developed when the evolution of the *zoophyte* is complete."

I assured her holiness that I considered myself the most favoured of men to be permitted to visit the sanctuary wherein the occult transmigration of life was being manifested. It was a rare experience!

Just then the goddess directed my attention to a flying root resembling a humming-bird. It was the far-famed *jalloast*, the semi-evolved humming-bird of Atvatabar. Other similar beings, half-root, half-bird, were seen perched in a bower of tree-ferns, whose waxy green fronds fell like an emerald cascade about the *jalloasts*.

From porcelain boxes suspended along the roof of the conservatory a perfect forest of strange plants depended, a species of *zoophyte* known as the *yarp-happy*, which seemed to be a combination of ape and flower. Its peculiarly weird, ape-like face was covered with a hood, and from the open mouth of each animal the tongue protruded. From the neck of the animal three long leaves radiated, the two lower leaves in each case terminating in claw-like extremities, which gave a weird expression to the *zoophyte*.

Right underneath these strange beings, The Lillipoutum.

119

there grew an immense quantity of spotted pouch-shaped plants, each having the head of a cat growing above the pouch. This peculiar *zoophyte* was known as the *gasternowl*. From either side of the junction of the cat-like head with the pouch radiated two speckled leaves. The tips of the ears terminated in frond-like plumes, and a peculiar plume like a crest surmounted the head.

A strange root known as the *crocosus* was developed into a perfect animal that crawled with four legs upon the floor. The animal was not unlike the lizard, or a diminutive crocodile, with an immensely long neck, which it held erect. The neck terminated in a bulbous head, with an open, bill-shaped mouth, not unlike the mouth of a pelican, while right below the jaws there grew a root-like appendage, that coiled around the neck. The animal possessed a root-like tail, and was a most interesting creature.

To enumerate all the wonders of the conservatory of plant transmigration at Tanje would be impossible. I saw the *jardil* (or love-pouch), an orchid resembling a pouch, with the face of a child growing therein, from which radiated rootlets and jabots of spiral fronds. I also saw the redoubtable *blocus*, an animal resembling

The Jugdul.

a jerboa, or kangaroo, whose only trace of plant existence was a few rootlets growing out of its back. The *funny-fenny*, or clowngrass, was a weed with veritable goblins growing on the stems. The goblins had long noses and wore high hats and lace collars, but were otherwise but plants with absorbent roots. They were so grotesque that I began to think that nature was laughing at me quite as much as I laughed at nature.

When leaving the conservatory I heard a chorus of tender voices like a band of spirits singing, whereupon the goddess directed my attention to a cluster of fairy girls that, like flowers, were growing upon the stem of a plant. It was a peculiarity of these fairy creatures to sing every time their goddess passed by, her spiritual atmosphere quickening them into conscious life and song. I was fairly dazzled with such a tribute of love to my gracious companion, and were the fairy flowers not sacred things I would have borne them away to exhibit such a trophy to the outer world.

This wonderful plant seemed more like the production of spirit power indulging in a weird fantasy of imagination, rather than an evolution of nature. It was a new experience to me to hear the little creatures sing in a tender chorus of adoration to the goddess and dance gleefully upon their stems. My guide fondled the strange creatures with her own fair fingers, and they seemed to me the greatest wonder I had yet beheld in Atvatabar.

The Yarphappy. "These," said the goddess, "are *gleroserals*, and I would gladly give you a spray were it not that removal from their tender habitat would kill them. But

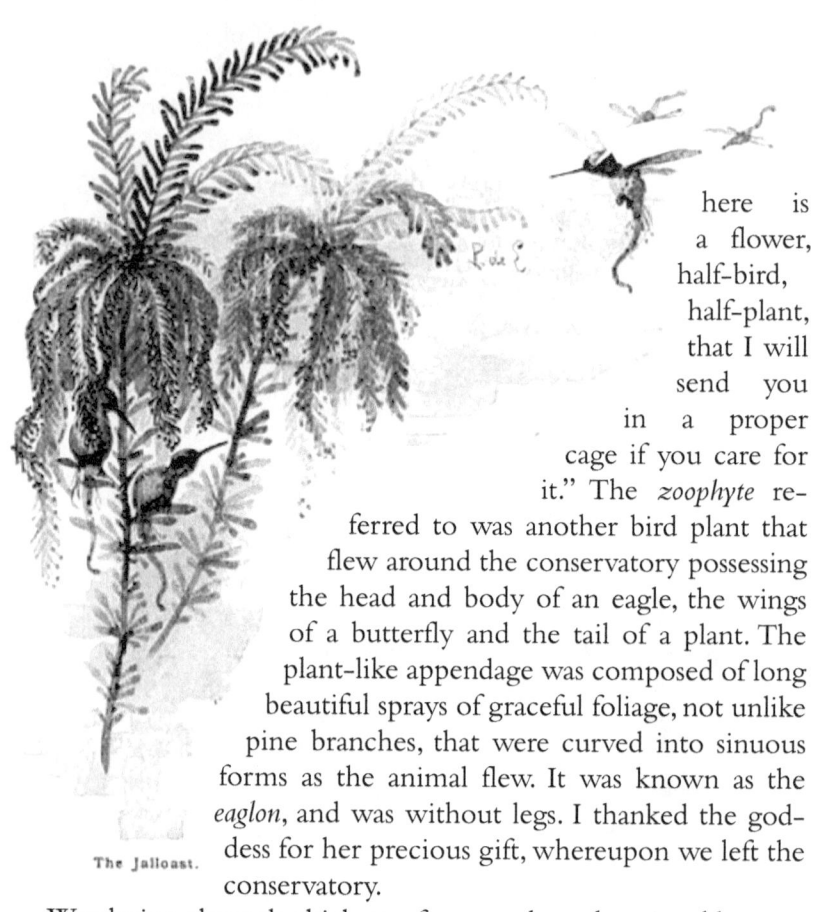

The Jalloast.

here is a flower, half-bird, half-plant, that I will send you in a proper cage if you care for it." The *zoophyte* referred to was another bird plant that flew around the conservatory possessing the head and body of an eagle, the wings of a butterfly and the tail of a plant. The plant-like appendage was composed of long beautiful sprays of graceful foliage, not unlike pine branches, that were curved into sinuous forms as the animal flew. It was known as the *eaglon*, and was without legs. I thanked the goddess for her precious gift, whereupon we left the conservatory.

Wandering through thickets of roses whose burning blossoms swooned upon their stems, we came upon a thick carpet of verdure that surrounded a hidden lake of clear, cool water. The rocky basin of the lake had been sculptured by human hands. Its margin was in outline a bold pear-shaped curve, that also curved upon itself, formed by an immense chiselling of the fundamental rock. In a little harbour of cut rock lay a pleasure boat, a curiously-wrought shell of silver that was propelled by *magnicity*. The goddess entered the boat, bidding me follow her. We sat together on an ample couch in the stern of the boat underneath a silver canopy. Touching a button, the boat moved swiftly over the water. It was a scene of rapture! Gazing into the depths of the water I saw the bottom of the lake sculptured in immense masses of flowers of stone, like the roof of a Gothic cathedral, but a hundred times more luxuriant. Around and above

us rose heights of blessedness filled
with all the thousand ecstasies
of leaf and flower. An islet bore
a little pagoda that stood in the
eternal noon a pillared jewel of
stone, silent and
beautiful. It was
half concealed
with festoons of creep-
ing plants whose flowers
were great globes
of crimson, yellow
and blue.

There
was around
me—
paradise,
and beside
me—ecstasy!

"You are pleased
with my garden?" said the
goddess.

"This must be the gar-
den of Hesperides that
our poets write of," I replied. "Here at last I have
found the ideal life."

The goddess reclined on
the couch in an attitude of
luxurious grace. Her every
gesture was at once heroic and
beautiful.

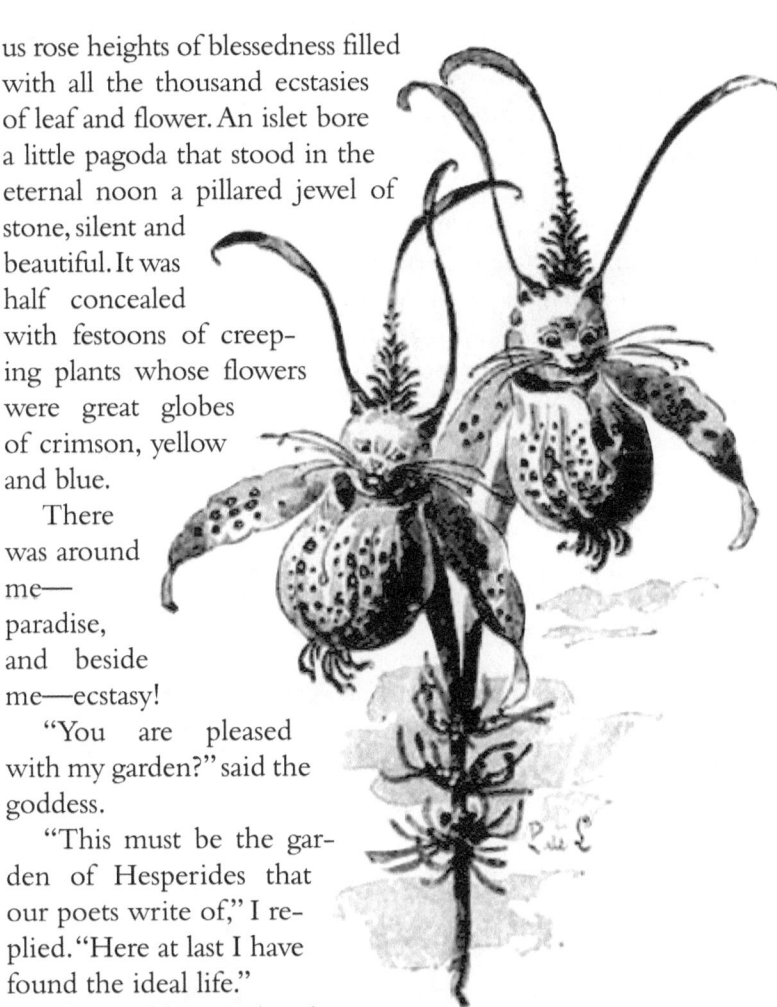

The Oasternowl.

"Tell me what your poets say of nature, life and love," said she;
"do they ever sing the delights of hopeless love?"

As the goddess uttered this last question I felt within me a
strange delight. There sat beside me, floating on that mysterious
wave, the idol of a great nation, the deity of its universal faith, a
divinity of power, glory and beauty, laying aside spiritual empire to

become the companion of a simple explorer of the internal world, her discoverer and her friend, by a most happy chance of fortune.

As these thoughts swiftly ran through my brain, and before I had time to reply, music, soft, weird, intensely intoxicating, was blown from among the tempestuous bloom of the paradises. The melody seemed the holiest thrill of hearts communing in the rapture of love! To explain the sweetness of the moment is impossible—the goddess was so alluring and serene. She kept her own emotions in the background as the result of a proud devotion to duty, and yet I felt swathed with a soul that seemed to have found an opportunity worthy the expression of its life.

A situation so daring, yet so tender, required an equally daring and reverent soul to meet it. I felt all its surpassing loveliness.

"Our poets," I replied, "have written of love in all its phases, describing the most spiritual passions as well as the most lustful. In poetry love may be any phase of love, but the reality is a compound of lust and spirituality, being rooted both in body and soul."

"Do your people," said the goddess, "never differentiate lust and love and obtain in real life only a spiritual romantic love such as we do in Atvatabar?"

"We believe, your holiness," I replied, "that such a love as you refer to is only to be found in a spiritual state and is the secret of disembodied blessedness."

"You must see Egyplosis," said she, "ere you depart from us, and there learn the possibility of ideal love in actual life."

The Crocosus.

"To discover such a joy," I replied, "will repay my journey to Atvatabar a thousandfold."

We alighted from the boat on a rocky margin of the lake that led into a labyrinth of flowers. Here we wandered at will, discovering at every step new delights. Lyone was not only a goddess, but also the fond incarnation of a comrade soul.

The Jardil or Love Pouch

CHAPTER 24

The Journey to Egyplosis

Never did time pass so rapidly or so happily as the days spent in the palace of the goddess. Although I met Lyone at the daily banquets and at our scientific discussions with the astronomers, naturalists, chemists, geologists, physicians and philosophers of Atvatabar, yet neither by look nor gesture did she betray the slightest memory of that ravishing scene in her garden only a few days before.

Again and again I asked myself, Was it possible that that calm and crowned goddess of the pantheon was a being that could feel thrilled with ordinary human ecstasy? Would I, most daring of men, ever be permitted to kiss that far-off mouth divine, and not be slain by one dreadful glance of contempt?

Our discussions terminated in an invitation by the goddess to accompany her in her aerial yacht, the *Aeropher*, to Egyplosis, whither, according to the sacred calendar, she must proceed to take part in the ceremony of the installation of a twin soul. Her holiness, their majesties the king and queen, myself and officers of the *Polar King*, to-

The Blocus.

gether with the chief minister Koshnili, the military, civil and naval officers, the poets, savants, artists, and musicians of Atvatabar, would sail in the yacht of the goddess.

A host of lesser dignitaries, including the sailors of the *Polar King* under command of Flathootly, would follow us in another yacht, called the *Fletyeming*. Each yacht had its own priest-captain, officers and crew of aerial navigators.

Each yacht consisted of a deck of fine woven cane, compact as steel, woven with great skill, with cabins, state-rooms, etc., of the same material erected thereon, and high bamboo bulwarks to prevent the voyagers falling off the deck.

The propelling apparatus consisted of two large wheels, having numerous aerial fans that alternately beat backward and cut through the air

The Funny Fenny, or Clowngrass

as they oscillated on their axes. The wheels were supplemented by aeroplanes, resembling huge outspreading wings, inclined at an angle, so that their forward rush upon the air supported the ship. They revolved with great rapidity, being driven by the accumulated force of a thousand *magnic* batteries, composed of dry metallic cells, especially designed for aerial navigation. Very little force was required to keep the vessel buoyed up in the air, owing to the diminished gravity.

It was discovered that the rarer metals *terrelium* and *aquelium* developed in contact, without salts or acids, enormous currents of *magnicity* without polarization or the development of gases. These metallic cells would run without attention or maintenance exerting *magnic* action, and could be stopped or started at any time without corrosion of metals or loss of energy, like the electric batteries on the outer sphere, but infinitely more powerful.

Aerial navigation was one of the great institutions of Atvatabar, and the goddess' yacht was only one of many thousand aerial ships that carried passengers, mails and light freight to and from every part of the country.

On such a machine as this we purposed travelling a distance of one thousand miles.

Five hundred miles west of Calnogor lay a range of lofty mountains, whose peaks pierced the upper strata of cold air. This region was the breeding-place of fearful storms that occasionally vexed the otherwise placid climate of the country.

Westward of the mountains, an elevated prairie or tableland extended for five hundred miles further, broken here and there into crevasses and canyons, the beds of mighty rivers. Beyond the prairie an irregular agglomeration of mountains and valleys stretched five hundred miles further until the ocean was reached which formed the western boundary of Atvatabar.

Egyplosis, or the sacred palace, stood on an island in a lake lying in a romantic valley of the central plateau, one thousand miles west of Calnogor. This was the destination of the *Aeropher*, the goddess making a special visitation to the palace of hopeless love.

No journey could have begun with better auspices than ours. We soared up the grand divide, underneath the brilliant sun, which threw the moving shadow of the ship on the earth beneath.

The Gleroseral.

Captain Lavornal, the inventor of the *Aeropher*, was resolved to outdo all former records in aerial navigation, and accordingly drove the *Aeropher* at a speed of eighty miles an hour.

The captain explained to me that he was using the wheels simply to lift the ship over the mountains. Once over these the wheels that were being used to lift the ship would thus propel her, when her normal speed of two hundred miles an hour would be reached.

Lyone was in a particularly happy mood. "I like aerial travelling so much," said she, "because it is the nearest mechanical approach to the nature of the soul."

"What relation to the soul can the ship possibly possess?" I inquired.

"Why, don't you see," said she, "that our travelling approaches nearer to that of the spiritual state than any other mode? We can at will sweep up into heaven or descend to earth. We are independent of obstacles. Rivers and roads, mountains and seas have no terrors for us. Then the infinite daring of it all—oh! it is to me delightful."

The Eaglon.

Higher and yet higher mounted the ship up the steeps of the continent until we plunged into a grisly pass. On either side the huge shoulders of the mountains lifted up forests of pines and cedars, whose colossal trunks seemed the gateways of a new world. The ship indeed possessed some of the attributes of a soul. It could plunge us into sublimity or death, lift up to the very sun itself, or, like a disembodied soul, skim the surface of the earth.

The mountains once crossed, we swept down their declivities toward the prairies with tremendous speed. The propellers seemed powerful enough to control the ship in the fiercest storm. The inner world lay spread out beneath us like a map in relief. There was a strange absence of shadow caused by a perpendicular sun that realized the climate of Dante,

"A land whereon no shadow falls."

Yet as the *Aeropher* swept onward her shadow could be seen drifting over cornfields, miles of rustling wheat and pastures where the cattle started and fled from the apparition in the sky.

We were admiring the beauty of the panorama beneath, when the sky became suddenly overcast with clouds, obscuring the light of the sun. This was so unexpected an occurrence that Lyone and myself looked at each other in alarm.

Captain Lavornal exclaimed: "Your holiness, I apprehend these clouds are the couriers of a hurricane!"

"Do you mean that we shall be overtaken by the storm?" asked Lyone.

"Most certainly," said the captain, "and I tremble lest anything should happen to your holiness."

"Do not fear for me," said Lyone; "even a storm is not insurmountable."

"Shall I descend, your holiness, or keep to our course?" inquired the captain with some trepidation.

"Keep to your course," replied Lyone.

Just then a hollow booming was heard, and then a fierce explosion in which the darkened sky became enveloped in a sheet of flame.

In a moment the cyclone struck the ship!

Some of the terrified voyagers shrieked and others remained silent, but all held tightly on to the nearest thing they could get hold of.

The ship lay at an angle of forty-five degrees from the plane of the rotating storm, having been caught by the wind with a fearful shock, snapping several of the cables that bound cabins and decks together. Strangely enough, the ship did not become a wreck, but was blown out of its course, the toy of the wind. We lost sight of the other ship containing the sailors, and could certainly only care for ourselves.

The cyclone proved to be a storm five hundred miles in diameter. The currents of air most remote from the centre did not sweep round in the same uniform plane. The entire circumference of wind was composed of two enormous waves each seven hundred and fifty miles in length and four miles in perpendicular height. It was as if the rings of Saturn had suddenly assumed a vertical as well as a spinning motion, and both movements of the storm produced an appalling splendour of flight hitherto unknown to human sensation. Can the *Aeropher* survive the roaring storm? was the thought of every heart. Bravery was of no avail with the destroying force that had so suddenly overwhelmed us.

CHAPTER 25

Escaping From the Cyclone

The ship, lifting her prow, would spring into the sky upon the bosom of the whirling waste of air. The sun was completely obscured by dense masses of flying clouds and we were deluged with torrents of water. The terror of the situation obliterated all thoughts of country or home or friends. All worldly consciousness had evaporated from the pale beings that in despair held on to the ship for life or death.

The ravages of the storm on the earth beneath could be heard with startling distinctness. We heard at times the roaring of forests and saw the shrieking, whirling branches in every earth–illuminating flash of lightning.

The goddess stood holding on to the outer rail of the deck, the incarnation of courage. She had risen to meet the danger at its worst.

The *Aeropher* having risen to an enormous height, being thrown completely out of the tempest as if shot from a catapult, turned to descend again. It flew downward like an arrow, filling every soul, save perhaps that of Lyone, with fear. All were resigned for death; there could be no escape from the destruction that threatened us.

All this time the centre of the storm had been travelling to the southeast, or about forty-five degrees out of our proper course. Suddenly the ship shot downward from the south-eastern limb of the storm, which almost reached the earth at this point. Gazing below, we discovered a fearful chasm in the face of the earth toward which we were rapidly flying. It was the canyon of the river Savagil, a merciless abyss ten thousand feet in depth.

Frightful as was the scene, it might yet prove our salvation if the ship could escape colliding with the precipitous walls. Were there no abyss we would certainly be dashed to pieces on the earth itself.

Suddenly the ship heeled over fifty degrees, flinging its living freight violently against the houses on deck and the lower rail. But we were saved! One side of the deck grazed the precipice as it plunged into the canyon. We had passed through the danger before knowing what had happened.

Lyone was stunned, but safe, the captain had a dislocated wrist, and others had broken limbs, but none was fatally hurt.

It was a terrible experience.

As the canyon of the river led in a north-easterly direction we did not emerge from the shelter it gave us to seek fresh conflict with the cyclone, but kept flying between the formidable walls. We soon knew by the returning sunlight and the silver clouds that the hurricane had died away.

The damage done to the *Aeropher* was quickly repaired. The ceaseless humming of the fans revolving on axles of hollow steel lulled our senses once more into dreamy repose.

"Ah," said Lyone, "this is life. I feel as though I were a bird or disembodied spirit. This aerial navigation is the realization of those aspirations of men that they might like birds possess the sky. Some have wished to enjoy submarine travel, to explore those frightful abysses of ocean where sea-monsters dwell; to behold the conflict of sharks in their native element, to see the swordfish bury his spear in the colossal whale. I prefer this upper sphere of sunlight and the dome of forests, mountains, and valleys of the dear old earth."

"You are right," said I; "the world into which we are born is our true habitat."

The walls of the canyon grew wider apart until we floated in a valley two miles wide. The meadow land below us was carpeted with grass and covered with clumps of forest trees, down the middle of which ran the river, green and swift. The walls of the valley here rose twelve thousand feet in perpendicular height, prodigies of stone, stained in barbaric colours by the brushes of the ages. Here and there triumphant cataracts flashed from the heights and fell in torrents of foam to the valley below. Sometimes a tributary of the river dashed furiously from the battlements above us into the abyss, flinging clouds of spray on the tops of the trees beneath.

THE GODDESS STOOD HOLDING THE OUTER RAIL OF THE DECK,
THE INCARNATION OF COURAGE.

The *Aeropher* maintained a uniform height of five thousand feet, sufficiently high to give us the exultation of a bird, yet sufficiently deep to allow the sublimity of the scene to fully impress us.

The musicians, who had hitherto remained in abeyance, now broke the silence of our progress with a swelling refrain. The music rolled echoing from granite to jasper walls in strains of divine pathos. We seemed to sail through the fabled realms of enchantment. In that little moving heaven, ceremony was dissolved into a thrilling friendship; the harmonious surroundings created a closer union of souls.

Above where I sat with Lyone there floated a flag of yellow silk a hundred feet in length. As it floated on the wind it assumed a varying series of poetic shapes, very beautiful to witness.

Sometimes there was a long sinuous fold, then a number of rippling waves, then a second fold only shorter than the first, then more rippling waves. It was a symbol of the soul and of the goddess, and represented the fascination and poetry that belongs to the adepts of Harikar. Its folds changed momentarily. At times there would be one large central curve like a Moorish arch, flanked on either side by a number of lesser arches. Again the flag streamed in throbbing waves, frequently blown by an intense breath of wind straight as a spear, crackling and shivering like a soul in pain. It responded not only to the motion of the ship, but had an independent life of its own.

"You see," said Lyone, "that the spiritual part of our creed is but the development of this independent life of the soul. The spiritual nature responds to the opportunity worthy of its recognition."

"That is but the mechanical law of cause and effect," I ventured; "where does self-sacrifice come in?"

"I do not quite understand," she replied; "self-sacrifice is the first law of the soul."

"What I mean," I said, "is this—having discovered your counterpart, do you adore despite the circumstances of fortune?"

"Most certainly," she replied; "there is the divinest self-sacrifice on both sides as far as the fortunes of each will permit. Ideally, the sacrifice is unlimited, but practically is limited as to time, opportunity and other circumstances."

"Is the counterpart soul loved in spite of disparity of circumstances, or is an equality of circumstances, such as rank, wealth and nationality, etc., a factor in the case?" I inquired.

"Outward circumstances have nothing whatever to do with the matter," said Lyone. "Friends, wealth, rank, everything is thrown aside in favour of the inward circumstance that the two souls are one."

"But," I urged, "you expose your spiritual creed to very violent shocks at times. The king of today may be a beggar tomorrow, and, besides, one or both of two souls may before they have known each other have been freighted with lifelong responsibilities. How, then, do you prevent a catastrophe to some one?"

"I admit," she said, "that as far as the every-day world is concerned, there are serious difficulties to contend with. But we avoid these by creating a little world of our own, exclusively for the cultivation of the spiritual soul. Just as some people apply themselves to physical culture to become athletes and show how grand the physical man may become, so we set apart a number of people as soul-priests to develop spirituality, or power over themselves and others and power over matter. It was for this object that Egyplosis was founded, to form a fitting environment for those who have achieved the ideal life. This life fully ripened, with its fresh and glorious enjoyment, can be maintained for a hundred years without diminution or loss of ecstasy."

"And do you mean that, after living one hundred years, beginning with your twentieth birthday, you are still only commencing your twenty-first year?"

"That is exactly what I mean," said Lyone. "I myself have lived ten years of Nirvana, and am yet only twenty years old."

I could well believe that such glorious freshness and beauty as hers was quite as young as she had represented it; but it was a strange idea—this achievement of an earthly Nirvana.

"Do you believe in the independent life of the soul after death?" I inquired.

"I believe that, as our bodies when they die become reabsorbed into the bosom of nature, to become in part or whole reincarnated in other forms of life, so also our souls are reabsorbed into the great ocean of existence, to also dwell, in time, wholly or in part in some other form of life or love."

CHAPTER 26

The Banquet on the Aerial Ship

The saloon, which was also the *salle à manger*, was situated in the centre of the ship. Thus the entire travellers could assemble together without disturbing the centre of gravity of the structure.

The saloon was composed of woven cane, and ornamented with a dado of sage-green silk, on which were embroidered storks, pheasants and eagles flying through space. An elongated table, also of wicker work, contained a sumptuous repast.

The goddess congratulated the guests on their safety, which proved that the skill that produced the *Aeropher* had successfully grappled with the difficult problem of aerial navigation.

The inventor of the *Aeropher* said it was the apex of mechanical skill. Invention had raised humanity from the depths of slavery, ignorance, and weakness to a height of empire undreamed of in earlier ages. Such material greatness expands the soul with godlike attributes. The ideal, inventive soul, the typical soul, was a god.

The poet said that the *Aeropher* was the symbol of that kind of poetry in which energy and art were in equipoise. It glorified mechanical skill. It had been prophesied that as civilization advanced poetry would decline. There was a period in the history of Atvatabar in which matters of taste, imagination and intellectual emotion had been utterly neglected by a universal preference for scientific and mechanical pursuits. The country was overrun with reasoners, debaters, metaphysicians, scientists and mechanical artists, but there were no poets. Such mechanical civilization was unfavourable to their development. The founding of such institutions as the art palace of Gnaphisthasia and the spiritual palace of Egyplosis had grafted on their modern life the soul life of more ancient times, until soul-worship had become the universal religion.

The goddess said that the aerial ship was the symbol of an ideal and passionate temperament resolved on discovering new spheres of spiritual beauty, so as to spiritualize the race. Such a soul ought to be free to surround itself with that atmosphere from which it absorbs life. It must choose its own weapons and armour, so as to be adequately equipped for the battle. In its eagerness to climb on discovering wings it must be accompanied by its own retinue of spirits, by enthusiastic and lasting friendships so consoling to its nature. Such was the idea of Egyplosis.

Captain Lavornal at this point stated that when the company regained the deck he would put the rotating wheel, placed at the stern of the ship, in motion, so as to produce the combination of a revolving as well as an onward flight.

"These wheels," said he, "will spin us around, and by means of our double rudder we produce both vertical and lateral undulations, which, combined with the rotary movement of the deck, will produce a delirious sensation. All the abandon of great and strong birds are ours. We can imitate the sonorous sweep of the *seemorgh*, who plunges with supreme majesty in the abyss of air."

"These elaborations of flight," said Lyone, "are not pursued merely for physical pleasure, but in a mysterious way they are the moulders of the soul itself. That essence, re-enforced with such subtle and powerful enthusiasm, develops sensibility and assumes a grandeur and ecstasy unknown to those who merely travel on the earth. Each gesture of flight is a stride nearer omnipotence, an attribute more godlike by reason of its supremacy over those obstacles that crush and overwhelm."

I shared the same seat with Lyone at the prow of the vessel.

The scenery had in our absence developed into more marked grandeur. Under the spell of an eternal morning, of such light as poets only dream of, there rose on either side of us consummate rocks and cataracts that signalled heaven. The swinging pillars of incredible streams leaped thousands of feet into the gulf beneath. They charmed us like glittering serpents. The gorge, the rocks, the cataracts, the heavens of the earth above us were a prodigal feast to which nature had bidden us.

Then the ship rose again toward the mammoth rocks,
adorned with the tapestries of falling wave.

As we explored the depths of the gulf the *Aeropher* assumed an undulating motion. For several miles the vessel kept descending, until we swept through an overwhelming jungle of wild flowers. There were acres of roses riotous in bloom, there was the trailing of wild peas sweet as honey, the blue of larkspurs, the fragrance of musk flowers, and the swaying cups of scarlet poppies.

Then the ship rose again toward the mammoth rocks that shimmered in the sunlight adorned with the tapestries of falling wave. Still upward we rose into the spell-bound sky, feeding on the savage sweets of nature, the rhythm of the golden cliffs, the echoes of the waterfalls. We were the associates of mighty pines that on the Theban peaks spread incomparable solaces for mind and heart. Then, as we descended from our extreme altitude, we began also to revolve with a splendid sweep of motion, until the landscape swam around us like a dream.

It was a delirious fantasy of airy clouds, fluttering leaves, songs of birds, milky avalanches, balsamic forests, and the awe-inspiring silences of revolving walls!

The intoxication of such wheeling flight filled us with a strange joy. Our journey became wistful, eager, breathless. We became poets, and the soul of a poet is a chameleon that takes its glow and colour from the surrounding infection. The motion that bore us in daring circles produced a euthanasia of mind and an exaltation of soul. The jugglery of flight under such conditions produced a Nirvana of soul and a Dharana of body. An exquisitely sweet whirlwind of emotion swept through I know not how many souls on the *Aeropher*, but certainly through the souls of Lyone and myself.

We both flew round and round like birds in intoxicating converse. During the progress of the flight, intellect, will and memory slumbered. I was deprived of the use of all external faculties, while those of the soul were correspondingly increased. Imagination and emotion were excited with rapturous energy. Lyone's eyes sparkled with a celestial joy. She was again the goddess in her ecstasy!

CHAPTER 27

We Reach Egyplosis

When I recovered my every-day senses the revolving motion of the *Aeropher* had ceased and our flight was confined to an undulating movement. I was holding the hand of the goddess, who had been in a hyperaesthetic condition herself during the gyrations of the ship, and when feeling her senses leaving her she had involuntarily grasped my hand. Our souls had been the recipients of the same rapturous joy.

When we were once more ourselves, Lyone was anxious to know something of the character of the women of the outer world. I talked to her about such women as resembled herself in spiritual fervour.

I described the Egyptian legend of Isis, the goddess of love, of life, of nature. I told her of St. Theresa, that blessed visionary, whose soul frequently experienced those voluptuous sensations, such as might be experienced when expiring in raptures on the bosom of God. I spoke also of pearly Eve, to whom, ere she had eaten of the fatal fruit, every moment was a delight, every blossom a wilderness of sweets. I spoke of Cleopatra, the haughty daughter of the Nile, the fervour of whose passion thickened into lust and death.

My story was interrupted by the arrival of the captain, who said: "Your holiness, we will reach Egyplosis in an hour."

"So soon," murmured the goddess.

"Is it the pleasure of your holiness that we alight at the private sanctuary or at the grand gate?" inquired the captain.

"At the grand gate, of course," said the goddess; "we must give our friends a royal welcome."

The captain bowed in obedience and disappeared.

The charms of our journey grew more and more interesting. In addition to the delights of discovery, I felt the rising ambition of a great joy in connection with Lyone. It was a daring thought, that I might possibly partake of a glorious camaraderie with the goddess, but when I thought that no stranger could possibly share a heart that belonged only to her own people, only to Atvatabar, I felt that Lyone was very far off indeed.

In a land where spiritual love was the prerogative of the priestly caste, strictly limited to the members of that caste, any priestly condescension or favour given to those outside the pale of the priesthood could have no meaning and was forbidden under penalty of death. Of course human nature is liable to err always, and it came to pass that the records of the legal tribunals of Atvatabar proved that many departures in soul fellowship took place between the most loyal inmates of Egyplosis and the outer inhabitants. The punishment for such offence to the most sacred law of Atvatabar, although terrible, was powerless to prevent such *mésalliances* of souls.

I knew that a spark of what might prove a mighty conflagration was already kindled in the bosom of the goddess. It thrilled me to know it, but only as the laws and customs of this strange country became known to me did I realize the tremendous risk in Lyone allowing her heart to betray any kinship, however remote, with mine. The greater the dignity, the greater the offence. The crime was sacrilege, and the punishment was death by the *magnic* fluid.

The goddess already belonged to her faith. She was love's *religieuse*. It was a cruel thing to seek her love when I knew it would perhaps bring her to an untimely end and stamp her name with everlasting disgrace. On the other hand, if the goddess, knowing much better than I the result of loving one not only outside of the sacred caste, but an "outer barbarian" as well, was brave enough to incur even the risk of death on behalf of her love, would I be so cowardly as not to follow her supreme soul even to martyrdom itself? And it might be that we might even raise a following large enough to defeat our enemies, and end in a greater triumph than either of us ever yet experienced.

Such were the thoughts that filled me when the aerial ship suddenly shot out of the chasm in which we had so long travelled and emerged upon the wide circular basin of the mountains about one hundred miles in diameter. In the centre of the high valley lay an immense lake, in whose centre stood a large island, everywhere visible from the shores, whereon stood the sacred palace of Egyplosis, the many-templed college of souls. We saw its pale green, gleaming walls rising from a tropical forest of dark green trees. Its gold and crystal domes reflected the sunlight dazzlingly, making the palace plainly visible all over that wide valley.

Egyplosis was a little city composed of an immense quadrangle, the supernal palace together with the subterranean infernal palace. The supernal palace was of enormous dimensions, being a square mile in extent, and was composed of over a hundred temples and palaces rising high in the air, the chief seat of soul worship in Atvatabar, and the home of twice ten thousand priests and priestesses.

The infernal palace consisted of one hundred subterranean temples and labyrinths, all sculptured, like the supernal palace, out of the living rock, and situated directly underneath it.

Our course lay in a direct line across the noble valley. It was the most diversified part of the country we had yet crossed, being broken up into hills and valleys, glens and precipices, fields and forests, lakes, islands and gardens, all composing a region of bewildering beauty.

The emotions awakened by my near approach to this strange place were keen and exciting. Now for the first time in history its mystery was about to be disclosed to alien eyes from the outer world.

Soon after entering the park we saw, some fifty miles to the north, the ship containing the sailors rapidly approaching Egyplosis. It had also escaped destruction by the cyclone, having doubtless followed us down the canyon we sought refuge in.

It was a new sensation to float bird-like over the enchanted fields in this most mysterious of worlds, toward a spot that has no prototype on earth.

A multitude of domes and crenelated walls grew into immense proportions beneath the boundless light. Egyplosis possessed in its palaces the enchanted calm of Hindu and Greek architecture, together with the thrilling ecstasy of Gothic shrines. Blended with these precious qualities there was a poetic generalization of the mighty activities of modern civilization. It was the home of spiritual and physical empire.

I wondered greatly what Eleusinian mysteries its courts contained.

LYONE WAS BORNE ON A LITTER FROM THE AERIAL SHIP TO THE PALACE.

I was indeed another Hercules visiting the realms of Pluto and the garden of Proserpine in quest of the immortal fruits of knowledge. Would I be successful in my quest, and bear back to the outer world some magical secret its nations would be glad to know?

Finally, we saw the clear and marvellous palace close at hand.

A hundred banners floated from its walls, and music from an army of neophytes on its towers saluted us.

The *Aeropher* swept over the lake, and, reaching the island, alighted on a marble causeway leading to the grand entrance of the palace. A thousand *wayleals* stood ranged on either side as a guard of honour. We had left the forest that largely covers the island, and on either hand stretched gardens of rainbow-coloured flowers, and here and there fountains sparkled in the sunny air.

Lyone seemed the impersonation of divine loveliness as she was borne in a litter from the aerial ship to the palace. On her head sparkled the bird of yearning, typical of hopeless love.

The high priest Hushnoly and the priestess Zooly-Soase of the supernal palace and the grand sorcerer Charka and the grand sorceress Thoubool of the infernal palace, surrounded by the chief priests and priestesses, magicians, sorcerers, wizards, theosophists, spiritualists, etc., gave us a royal welcome, and were jubilant at the return of the supreme goddess to Egyplosis.

CHAPTER 28

The Grand Temple of Harikar

Twelve of the most handsome priests and priestesses constituted the guard of twin-souls in waiting to the goddess, and these escorted her into the grand court of the temple palace. Over a gigantic archway were sculptured the words *Dya Pateis omt Ami Cair*, which meant *two bodies and one soul*. This was the motto of Egyplosis, the expression of ideal friendship and indicative of a system of life the reverse of that of the outer world of Atvatabar, which had for its motto, "One Body and Two Souls."

The architecture of the supernal palace was of amazing proportions and solid grandeur. Its aggregation of temples was sculptured out of one mighty block of pale green marble. The vast quadrangle seemed a tempest of imagination and art, whose temples, terraces and towers were the expression of the infinite souls that formed them. The colour of the stone was beautifully relieved by broad bands of the vermilion metal *terrelium*, that plated the walls with several parallel friezes, which lent an amazing splendour to the scene, and made us feel as though we were entering some palace of eternity, where magnificence has no end.

We had no time to examine the marvels spread before our delighted eyes, for, on the conclusion of our reception by the great officers of the palace, we were conducted to chambers set apart for our use, to rest and refresh ourselves to witness the exercises attending the installation of a twin-soul on the following day.

The chief temple at Egyplosis was interiorly of semi-circular shape, like a Greek theatre, five hundred feet in width. It was covered like the pantheon with a sculptured roof and dome of many-coloured glass. The roof was one hundred and thirty feet above the lowest tier of seats beneath or one hundred feet above the level of the highest seats beneath. The walls were laboriously sculptured dado and field and frieze, with bas-reliefs of the same character as the golden throne of the gods that stood at the centre of the semi-circle.

The dado was thirty-two feet in height, on which were carved the emblems of every possible machine, implement or invention that conferred supremacy over nature in idealized grandeur. Battles of flying *wayleals* and races of *bockhockids* were carved in grand confusion. It was a splendid reunion of science and art.

Higher up the field space, which was fifty feet in height, was broken by a gallery or cloister behind a tier of splendid pillars, themselves carved with the emblems of art. The hidden wall, as well as those portions above and below the cloister between dado and frieze, were covered with endless representations of the creations of art. Heroic eurythmic figures representing poetry, music, painting, architecture, etc., formed a mighty symposium.

Highest of all, the enormous frieze, fully sixteen feet in width, was one mighty band of solid *terrelium*. This had been cast in plates having sculptured symbols in high relief of the sublime emblems of Harikar, and portrayed scenes from the idealities and mysteries of Egyplosis.

There were represented the fine and perfect figures of magicians in the midst of their incantations, of sorcerers raising souls to life again; there were visions of the sorcery of love in all its moods, and of the rapt practices of twin-souls generating a creative force in batteries of spirit power.

Above all rose the dome whose lights were fadeless. The pavement of the temple had been chiselled in the form of a longitudinal hollow basin, containing a series of wide terraces of polished stone, whereon were placed divans of the richest upholstery. In each divan sat a winged twin-soul, priest and priestess, the devotees of hopeless love. On the throne itself sat Lyone, the supreme goddess, in the semi-nude splendour of the pantheon, arranged with tiara and jewelled belt and flowing skirt of sea-green *aquelium* lace. She made a picture divinely entrancing and noble. Supporting the throne was an immense pedestal of polished marble, fully one hundred feet in diameter and twenty feet in height, which stood upon a wide and elevated pavement of solid silver, whereon the priests and priestesses officiated in the services to the goddess. On crimson couches sat their majesties the king and queen of Atvatabar, together with the great officers of the realm. Next to the royal group myself and the officers and seamen of the *Polar King* occupied seats of honour. Behind, around and above us, filling the immense temple, rose the concave mass of twin-souls numbering ten thousand individuals, each seated with counterpart soul.

As I gazed on those happy terraces of life, youth, love and beauty, I felt exhilarated with the sensations the scene gave rise to.

The garments of both priests and priestesses were fashioned in a style somewhat resembling the decorative dresses seen on Greek and Japanese vases, yet wholly original in design. In many cases the priestesses were swathed in transparent tissues that revealed figures like pale olive gold within.

The grand sorcerer Charka and the grand sorceress Thoubool occupied a conspicuous divan upholstered with cloth of gold. The sorceress was a grand beauty, neither blond nor brunette, but her complexion would, chameleon-like, change from a rosy white to a clear golden hue. Her hair was bright copper, gleaming like strands of metal. Her eyes changed colour incessantly, being successively blue and black.

Her robe was a pale green silk, bound at the waist with a heavy cincture of gold. She wore a necklace of many-coloured gems.

The grand sorcerer wore a robe of moss-green velvet embroidered with *appliquéd* white silk lace, resembling lotus bloom. Both wore diadems of emeralds. Other twin-souls were arrayed in equally splendid attire, and seated on couches whose upholstery accentuated or harmonized with their fair occupants. Whatever the colour selected, I observed that each twin-soul priest and priestess wore robes of a consanguineous hue, however the individual stuffs might vary in texture or quality. I also observed that in no case were the laws of taste in colour violated, and unerring instinct had guided every priest and priestess in achieving the most piquant harmonies of colour. With garments in simultaneous contrast each twin-soul sat on a couch upholstered in fabrics in pure contrast of colour.

How I wished some great painter of the outer world could transfer to canvas that conflagration of beauty.

Several twin-souls, with garments that seemed beaten gold,

reclined on black velvet couches beside us. On an immense divan of white velvet near by sat a group of priests and priestesses arrayed in stuffs that were the strangest tones of purple, brown, violet, green, and red. A twin-soul in golden maize sat on a dark purple couch. A twin-soul in ecru sat on a salmon-coloured couch, while a twin-soul in *myosotis* blue reposed on a couch of the colour of Australian gold. Celibates and vestals in russet robes luxuriated on couches of magnolia green.

It was evident their artists possessed a happy skill in creating such harmonies of costume. Sculptor, upholsterer and *couturière* formed the trinity of genius that wrought marvels of form and colour.

Harikar, the Holy Soul, was the deity, who was symbolized by the goddess, and ministered to by such a retinue of souls. No doubt Harikar was mightily pleased at such a tribute of wealth, love and beauty. As far as an individual could appreciate such splendour, I must testify it was an eminently thrilling oblation.

The votaries themselves were no solitary ascetics who practised heroic mortifications to obtain dominion over life or nature. Instead of the pale devotee who in other creed cultivates the desire to get away from all things earthly, and whose every effort is to extinguish pleasure in life, every *theopath* of Harikar cultivated a Greek perfection of body, as well as a Gothic intensity of soul. By what powerful incantation were the priests of Egyplosis able to overcome the law of the outer world, that all joy must be paid for in pain, and that the joy was nearly always too dear at the price given?

CHAPTER 29

The Installation of a Twin-Soul

The sacred musicians of the temple surrounded the throne in solid circles each arrayed in lordly attire.

They flourished instruments of gold, that rang out music of such depth and clearness of tone as to melt every soul in that vast audience into one thrilling whole. The sounding song was the incarnation of all things majestic and glorious. In its breathless measures were born the spirits of conquest, pride, inspiration, love and sympathy. The thrilling climax was wrought of passages eloquent of love, tenderness, reverence, joy, adoration and poetry.

Again, with the music becoming more refined, a choir of singers in the high cloister in the walls sang as they walked a refrain of purifying sweetness. It was a wail of fidelity and love, and both song and music moved in perfect accord.

Thereafter music alone was heard, when the high priest Hushnoly, and the high priestess Zooly-Soase stood before us on the silver pavement beneath the throne.

The blue-black hair of the high priestess fell around her olive face and shoulders like a cloud of darkness. She wore a robe of coral-red silken gossamer, that with its foldings shivered like quicksilver, revealing a figure of olive marble beneath. Her shoulders, arms and breasts, soft and heavy in mould, were dimly seen beneath their coral veil. Her profile was perfect. Her eyes were jewels of swart fire. Her eyebrows made perfect arches above them, enhancing the beauty of her face. Her mouth was fine and tender, and her lips red with kisses. The high priest, whose noble features were olive-green in hue, wore a splendid opaque silk *burnous* of camellia-red, of heavier texture than that of the priestess. He wore boots of scarlet lacquered leather. Both wore diadems of *kragon*, the precious stone.

A stone altar curiously carved, on which stood a green bronze turtle of large size, occupied one side of the front of the pavement. The turtle held its head stretched upward, and through its open mouth a thin stream of blue smoke ascended. On the wide flat back of the turtle lay an open volume, the sacred book of Egyplosis.

The priest and priestess stood beside the altar, each reading an alternate stanza from the ritual of the goddess. While reading, the priests with loud voice followed the intoning of the high priest, and the priestesses that of the high priestess, as follows:

The Ritual of Hopeless Love

Priests: Harikar is the supreme soul, and the goddess Lyone his supreme incarnation. Equally free from asceticism and indulgence, she treads the golden path.

Priestesses: Let us joyfully obey our adorable goddess, who commands us in all manner of spiritual joys; let us follow her glorious example, preserving purity of heart and life.

Priests: Let us adore a cupid agonized, worshipping the goddess of hopeless, tender, romantic love. Let us, with our counterparts, the most lovely of maidens, become twin-souls for evermore.

Priestesses: Let us love the shapely and active youths, the young men of soul and intellect, likewise those of courage and daring, whose hearts and minds are in complete unity.

Priests: Let us add splendour of body to greatness of soul. May we excel in the chase, the dance and the race. Let us drink ambrosial wine, and eat the juiciest of meats, and clothe ourselves with the finest and strongest of tissues.

Priestesses: Let us have a beautiful companionship with our counterpart souls. Let us rejoice in the sun, in the free winds of the sky, in the glory of flowers, in the pride of horses and elephants richly caparisoned. Let us treasure jewels. Let us possess emeralds, turquoises, diamonds and rubies. Let us array ourselves with marvellous stuffs, dyed with the richest colourings.

Priests: Let us here in search of the ideal find an ever-in-

The Priest and Priestess stood beside the altar, each reading
an alternate stanza from the ritual of the goddess.

creasing Nirvana of blessedness. Goddess of souls, lead us to imagine higher and holier exaltations; keener and more blessed raptures!

Priestesses: Sweet mother of souls! teach us to cultivate consoling friendships with sympathetic hearts. Give us longings for the utmost depths of love and tenderness; let us possess fervid and impassioned souls.

Priests: Let us create a paradise wherein life is one long intoxication of love, beauty and soul-culture, found in the fascinating converse of soul with soul and intellect with intellect.

Priestesses: May rapturous energies spring from hopeless loves! May the yearning for inaccessible pleasures fill us with blessed extravagance and holy madness.

Priests: May we, firmly poised on virtue, become possessed of noble, delicate, enormous souls. May the meeting of spirit with spirit be too ecstatic for words to express. May vows be written in each other's hearts. May the jewelled ring bind soul and soul, and in the commingled life may the holy compact be known, that a perfect circle of souls has been consummated.

Priestesses: Secure by our compact and our vows from tasting of the forbidden fruit, may we always possess the happy intemperance of never-satiated souls.

Priests: May the sorcery of love procure for us the shuddering sensibility of sorrow, without its agony, as we possess the perfect delight of day without the cold and lugubrious shadows of the night.

Priestesses: Contact with life begets love, and love begets sensation, and sensation desire, but reason and culture control desire and so preserve the endless sweetness of our joy.

Priests: The real mortal, the ideal divine. The real awakens desire, the ideal feeds it. The real is the maimed, the halt and the blind; it is the sepulchre of faith; the poor, the tawdry, the miserable, it is the measure of our imperfect attainment of the ideal.

The ideal is the supreme made possible by love and charity. It is wide as imagination, perfect as love, calm as death. It is the unchangeable and the immortal.

The real with its disappointments is soul shattering, but the ideal is perennial life.

The more inaccessible the pleasure, the keener the delight in its pursuit.

In love, accessibility is death.

Priestesses: By losing the real we obtain the ideal. What others strive for we possess. Praise to Harikar for the most glorious of men, for precious viands, odoriferous wines, rare and costly jewels, marvellous stuffs, and the hundred temples and gardens of Egyplosis! Praise to Harikar for our counterpart souls!

Priests: Praise to Harikar for the loveliest of women, noble, cultured and tender, with whom Nirvana is ecstasy.

Priestesses: Nirvana is the consummate gift of Harikar, the one everlasting sweetness!

* * * * * * * *

During the intonation of the ritual, the twin-souls put into practice the manifestations of those endearments prayed for, and which they certainly seemed to possess.

Throughout the entire congregation, priest and priestess, enfolded in each other's arms, swayed caressingly together and rapturously kissed each other. The fondest sighs were heard amid the recitations, and the faces of lover and beloved were flushed the colour of rosy flame. A tempest of restrained passion shook the entire congregation.

What wonder, that, ruled by such a faith, each twin-soul splendidly apparelled, in such an edifice, should grow rich and strange, bold and delicate, and exhibit the intemperance of emotion excited by sensations so multiplied and extreme? I then saw a new meaning in the grandeur and efflorescence of the sculptures of the temple. I saw in the profuse decorations, in the arabesques so fantastically entangled and unrolled, a manifestation of the delicate sensibility that created them.

Not only were real or natural objects idealized in art, but also conventional art, or the record of what nature suggests, as well as how she appears, to the soul of the artist. And what must have been the infinite wealth of suggestion to such souls as these to account for such mouldings and traceries on wall and roof, and such wealth of colour in attire, reflected and duplicated in the jewelled windows of the dome. Here were souls fitted by nature and art to fuse and create the suggestions of nature into shapes of eternal beauty. These flamboyant shapes and mystical colours presuppose the strange illuminations that had pierced tender and extravagant hearts.

CHAPTER 30

The Installation of a Twin-Soul
(Continued)

While priest and priestess were folded with mutual emotion two
of the loveliest souls took the place of the high priest and priestess on the silver pavement. The girl was young and tender, golden
white in complexion with crimson lips. Her figure was swathed in
a vermilion robe, on the breast of which was embroidered in outline a sea-green sun whose swaying rays reached the furthest parts
of her garment. Her pale blue hair was crowned with a chaplet of
daffodils. The youth wore a robe of scarlet silk embroidered with a
golden sun similar in design to that of the priestess. His pose was
singularly noble. These two souls were about to become priest and
priestess, and, after having taken the vows of hopeless love in presence of the goddess, high priest and priestess and congregation
of twin-souls, they sang the following anthem, accompanied by a
wailing storm of music from several hundred violins, entitled:

The Twin-Soul

Priest

Love is a heated furnace that devours
The thickest ice; love is a sweet moist wind
That cools the fevered desert with its balm.
There is no rain nor heat, yea, even snow
Is warm and rosy to ideal souls
That shudder in life's sweetest ecstasies.
If love, that makes ideal life, that dwells
In fragrant silences, makes green the grass,
And far more tender the diviner flowers,
It surely makes both bold and delicate

The warm superiority of flesh
Of that strange, sacred soul that dwells with mine.

The clear, yet golden whiteness of the form
That shines through pale green diaphane,
Showing its pliant beauty, is the dress
Of that rapt soul that is all tenderness.
Her brow is crowned with wistful daffodils,
Making her fair face fairer, and her eyes
Are clouded sapphires; yea, her perfect lips
(Whereon my soul will dwell for evermore)
Clear blood-red rubies! The sweet hand holds
Red poppies and blue lotus, and the soft
And sulphur blossomed wind flower. If such dress
Enshrine a soul as perfect, if the curves
That make her form voluptuous describe
The splendour of her soul (and this I know),
Love has no purer temple, nor more sweet!

The priest had sung alone so far, and now both priest and priestess joined their voices in a marvellous song. Wilder, sweeter and more intense, the violins stormed and wailed pathetic whirlwinds of ecstasy. At times their insufferable moans caught the excited hearts of the audience, and twin-souls in their passion would rise on their wings and, revolving, sweep around the amphitheatre locked in each other's arms.

Priest and Priestess

Sharper than pain, we love, and the caress,
Keener than torment, overmaddens us!
There is no fasting when our feverish lips
Meet in the shock that strikes the spirit dumb
With swooning raptures! The dilated soul,
Intemperate with the enormous moan
Of passion, would outleap the strenuous will.
The flesh, transfigured with the crisis, reels,
Stretches the chain of duty and would leap
To grasp the tempting and forbidden fruit,
Were not that virtue is our comrade now.

We lift our eager faces to the sun
And feast on life and in each other's souls

Luxuriate, confounded with delight.
For us no mouldy cloister waits its prey,
Nor cave of darkness, where existence mourns
And dies beneath its scourgings. We have made
Our grim novitiate with reality.
Have known its agony, for we were born
So eminent for rapture, that the pain
All men inherit desolated us
And spread a living terror in our souls;
So that through clouds of everlasting woe
Scarce came the gleam of gladness or of love,
And earth was pitiless, and brutal souls
Who cannot feel there ruled. Oh, the wide world,
Degraded by ignoble brutishness,
Could yield no tendernesses infinite
For we who feed on rapture. Thus it was
Our souls on meeting, in the thrilling kiss
Were fused in indissoluble embrace;
We who were famished, in ideal love
Found sustenance and passed from death to life!

The song was perfect. The strange, fresh accents of the singers, so full of love and passion, melted every heart in the temple with their ecstasy. One might hear such measures without thought of lapse of time or of worldly concerns. Ah! if one could hear such melody forevermore! With a burst of dramatic joy the singing of the last stanza revealed whole worlds of rapture.

Reincarnated in an earthly heaven,
Now have we reached Nirvana, now
Above us open the wide gulfs of joy,
And luminous and glorious round us blow
Millions of flowers; while afar there shines
The mighty splendour of the exhaustless sea!
We dwell in breathless joys, thrilled through and through
With majesty and sweetness; we have grown
Athletes of joy in our Agapemone:
Eager and breathless, we have found at last
The fount of youth, the magical Arjeels;
Fruits of organic gold amid the leaves
Sparkle, and around our island home

Are spread the veritable golden sands
Whereon our happy feet tread evermore!

The singers disappeared, and in their places a hundred wondrously-arrayed figures moved in the dance of pure being on the silver pavement. Lithe as leopards, with unclad limbs and feet, priest and priestess danced all the ecstasies of Egyplosis. The dancers were so young, so fresh, so tender, so beautiful, and so innocent, that it was a supreme joy to behold them. Rapture grew universal and lovers cried with hysterical shudderings. The rainbow-coloured throng, moving to the music of the golden instruments, flashed upon the pavement like joy taking possession of the world!

I felt intensely sad for Lyone, who sat like a statue of golden marble, gazing on the abyss of joy beneath. Had the goddess no lover to press her to his heart amid the universal rapture? Alas! the immense dignity of her position and the unalterable laws of Atvatabar alike prevented any single soul from feeding the intense hunger that consumed her. Accompanying the dancers, the unseen choir in the cloisters began to sing a new opera of love, and the strains of an "*Ave, Lyone, bona dea,*" stole upon the senses like the bewildering sighs of angels, making one ache with delight. A story of romantic love once more sculptured the faces of priest and priestess with angelic beauty, as it rose on wings of song and swept in delightful moans upon the carven stone.

It was a memorable scene, one never to be forgotten! The hieroglyphic walls, carved in high relief with the instruments of empire, the dome with its ten thousand fadeless lights, the terraces of twin-souls radiant with delight, the marvellous dancers, the superb music that seemed to shake the heart of the solid stone that enclosed us, and high over all the supreme goddess in whose honour all this adoration was made, seated in bliss on the throne of the gods—such was the situation at that moment. It was a monstrous and a splendid joy!

Suddenly a roar of invincible music issued from gigantic tubes that pierced the body of the throne itself with fresh and warlike explosions of melody. I was filled with a maddening delight, until consciousness could hardly bear the strain any longer. I cried aloud, amid a Chimborazo of song, a hundred-cratered Popocatapetl of sweet strains. The audience, enraptured with the climax, became an inferno of passion, laughter tears and felicity!

CHAPTER 31

The Mystery of Egyplosis

The palace of the goddess at Egyplosis was a component part of the vast quadrangle known as the supernal palace. The view therefrom embraced the wide inner garden of the entire palace of temples, discovering jungles of shrubs and flowers of all imaginable hues, interspersed with lakes sleeping in their marble basins like enormous jewels. Fountains of solid silver gushed forth a brilliant foam of waters amid the embowering foliage, and there glad priests, in the society of priestesses sweeter than the flowers themselves, dreamed life away in enthusiastic peace. Surrounding all was the high and glorious palace, forming a background, on the design of which imagination and art had been entirely exhausted.

The scene the day following the Ritual of the installation of a twin-soul in the temple of Egyplosis was a boudoir in the palace of the goddess. It was a large apartment, whose walls were hung with panels of rose-coloured velvet, embroidered with gray-green silk foliage. In one large tapestry, the hands of loving priestesses had embroidered a scene in the garden of Egyplosis. On a dais, upon a couch of soft red silk upholstery sat Lyone, swathed in draperies of shrimp pink and pale peacock green, embroidered with ivory-white silk. A large terra-cotta silk rug, whose only ornament was an elaborate border, covered the floor. The goddess wore a belt of *aquelium* serpents having tulips in their mouths. Heavy *terrelium* bracelets adorned her wrists, and she wore a diminutive tiara on her head.

I sat on a luxurious seat, the sole guest of the goddess. I was rapidly learning from the divinity the mystery of Egyplosis. I was especially anxious to find out how the jewel of one hundred years of youth could be grafted into the ordinary existence. An idea so splendid seemed to be the germ of earthly immortality. We were discussing the subject of hopeless love, and I asked her if she considered life and love were the same element.

"Life and love are synonymous," she replied. "By love I mean the spiritual, ideal, romantic passion that is hopeless."

"Yes," I replied, "but does not the idea of inaccessibility create a worthless desire, that is, a desire for something that is forbidden or unattainable? The majority of men, I think, will prefer an every-day love with all its risks and imperfections to the shadowy ghost of a hopeless love. The hopeful love does no violence to nature such as is contemplated by the hopeless sentiment."

"You hardly understand me," said she; "the pleasure we aspire to is superior to any physical delight, and is an end in itself. It is romantic love, that blooms like a single flower in the crevices of a volcano. It is the quintessence of existence, the rarest wine of life, the expressed sweetness of difficulty and repression and long-suffering, the choicest holiday of the soul. We are willing to pay the price of hopelessness to taste such nectar. In the every-day world such joy only rarely exists. Interest, indulgence, ambition, fortune, time, temper and marriage destroy it. Youth, captivated by a beautiful face or a winning smile, thinks it has discovered its true counterpart, and so takes possession of the prize. It finds afterward it was mistaken, and all its life thenceforth becomes miserable."

"But," I replied, "if the world at large had discovered that your theory of love was the true one, it would long since have acted on its discovery and put no destroying restraint or obligation on so precious a possession. But the world found that a thousand accidents would infallibly open the eyes of both parties to the fact that they possessed but few qualities in common, or in counterpart, and with such knowledge of good and evil they would infallibly separate. Hence the foundation of society would be torn asunder and the rising generation of helpless children become orphaned of home, the very bulwark of life. Society must have assurances that people do not get married simply as an experiment, but are willing to honourably undertake the mutual sacrifices their act carries with it."

"I have already admitted," said she, "that the joy of spiritual love hardly ever exists in its virgin force in the every-day world. I admit that the necessary regulations of society, although they tend to destroy it, must be enforced. The Atvatabar nation rests on the marriage idea. At one time in our history the people strove for ideal love and overthrew the ordinary marriage yoke without the restraint of reason. Law and order disappeared and social chaos reigned. The land was filled with the wailings of orphans whose parents had deserted them, and men and women formed new associates every day. Unbridled license devastated the country. Our lawgivers re-established the law of marriage as being the only law suitable to mankind. Man in the aggregate had not developed to a state in which the consummation of marriage could be dispensed with. Yet there were many among those who had advocated ideal love worthy of their theory. Although married to each other, they had remained celibates. For these Egyplosis was founded, for the study and practice of what is really a higher development of human nature and in itself an unquestionable good. It is the most powerful element in the production of creative energy of soul and personal beauty. As you will have observed, all our devotees are singularly beautiful in form and feature and possess spirit power to a high degree."

As the goddess spoke a few threads of her bright blue hair had strayed across her face. Her beautiful eyes flashed with a royalty of truth, tenderness, magnetism, and feeling. She was the living illustration of her claims for Egyplosis.

"What you say," I replied, "illustrates that ordinary marriage, with all its limitations and, infelicities, is absolutely necessary for the well-being of society. Marriage is simply the application of reason and morality to blind, passionate nature. The home circle is the origin of nationality, progress, and wealth. Ideal love, wrested from the dragon of difficulty, is, I think, but rarely tasted in so real, so practical an institution. This is the experience of the nations of the outer world, and how much better for man that it is so? A roadway in proportion to its rhythm of undulation becomes useless, hindering travel rather than accelerating it. So also with love. When settled in the calm security of marriage the mind is freed from the romantic extravagance, the torture, the delight of hopeless sentiment. Thus men are free to devote themselves to the more serious purposes of life and achieve wealth and fame for themselves and their families. I am, nevertheless, curious to see how your institution is conducted, for hopeless love seems to me one of the most disquieting things in life. Its victims, happy and unhappy, resisting passion with regret or yielding with remorse, are ever on the rack of torture. They resemble the devotees of certain idols, who pierce themselves with cruel hooks and swing aloft in honour of their god. It may be pleasure, but not one in a thousand will ever achieve that degree of soul exaltation and physical abnegation to think it so."

"And yet not one in a thousand, not one in a hundred thousand lives in Egyplosis," said the goddess.

"The men who achieve anything," I continued, "good and great in the world, the men who build empires, discover ideas, who both rule and populate nations, are all rewarded by a hopeful love. It is only a hopeless love that sets up its mirage of false and never-to-be-obtained joys. Hence, I ask you the question, What of Egyplosis?"

The goddess smiled at my controversial attitude, "It is the old question," she replied, "of conventionalism *versus* art, of economic institutions *versus* nature and life. Just as we endeavour to rescue spontaneous invention and originality from the disease of the tasteless and laborious productions of a mechanical civilization, so we labour to create an earthly home for the soul in a world where superficial necessities will stifle it out of existence. There was a time in the history of Atvatabar when people talked of art and love, both of which did not exist. The octopus of commercial, mechanical and economical life had strangled the soul and all its attributes. Men fought for treaties of commerce, treaties of marriage, deeds of property, and all the while acted in defiance of their obligations. They cheated each other, lied to each other, deserted each other incessantly. Love had taken wings and fled. Art had lost its language and its cunning. Life was no longer illuminated with splendid ideals. It was no longer arrayed in the fair and fascinating garments that only the soul can weave. History was no longer glorified by paintings and sculptured reliefs. Religion was no longer symbolized in the solemn magnificence of architecture, or sculptured shrines of gods. Articles of daily use were made solely to make a profit, and the widespread use of machinery was destroying the art, the soul, the pure life of the people. A paternal government, seeing the tyranny of commercialism and the possible extinction of the soul itself, has wisely, in the spirit of patriarchal hospitality, established the art institution of Gnaphisthasia and the religious institution of Egyplosis, for soul development in harmony with the high destiny of mankind. Harikar, or developed soul, is the natural sequence of the development of the soul and intellect, achieving the supreme virtue of spiritual perfection, or dominion of the passions of the body and the forces of nature. Love was the one great end of our religion, for life is love."

"I value your creed," I continued, "to the fullest extent. I value the idea that every intellect shall enfold a soul. You practise the doctrine that hopeless love is that phase of the passion that contains the most delirious possibilities of joy, yet, allow me to ask, have you never discovered that there may be disappointments for even such guarded emotions as yours? Are your neophytes perfectly happy? We find, in the outer world at least, that no state or condition in life is perfectly pleasurable. Their joys die of their own ennui if for no other cause. We find happiness like a flower; it has its period of bloom and decay. The more intoxicating the beauty the shorter its life. Happiness long continued grows common, fades and dies. Then again the human soul is always in a fever of unrest. It always thinks what is beyond its reach is liberty. As one of our poets has expressed it:

"Oh, give me liberty!
For even were a paradise itself my prison,
Still would I long to leap the crystal walls!"'

As I spoke I saw that the goddess was an eager listener to my words. Was it possible that she might have an idea that even Egyplosis might indeed be a prison? But, then, her position, her vows, recalled to her the fact that she was love's *religieuse*, an indissoluble part of the temple of love itself.

The goddess replied, that sometimes impatient spirits had entered the palace, but any incorrigible cases of insubordination were either imprisoned in the fortress beneath the palace or were expelled into the outer world. The neophytes entered the temple college while under twenty years of age. Each soul, thereafter mingling freely with five thousand of the opposite sex, chooses in a month its counterpart for life, thus forming a complete circle. The choice must be approved by a council of "Soul Inquisitors" who, before the lifelong union is made, see that both possess all the elements that will produce a high, holy and pure blending of thought, feeling, emotion, joys spiritual and intellectual, whose every breath will be an ecstasy, and at the same time possess reverence for each other and the power of resistance to passion and are able to walk in the pure path.

"Do you not think," I replied, "that the temptation being ever present, the struggle in the soul must in time exhaust and enfeeble the moral powers, producing disastrous consequences?"

Before the goddess could reply, a terrible commotion was heard in the palace garden. The shrieks of a woman mingled with the loud voices of men were heard in furious clamour, and one of the royal guards entered the palace chamber in breathless haste.

CHAPTER 32

The Sin of a Twin-Soul

"Your holiness," said the captain of the sacred guard, as he entered the apartment, "the twin-soul Ardsolus and Merga has sinned against the laws and religion of Egyplosis. I crave permission to bring the guilty pair before the goddess with the evidence of their guilt."

The goddess, answering quickly, ordered the priest and priestess to be produced.

The captain thereupon commanded his *wayleals* to bring the prisoners into the audience chamber.

Shrinking between her guards, the priestess Merga appeared bearing in her arms a lovely babe, a rosy duplicate of herself. Following her came the priest Ardsolus, also a prisoner.

The priestess was the picture of petite girlish beauty. Her delicate rose complexion was flushed with a feeling of shame, and her handsome hazel eyes, dilated with vexation and sorrow, were filled with tears.

Her lover was tall, straight and athletic, with a proud, fine-cut face. The down of manhood was just showing itself on his upper lip.

"I feel sorry for you both," said the goddess; "did you weary of the joys of Egyplosis?"

Ardsolus threw back over his shoulder a falling fold of his white *bournous* and, drawing himself proudly up, replied: "Yes, your holiness, our life here is imprisonment. We have grown weary of its restraint and are eager to return to the outer world with all its cares and freedom."

The chamberlain at this moment announced the arrival of the high priest Hushnoly, the secular, as well as the sacred governor of Egyplosis, and the high priestess Zooly-Soase, who both entered the presence chamber. Hushnoly, saluting the goddess, announced that he had come in search of the erring twin-soul. The high priest was astonished beyond expression at finding sin and shame in so glorious a retreat.

Addressing the weeping girl, he said: "Do you know, my child, how unfortunate you have been? You have committed the unpardonable sin in the temple of hopeless love. Did you not think of your lifelong vows of celibacy and of the deep and tender joy of romantic love?"

Merga only replied by clasping her babe still closer to her breast and bathing it with her tears.

"What excuse do you offer for your crime against yourself, your religion and your fellow-priests?" demanded the high, priest of Ardsolus.

"Your highness," said the youth, "we have, after due experience of our vows, arrived at the conclusion that such vows are a violation of nature. Everything here bids us love, but the artificial system under which we have lived arbitrarily draws a line and says, thus far and no further. Your system may suit disembodied spirits, if such exist, but not beings of flesh and blood. It is an outrage on nature. We desire to leave Egyplosis and return to the common ways of men. We may be there unfortunate, but we will be free. This rarified atmosphere stifles us."

The high priest was horrified. Never before had a twin-soul been so sinful, so contumacious. It revealed a state of things too terrible to contemplate! If such conduct became contagious, it meant the ruin of Egyplosis.

I could detect, however, in the sight of the goddess a certain sympathy for the prisoners which, perhaps, it would just then be very impolitic for her to reveal. It was clear that beneath all this ideal joy lay a slumbering volcano of passion that only awaited a favourable moment for a fierce outbreak. The laws of this strange faith seemed not to have contemplated that to avoid temptation is the only security of moral strength, and that to seek temptation is to paralyze the moral fibres of the soul. The high priest grew pale with excitement.

"Are you aware of the enormity of your offence?" said he to the defiant youth. "For a moment of sinful delight you destroy your interregnum of a hundred years of blessedness, and you, each of you, have delivered a blow at earthly immortality. The success of our religious system is proven by the fact that we have already lengthened the life of our *hierophants* one hundred years, or twice the duration of life in the outer world of Bilbimtesirol. This is the last of many outbreaks of malfeasance to vows made in deliberation, and a fresh exhibition of treason in the sacred college of souls."

"I tell you this," said the youth in reply, "you are slumbering on the edge of a volcano. There are thousands of twin-souls ready to cast off this yoke. They only await a leader to break out in open revolt!"

"Then, sir, we will take care that you are not their leader; we shall suppress you, as we have all similar cases, in the cells of the fortress. Neither Egyplosis nor Atvatabar will hear of your crime. His majesty the king will, I have no doubt, acquiesce in the wisdom of such sentence."

"The punishment is no greater than the crime," said the high priestess. "I despair of Egyplosis if such crimes become frequent. What will our goddess think, what will Atvatabar think of our holy temple when its own priests, the sacred devotees of Harikar, the ministers of the supreme goddess and teachers of the people in their holy religion, are found traitors? Will the government support rebellious and sinful souls in every luxury for the senses, with every possible means for developing and achieving spiritual mastery over the physical world, on the sole condition of hopeless love? It will not. Hence, I say, this disobedience must be quenched in the spark, or it will break out in ruin to our whole religious institution."

"Your punishment," said the high priest, "unless you will repent of your misdeed, give up possession of your offspring, and live ever afterward as holy priests of hopeless love, will be separate and solitary confinement for life in the fortress. You will both be simply obliterated from the world."

As the high priest uttered these words the mother-priestess gave a cry of terror, and, grasping her infant convulsively, gazed with an appealing glance at the goddess.

"We refuse to live as hypocrites," said the youth; "we are no longer twin-souls—we are man and wife and demand to be set free."

"Will you, each of you," said the goddess, "renounce that obedience that makes you factors of deities? Will you dethrone ideal love? Will you throw away palaces and gardens and flowers? Will you forswear the delight of the companionship of twin-souls?"

"We wish to be set free, your holiness," said the youth with firm, set lips.

"Do you no longer value the secrets of magic and sorcery? Do you renounce initiation into the secrets of nature to possess creative force to taste the elixir of life, the secret of the transformation of metals, and, above all, the blessedness of Nirvana? Knowing that love dies in possession do you desire to step forth from paradise into a hard, cold, realistic world, where every experience is a spear driven into the flesh?"

"We dare our fate!" replied the youth. "We ask you, goddess, to set us free."

"I will bring you both before the spiritual council," said Hushnoly, "and, as you are aware, the sentence of the council as provided by the constitution of Egyplosis will be that you, each of you, be imprisoned in separate cells for life, and the child removed and cared for in a distant part of the kingdom. You will henceforth be obliterated from life."

The lovers convulsively embraced each other, the beautiful Merga weeping bitterly.

"We will accept the punishment," said Ardsolus, "because we will give courage to the many twin-souls already imprisoned and also to those who as ardently desire freedom as ourselves. They will never forget that we are fighting their battle against a monstrous wrong."

"Guards, remove the prisoners," said the high priest.

"Can nothing that I may say mitigate their punishment?" said the goddess.

"Your holiness is aware," said Hushnoly, "that the laws of Egyplosis admit of no other interpretation than that prescribed for such a case as this. The foundation of the religion of Atvatabar must be preserved at any cost."

"I urge for mercy," said the goddess, who honoured the prisoners with her tears.

CHAPTER 33

The Doctor's Opinion of Egyplosis

My experiences in Egyplosis were teaching me that even the most perfect human organizations contain the elements of decay and death. The human soul at variance with its own physical condition was hardly the best ideal of a god. Here was happiness piled upon happiness, yet the recipients thereof were not happy. Disappointments and suffering are natural to man because life is supported on difficulty, and a long-continued happiness is the sure forerunner of disaster. The reaction of misery lies somewhere concealed from the eye of happiness, and if it does not at once show itself, it will later on. Even in well-guarded happiness, if one single pleasure be omitted, we experience more regret at its absence than pleasure over the bounties we enjoy. Hence, a large proportion of twin-souls were not wholly in love with their life in the temple of souls, however enamoured they were of each other. Almost absolute freedom of action, freedom from care, physical and mental exercises, soul development, the practice of magic, the most alluring investigation of mental and spiritual themes, the study and practice of art in all its forms, and the investigation of inventive mechanism; a palace to live in, with vast galleries of paintings and sculptures, salons for music, and schools of science, libraries filled with the rarest works of history, literature and poetry, and, most precious of all, the daily dalliance with counterpart souls, could not make these people happy. The one thing denied, which any reasonable man would say was simply the price paid for all this glory, was considered the greatest of all misfortunes. The imagination has a strange habit of passing lightly over happiness possessed and settling down upon a little thing beyond reach and exaggerating it to the utmost.

The imprisonment of Ardsolus and Merga created a profound sensation among the ten thousand inmates of the palace. Sentiment was divided so much that two political parties were formed—those who believed the erring lovers had met a just fate, and those who thought the system at fault in providing no means of immediate escape, when to reside in the palace became imprisonment and a living death to certain souls. The latter party was composed of the more youthful section of the priesthood, who sympathized with the unfortunate lovers. These latter would have got up a demonstration in their favour did not the stern rules of Egyplosis suppress any such outbursts of popular feeling.

On the day following the imprisonment of the erring twin-soul, the question was being discussed in the apartments occupied by the officers of the *Polar King* and myself. We had been lodged in a noble building not far from the palace of the goddess, while the sailors were quartered in the fortress of Egyplosis, in company with the *wayleals* of the palace itself.

"Your opinion of Egyplosis has possibly undergone a change since the day of our reception," said the doctor.

"Well," said I, "I suppose the longer we stay here the more exact will be our knowledge of this peculiar institution."

I had considered Egyplosis as a successful institution for developing the human soul. Certainly Harikar with his beloved attributes required a fit home for his complete development.

I had praised their oasis of love, of refinement, of rest, and of beauty, and even ventured to assert that such a paradise was the outcome of the love and purity of twin-souls. I forgot in my enthusiasm the possibility of the soul being satiated with pleasure, that life is a warfare ever seeking but never gaining repose, and that we are led more by our passions and illusions than our judgment. I forgot that while man resists pain he always yields to pleasure. I forgot that he was created for difficulty, which is the oxygen that feeds the flame of endeavour, and that difficulty alone can develop efforts which pleasure so easily destroys.

"I am of the opinion," said the doctor, "that this institution is founded on a perversion of human nature. This so-called hopeless love is, as we have just had proof, one of the most disturbing elements in life. Its victims resemble Tantalus, who, though steeped to

171

the lips in water, can never drink. They are the unhappy devotees of an idol, and, like the Hindus, stick into their sides the hooks of a cruel passion and swing aloft in torture to the applause of an admiring crowd."

"You evidently do not reverence hopeless love?" I remarked.

"I consider Egyplosis," he continued, "but a nervous asylum on a large scale. This nervous temperament, with its hysterical raptures and tears, its painful sensibility, its exalted spiritualism and irresistible sympathy, departs so far from the steady temperate sphere of action that can alone sustain alike the pleasures and disappointments of life as to become the object of pity. These are the marks of a mental disease. Ultra-romantic ideas and whimsical and unaccountable tastes are attributes of this temperament. It is a kind of insanity, not the insanity proceeding from hopeless mental aberration, but founded on a systematic train of ideas born in a heated enthusiasm. It may lead, however, to hopeless insanity."

"Doctor," said the astronomer, "you are taking a very cold-blooded view of the subject. You seem not to have discovered that the life here is ideal. From what you say one would think that love is a species of insanity."

"That is precisely my idea," replied the doctor. "Haven't you observed how foolishly people act when in love? All ordinary human prudence and judgment are thrown aside. Love pares the claws and pulls the teeth of man as a rational animal. Love is supreme folly."

"I think," said the astronomer, "the climate of this country has something to do with the present institution. You see that the sun here never sets, and, were it not for his diminutive size, would infallibly turn the entire interior world into a desert, such as the moon is at present, where the outer sun's heat falls for fourteen days on the one spot without intermission, completely blasting her territories. The mild yet incessant heat of Swang creates a fervour of blood and a romance of temperament unknown in lands possessing night, hence the practices of Egyplosis are a natural result of climatic conditions. The appetite for ideal love has been created by the climate, and the religion of the country very naturally responds to the craving of such appetite. Who knows what excesses might not obtain if no such restraint were imposed on the most gallant youth of the country."

"I think," said the naturalist, "that the proper thing to do would be to have their people imitate the conduct of Jacob of old and Rachel. Jacob worshipped ideal love in the person of Rachel for seven years and then married, her. If our commander would only propose such a scheme to the supreme goddess it might possibly be favourably considered."

"Do you really suppose," said I, "that I possess any influence with the goddess, or that any recommendation of mine would be able to change the constitution of Atvatabar?"

"Well, sir," said he, "if you will allow me to make the remark, I think the supreme goddess takes quite as much interest in you as you do in her, and would treat your opinions with great respect."

"You think more than I have ever dared to think," I replied, "and your thought savours of sacrilege. The goddess belongs to her faith, her country. To prefer an individual soul is to dethrone herself as goddess and meet a painful death."

"In any case, whatever happens, you can rely on the fidelity of your followers," said the naturalist.

The subject was fast becoming embarrassing and I merely said: "Gentlemen, I am assured of your fidelity; so please let us dismiss the subject."

The hour for rest having been sounded, I sought my couch, but not to sleep. The remarks made by my companions, emphasized by my growing fondness for the goddess, set me to thinking what the end would be of our discovery of Atvatabar. I wondered if Lyone was not, as sung by her devotees,

A chrysalis eager to hover
And fly from her prison away.

Could it be that the goddess might possibly, if an occasion worthy of such a step presented itself, fly from Egyplosis, renounce her throne, her crown, her sublime office of supreme goddess of Harikar, and with me retire to some far-off country, braving in the meantime the almost certain prospect of death. For her sake I felt I could meet any situation, however terrible, but for my sake would she throw aside her unparalleled dignities? Even if in trying to escape we outflew in my own vessel their ships of war, we could never escape the ubiquitous *wayleals*, the *magnic*-winged troops that could fight equally well on land or sea.

Bah! I said, such a dream is idiotic. When I thought of the splendour of the position that she would be obliged to renounce for the sake of her love for the passing stranger, and of the awful penalties that awaited transgression in one so exalted, I considered that no craving of passion should dare to resist such difficulties.

Here duty was resistance. Nowhere is man exonerated from the penalty of having to pay a price for his possessions, and even possession itself is not happiness. Better, I said to myself, to depart in peace than encourage the goddess in a desperate enterprise, if indeed she had any such desires as my vanity attributed to her.

CHAPTER 34

Lyone's Confession

The following day I again met the goddess in the same magnificent apartment in her palace. She was in a contemplative mood. A white robe of the finest silk enveloped her, showing to full advantage her superb figure. Her silky, shadowed eyes shone with a mild translucent light. The ripe beauty of her face was somewhat pale, for some tearful memory possessed her. Over her shoulders fell the torrent of her hair, while on her brow gleamed a diminutive diadem whose central part was fashioned like the throne of the gods. She wore a heavy necklace of shrimp-pink pearls.

As we reposed on wide, luxurious couches a maiden of rare beauty brought us dishes of curiously-prepared meats and wine of the finest vintage in flagons of gold. From distant cloisters came wafted the echoes of singing priestesses breathing their intoxicating *Amens*.

Lyone had been reciting her past soul experiences, now and then pausing as the story would grow more sacred. To me the revelations of the goddess were of breathless interest. I dare not urge her too forcibly, fearing to break the spell of her confessional mood.

She was pleased to say that my advent in Egyplosis had revived the past as no other event of late times had done. She was willing to recall the sweet experiences of her early life, prior to her elevation to the throne of the goddess.

I knew she was in that mood when confession to a kindred soul is most consoling to the heart. I urged her to continue the story.

"Well," she continued, "my parents, who were people of importance in Calnogor, had destined me for marriage and the outer world, but before I even knew of Egyplosis I had a day dream. I saw with my waking eyes this temple-palace as one might see it in a picture, splendid as the reality. I saw myself with a youth of noble aspect standing in a court of the garden, and his arm was around me. He was tall and shapely as a palm tree and was all tenderness and devotion. The picture vanished, yet its influence remained. It utterly transformed me from the undreaming girl that I was to a soul active and ardent, already experienced in what life really was. I learned that the mystery of life was love, and longed for spiritual companionship with an inmate of Egyplosis."

"Was the dream fulfilled as you expected it would be?" I inquired.

"Exactly as I anticipated," said Lyone. "I entered Egyplosis in spite of the earnest desire of my people to remain in the outer world and lead a life of barren conventionality."

"Had you not learned," I inquired, "that it was impossible to overleap the purposes of nature without paying a penalty therefore, that ideal passion will in time give way to the commonplace, just as water follows the law of gravity?"

"I knew nothing but that ideal love might be eternal. It is the passion that makes a goddess human and the mortal divine. Within a month after entering the temple walls I discovered the very reality of the image I had seen years before. He was my twin-soul, my lover, my god. At our first meeting we simultaneously burst into tears. It was an ecstasy in which the body did not participate to any marked extent, but belonged purely to the region of the soul. We accepted the vows made at the installation of a twin-soul and became a completed circle."

"Being the goddess," I said, "your lover must have died?"

"He died some years ago," she said, "and on his death, by reason of my widowhood, my gifts, my spirituality, my love and my beauty, I was elevated to the throne of the gods when vacant, and was worshipped as supreme goddess of the faith. It is utterly against our laws for a goddess to choose another counterpart; she is supposed to belong only to Harikar, the ideal soul whom also she symbolizes; hence I am obliged to dwell largely alone."

"You doubtless regret the loss of your earthly counterpart?" I urged.

"Regret it! Ah, that was life!" she said, "for my soul then knew what spiritual freedom means. I experienced ecstatic agonies, bliss was pain and pain paradise. I flew as a bird full of anguish, bearing treasures of love and tears. I desired self-sacrifice, I wanted to smile on every one, to help every one. I loved life; I had no fear of death. My capacity for rapture seemed to expand continually. Every scene I gazed upon trembled in a new blaze of delight. Thoughts, like lightning, rent open new worlds of passion and tenderness, wherein I moved as a goddess peerless and supreme. But when the tomb closed upon my heart of hearts I begged them to lay me by his side and seal the door upon us forever. The glory of life had departed, and day after day I swooned upon the sarcophagus that held my treasure, my life."

Lyone was unusually excited, and to divert her attention from the past I spoke of the present, of her proud position as supreme goddess of Atvatabar.

"How does it affect you," I exclaimed, "to be the recipient of such adoration as you receive as goddess?"

"At first it was soul maddening," she replied; "I thought I should never be able to sustain such adoration. My soul, blinded and bewildered by the incense of song and prayer, seemed unable to bear the intoxication. Even yet, as I sit upon the throne of the gods, fantastic, astonishing emotions thrill me into swooning away. Oh, it is incomparably glorious to hear around you those earthquake surges of prayer, to see souls quivering with adoring love. I feel at times as though I were the cone of a volcano radiating fire and flame into a burning sky!

"Then, again, I smile, and feel as I smile that I have power over life and death—oh, you do not know what love is—you do not know its tremendous power until you feel its splendid flame breathed from ten thousand souls clasping your shrieking soul in a blood-crimson embrace! If thoughts be things it makes me a creator. If thoughts can chisel matter, then I am gracious in face and figure. Men say my flesh is smooth as marble, soft as velvet, and bright as gold, even as the forms of our priests and priestesses are sculptured and coloured by the thoughts of love.

"Only a goddess knows such thoughts as hers that burn in the soul like fluid gold. Imagination fills me at times with vast and phantasmal splendours. Adoration glorifies me like light raining on the palms and palaces. I see shapes of burning sweetness, and the air around me is laden with the caresses of heavy, strange perfumes. Unclothed raptures, exquisitely soft and tender, surround me, like heaven opening its wings of flame upon the world. Happy voices, ringing in the sensuous arcades of music, fall on my ears, the blown spray of immortal friendships.

"Yet, is it not strange that all these delights, violent and glorious as they are, do not wholly satisfy the soul? I continually long for something sweeter yet. It seems the greater the joy the more enormous the capacity, and no joy completely fills the ever-expanding soul."

"You think," said I, "that even the rapture of a goddess is not wholly adequate to create a feeling of repletion of satisfaction in a soul such as yours?"

"It is contrary to our laws to think so, yet at times I know I could forego even the throne of the gods itself for the pure and intimate love of a counterpart soul."

"You are not so desirous of the human soul in its collective form as you are of individual soul wholly yours?" I ventured, shaken with a quivering thrill.

"The soul ever seeks that which is beyond and individual," said Lyone; "having once loved the individual soul, I know what such holy rapture means."

"What are the difficulties to be surmounted in your quest of a counterpart soul?" I inquired, with a secret delight.

"The sacrilege of a goddess becoming attached to the individual to the exclusion of all other individuals. The goddess-elect must have been a novitiate and priestess of Egyplosis and the survivor of her counterpart soul. Her experiences as a noble and pure priestess, together with special beauty and popularity, are the conditions for the peerless office of supreme goddess and incarnation of Harikar. By her vows she can never again become the exclusive possession of any one soul. She belongs to Harikar, the universal soul."

"And what is the punishment for renunciation of your office and attachment to another soul?"

"A shameful death by *magnicity* for the twin-soul. No goddess can resign her office. No goddess can seek a lover and live."

"Not even an ideal affinity?" I asked.

"Why, even ideal affinities who forget themselves are punished with lifelong imprisonment, and their names blotted out of the priesthood as though they were dead," said Lyone.

"Are there many such transgressors of their vows in Egyplosis?" I inquired.

"There are, I believe, some five hundred twin-souls at present immured in the dungeons," said Lyone.

"Poor souls!" I murmured, "their apostasy was but their reformation."

"I often think of them," said Lyone, "but I know I can never liberate them except by my own successful apostasy. And yet when all else is peaceful and happy, or at least appears so, why should I become the leader of an insurrection that would precipitate a hundred times more misery on the nation, to say nothing of the possibility of defeat?"

I saw that a crisis had come to Lyone, a tremendous debate agitated her soul. I forbore treading further on the sacred ground. She, with true delicacy, was striving to hide the intensity of her proud unrest. I felt that in time she would have the courage to take the irrevocable step that led to freedom or death.

As I sat devouring every word spoken by Lyone I felt a strange power surrounding me, an emanation of the soul of my beloved friend. I resisted for a long time a sacrilegious desire to fling myself at her feet and clasp her in my arms. I thought of her supreme dignity, her love for her faith and her people, and I knew one cold glance from her eyes would pierce me through and through like a sword. The more I thought of my position at that moment the more amazed I became at the audacity that led me to ever think of claiming the soul of the goddess as mine, much less my encouragement of an enterprise so desperate as we had already assuredly embarked upon.

As I gazed in adoration at the splendid soul before me the scene through the open windows seemed to grow more ideal. There was a new glory in the gardens around me, a finer flashing of fountains in the sunlight, and a bolder chiselling of palaces and temples. Beyond and above there wheeled the roof of the world, with its still more prodigious forests and mountains and a wider expanse of gleaming seas.

HER KISS WAS A BLINDING WHIRLWIND OF FLAME AND TEARS! IT WAS THE PROCLAMATION OF WAR UPON ATVATABAR. THENCEFORTH WE BECAME A NEW AND FORMIDABLE TWIN-SOUL.

I sprang forward with a cry of joy, falling at the feet of the goddess. I encircled her figure with my arms and held up my face to hers. Her kiss was a blinding whirlwind of flame and tears! Its silence was irresistible entreaty. It dissolved all other interests like fire melting stubborn steel. It was the proclamation of war upon Atvatabar! It was the destruction of a unique civilization with all its appurtenances of hopeless love. It was love defying death. Thenceforward we became a new and formidable twin-soul!

CHAPTER 35

Our Visit to the Infernal Palace

The infernal palace was a congregation of subterranean rock-hewn temples under the spiritual control of the grand sorcerer Charka and the grand sorceress Zooly-Soase.

The grand sorcerer's dominion was directly underneath the supernal palace of Egyplosis. An ornate pagoda of stone covered the entrance to the underground palace. The descent was by means of a wide gradient of polished marble, and there was also an elevator car, beautifully decorated with electro-plated sheets of gold and lit by electricity, which was the most rapid means of descent to the pavement beneath, a distance of two hundred and fifty feet. The procession of twin-souls and attendants, who carried Lyone and myself in a splendid litter of gold, entered the palace by means of the inclined marble highway whose sculptured walls were radiant with electric light. The many temples of the underground palace were devoted to the most occult worship of Harikar. There was an immense central edifice whose roof, supported by lofty columns, and sculptured in fantastic beauty, rose two hundred feet above the pavement. Here electric suns lit up what was merely the vestibule of a hundred temples all hewn from the same pale green marble, the *aquelium* floors glimmering like a fathomless sea.

As we entered this splendid abode of sorcery, we were received by the august officials of the sanctuary. The grand sorcerer Charka was a man of imperial presence, gracious and subtle. His flesh was of the hue of silver bronze and he possessed noble features. His hair was blue and his blue beard was trimmed into a rounded semi-circle on his chin, while his moustache spread nobly on either side of his lips. He wore a robe of emerald blue silk, embroidered with silver flowers. The grand sorceress, Thoubool who accompanied him, possessed the complexion of a pearl, was arrayed in a robe of celestial blue silk, and, like the grand sorcerer, wore a diadem of rubies.

Our reception was extremely gracious, the grand sorcerer saying he felt highly honoured with our visit.

As we passed down the palace pavement, an immense bell opened its mouth of gaunt and glorious bronze. Soft explosions of music swept in thrilling moans through temple and cloister, the echoing walls resounding with *ritournels* of enthusiastic peace. As if inspired with passion, I could hear the bell swing and roll on its delirious pivot uttering its deep-sounding fantasy.

I saw, illuminating the sculptured archway of each temple on either side of us, the name thereof in letters of incandescent light. I saw the names Amano, Biccano, Demano, Hirlano, Kilano, Pridano, Redolano, Ecthyano, Oxemano, Jiracano, Oirelano, Orphitano, Cedeshano, Padomano, Jocdilano, Nidialano, Bischomano, Omdolopano and many others, indicating the various departments of soul development to which each temple was dedicated.

The sorcerer waved his wand and suddenly a band of priestesses appeared on the pavement moving in strange and fantastic measures. Their attire consisted of low-cut circles of bright and beautiful stuffs with short skirts, having in front of each a sheaf of heavy folds that expanded and fell as the dancer moved. All wore jewels and rings of precious metals on wrists and ankles. Their faces, perfect in feature, were pale rose in colour but marvellously delicate. Ranging themselves on either side of the immense aisle, they formed a delightful guard of honour for the grand sorcerer and his retinue.

They were not only souls, but the materializations of souls, that danced and sang as when on earth. They were souls of former priestesses reincarnated by the sorcerer and who vanished when we reached the entrance to the temple of the labyrinth. It certainly was a delicate and super-excited imagination that wrought the splendid archway through which we passed into the grotto garden beyond. Neither Greek nor Moor, Hindu nor Goth ever conceived such arabesques as were sculptured on the walls of the entrance to the holy of holies.

In the garden, hewn from the solid stone, were interminable thickets and hedges enclosing labyrinthine walks. There were open spaces in which stood veritable trees with strangest leaf and flower, branch and stem delicately chiselled from the solid rock. There were also acres of grass and flowers, wonderful creations of art. There were rose bushes, heavy with their eternal bloom, the flowers stained crimson as in life and the leaves their varying gradations of green.

Fruit trees, with pale pink flowers and leaves light and dark green, stood amid the green grass that never waved in the breeze. An immovable streamlet ran down its bed of carved irregularities between flowery banks and underneath a bridge formed of a single arch.

I looked up expecting to see the sky, but my gaze met the solid heavens of stone, and I knew again I was in a cavern. The feeling was somewhat suffocating. The garden was lit by an electric sun in the centre of the roof two hundred feet overhead. The pathway, wide enough for six people abreast, led by labyrinthine dells to the pagoda of the sorcerer, which stood in the centre of the garden. The mazes of the pathway were so numerous that none save the initiated, when once in the labyrinth, could find their way out again.

It was a weird experience to find myself walking between the master twin-souls of that subterranean paradise, exploring its many mysteries.

We arrived in due time at the entrance to a mighty temple at the further side of the labyrinth, whose bronze door suddenly opened to receive us, and the sorcerer bade me enter.

Passing through a pillared porch we entered a wide and lofty space lit by tall windows and a roof of many-coloured domes of glass that threw wonderful lights on the polished *aquelium* floors of the building. The light that shone through window and dome was produced by myriads of electric incandescent lamps that glowed in recesses of the rock behind each window. This was the inmost shrine of the sorcerer.

As I walked toward the centre of the mysterious temple the sorcerer inquired if creative magic was cultivated on the outer sphere.

I informed the sorcerer that necromancy, divination, magic, clairvoyance, esotericism, and theosophy were things known and practised in many countries. "But," I added, "the idea there is that of self-abnegation and miracles are only to be performed by ascetics who practise the most rigid austerities. Men who desire to possess occult power live in complete solitude, subjecting themselves to cruel mortifications. They abstain from all fellowship with their kind, they try to live even without food. They absolutely mourn existence, avoiding all contact with everything earthly. They hope by renouncing all the actions of life to enter more and more into the spiritual existence. They believe they can build up an enormous soul out of the ruins of the body."

"Do you find that such a method produces a high development of creative power, love, justice, conscience, truth, temperance, order, and benevolence?" said the grand sorcerer.

"I cannot say," I replied, "that the devotees to whom I refer are conspicuous for those qualities, certainly not for a highly active state of such qualities. Their abnegation develops fanaticism, which is intemperance itself, and fills them with hate toward those outside their creed. The starvation of every appetite of pleasure withers up the appreciation for every form of human delight."

"Then what virtues are derived from ascetic practices?" inquired the sorcerer.

"Certain virtues of a negative order," I replied. "The adepts claim to have power to create and transport matter; a claim which reliable history does not, except in a few cases, recognize, and in a very limited sense they have power to separate the soul from the body. While the body remains in a comatose state, the soul traverses space, holds consultation with similar souls, and returns to its mansion in the body again."

"Your magicians," said the sorcerer, "weaken or kill the body without imparting corresponding power to the soul. Now we of Atvatabar believe that the body should be developed equally with the soul. We believe that contact with the noblest and best of earthly things develops power and beauty. We feed both body and soul on the perfection of things, that both may thereby absorb perfection.

"In the brilliant activities of the supernal palace, and in the golden calm of the infernal palace, priest and priestess, as twin souls, naturally intermingle in the enjoyment of a long Nirvana of ecstasy. We have not only the occult power to perform miracles like the ascetics of the outer sphere, but the soul possesses an enormous development of every noble quality without which our golden century is impossible. We are able by means of our baths of life to obtain a hundred years

THE LABYRINTH WAS A SUBTERRANEAN GARDEN, WHOSE TREES
AND FLOWERS WERE CHISELLED OUT OF THE LIVING ROCK.

of glorious youth, during which period age and decay of the body is suspended. Our devotees when they arrive at the age of twenty years, when youth is fully developed, begin their Nirvana of blessedness and love. They do not grow older during these years. The eye is as bright, the pulse as bounding, the heart as lively, the complexion as pure and lovely, the feelings as fresh, at the end of the interregnum as at its commencement. Then when the golden century is exhausted, the body begins to be twenty-one years old."

"Do you mean that a man who has lived one hundred and thirty years is but thirty years old?" I inquired.

"Precisely," said the sorcerer; "why should we call a period age in which there is no change?"

"Do all souls live until their century of youth is accomplished?"

"Not all souls. Many die of accident or in consequence of sin. With some, Nirvana consists of but a single day's felicity, with others a month, or a year, up to a hundred years. It is the ideal for which we strive, and there is no reason why the body should not live one thousand years as well as one hundred, when vitality becomes more developed."

I was astonished at the remarks of the sorcerer, and yet I remembered the case of Adam, Noah, and Methuselah. I told him that men on the outer sphere had lived almost one thousand years.

"You may be sure they never practised the austerities of the ascetic life you have just mentioned. They must have enjoyed life always turning their faces to the sun."

"I think one hundred years a great step toward immortality," I remarked.

"At twenty years the body is developed, but even a hundred thousand years will not develop the soul. Think of the development involved in having power over disease and death, power to create substantialities of matter!"

"Do you create matter?" I inquired breathlessly.

"I will show you what we can do," replied the sorcerer; "if you will follow me."

The sorcerer led the way to seats upon a platform of silver, on which stood in terrific grandeur the figure of a *hehorrent*, or dragon of gold, whose eyes were blazing rubies. He stood before the dragon, at least twenty feet above the pavement of the palace.

Presently the sorcerer shouted with a loud voice, "My host! my host!" and at once several thousand twin souls thronged into the immense temple, dancing with naked feet on the polished *aquelium* pavement. Beneath the monster miles of wire were wound in a coil, and to the wire were attached twenty thousand fine wires of *terrelium*, each wire terminating in a *terrelium* wand. These wires were held one each by priest and priestess, who began to move in a strange dance on the pavement and sing an anthem to Harikar. As they moved more and more rapidly the clamour of bells arose, and explosions of sound, like bullets rained upon drums, shook the building. In the semi-darkness the body of the *hehorrent* seemed to quiver, and, as I gazed, lo! a shower of blazing jewels issued from its mouth. There were emeralds, diamonds, sapphires, and rubies flung upon the pavement, scintillating with fire the colours of the stones themselves!

The sorcerer, waving his *terrelium* wand, shouted, "Hold! It is enough!" and the séance was at an end. He received the jewels that had been collected by his *hierophants*, and descending, offered me a splendid ruby as large as a hen's egg. I looked at him with awe, as I felt its size and weight. He simply said, "These jewels have been created by spirit power."

"Do you," I gasped, with a feeling of mingled exultance and fear, "do you create matter?"

"The abnegation of hopeless love is the source of the spirit power by which we create matter such as this," replied the sorcerer. "The twin-soul is the cell that generates the creative force."

"And can you create other matter than jewels?" I eagerly inquired.

The sorcerer gazed at Lyone for a moment, who had been strangely silent in the presence of her most powerful spiritual co-adjutor, and then replied: "Yes, we can create all things if necessary. We can, for example, create islands in the sea, with mountains, forests, lakes, valleys, winding walks and thickets of flowers, palaces and pagodas."

I was breathless with excitement at such a reply. "Oh, that I could see such an island," I rejoined, "and tread, if but for a single hour, its ecstatic shores!"

"You can both see it and walk upon it, if the goddess so wills it," replied the sorcerer. "What is the command of your holiness?" he inquired.

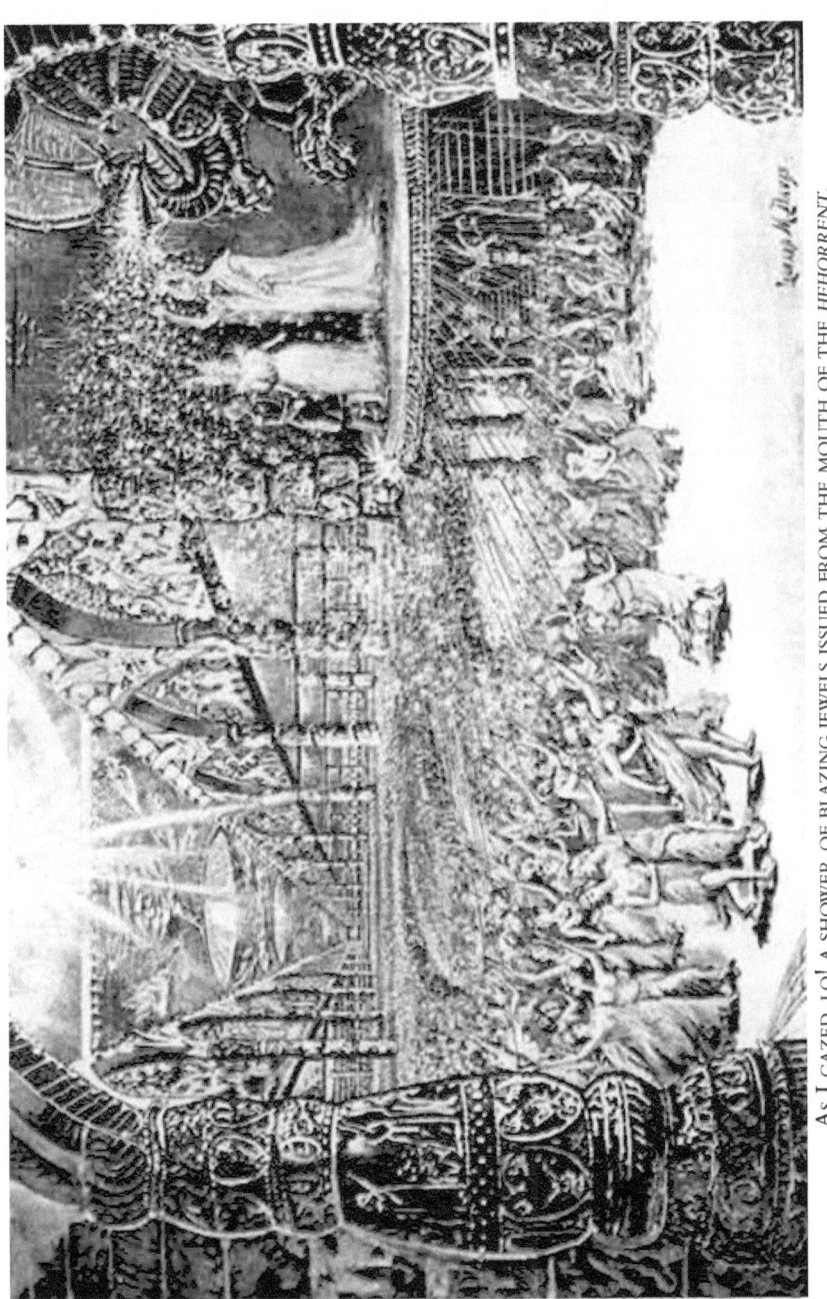

As I gazed, lo! a shower of blazing jewels issued from the mouth of the *Hehorrent*.

"I would like the commander to see Arjeels, if your priests and priestesses are willing to perform the necessarily arduous ritual involved in its creation," replied Lyone.

"My *hierophants*," replied the sorcerer, "are only too happy to serve their goddess at all times, and I will at once command them to prepare to execute the ritual for creating the magical island of Arjeels."

"Your devotion," said Lyone, "fills me with the purest joy."

As we conversed, the large ruby I held in my hand had grown considerably less in size, as though the elements of which it was composed had to a degree evaporated as unseen gases, so that in a short time the jewel might wholly disappear. The sorcerer, anticipating an inquiry as to its disappearance, stated that all objects created by spirit power could only be maintained in their full material splendour so long as they were sustained by the power that gave them birth. The creations were not additions to already existing elements; they were simply focalizations of matter from the elements of the surrounding world, held together by the force that withdrew them from their normal habitat as long as the spirit power remains supplied. The jewels would in a few hours cease to exist, because they were not enfolded with the power that produced them.

"As to your magical island," said I, addressing Lyone, one of whose titles was Princess of Arjeels, "where is your principality situated?"

"It is located anywhere in the wide sea," said Lyone.

"Do you mean to say," said I, "that Arjeels is not a real, veritable island of the ocean, but only a ghostly island, a mirage that retreats as we approach it, a fantasy of the imagination?"

"Arjeels is a real island, with real rocks and waterfalls, lakes and forests, birds and flowers. There is a real palace, and all the appurtenances of an ideal life. All this is a materialization of the ideal desires."

I was astonished at her reply. "Once called into being," I inquired, "how long can the island exist?"

"So long as the twin-souls support it by never-ceasing ecstasy, so long as they perform their magical dances on the *aquelium* floor of the temple of the dragon, holding in their hands the *terrelium* wands. Once the island becomes materialized it requires thousands of twin-souls to sustain and preserve its reality, and it only vanishes when the twin-souls are utterly weary of their ecstasy."

"And when the twin-souls grow weary of their joys, what becomes of the island and its glories?" I inquired.

"We can preserve the island for a long time," said the sorcerer, "by having fresh dancers take the place of those that are exhausted, but after the lapse of a month, or longer, when all are utterly vanquished with fatigue, the spirit power becomes exhausted and the island disappears upon the sea."

I rose and enthusiastically grasped the sorcerer by the hand. "Ah, dear sorcerer," said I, "will you show me this magical island?"

"The command of the Princess of Arjeels," he replied, "will be obeyed."

CHAPTER 36

Arjeels

I was full of impatience to witness the creation of the magical island, where with Lyone I might find ideal delight. It was necessary, however, for the grand sorcerer to make ample arrangements, not only for the generation of sufficient spirit force to create the island, but also a force sufficient for its continuance for an indefinite length of time. It was absolutely necessary that there should be a reserve force of ten thousand twin-souls to take the places of the original legion of souls, when they would become weary of their ecstatic labours. Only once before had Arjeels been created, and it was thought a most wonderful thing that the sorcerer could preserve its existence for a single day. Now it was contemplated to sustain the island for months, and this required a continuous as well as a lavish expenditure of spirit power.

The sorcerer had enlisted his full quota of twin-souls, and prepared them for their heroic duty. The *terrelium* wand held by each soul was connected with the wires of a *helic* having immense coils of *terrelium*, that held by a rampant *hehorrent* of gold, formed an immense spiritual battery in the centre of another subterranean temple. Wires led from the battery underground across Atvatabar to the city of Mylosis, on the seacoast most remote from Kioram, a thousand miles from Egyplosis. The sorcerer announced a few days after the visit to the infernal palace that he was ready to accompany us to Mylosis, whither the queen's golden yacht had been sent to meet us.

The aerial yacht of the goddess flew swiftly over Atvatabar, bearing the precious Lyone, the grand sorcerer Charka, and myself to the far seacoast, the first stage in our journey.

The brightly flashing seas, the rose-coloured sun, and the transcendent concave of the earth encompassing us, with the near tropical splendour of the country, made a scene of long remembered joy. But these objects, so glorious in themselves, were made still more splendid by the love that reigned in the souls that contemplated them.

In due time we reached Mylosis, where we found the royal yacht and a reverent crowd of people awaiting us.

The sorcerer lost no time in connecting the subterranean wires with a cable of *terrelium* on board the yacht, and, this being done, we immediately set out to sea, followed by a crowd of pleasure ships, conveying a host of people anxious to witness the miracle about to be performed.

We anchored the yacht at a distance of fifty miles from the coast. The grand sorcerer, surrounded by his acolytes, held in his hand a thick rod of *terrelium*, the extreme end of the cable, whose further extremity was connected with the battery in the Temple of Reincarnation at Egyplosis. An exchange of messages along the wire informed us that the ten thousand twin-souls had already begun their dance of Pure Being upon the pavement of the greater temple. Immediately a stream of flame leaped from the end of the rod, like water spouting from a tube under enormous pressure.

"Now," said the sorcerer, "by virtue of the spirit power in this cable, what I will to exist, will exist. I will that the magical island of Arjeels shall rise above the waves."

"I wish the island," said Lyone, "to have an elevation of five thousand feet in the centre, and at an elevation of four thousand feet fill a crater of the mountain with a lake of cool water surrounded by aerial gardens, and on the shore place a palace of rose-coloured marble, luxuriously furnished, with servants to wait upon us. All else may be according to your own fancy."

"As your majesty wishes," replied the sorcerer, and as he spoke, a high mountain rose instantly from the sea a mile away, creating enormous waves, that threatened the safety of the yacht and the congregated vessels. A feeling of awe silenced the host of spectators.

Instantly, as quickly as the sorcerer moved his wand, the mountains became clothed with forests, and high up on the shoulder of the central peak appeared a palace of rose-coloured marble, whose

"By virtue of the spirit power in this cable," said the
sorcerer, "I will that the magical island of Arjeels
shall rise above the waves."

supernatural architecture seemed a celestial dream. The island was thirty miles in length and about fifteen in width. From immense cliffs, foaming waterfalls flung themselves downward to the sea. Dazzled with their blinding beauty, we saw ravines engorged with flowers. In green and glorious blessedness the island lay before us, complete, like an enormous emerald in a setting of blue sea. We were so awe-struck with the labours of the sorcerer, that it seemed a sacrilege to set foot on the miraculous shores of Arjeels.

At a sign from the sorcerer, the captain of the yacht fired one hundred guns, and the vessel moved toward the romantic island. We came close up to a white marble wharf, and Lyone and myself alighted upon the sacred retreat. Everything seemed so natural, that we could scarcely believe the solid rock to be sustained by self-sacrificing love.

The adorable sorcerer remained on board the vessel, as it was impossible for him to leave his post of duty for a moment, while the dazed yet happy inhabitants of Mylosis departed homeward in their vessels.

It was arranged that when the spirit power that sustained the island would become exhausted, owing to the utter weariness of the twin-souls, the firing of a gun on board the yacht would be a signal that Arjeels would disappear from upon the sea.

The moment both Lyone and myself stepped upon the magical soil we felt an instantaneous increase of health and vigour. We did not at first use our *magnic* wings for flight, but walked along paths that wound around the beach of golden sand, shaded by towering palms.

After remaining for a time on the margin of the sea we rose on our wings, and, like birds, encircled the island, rising ever higher until we alighted before the palace created for Lyone, a gem of the rosiest marble, covered with a dome of gold that flashed around it the light of the sun. The architecture was broad and heavy with splendid carvings, and surrounded by a pillared portico. The palace stood on the shore of a beautiful sheet of cool water; elsewhere its shores were thickly clothed with tropic foliage and aerial gardens of the greatest beauty.

We had reached at last the holy of holies of ideal attainment, a retreat of bewildering beauty. The weird and splendid proportions of the palace, with its domes and towers ornamented with sculptured arabesques, rising from the soft waters of the lake, a veritable Fountain of Youth, all surrounded by the green and gleaming forest and gardens without end, filled our souls with a new rapture. Everything was so perfect and peaceful, so rich with life and beauty, so fresh and sparkling, so unspeakably happy, that I said, "This is the end of all toil and ambition, this is the perfect flower of life. Here is the lake of immortality, and here the fabled gardens of the Hesperides."

Rayoulb, the chamberlain of the palace, and his acolytes, who received us, were also the product of spirit power, the reincarnation of former inmates of Egyplosis. They awaited us before the palace, announcing a feast had already been prepared for us.

The interior of the palace revealed new wonders. Wide and lofty chambers were hung, some with woven and painted tapestries, and some plated with sheets of gold, illuminated by electricity with many-coloured designs in precious metal. Others were decorated with tender and brilliant frescoes, in which the transparent plaster seemed to hold in its depths the tones of gold, of ultramarine and vermilion, in fabulous scenes. Woven and painted tapestries clothed the walls of still other chambers, representing in entrancing colours the most occult mysteries of Egyplosis. The banqueting chamber had a dome of enamelled glass, that softened the light with many a caressing colour. Porcelain vases, gorgeous in depth and richness of colour, containing plants of the richest bloom, added to the apartment their decorative grace. There were also an art gallery, a library, and a museum of jewels.

On one side of the palace a square cloistered arcade surrounded a marble court. In the centre of the court lay a square pool of crystal water, whose basin had been chiselled out of the solid rock. The pool was fed by a wide water-fall falling down a precipice on the pavement. Here also were several pagodas containing chimes of bells and large oblong vases of stone filled with blooming flowers.

Amid such splendour I began to realize that love has the power of spiritualizing all things, of interfusing them with its own rapture. Under its flame all colours brighten, all movement becomes divine, all labour seems holy. The sea attains a deeper blue, the shores a brighter green, the beloved one becomes more beautiful, more delicate and supernatural. Love, indeed, is an ultramarine and ultramontane joy!

"This delight," said Lyone as she lay in her boudoir, plunged in delicious blessedness, "fills my soul with universal peace. Hitherto pained with the chagrin of life, I welcome this unwonted repose. Oh, I am supremely happy!"

"This expedition," I replied, "is not to observe the transit of Venus, but the possession of Venus, to weigh each other's souls and read the poetry written in every fold of the heart. It would be the perfection of life if such reality of the ideal could surround us forever, but in a world where the worm doth conquer, where the storm wastes the flower and herb, such felicity is purchased only by the sacrifice of ourselves or of others. But while it lasts let us prize its ineffable joy. Hitherto," I continued, "philosophy has said that if we do not want to be undeceived we should never visit the haunts of imagination, for the fruits thereof are ashes, but we will create a new philosophy, that will assert that the haunts of imagination are ideally real, that the veritable Fountain of Youth has been discovered, that Eldorado may be won."

The following day found us floating on the lake before, the palace in a beautiful *magnic* boat. Musicians occupied a pagoda overlooking the lake, and made the air sweet with their music. The lake seemed to fill the crater of an extinct volcano, and miles away on its further shore rose the lofty precipices of a mountain crest. It was most delightful to float on its profound wave, at an elevation of four thousand feet, and yet see the sea beneath us, and we surrounded with all the glory of the interior world.

Birds, gorgeous as humming-birds, resplendent in burnished hues of purple, garnet, and green, would flash amid the flowers, or chase each other over the water. As for ourselves, we no longer feared our own holiest emotions. Our deepest feelings were then in the foreground. The mysterious carmine on the palpitating lips of Lyone was the symbol of a warm, delicate, super-excited soul.

Lyone grew day by day more and more beautiful. She resembled the colour of a deep and mysterious gold. I crowned her brow with flowers and wreathed her azure hair with wistful daffodils.

Another day we rode on soul-created horses to discover the odoriferous retreats of the island. The pathways wound through flowery ravines, that looked out upon the sea. The sweet cool air that filled the splendid gloom of the palm woods seemed the essence of gladness. What glorious vistas opened amid the luminous green of the forest! The murmur of music filled the infinite ways of the island as our cavalcade wound round its peerless hills or plunged into its abysses of flowers. The spell of an ideal land was upon us, and we experienced sensations hitherto unfelt in life.

"This," said Lyone, "is the ideal climate. Everything has become transfigured; even the light of the sun is softer and more blessed."

"And the goddess of Atvatabar," I replied, "has become more delicate, more supernatural, and more holy."

The island was one vast garden of tropical fruits and flowers, without the malaria of decay. Everywhere nature, carefully assisted by art, assumed the rarest beauty. Everything that savoured of ruin and decay was non-existent. There were no wild or poisonous animals. No deadly serpent was coiled upon the branches, nor did poisonous insects crawl on leaf or flower. Forests of trees of a strange tropical vegetation abounded. There were the *fruha*, resembling dates; the *caspariba*, resembling bananas; the *dulra*, resembling limes; the *jackle*, resembling lemons; the *congol*, resembling oranges; the *velicac*, resembling bread-fruits; the *persar*, resembling custard apples; the *phyorbal*, resembling cocoanuts; the *gersin*, resembling *mangosteens*; the *huflar*, resembling coffee; the *solru*, resembling plums; and *presuveet*, or tamarinds lining the route. Fruits such as the *troupac*, or citron; *dewan*, or guava; *orogor*, or mango; and *ryeshmush*, or plantain gleamed amid the embowering foliage, and gardens of *squangs* and the pineapples, aloes, nutmeg, cloves and spices of Atvatabar, were on every hand.

One day, when floating on the lake, we heard with surprise and infinite sadness the discharge of a gun, the signal that the island was at an end. Spreading our wings, we awaited the catastrophe.

Suddenly a roar of thunder startled us, and Arjeels, with its majestic cliffs, its green forests and rivers of flowers, fell in one dissolving crash, and faded from sight. The lake and boat fell from beneath us so rapidly, that we would have fallen headlong into the sea had not our wings saved us. There flowed where the island had stood a circular wave rushing to a focus. There was an upward spouting pillar of foam, and all again was placid sea!

We flew downward to where the yacht awaited us, and alighting on board, soon reached Mylosis.

CHAPTER 37

A Revelation

Alas for the brevity of earthly joys! The noble priests and priest-esses had made a heroic effort to sustain Arjeels, but a month's incessant labours had quite exhausted their powers, and the glorious island vanished, with all its ideal sweetness. As if to intensify our sadness, when we reached Egyplosis again, we found the high priest Hushnoly, impatiently awaiting our return to secretly report the proceedings of a late council of the king and government, held in the council chamber of Egyplosis.

I knew by the appearance of Hushnoly that something unusual had happened. He hesitated to unfold his secret until requested to do so by the goddess.

"It is a serious business," said Hushnoly, "and I have been commissioned by his majesty to know the full meaning of the step both your holiness and His Excellency are about to take, and see if there is no possibility of averting the terrible calamity, that overhangs Egyplosis."

"Tell me," said Lyone to the high priest, "what the council has been discussing, and what it has determined upon."

"Your holiness," said he, "I should inform you that Koshnili, as chief minister of Atvatabar, has received a report from his winged spies, charged with the duty of watching the movements of His Excellency and retinue ever since their arrival in Atvatabar. His duty made it necessary to discover the real object of the illustrious strangers in visiting our country, and consequently their actions have been carefully watched and reported."

"And of course," said I, "my constant association with the supreme goddess, has led Koshnili to suspect me of designs inimical to the welfare of the kingdom?"

"Listen to the report made by Koshnili," replied Hushnoly, who unrolled a document he held in his hand, and read as follows:

To His Majesty, King Aldemegry Bhoolmakar, of Atvatabar, greeting:

Your faithful minister begs to report that his private *wayleals* have followed His Excellency, the alien commander, Lexington White, and followers from their arrival in Kioram until their reception at Egyplosis. The illustrious strangers, after landing on our soil, travelled by sacred locomotive from Kioram to Calnogor, and were there the guests of your majesty, after which they attended a feast of worship to the supreme goddess in the Bormidophia. The illustrious strangers were then received by her holiness in her palace of Tanje. While lingering here my *wayleals*, from the ramparts of the palace, saw His Excellency the alien commander, in company with her holiness, enter the silver pleasure boat. Their long-continued interview in the palace garden testified that a mutual affinity had drawn the illustrious personages together. From later observation my faithful *wayleals* are convinced that in the palace garden of Tanje was begun the awful possibility of a twin soul of our deity, and the alien commander, and the consequent apostasy of the supreme goddess, and her renunciation of Harikar.

My faithful *wayleals* further report that while travelling on the aerial ship from Calnogor to Egyplosis, they obtained further evidence of the consummation of a deific and alien twin soul. The principals sat apart from all others, on a seat at the prow of the vessel, and the report of their conversation will justify your majesty in believing that a sacrilegious twin soul already exists in defiance of civil and religious law, her holiness and the alien commander being the illustrious components.

Awaiting the further commands of your majesty, I remain, with profound veneration,

Your majesty's faithful servant,
Koshnili

I gasped for breath at hearing so brutal a dissection of our hearts. I was thunderstruck. I could only ask Hushnoly what he had to say on the situation.

"That you love each other, I need not ask," said he; "that may be taken for granted. But I might ask, do you each of you fully recognize the position you stand in? Do you know that your conduct menaces the throne of the gods itself? I can understand the violence of love for a human soul in the breast of the goddess, but what of her renunciation of Harikar?"

"If not already convinced," I said, "I think her holiness will soon see that all this monstrous system of hopeless love is tottering on its throne. It is an artificial society, that must in time, of its own accord, crumble to pieces."

"His majesty," said the high priest, "has departed with his retinue to Calnogor, and has called a council of the government to consider the situation. He held that the rank of the individuals who have offended against the sacred code of Atvatabar, and the monstrous impiety of the offence itself, constitutes a subject worthy of the most serious consideration of the government. His majesty was extremely angry on hearing the report of Koshnili. He characterized Your Excellency's conduct as unworthy of the hospitality you had received, and as involving the ruin of both the supreme goddess and yourself."

"What did Koshnili say when presenting the report?" I inquired.

"Koshnili said that the affections of their beloved goddess had been withdrawn from their only legitimate object, Harikar himself, and had been appropriated not even by a holy priest of the temple, not even by an ordinary citizen, but worse than all, by an infidel, a heathen, an adventurer and a stranger, emanating from some *terra incognita* that might, owing to the fatal discovery of Atvatabar, one day send its hordes to ravage the country with fire and sword. The council," he continued, "knew the penalty for such treachery and abuse of hospitality on the part of a desperate and fanatical stranger, as well as such apostasy on the part of the goddess. He demanded the immediate arrest of the guilty parties. The king had sufficient evidence to convict and execute both individuals by reason of their high treason against both the government and faith of Atvatabar."

"Did the king approve of Koshnili's demand?" I inquired.

"His majesty," said Hushnoly, "said that a matter of such importance required the greatest circumspection. Her holiness was known to be the most pious and popular supreme goddess that had ever sat on the throne of the gods, and although it was evident she had insulted Harikar, still if the quiet expulsion of the strangers from Atvatabar soil would prevent further disgrace of their faith and country, he would prefer to issue a decree of expulsion, rather than a decree for the arrest of both commander and goddess. To reduce the possible calamity now overhanging the nation to the least possible proportions, it would be necessary to act at once, rather than to await the development of more complete evidence of affection between the guilty parties."

Admiral Jolar deprecated the violent measures advocated by Koshnili, and supported the idea of the king, to quietly expel the strangers. He said that if the decree of expulsion were entrusted to him, he would see that it was carried into effect without delay. The council could rely on the royal fleet doing its duty.

Koshnili was angry at his idea of immediate arrest not being acted upon. "Suppose these strangers," he said, "refuse to leave, and being warned by your royal mandate so fortify themselves by stirring up an insurrection in favour of her holiness, that might possibly defeat the royal arms, and, in the end, we ourselves be sacrificed by our present timid vacillation. The crisis is a serious one and demands a desperate remedy."

"The Governor Lapalme," said Hushnoly, "rebutted the arguments of Koshnili. He pointed out that the laws of hospitality demanded that the strangers should receive consideration at the hands of the king, even if guilty. They might receive fair warning to depart, after which, if the commander prove contumacious, more stringent measures could be taken. Should the commander, in defiance of the royal mandate, endeavour to consolidate his affection for her holiness, doing further sacrilege to our faith, ecclesiastical law has the remedy of death for those who would dare dethrone our faith, and lead our beloved goddess to take the irrevocable step of abandonment of her supreme office. After considerable discussion, it was decided to act on the suggestion of his majesty the king, that without bringing the matter before the Borodemy, a decree of expulsion be handed Admiral Jolar, for execution on the parties to be expelled from the kingdom. The decree is already in the hands of Admiral Jolar for delivery to Your Excellency."

CHAPTER 38

Lyone's Manifesto to King and People

"Might I ask your holiness," said the high priest, "if you will really take so determined a step as that indicated by the action of the royal council? The thought of such a thing strikes me dumb with fear."

"Hushnoly," said Lyone, "I have ever found you faithful to my interests, and I will now confide in you my purposes. You are a man of wisdom, calm and conservative, and can rest happy in the possession of your counterpart soul. Your character has become moulded by your long novitiate until you have become a part of the institution itself. To think of any other state of things is to you an impossibility. On thousands of souls here, your inflexible laws have only developed a rebellious energy that will some day utterly destroy the fabric of Egyplosis. The true union of souls is not artificial restraint and the present calmness is only the pause that preludes the explosion."

"But do you, supreme goddess, indeed desire to leave us forever? Will you profane your holy office? Will you despoil the temple of ideal love?" said Hushnoly, with emotion.

"You think it monstrous," said Lyone, "that I should desire to uproot principles so fixed and permanent. You can judge, then, how fierce must be the passion that causes me to antagonize duty consecrated by the ties and memories of my holy office."

"To break away from a responsibility so supreme," I said, "argues alone an extraordinary force. Your very system creates just such a love as this. Here souls are required to meet in rapture, and yet to stand balanced, as it were, on the thin edge of naked swords, and fall neither this way nor that. The development of a purely romantic love effeminates the race. The example of Egyplosis if carried out universally would obliterate the nation in one generation. The nation is wiser than its creed. Let us therefore choose the wiser path."

"It was the dream of your noble parents," said Hushnoly to Lyone, "to see you supreme goddess of Egyplosis. When you obtained this peerless honour they died. Your mother, dying, implored you to remember your vows, and to be ever true to your high office. 'Love only duty,' was her last sigh. If you love aught else, there is but a cruel death for you, and your memory will be an everlasting disgrace. Will you, the ideal of hopeless love, be the first to prove faithless?"

"What you say is true," I said, replying for Lyone, "but what is duty? Lyone not only owes a duty to her office, but also to herself. Her duty to herself is to rise up and break down this monstrous environment that chains down her soul, and her duty to these ten thousand souls is to tell them that an institution that constantly antagonizes nature is immoral. Here refined souls," I continued, "seek the cloister, not for peace, but for ecstatic anguish. They love and weep, and thus agitated they grow at once weak and violent, and can never accommodate themselves to the serious purposes of life. Thus sacrificed on the altar of a false god, weary of a life of barren blessedness, you will discover, if you but seriously inquire into it, that this palace is purely a prison for thousands of noble souls."

As I spoke, Hushnoly clasped his head with his hands and groaned. "With the downfall of Egyplosis," he murmured, "farewell delights, farewell tendernesses, farewell mystical, chivalrous love!"

"Do not be so dejected," said Lyone; "your imagination gives you but a capricious view of the future, which will be even nobler than the past."

The high priest could hear no more, and left us seized with affright as to the future, and mourning the anticipated downfall of Egyplosis.

Lyone, far from exhibiting fear, grew enthusiastic over our projected *coup d'état*, that would certainly, if successful, create an organic change in the constitution of the kingdom.

We discussed the situation at length, and determined to leave Egyplosis for Calnogor forthwith.

I could in some measure appreciate the struggle undergone by Lyone necessary to sever her forever from so ineffable a retreat. But passion was stronger than environment, and it was duly announced that the supreme goddess and the commander of the *Polar King* and their immediate followers would leave for Calnogor forthwith.

Our departure from Egyplosis was attended with impressive ceremonies, our journey to Calnogor being made in the aerial ship of the goddess.

On our arrival at Tanje we discovered that the king and government had held their council unknown to the people. We did not think it expedient either, just then, to make public the determination of the goddess. I ordered my officers and sailors to Kioram forthwith to take command of the *Polar King*. My instructions to Captain Wallace were to have the ship fully supplied with stores, and remove her from the basin where she lay into the outer harbour of Kioram, and there await further orders. After a considerable period of inactivity the ship's company were nothing loath to get on board again with the prospect of another voyage. I confided to the officers the possibility of our being engaged in hostile operations, and ordered the ship to be put in fighting trim without delay. The officers and men were tendered the dignity of riding to Kioram in the sacred locomotive, and their departure was made amid the enthusiasm of the populace.

As for myself, I remained at the palace of Tanje, the residence of the goddess, to assist Lyone in preparing her manifesto to the people.

It was a painful crisis for her, who was the symbol of ideal love, to be the first to renounce its delights for the sake of an every-day union with a beloved soul.

For days her decision trembled in the balance. Her avowal of being led captive by human love would be a national catastrophe. She trembled for her ten thousand devotees in Egyplosis. It seemed a cruel and heartless trampling under foot of throbbing hearts that were thrilling with faith in their goddess. When I saw Lyone prepared to abandon Egyplosis for my sake, when I knew she would forever resign that splendid throne swept by whirlwinds of adoration, for the sake of being clasped to my heart, when I saw her risk even life itself for the simple love of one adoring heart, I then knew what love really was. It was, as Dante says,

Joy past compare, gladness unutterable,
Exhaustless riches and unmeasured bliss.

At last the decision was made. Lyone had decided that the ideal love of Egyplosis was only suited to disembodied spirits, and not for those breathing elements of matter that are unable to exist in the spiritual state.

The following was the text of her manifesto to the king, Borodemy and people:

The Avowal of Lyone, Supreme Goddess of Atvatabar, Holy Ruler of the palaces, Supernal and Infernal, of Egyplosis, Queen of Magicians, Mother of Sorcerers, Princess of Arjeels, etc., etc., to His Most Excellent Majesty King Aldemegry Bhoolmakar and the People of Atvatabar.

The supreme goddess presents her respectful salutations, and desires to inform his majesty the king and the people that her ardent soul, sensitive to the tender feelings of human affection, desires to live no longer without a counterpart soul. The love of ten thousand souls does not satisfy the craving for the love of but one soul. She has been told to love Harikar the unseen. She reaches out her lips, but they do not meet with love's delirious kisses. Her heart, withering within her because of soul loneliness, has taught her to seek liberty, to love the soul of her choice.

She resigns her seat on the throne of the gods, as goddess, having discovered her counterpart soul.

She hopes that reform and not destruction will guide the king and his ministers in dealing with Egyplosis at this crisis.

Given at her palace of Tanje in this, the eleventh year of her deification as supreme goddess.

Lyone

This memorial fell upon the people like a shell of *terrorite*. No one had ever suspected the crisis was so real. The king had lulled himself with the belief that, as my sailors had already departed to embark on the *Polar King*, I would possibly quietly follow them, and leave the country without his having the trouble of even asking me to go. The message of the goddess, however, opened his eyes to the true state of things, and I forthwith received the following decree from his majesty, at the hands of Jolar, admiral of the royal fleet:

Aldemegry Bhoolmakar, King of Atvatabar, to His Excellency Lex-
ington White, Commander of the ship Polar King, etc., etc., greeting:

It having come to our knowledge that you, the said Lexington White, have conceived an affection for the sacred
person of our illustrious supreme goddess, Lyone, spouse of
Harikar, holy ruler of Egyplosis, mother of sorcerers, etc.,
in defiance of our holy faith and laws of this our realm, and
furthermore it having come to our knowledge that the said
supreme goddess has so far forgotten her holy duty as to re-
ciprocate your affection, be it known to you that the penalty
prescribed by the laws of this our realm for your heinous
offence (which is sacrilegious treason) is death by *magnicity*,
for both guilty persons.

To inform you of the law and the penalty for your crime,
and to give you an opportunity of renouncing your affection
for our supreme goddess, and for your immediate departure
from the soil of Atvatabar, we send you this our decree, commanding you as follows: That you forthwith renounce your
treasonable affection, love and interest in the personality of
said supreme goddess. That you embark, together with your
officers and seamen, on board your ship, the *Polar King*, within one week from date hereof, and forever leave our realm
of Atvatabar and the surrounding seas thereof. You must not
again return to this our realm in any manner whatsoever, or
send messengers, or correspond or conspire with any inhabitant thereof, particularly with our said supreme goddess, under
penalty of death, both for yourself and for your entire crew.

Given at our palace in Calnogor, in this fifty-sixth year
of our reign.

Aldemegry Bhoolmakar
King of Atvatabar

I received the document from the hands of the admiral with
deep respect, and requested him to assure his majesty King Aldemegry Bhoolmakar of my profound regard and deep gratitude for
the hospitable reception we had received from his majesty and his
people during our stay in the glorious kingdom of Atvatabar.

I stated that we were at present in the act of leaving their country on a voyage of further discovery, but could not say that we

would not again return to Atvatabar. We should be most happy to obey the command of the king, but should we receive a message to return from the supreme goddess ere we left the interior world, we might possibly return, notwithstanding the royal command, and brave the wrath of his majesty.

"In that case," said the admiral, "it would be my duty to prevent you from landing on Atvatabar soil; and should you succeed in eluding the vigilance of the fleet, your apprehension and that of your people by his majesty's *wayleals* would mean the execution of your entire party. We are a proud nation, and our army and navy are invincible."

I thanked the admiral for his well-meant warning, whereupon he withdrew from the palace.

CHAPTER 39

The Crisis in Atvatabar

The manifesto of Lyone had precipitated an historic crisis in Atvatabar. The king awaited my leaving the country with the utmost impatience. He made every effort to prevent the news from reaching the public, hoping that when I took my departure the goddess would be amenable to the laws of the realm, and the faith be thus preserved.

The more that Lyone and myself discussed the situation, the more apparent it appeared that we could not now draw back from the position we had taken. It was absolutely necessary to provide a following in case the government attempted arrest, or the execution of either or both of us. Trusty messengers were despatched to the high priest, Hushnoly, the grand sorcerer, Charka, the lord of art, Yermoul, and the other friends of Lyone, informing them of the step she had taken, and asking their support in case any violence were offered her.

I advised Lyone to have her agents collect and transmit to Kioram all munitions of war. Some of the royal *wayleals* were armed with spears, and others with swords and shields. All battles were fought in the air, by reason of the *wayleals* being able to fly, as their movement on wings was more rapid than movement on foot.

As already stated, the ordinary spear of the king's *wayleals* was very effective, by reason of its discharging a magnetic current into the body, causing instant death. With a view of arming the army of the goddess with a more potent weapon than *magnic* spears, I quietly had agents purchase for immediate transmission to Kioram vast quantities of iron, and the material for making gunpowder, which happily existed in great abundance in Atvatabar. My idea was to start a manufactory for firearms, which were unknown to the interior world, and arm every man with a magazine rifle—a portable *mitrailleuse*, in fact.

209

While engaged in discussing the plan of defence with Lyone the crisis was precipitated by the press of the country finding out the *coup d'état* of the goddess. With a view of placing the government in the most favourable light before the people, the chief organ of the king, *The Calnogor Jossidi*, published a fierce editorial condemning the action of the goddess, and reviling what it was pleased to call "the contumacious invader and despoiler of Atvatabar." The article ran thus:

Impious Sacrilege!
Astounding Apostasy!
The Supreme Goddess Refuses Further Worship, and Has Degraded Herself by Seeking Marriage With an Alien Lover!
What is Faith, If Deceit Be Our Deity?

The sweet, the noble, the pure, the exalted worship of holy love, and of its hitherto most perfect symbol, the Goddess Lyone, is threatened with extinction, if it be not entirely destroyed. That sweet and perishable affection that fills the breasts of lovers, which has been for ages conserved, expanded, and wrought into an enduring fabric of religion in the sacred temple of Egyplosis, is about to utterly perish by a mad act of apostasy on the part of the deity herself. Whither now will tender and faithful hearts turn to find a refuge for all that makes the life glorious? Our ideal soul has sunk into degradation! She has flung herself from her proud and happy throne, wounding our faith with impious sacrilege!

Never before in the history of the world has the treachery of a goddess been manifest; we have had occasion hitherto only to mourn the apostasy of the worshipper. Now what avails our worship, if the object of our adoration fails us in the hour of need? Who is to console the bereavement of millions, when their consoler has hopelessly abandoned them? We say to both his majesty the king and government, follow the iconoclasts with the sword of justice; no punishment is too severe for such perfidious workers of iniquity! Death on the *magnic* scaffold is the penalty for the infatuation of the goddess and her atheistic lover! Wanting both men and money, the standard of revolt will be brought down by the first blow, and his majesty's troops can be relied upon to bring the rebels to swift justice. Let them be covered with eternal infamy who will support this fearful apostasy!

It became necessary for Lyone to publish the following manifesto to the nation, stating briefly the reasons that led to her renunciation of Harikar, to become the apostle of a new creed of one body and one soul:

Lyone, who has been until now Supreme Goddess of the faith of Harikar, to her faithful people, greeting:

I, who have been exalted to the high seat of honour on the throne of the gods, as the incarnation of the supreme soul, having received divine honours at your hands, desire at this crisis to make known to you the nature of the reform I seek to establish in the faith and worship of Atvatabar.

I do not seek to annihilate your faith, with all its tender and memorable qualities. I simply seek to reform such religion, making it more natural, more holy. All things that exist do change; if they do not rise to greater glory, they must sink to profounder shame. I, who have been your goddess during a long and blessed Nirvana, know how much you love me. I know that round my throne a tempest of passion has swept for years, filling me with its ecstasy. But I hasten to tell you that the delights of Egyplosis have been purchased at a fearful price. The sacrifices of its priests and priestesses have proved to me that even the retreat of ideal love can be as inexorably cruel as the outer world. So harassing have been these sacrifices that some could not bear their burden, and at this moment five hundred twin souls are confined in the dungeons of Egyplosis because they transgressed the vows of their novitiate. Of what avail are tender, chivalrous delights, if nature, if reason, be outraged in producing them?

Those who have remained steadfast to their vows, have grown sickly and morbid, feeding too long on fantastic ecstasies. Despondent and unreal in mind, delicate and nervous in body, they only appear rich and radiant in some brief ceremonial, while their every-day life is shuddering, tearful, and unstable, and utterly unfit to cope with the struggle of ordinary existence.

Therefore it is that one moment of pleasure is purchased by whole days of pain, and the oscillation between such extremes racks and ruins the dearest souls.

The motto of the new faith for Egyplosis, 'One Body and One Soul,' founded on the ordinary marriage rite, will restore to priest and priestess the steady and temperate possession of their souls which gives society that virile force necessary to its very existence.

By the memory of our mutual love, I claim the support of my faithful priests and priestesses, worshippers and people, in the coming struggle.

Lyone

The manifesto of the goddess, published in all the papers of the kingdom, created a profound sensation. It was the first discovery to millions that their religion had been weighed and found wanting. Although many were aware of its excesses, they saw that, despite every regulation, the hornet was in possession of Hesperides, prepared to sting the hand that reached for the golden fruit. They learned that passion led to agonized exaltation, and that the moral fibres of the soul became paralyzed by fierce temptation and inordinate spiritual delights. They saw that restraint of rapture and a more natural basis for the fellowship of the sexes were reforms imperatively needed, if the religion of Atvatabar were to remain an elevating and purifying force. Their creed must be reformed, both in faith and practice, and who so capable of introducing such a reform as Lyone herself?

The power of the deep-rooted conservatism of those who had nothing to gain by the change, the fear of the merchants that civil war meant their financial ruin, of a king jealous of his authority, and of the supremacy of existing laws, were the forces that would oppose the power of the goddess to carry out her reforms.

I began to accuse myself of being entirely responsible for all this disturbance in a peaceful country. Had I never discovered Atvatabar, Lyone might never have desired to disturb the existing order of things, but would have remained an agonized and crowned goddess, wedded only to Harikar, in a temple of eternal celibacy.

I knew, however, that all this was changed. I knew it by her sighs at our first meeting in the garden of Tanje, which, to remember, again and again made me thrill and shudder with joy.

CHAPTER 40

My Departure From the Palace of Tanje

The week of grace allowed me to leave Atvatabar had already expired ere it had seriously occurred to me to actually leave the palace. The commotion in the nation consequent on the publication of the manifesto of king and goddess was so great, and the necessity of advising Lyone in the crisis so urgent, that I did not take leave of her until the time for my departure was exhausted. One thing that made me somewhat careless of arousing the royal danger was that the *Polar King* with her *terrorite* guns could command Kioram in spite of the royal fleet, although it numbered one hundred vessels. Fortunately the royal fleet had not yet learned the use of gunpowder, their guns being discharged with compressed air.

A despatch from Captain Wallace stated that the ship was lying in the outer harbour, well equipped either for a long voyage or probable hostilities.

With the view of allaying the excitement of the people, the king published a statement that the alien commander and his retinue had been ordered to leave forthwith. As for Lyone, the crisis had in no wise terrified her; she felt assured, however, that "the beginning of the end had come."

"Are you not afraid of lifelong imprisonment or death in case your cause has no supporters?" I asked.

"They can do me no harm," she replied, "for the entire priesthood of Egyplosis, the Art Palace of Gnaphisthasia, and thousands of sympathizers among the people themselves, will rally to my flag when the hour of danger comes."

"You can depend on my operations at sea," said I, "in your behalf. Although I have but a single vessel, I will fight the entire fleet of Atvatabar. One shell of *terrorite* has more power than a thousand of their guns. I will destroy Kioram, if need be, to bring the king to submission."

Before leaving Lyone, I drew up a plan of campaign for the coming struggle. Hushnoly, the high priest, although conservative as regards the affairs of the priesthood, was really a trusty friend of the goddess, and would assist the grand sorcerer in commanding a wing of the sacred army.

The liberated priests and priestesses would fight like lions for the cause for which they had been imprisoned. The palace of Gnaphisthasia would also furnish its battalions, led by Yermoul, lord of art. Then, among the fifty millions of people there were perhaps twenty millions in favour of reform, who would contribute a large army in support of Lyone.

"It is by no means certain that a civil war will take place, even to secure the proposed reform," said Lyone. "The people may leave it to the Borodemy and the law to settle the matter."

"And what would be the result in such a case?" I inquired.

"Well, if I persisted in my demands, and no insurrection took place," said Lyone, "the king might put me to death as the simplest way of ending the matter, and appoint another goddess in Egyplosis."

"They will never hurt a hair of your head while I live: I swear it!" said I, with considerable emphasis.

Lyone smiled at my enthusiasm, and refused to permit me to linger longer with her. We understood each other perfectly. I saw that when Lyone had once made up her mind on a certain course, there could be no retreat. She cared not any longer for a dead throne, for even the worship of the multitude could not feed her famished heart. She must have a beloved soul, consecrated to herself alone, between whom would vibrate the music of great thoughts and tender emotions.

Lyone had declared war upon hopeless love. This was a necessary consequence of her altered position. Egyplosis, founded on a brilliant theory, had in practice become a prison, and she must open the doors to let its prisoners free.

Just as I was leaving the palace I received a message from Hushnoly stating that the king had secretly ordered my arrest, and to be circumspect if I wished to reach Kioram free.

Attended by a guard of *bockhockids* faithful to Lyone I set out for Kioram, taking a circuitous road to avoid Calnogor. I had been informed by Hushnoly that mobs of excited and bloodthirsty *wayleals* were flying about the metropolis, shouting "Death to the foreigners!" Mounted on a magnificent, majestic steed of great power, I led my little band at a furious pace. The *bockhockids* with each stride of the leg covered a distance of sixty feet, and could travel easily seventy miles an hour without appearing to run very quickly.

About an hour's travelling brought us abreast of Calnogor, and soon afterward I heard shots fired and the noise of a conflict. Making an aerial detour, I discovered a combat between a dozen *wayleals* on the one side and a crowd of *wayleals* on the other. I noticed that as fast as the individuals of the larger body were fired at by a weapon in the hands of the smaller company they at once became lifeless, either falling to the ground or hanging limp in the air supported by their still vibrating wings. Being intensely curious to see the *wayleals* using revolvers, I ventured with my men nearer the mêlée, and coming near the flying warriors, I discovered to my surprise and horror that the smaller band of flying men was a company of my own sailors, led by Flathootly, fighting back to back a swarming mass of *wayleals*.

The brave fellows fought like lions. No sooner did a *wayleal* approach a sailor with his deadly spear than he was shot. My men, fighting such fearful odds, for the enemy numbered several hundreds, could not long maintain so unequal a combat, notwithstanding the superiority of their weapons. It was only a question of time when their ammunition would be exhausted, and their spears would then be their only weapon, and I had evidently arrived in time to relieve them. Flathootly was shouting to the enemy, "Shtand back, or Oi'll shoot yez!" when I approached. The sailors cheered to see me flying to their relief, and at that moment the enemy, recognizing in me the very man they wanted, swarmed around to prevent my escape. My *bockhockids* drew their spears, and the sailors used their revolvers freely, and forming a flying ring, effectually protected me from the onslaught of the king's *wayleals*. I rallied my entire company, who received the rush of the *wayleals* with a discharge of revolvers and *magnic* spears, by means of which we killed several. Again and again the enemy fell upon us with renewed fury, shouting their war-cry of *"Bhoolmakar!"* They evidently meant to harass us until re-enforced by a detachment of the royal troops strong enough to capture us.

A *wayleal*, in an unguarded moment, struck me on the shoulder, fortunately with only one point of his spear, drawing blood. Flathootly, who saw the blow, emptied his revolver in his breast, and he fell to earth a dead man. I was surprised that the enemy had not already annihilated my men, for, notwithstanding their fear of the sailors' revolvers, three of the sailors had been killed. It was terrible news to think of my brave fellows being slaughtered, but I was determined to have revenge. I singled out Gossody, the leader of the *wayleals*, and rushing forward on my *bockhockid*, aimed at his head with my revolver, and instantly killed him. The death of their leader paralyzed the *wayleals* for a time. Before they could recover from their surprise, we killed a number of them. The enemy, once more rallying, made a fresh attack. They hoped to either kill or capture us by sheer force of superior numbers. We killed dozens of them, but at a fearful cost. Six of the *bockhockids* and three more of our own sailors bit the dust. It was quite evident that it would be only a question of time before we would be completely annihilated. I saw that it was necessary for us to reach Kioram without further fighting. We could not afford to risk the life of another man, even to gain a complete victory. I therefore ordered a flying retreat. The *bockhockids* were arranged in a circle, in the midst of which flew our sailors. We struck out for Kioram with the speed of the wind, pursued by an ever-increasing horde of *wayleals* thirsting for our blood. Such was our speed of motion that the thrusts of the enemy were ineffectual. It was a magnificent sight to see the giant machines, like flying cranes, devouring distance with their wings, each ridden by a winged warrior. Wearied and exhausted with our fight, and still longer period of flight, it was a welcome sight to see beneath us the city of Kioram, and the *Polar King* riding at anchor in the outer harbour, beyond which lay the royal navy of Atvatabar.

When within sight of the city the enemy unexpectedly gave up the chase, and did not follow us further. We soon gained the ship, and in a short time our *bockhockids* decorated the masts and rigging. The story of my imprisonment and the massacre of the six sailors of the force sent to escort me to Kioram was soon told, and a more determined crew never trod the deck of ship of war. We would teach Bhoolmakar a lesson he would never forget!

CHAPTER 41

We Are Attacked By the Enemy

Captain Wallace and the entire ship's company were overjoyed at my escape from the clutches of the enemy. The loss of six of our brave sailors was a terrible calamity in any case, but still more so in view of the impending attack by the enemy's navy.

We had a good stock of gunpowder on board, and the ship's mechanics under Professor Rackiron began the construction of a series of machine guns, each weapon having one hundred rifled barrels arranged in circles around the central tube. Twenty-five of these guns were constructed. To each tube was fitted a magazine, with automatic attachment, so that one man could handle each weapon, that would throw five hundred balls with each charge of the magazine.

The *fletyemings* of the royal navy possessed the advantage of numbers and ships, so that it was necessary for us to have the advantage in point of arms. Our monster *terrorite* gun and the *terrorite* battery gave us also an immense advantage over the gunpowder batteries of the enemy. Thus equipped, we were more than a match for any ten ships of the enemy. But when we saw one hundred vessels, the smallest of which was as large as our own, and many twice our size, bearing down upon us in battle array, we felt our chances of escape, not to mention victory, were hardly worth calculating.

It was a splendid scene for a naval battle. The harbour of Kioram was a bay fully fifty miles in diameter, and here lay the royal fleet, whose hulls of gleaming gold shone on the blue water, while beyond rose the brilliant whiteness of the sculptured city.

Captain Wallace had the ship ready for action. Every soul knew it was a life-and-death struggle. The sailors knew that success meant wealth beyond the dreams of avarice. For myself, the prize was something more worthy of our desperate courage—it was the priceless Lyone, possessed of a divine personality. Her life, like my own, hung in the balance. Should I win the battle, we would win each other. Should I fail to conquer, there was but one kind of defeat, and that was death.

Every man stood at his post in silence. Flathootly had command of a company of sailors. Professor Rackiron superintended our chief arm of defence, the *terrorite* guns—weapons, like our revolvers, fortunately unknown in Atvatabar. We had a large quantity of explosive *terrorite* on board, in the shape of shells for our guns. The shells contained each the equivalent of 100 pounds of *terrorite*—that is to say, they would each weigh 100 pounds on the outer earth, while the shells of the giant gun weighed 250 pounds each. The iron hurricane-deck, that did us such service in the polar climate, was put up overhead, as a protection from the onslaught of a boarding crew.

The ships of the enemy advanced proudly in a double line of battle. On the peak of each floated the ensign of Atvatabar, a red sun surrounded by a wide circle of green, on a blue field.

On the *Polar King* floated the flag of the goddess, a figure of the throne of the gods in gold, on a purple ground.

When but a mile off, we could see the guns on every ship pointed and ready for the attack. The enemy suddenly broke into the form of a semi-circle. It was the design of Admiral Jolar to surround us and capture or destroy the *Polar King* by sheer force of numbers. We allowed the formation to proceed, until the entire navy of Atvatabar surrounded us in an enormous circle.

Having executed this manoeuvre, a boat put away from the admiral's ship and approached us. In a short time it reached our vessel, and the captain of the admiral's ship, with several officers, came on board.

The captain demanded my unconditional surrender, "in the name of his majesty King Aldemegry Bhoolmakar of Atvatabar." I had been declared "an enemy of the country, a violator of its most sacred laws, a heretic in active destruction of its holy faith, and a fugitive from justice." The captain, as the emissary of the admiral, demanded the immediate surrender of myself and entire company.

I asked my men if they were prepared to surrender themselves to the enemy. Their fearful shout of "Never!" disturbed the silence of the sea, and must have been heard by the distant enemy.

"You hear the reply of my men," I said to the captain. "Tell your admiral that the commander of the *Polar King* declines to surrender."

"Then," said the captain, "we will open fire upon you at once. We mean to have you dead or alive."

"Give the admiral my compliments," said I, "and tell him to open the fight as soon as he likes."

The captain and his staff rapidly disappeared, and we knew that the fight was certain. The officers had no sooner reached the admiral's ship than a report was heard; and a ball of metal crashed upon the hurricane-deck overhead, tearing a large hole in it, and then plunged into the sea. This was the signal of war. Before we could reply, the *Polar King* was the target of a general bombardment from all points of the compass. The balls that struck us were of different kinds of metal—lead, zinc, iron, and even gold. Although the range of their guns was accurate, yet, owing to the loss of gravity, the shots had but little effect on the plating of the vessel. Some of the sailors were severely wounded by being struck in the limbs with the large missiles hurled upon us, and I saw that if the enemy couldn't sink the *Polar King* they could at least kill us, which was even worse.

I gave orders to Professor Rackiron to train the giant gun on the admiral's vessel. The discharge was accompanied by a slight flash, without smoke, and we saw the deadly messenger make its aerial flight straight toward the admiral's vessel. It entered the water right in front of the ship, and in another instant an extraordinary scene was witnessed. The ship, in company with a vast volume of water, sprang into the air to a great height, with an immense hole blown in the bottom of the hull. Falling again, she sank with all of the crew who did not manage to fly clear of her rigging. After the vessel disappeared, the last of the waterspout fell upon the boiling sea.

It was a great surprise to the enemy to see their best ship destroyed at a single blow. The effect of our shot completely paralyzed the foe for the moment, for every vessel ceased firing at us. At first it was thought that the admiral had gone down with his vessel, and until a new admiral was in command the battle would be suspended.

THE SHIP IN COMPANY WITH A VAST VOLUME OF WATER
SPRANG INTO THE AIR TO A GREAT HEIGHT.

During the confusion we ran the *Polar King* through the breach made in the circle of the enemy, keeping his ships on one side of us. I determined to try the tactics of rapid movement, with the steady discharge of the *terrorite* gun, hoping to destroy a ship at every blow.

It soon appeared that Admiral Jolar was still alive, he having escaped from his ship in mid air, with his staff and a number of *fletyemings*, by means of their electric wings. He had alighted on the ship of the rear admiral, where he hoisted the pennant of the admiral.

The enemy was now thoroughly alive to the necessity of destroying or capturing us. I saw it was a mistake in allowing ourselves to be surrounded in a bay only fifty miles wide. To fight so many ships required ample sea-room, to avoid the possibility of being captured.

The admiral sent ten ships to guard the mouth of the bay. It was a satisfaction to know that the torpedo was also unknown in Atvatabar, else our career would have been cut short. The *Polar King*, running twenty-five miles an hour, was followed by the enemy's fleet, which, although slower in movement, had the advantage in numbers and could possibly drive us upon the shore. After sailing as far east as we cared to go, the *Polar King* lay to, awaiting a renewal of the battle.

CHAPTER 42

The Battle Continued

The royal fleet formed a wide semi-circle a mile off, and reopened its guns upon us. An unlucky shot struck one of our seamen and cut off his head. A perfect storm of shot rained upon us, so destroying our hurricane-deck that it was no longer of any protection to us. The enemy, encouraged by their success, closed in upon us. What we feared most of all was an attack by the wing-jackets, against whom neither our heavy guns nor superior speed would much avail.

Professor Rackiron aimed the giant gun right in the centre of the enemy's line of battle. The shell struck the middle ship and exploded. All three vessels were scattered half a mile apart, and made complete wrecks. The *Polar King* darted forward to pass through the breach made in the enemy's line. We found this a matter of difficulty, for the enemy, seeing our move, closed the gap in front of us. The ships ahead would have barred the way, but to prevent their doing so, we threw a shell of *terrorite* over the bow of the ship into the water. The sea rose on either side fully half a mile into the air, in solid pillars of water. In the confusion, we burst through the ranks of the enemy and were once more in open water.

The admiral must have been exasperated at our escape. He followed us as before, in close rank, firing as he came. We now saw that he was about to change his mode of attack, for, hovering in the air, a rapidly-growing swarm of *fletyemings* were preparing to give us a hand-to-hand combat. Each vessel furnished a certain contingent to the attacking force, until the aerial battalion numbered about five thousand men. Our position seemed hopeless. What could less than eighty men do against a host of ten thousand? At close quarters our *terrorite* guns would be useless.

223

With loud yells the *fletyemings* swept down upon us. Fearing our guns, they kept open rank and spread around the ship. Aiming at the densest part of the enemy, we destroyed about five hundred of them, but, quickly rallying again, they were upon us.

We were ready for them. Our battery of twelve *terrorite* guns, including the magazine guns and musketry, rang out a terrible discharge. Under the withering fire and fearful explosions our foes fell back, and the sea around was strewn with dead and wounded bodies. Luckily for us, the only weapons possessed by the enemy were their *magnic* spears. The wing-jackets, rallying again, swarmed upon the rigging and covered the ship like a cloud of vultures. Ere we could again discharge our guns, several of our men were beaten down by sheer force of numbers. They made splendid use of their deadly spears. The ship's crew, re-attacked between the discharges of the guns, were many of them stunned and killed—the enemy after each discharge renewing the attack, being constantly re-enforced from the fleet. It was possible that we would be conquered by the fearful odds against us.

Our ability to keep up a fire from our guns grew more and more difficult, owing to the incessant attacks of the enemy and the vast accumulation of their dead bodies on deck. The spears of our foes were more formidable weapons than we had supposed, for their touch was death. It was evident, notwithstanding the carnage, that our men would be obliged to surrender, owing to sheer exhaustion. As soon as a wing-jacket dropped from the ranks of the enemy another took his place; our guns covered the sea with their dead bodies. The admiral was determined to conquer us at any cost, for he rightly surmised our victory would be a terrible blow to Atvatabar.

To remove ourselves as far from the fleet as possible, I directed the ship at full speed ahead for the outer water. The ten ships that lay across the entrance to the harbour would have to be destroyed, notwithstanding the ceaseless attack of the *fletyemings*, who followed our every movement. We acted solely on the defensive, and managed, while repelling the most furious onslaughts, to throw overboard the dead bodies of the enemy.

In the midst of constant fighting we managed to get the *terrorite* guns into position again, and when within a mile of the blockade fired the entire battery into it. Our shells sank every vessel they struck and broke several others from their moorings. Several more shots destroyed the remaining vessels, but only leaving their crews like a swarm of hornets free to attack us, This, however, was a minor matter compared with possessing the freedom of the outer sea. We rushed over the spot where the ships had been anchored, and soon left the pursuing fleet far behind.

The wing-jackets, re-enforced by the crews of the blockading fleet, renewed their attack. Having learned the terrible power of our magazine guns, they contented themselves with making attacks on unguarded points. But fifty sailors were thus engaged, while the remainder of the ship's crew, including the officers, worked the guns with a will, The revolvers of the enemy disabled us considerably, but by firing our magazine guns in every direction we kept the ranks of the flying enemy pretty well thinned out.

Our tactics were to keep the foe divided, if possible, and destroy the attacking force in detail. So long as the sailors could stand by their guns we were safe. We could outstrip the fleet in speed, thus reducing the chances of our immediate antagonists being re-enforced, for those who at first attacked us melted rapidly before the withering fire of our batteries.

Finding themselves unable to secure the ship, even with such enormous sacrifice of life, the *fletyemings* suddenly retreated to the fleet, leaving us free to rest ourselves and look after the wounded.

The terrible strain of the fight had utterly exhausted the sailors, who had fought for fifty consecutive hours, without rest or refreshment. We tumbled overboard the dead bodies of the enemy who had fallen upon the deck, and buried eight of our own sailors who had been also killed. Several men were wounded about the head and neck with spear-thrusts that had failed to kill, but none seriously. Captain Wallace got an ugly wound in his neck, but it was not sufficient to keep him from duty. Flathootly, in slaying a *fletyeming*, received a wound in the hand that required the attention of the doctor. Professor Rackiron and Astronomer Starbottle passed through the fight unscathed, while Professor Goldrock suffered from a broken leg. Our helmets, provided originally for triumphal purposes, had proved of the greatest possible value, and saved many a life on board the *Polar King*.

All this time we lay in full view of both the enemy's fleet and the entire kingdom. It seemed to us a strange thing that the admiral did not continue the fight with his reserve of *fletyemings*, who could easily outstrip the ship in their flight. He still possessed thousands of wing-jackets who had never been engaged in actual conflict, who might have relieved their exhausted comrades and in time have forced us to surrender.

Was the supine conduct of the admiral caused by a panic at our power of havoc or, did he think my retreat to sea really an effort to escape the country?

If his truce was caused by a belief that he was unable to cope with us he might have called the *wayleals* of the king to his assistance, but possibly the pride of the service prevented an alliance with the army for naval conquest, more particularly where the naval forces outnumbered the enemy two hundred to one.

The scene of battle lay in full view of the entire nation, just as the kingdom lay in full view of ourselves. The nearer inhabitants could see the movements of the ships and the sailors, and the progress of the battle, so far, was known to every one. If the impression was favourable to the *Polar King*, doubtless there would be a demonstration in favour of the goddess; if not, it would be because the capture of our ship was considered certain.

We lay to, at a distance of ten miles from the enemy's fleet, awaiting the renewal of hostilities.

CHAPTER 43

Victory

The enemy, finding we were not disposed to leave Atvatabar, began to move down upon us once more in battle array. The royal fleet consisted of seventy ships, the former thirty having been either sunk or disabled by us. As for ourselves, the hurricane-deck, masts and rigging had been hammered to pieces, but the hull was sound, the sailors enthusiastic, and the *terrorite* guns unharmed and our spears invincible.

As the enemy approached us their ships began to move wider apart, with a view no doubt of circumnavigating us, and then close in upon the *Polar King* as before. Another squeeze of this kind might prove fatal, consequently our plan was to keep the enemy at a safe distance and on one side of us, and destroy his ships one by one with our guns while out of range of his fire, if possible.

The admiral did us the favour of keeping around his ship half a dozen vessels by way of protection, and in this manner drew near. We were determined to bring the engagement to a close as soon as possible by striking the enemy a terrible blow. As soon as their vessels drew within range we struck the central group with a shell from the giant gun. The explosion worked a tremendous havoc among the congregated vessels, but without waiting to learn its full effect I ordered twenty shells to be fired into the central mass in quick succession.

The result was appalling. The great want of gravity caused a vast irregular mountain of ships and water to be piled high in the air. We could hear the shrieks of drowning and dismembered *fletyemings*. Volumes of water shot to tremendous heights, became detached from the main mass, and floated in the air for a time in liquid globes.

It was some time before the whirl of wrecked ships and angry water, filled with perhaps thousands of wing-jackets, subsided to the level of the ocean again. The ships sank beneath the water, on which floated hundreds of dead bodies. Those *fletyemings* who had escaped accident or death, headed by Admiral Jolar, who was still alive, formed themselves into a compact mass as they hovered over the scene of the disaster for a final hand-to-hand attack. Re-enforced by thousands of *fletyemings* from the then unharmed vessels, they approached with yells of *"Bhoolmakar!"* Finding their ships useless, they were determined to fling themselves in heroic sacrifice upon us in such numbers as to crush us.

This was precisely their most dangerous form of attack, but we could only await their coming. As the living mass of men approached we saluted them with another discharge of shells, which exploded in the very heart of the unfortunate host. The carnage was dreadful, and hundreds of dead bodies fell into the sea. Admiral Jolar was killed, and without their leader the *fletyemings* became demoralized. Ere they could rally again, we were about to fire another round of shells, when Rear Admiral Gerolio, with a few *fletyemings*, left the main mass under a flag of truce and approached us.

We were nothing loath to receive their message. Alighting on deck, the rear admiral informed me that owing to the loss of their admiral they were disposed to cease fighting provided I would leave the country forthwith.

"Then," said I, "you wish to report that you defeated us by driving us from the country?"

"I shall report that it was a mutual cessation of hostilities," said he.

"It has cost us too much to give up the fight now," I said. "One of us must surrender."

"Do you surrender, then, to His Majesty Aldemegry Bhoolmakar, King of Atvatabar?" eagerly inquired the rear admiral.

"Do you surrender to Her Majesty Lyone, Queen of Atvatabar?" I replied.

"We make no such surrender," said he, very much surprised to know that Lyone had been proclaimed queen. "If we cannot conquer you by force of arms we have ships enough to starve you into submission."

"We care nothing for your ships," I replied, "we will destroy them one by one."

"You may sink our ships," said the rear admiral, "but you will never conquer our *fletyemings*. We will begin a hand-to-hand conflict that will not cease until you and your entire crew are killed or are our prisoners."

"The truce is at an end," I replied. "Return to your ships immediately."

The rear-admiral and his staff rose on their wings, and in a short time regained the cloud of naval warriors that hung in the air half a mile away.

During the truce the ships of the enemy had drawn nearer and at once opened fire upon us.

A well-aimed shot struck us under the water-line, penetrating our armour, and going clean through the side of the vessel. The central compartment rapidly filled with water. It was a fatal blow, for although the fore and aft compartments would keep the ship from sinking, yet it soon put out our boiler fires and left us a helpless hulk upon the water.

The main deck, containing our *terrorite* guns, was on a level with the water, and a quantity of *terrorite* and gunpowder rendered useless. We were in a terrible position, for our small stock of available ammunition would be soon exhausted. The enemy soon discovered the effect of their blow, and closed around us like vultures hastening to their prey. We suffered a terrible bombardment, that killed more of our men, and finally the *fletyemings* closed around us in swarms to annihilate us.

Resolved to sell our lives dearly, we received them with a discharge of our magazine guns. They quickly rallied and renewed their attack, but as long as our ammunition lasted were afraid to come to close quarters. At last we drew our revolvers and the hand-to-hand conflict began. Some of the sailors used their cutlasses with good effect. We had proof that the magnetic spears in close quarters were terrible weapons. As I saw my men falling around me I felt that the game was up. I thought of Lyone, and the thought would not let me surrender. I was already wounded in the shoulder and body, and stunned, while the enemy was swarming in greater numbers than ever. Must we surrender?

Suddenly, at that moment, a shell came screaming through the air and exploded above the ship, right among the *wayleals*, killing twenty or more.

Merciful heavens! Can the enemy, after all, fire shells at us? But why use them when the fight is practically over, and why fire them among his own *wayleals*? Another and another shell exploded among the *wayleals* around us, and finally a regular tornado of them exploded all around the *Polar King*, putting the enemy completely to flight.

As soon as the air was cleared around us, I saw to my intense astonishment two friendly vessels, one of which bore the flag of the United States and the other the flag of England, firing shells at the enemy. I then knew the cause of our deliverance, and shouted for joy. My men—all that were alive—rose and cheered our comrades from the outer world! The excitement was overpowering! We could only, amid tears of joy, salute them and signal them to keep up the fight. We were saved!

A well-aimed shot from the Englishman sank still another vessel. This fresh disaster received from the strangers seemed to completely unnerve the enemy, for, strange to say, every ship afloat struck its colours in surrender! It was well that the rear-admiral did so, for it would have been only a question of time until his whole fleet would have been destroyed.

The *fletyemings* retreated to their ships, and in a short time the gold-plated ship of Rear-Admiral Gerolio, under the flag of truce, came alongside our vessel. The rear-admiral and his staff came on board, and delivered up his sword in token of surrender.

"You surrender to me as admiral of Her Majesty Lyone, Queen of Atvatabar?" I said.

"I do," said the rear-admiral, "and am willing to devote my services to the cause of her majesty."

"Will your *fletyemings* as well as yourself swear allegiance to Queen Lyone and her cause?"

"We swear it!" yelled the *fletyemings* of the rear-admiral's ship, and, at a signal from their leader, the flag of the new queen took the place of the flag of his deposed majesty, King Aldemegry Bhoolmakar.

In a moment the entire fleet exhibited the flag of her holiness as the symbol of their new allegiance. This was a gratifying victory, as it procured for our cause more than sixty fully manned vessels of war and twenty-five thousand *fletyemings*.

Lyone was mistress of the seas!

"How came you to surrender at this juncture?" I inquired of the rear-admiral.

"Well, sir," he replied, "we have already lost more men and ships than if we had been engaged with an enemy similarly armed and having as many vessels as ourselves, and when the strange vessels came to your assistance we saw it was useless to prolong the fight. We saw that with your terrible weapons you were invincible. You can destroy us and we cannot destroy you, therefore I concluded, as rear-admiral of the fleet and successor to Admiral Jolar, who was killed in battle, that it was throwing life away to continue the fight. I saw, furthermore, that with you as the champion of the goddess her cause would succeed, and I wanted to be the first to render homage to her majesty."

"You have acted well," I replied, "and to reward your action, I now, in the name of her majesty, appoint and proclaim you rear-admiral of the fleet of Lyone, Queen of Atvatabar."

This announcement was received with frantic cheers by the sailors of both vessels.

Now that I was master of the sea, I intended to immediately extend my operations to the cause of the queen on land, and assuming the dignity of admiral, appointed Captain Wallace of the *Polar King* also rear-admiral of the fleet.

This announcement was received with the firing of guns and tremendous cheers.

"Rear-Admiral Wallace, Rear-Admiral Gerolio, and myself," I said to the sailors, "will determine the question of who will become the remaining high naval officers, and now that the battle is over, let us see that our wounded are properly cared for and all ships afloat put in proper repair."

It was a glorious victory!

All this time the two cruisers who so fortunately arrived in time to turn the tide of battle in our favour were rapidly approaching us, firing guns in honour of our victory. I acknowledged their arrival, as well as their valuable services, by having the royal fleet drawn up in double file, between which lay the *Polar King*, and ordering every vessel to give the strangers a salute of one hundred guns.

My anxiety to learn more of our allies was so great that I despatched two of my most active wing-jackets to the strange vessels to procure accurate information concerning them and their object in visiting the interior world. The *wayleals* returned with the information that the vessels were the United States ship of discovery *Mercury*, commanded by Captain Adams, and the English ship of discovery *Aurora Borealis*, commanded by Sir John Forbes. Both were fitted out by their respective governments to explore the interior world consequent on the report of Boatswain Dunbar and Seaman Henderson, the only survivors of the twelve men who left the *Polar King* when in the Polar Gulf. The respective commanders, officers and men of the incoming vessels were delighted to know that the *Polar King* was not only safe, but had discovered Atvatabar, and that its commander was at present king of the realm. This was the substance of the despatches sent me by Captain Adams and Commander Forbes, and addressed, "To Lexington White, Esq., Commander of the *Polar King*." Captain Adams stated that Boatswain Dunbar was on board his vessel as pilot, accompanied by Seaman Henderson.

Owing to the waterlogged condition of the *Polar King*, we could only wait the arrival of the vessels. When near at hand, a simultaneous salute of guns reverberated upon the sea, which must have been heard in all Atvatabar. Amid the smoke and noise of the roaring guns, steam launches had put off from the *Mercury* and *Aurora Borealis*, and in a very short time the commanders of both vessels stood upon the deck of the *Polar King*, accompanied by their respective officers. I embraced Captain Adams and Commander Forbes, and introduced the strangers to Rear-Admiral Wallace, Rear-Admiral Gerolio and staff, who were no less delighted and surprised than myself to receive visitors from the outer world. When the commanders reached the deck of the *Polar King* the cheers of the American and British sailors, mingled with the shouts of our *fletyemings*, made a soul-stirring scene.

In fact, I was already beginning to think the outer world a more or less mythical place, and thought the doctrine of reincarnation had an illustration or proof in myself. After all, the outer world really existed, and, strange as it seemed to the Atvatabarese, there was really an outer sun and live beings like themselves, only physically more vigorous.

It was necessary to set out at once for Kioram, as the *Polar King* was in a sinking condition.

Every man had been either killed or wounded. We made a total loss of sixty men, including the ten who left the ship in the Polar Gulf, thus making the entire company of the *Polar King* but fifty souls.

As for the ship, her plating was burst apart in many places and full of started bolts, caused by missiles of the enemy. The central compartment was filled with water, and the masts, sails, smoke-stack and hurricane-deck were practically destroyed.

Many of the guns were not struck once in the entire fight, and were ready for active service any moment. The *terrorite* battery was partially submerged, but still in good condition.

Captain Adams and Sir John Forbes both craved the honour of towing the *Polar King* into port, to which I willingly assented.

As admiral, I at once assumed command of the fleet, which I ordered to make sail for Kioram without delay. The fleet fell behind in good order, and followed the *Polar King*, bearing the victorious flag of the queen.

CHAPTER 44

The News of Atvatabar in the Outer World

The kingdom of Atvatabar lay before us like a continent drawn upon a map, or, rather, upon the interior surface of a sphere or globe, everywhere visible to the naked eye. Its green forests, its impressive mountains, its rushing rivers, its white and many-coloured cities, its wide-stretching shores, fringed with the foam of an azure sea, lay before the astonished eyes of our visitors.

When within a few miles of the city, Governor Lapalme, accompanied by Captains Pra and Nototherboc, advanced to meet us in a large magnetic yacht, bearing the flag of Lyone. The governor hastened to inform us that, in view of our victory, the city of Kioram had declared its allegiance to the cause of Lyone, and invited myself and officers of the fleet, as well as our distinguished allies from the outer world, to a banquet in the fortress of Kioram. This news gave me great satisfaction, as the city would be a splendid base of military operations. The officers and seamen of the *Mercury* and *Aurora Borealis* created quite as great a sensation in the streets of Kioram as did the victorious sailors of the *Polar King*.

Landing on *terra firma*, Governor Lapalme took the opportunity of showing our guests the beauty of his *bockhockids*, who formed a guard of honour to the fortress, where we were all royally received.

The two captains, together with their officers and sailors, were astonished at the multitude of strange objects shown them. Captain Adams would not remain satisfied until he was accoutred with a dynamo and a pair of *magnic* wings, with which all the sailors and soldiers of Atvatabar were supplied as part of their uniform. He was shown how the battery of metals gave motion to the dynamo, which in turn acted on the steel levers connected with the ribs of the wings. Although the worthy captain was of considerable weight, yet his astonishment at being able to skim through the air like a swallow was great. No sooner did he touch the button than all his preconceived notions of locomotion were destroyed, and he gasped with fear at his own prodigious motion. The two facts of unfailing movement of wings and exceptional buoyancy of body soon made him a fearless rider of the wind. He alighted on the earth with the greatest enthusiasm over the success of his experiment.

The *magnic* spear was another surprise for our guests. Sir John Forbes was astonished at my being able to fight the *fletyemings* so long, armed as they were by so potent a weapon of death. He would certainly recommend its use in the British army and navy on his return to England. Our allies were surprised at everything they saw, particularly at the rapid movements of the *fletyemings* or wing-jackets of the royal navy. They thought it an extraordinary thing the sailors should fly by *magnic* wings.

After the banquet Captain Adams, who was a fine type of an American seaman, bold, alert and courageous, gave us an account of how both the United States and England came to send ships into the interior world. It appeared that the story of Boatswain Dunbar first published in the New York papers, that the *Polar King* had sailed down the Polar Gulf *en route* to an interior world, had created a tremendous sensation on the outer sphere, and all civilized nations immediately fitted out vessels of discovery to follow up the *Polar King* and make discoveries for the benefit of their respective governments. So far as any one knew, only two vessels had succeeded in entering the interior sphere.

The recital of Captain Adams was frequently interrupted by Sir John Forbes, the British captain, a courageous officer, who possessed all the stately dignity of his race. He stated that since the discovery of America by Columbus no other event had awakened such unbounded enthusiasm as the discovery of a polar gulf and an interior world.

"I am most of all interested at present," said I, "in the story of how Dunbar reached civilization again after parting with us. I forgive you, Dunbar," I continued, addressing him, "for your mutinous conduct, and now let us hear the story of your adventures in the Polar Sea."

"Admiral," said Dunbar, "had we known the terrible hardships we would have to endure in making our way home, chiefly on foot and at the same time burdened with the boat, we would never have left the ship. But you must thank me for the presence of the two ships that are here today and for the fame you already enjoy in the outer world."

"It's something tremendous," said Captain Adams.

"How did your geographers receive the news of the interior world?" I inquired of Sir John Forbes.

"I need not say that the English geographers, in common with the entire nation, were greatly excited at the news. The Royal Geographical Society have already made you an honourary member, and it was actually proposed at one of the meetings that the government should proclaim a special holiday as a day of rejoicing for so great a discovery. This would certainly have been done but for the fact that the story rested entirely on the testimony of two sailors, and that any public rejoicing should be postponed until the story of the sailors would be verified by a special expedition sent from England. Of course, many people think that Dunbar's story is a fable or a hallucination that he himself believes in. On the other hand, hundreds of professional and amateur astronomers and geographers are proving by mathematics that the earth must be a hollow sphere, and the story of the open poles an entirely physical possibility."

"The people of the United States," said Captain Adams, "are almost unanimous in the belief that the interior world is a veritable reality, and it only requires a return of my ship to convince every one that Dunbar's story falls very short of the glorious reality."

"There is no man more famous today than Lexington White, Admiral of Atvatabar!" said Sir John Forbes.

"I thank you, gentlemen, for your kind words," said I; "and now for Dunbar's story."

"I think, admiral," said Captain Adams, "that if I were to read you the article containing Dunbar's story written by a special commissioner of the New York *Western Hemisphere*, who was the first to interview Dunbar at Sitka, on learning of his arrival there, it would be perhaps the best narration of his perilous adventures." As the captain spoke he drew a copy of the *Western Hemisphere* from his pocket.

"By all means," I replied, "let us hear what the press said about Dunbar and his adventures."

Thereupon Captain Adams read the New York *Western Hemisphere's* account of Dunbar's adventures, as follows:

An Astounding Discovery!
The North Pole Found to be an Enormous Cavern, Leading to a Subterranean World!
The Earth Proves to be a Hollow Shell One Thousand Miles in Thickness, Lit By an Interior Sun!
Oceans and Continents, Islands and Cities Spread Upon the Roof of the Interior Sphere!
Boatswain Dunbar and Seaman Henderson, of the Polar King, Having Deserted the Ship as She Was Entering Plutusia, Have Arrived at Sitka, Alaska, in a Desperate Condition, and Have Been Interviewed by a Western Hemisphere Commissioner
They Say Lexington White, Commander of the Polar King, is at Present Sailing Underneath Canada on an Interior Sea!
Tremendous Possibilities for Science and Commerce!
The Fabled Realms of Pluto No Longer a Myth!
Gold! Gold! Beyond the Dreams of Madness!

The story of the discovery of Plutusia and the Polar Gulf, as told by the two shipwrecked survivors of the mutineers of the *Polar King* now at Sitka, Alaska, to the *Western Hemisphere*, will form an epoch in the history of the world. The renown of Columbus and Magellan is overshadowed by the glory of Lexington White, a citizen of the United States, who fitted out a ship for polar discovery, and, taking the command himself, has unravelled the mystery of the North Pole, discovered the Polar Gulf and the interior world.

Having penetrated the Polar Gulf about three hundred miles, and having discovered the interior sun, a fear seized on a number of the sailors, among whom were Boatswain Dunbar and his companion, Henderson, who are the only survivors of twelve men who left the *Polar King* in an open boat to return home again, and to whose safe arrival in

237

Sitka the world is indebted for news of the important discoveries that had been made.

Dunbar and Henderson arrived in Sitka in a very forlorn condition, almost starved to death and utterly exhausted with their terrible journey homeward. They seem to forget largely the incidents of the journey outward in the *Polar King*, but have a very clear recollection of their own individual experiences in returning to civilization again. Dunbar, with his eleven associates and the Eskimo dogs, were no sooner cut adrift from the *Polar King* than they began to realize their terrible position. Borne on the breast of the immense tidal wave that vibrated up and down the polar cavern, they were tossed helplessly to and fro, now flung almost out of its mouth and again sucked back into its midnight recesses. They floated for days in the gigantic tunnel of water that threatened to collapse any moment and overwhelm them. They would fain have returned to the ship, but the breeze blowing out of the cavern wafted them far from their comrades, and they therefore bent all their energies to the task of getting home again. The light of the polar summer that lit the mouth of the gulf was their guide that led them back to the old familiar world.

Happily for the adventurers, the direction of the wind continued favourable to their voyage. They made about a hundred miles a day, and in five days reached the edge of the outer ocean. Here again the grandeur of the scene appalled them. Let the reader imagine a little boat carrying twelve souls out of that monstrous cavern five hundred miles in diameter. Think of fifteen hundred miles of ocean forming the mouth of the world that shone in the Arctic sunlight like molten silver surrounding an abyss of darkness.

Dunbar and his companions had no sooner emerged from the gulf and seen once more the light of the sun—our own sun—than they wept for joy. But again, when they thought of the terrible barrier of ice they had to cross again they began to wish they had remained with the *Polar King*. Thus man fluctuates between this or that impulse, as he is moved.

'I say, captain,' said Walker, one of the men, 'don't you

think it about as safe to go back and find the ship as to run the chance of being frozen to death on the ice?'

'Well,' said Dunbar, 'when we left the ship everybody knew it was for good. Our shipmates have chosen their course, as we chose ours, and it's too late to go back now. As likely as not she may have struck a rock and has gone to the bottom by this time.'

As the boat cleared the cavern the sea fell down before them, until at noonday the sun itself was visible, a joyful proof that they had at last gained the normal surface of the earth again.

When three days out of the gulf, the weather grew suddenly colder, and the sky became obscured with clouds, completely hiding the sun from sight. A furious snow-storm overtook the voyagers, who, benumbed with cold, wished they were only back again under the hurricane-deck of the *Polar King*. Fortunately, the wind blew steadily toward the Arctic Circle, bringing them nearer home, but such was the anxiety and suffering caused by insufficient protection from the inclement climate that they cared not whither they drifted, so long as they could keep alive.

By the help of a little oil-stove they boiled their coffee under a sail, which, spread horizontally above them, in some measure kept the snow from burying them alive.

The storm spent its fury in twenty-four hours, and when the air grew clear again they were saluted with the sight of that enormous ridge of ice through which the *Polar King* found a passage a month before. The ice was heaped up with the purest snow in places twenty feet in depth. Thousands of icy peaks and pinnacles, as far as the eye could reach, pierced the sky. Under other conditions the sight would have been sublime, but to men frozen and famished with insufficient food it was a scene of terror.

The icy range was flanked by an ice-foot varying from thirty to sixty miles in width, and from four to fifty feet above the sea-level.

Here was the problem that confronted Dunbar—he had to travel over at least thirty miles of icy splinters over an

WE SLOWLY DRAGGED OURSELVES ACROSS THE RANGE OF ICY PEAKS.

ice-foot whose surface was broken into every possible con-
tortion of crystallization. There were mounds, hummocks,
caverns, crevasses, ridges and gulfs of the hardest and oldest
ice. Then when this barrier was crossed there was the icy
backbone of the whole system, five hundred to a thousand
feet in height, to be crossed, as there was no lane or opening
to be discovered through so formidable a range of ice mountains. Even if he succeeded in crossing the same, there would
certainly be an ice-foot of perhaps greater dimensions than
the one before him to cross, and that might prove to be only
a valley of ice leading to other and still more inaccessible
cliffs to be surmounted.

'This is no place to die in,' said Dunbar, 'and so, boys,
we've got to hustle if we ever expect to get home.'

'Ay, ay, sir,' said his companions, but when they reached
the ice they found that having remained in a cramped position for a month in the boat had incapacitated them for
walking.

It was also found that Walker's feet and those of four other
sailors had been frostbitten, and that they were totally unable
to be of any service to themselves or the others.

The outlook was mournful in the extreme. The only
thing that cheered them was the constant sunlight, and even
that consolation would depart in another month, and if in
the mean time they did not get away from the ice, hunger
and the awful desolation of a polar winter would terminate
their existence.

There was no chance of starting on their journey until
they got accustomed to the use of their limbs, and so they
built a hut of blocks of ice, which were solidly frozen together by a few buckets full of sea water thrown over them.

The dogs were glad to get on the ice again, and scampered
about totally oblivious of the fact that the supply of pork was
getting very low, and unless they got some fresh meat very
soon they would be obliged to feed on each other.

They remained a fortnight in their Arctic abode exercis-
ing themselves by cutting a passage in the ice. During this
time four of the sailors died. Finally the remainder, packing

everything into the boat, yoked the dogs thereto, and started in anything but hopeful spirits on their arduous journey.

It was found that Walker had to be carried along, but he did not long continue a burden to his associates, for on the fourth day of the march he died, and was buried in the snow. It was a toilsome journey. Almost every foot of the way required to be hewn out of ice as hard as adamant.

"The dogs suffered greatly from insufficient food and tireless exertion. Several died from complete exhaustion, and were greedily devoured by their fellows.

After desperate exertions, Dunbar and his company, now reduced to seven souls, gained the crest of the ice range and had the satisfaction of seeing open water not twenty miles away. It took some time to discover the best route for a descent, but at last they reached the level of the ice-foot beyond, and struck for open sea. A fortunate capture of several seals re-enforced their almost exhausted supply of provisions.

Dunbar cared nothing about latitude or longitude or scientific information in such a desperate fight for life. It was a joyful moment when he and his companions launched their boat safe into the sea again after the incredible toil of dragging it forty miles across the splintered ice peaks and the terrible ice-foot north and south of the *paleocrystic* mountains.

Dunbar hoisted his sail, abandoning the few dogs who yet remained alive, and with his unhappy companions steered for Behring Strait, first making for the coast of Alaska that faces the desolation of the Arctic seas.

It would be impossible to describe the horrors of that lonely voyage. The terrible struggle with five hundred miles of ice-floes, with snow-storms that piled the snow high upon the voyagers, and the ferocious cold, proved too much for five of the seven sailors, and one by one the poor fellows died, and were thrown overboard.

Only two men—Dunbar and a sailor named Henderson—emerged from the Arctic Sea, arriving in six months from the time they left the ship, in Sitka, Alaska.

CHAPTER 45

The Voyages of the Mercury
and the Aurora Borealis

"It was a most fortunate thing that any of the men could live until they reached civilization," I said, when Captain Adams had finished his reading of Dunbar's story in the paper.

"It was solely due to that fact that we are here at present, admiral," replied Captain Adams. "No sooner was the story published than the greatest possible excitement arose both in America and Europe. The United States and Britain felt chagrined that a private citizen had been able to achieve what the greatest nations on earth, with unlimited men and money, were unable to accomplish. To satisfy popular clamour the United States, Great Britain, Russia, France, Germany, Italy and Spain each fitted out separate expeditions to follow in the wake of the *Polar King*. These were manned with former Arctic navigators, and were in each case commissioned and fitted out regardless of cost to explore the interior world and lay the foundation of future conquest and commerce. The Secretary of the United States Navy, at Washington, sent for Dunbar and Henderson, and forthwith employed both as pilots for the *Mercury* expedition under my command."

"How did the English people receive the news?" I inquired of Sir John Forbes.

"It is useless to say, admiral," he replied, "that the story of the *Polar King* was the sole topic of conversation for weeks throughout the United Kingdom. The Royal Geographical Society, the Royal Astronomical Society, and the Travellers' Club, all sent special deputations to the government, asking for the fitting out of a ship to undertake British research, which might possibly accompany the United States vessel having the pilots Dunbar and Henderson on board, and thus partake of the advantage these guides would naturally give the United States vessel.

"The British Government," continued Sir John, with a smile in his eye, "saw at once that British interests in the interior world must be protected at all hazards, and gave the Lords of the Admiralty full power to act.

"My fame as an Arctic navigator and as the discoverer of the bones of the great Irish Arctic hero, Montgomery, and those of his men, in a cabin on Prince Albert's Island, caused the Lords of the Admiralty to place at my command the frigate *Aurora Borealis*, manned by experienced Arctic sailors.

"Negotiations were opened with the United States Government, whereby the *Aurora Borealis*, by proceeding up the northwest passage along the route followed by the Montgomery expedition, might meet the *Mercury*, who would enter the Arctic Sea by way of Behring Strait. It was arranged, as Captain Adams is aware, that each vessel should proceed direct to latitude 75 N., longitude 140 W., and there await the other vessel."

"You are right," said Captain Adams, "for my instructions were of the same nature. The *Mercury* was fitted out in Brooklyn Navy Yard, and as soon as her complement of two hundred and fifty officers, explorers, scientists, press correspondents and seamen was enrolled, and her stores fully shipped, I was instructed to proceed by way of the Nicaragua Canal to San Francisco for further orders and stores. Leaving San Francisco I next touched Victoria, B.C., and finally at Sitka, Alaska, for final orders. The entire winter had been consumed in getting ready, and by May 1 I cleared for Behring Strait, steering straight for the rendezvous in the Arctic Sea where we had arranged to meet by June 1. I was first on the spot, and had the good fortune of only having to wait a week before we sighted the *Aurora Borealis*."

"And then," said Sir John, "began the real work of the voyage. All had been plain sailing so far, but it was clearly impossible for any vessel to reach the Polar Gulf unless a lead was discovered in the ice barrier similar to that so fortunately discovered by the *Polar King*. It was here that the services of Dunbar as pilot came into requisition. Captain Adams had got him to mark on the chart as near as possible the location of the chasm in the ice mountain discovered by the *Polar King*. That once rediscovered, we could succeed in following the *Polar King*; but should we fail in our quest, all further progress would be impossible. I often said to Captain Adams that I considered Lexington White as one of the most fortunate of men. It was nothing short of the miraculous that you should discover a newly-rent passage through the barrier of ice that for ages has guarded the sublime secret of the pole. Only once in all the eternity of the past did the gate of that thrilling Arctic zone open itself to humanity, and by a miracle of fortune you were on the spot at the right moment, ready to enter that open door. That fact alone emblazons you with glory. But to my story. How were we to discover the same or a similar lead to the north? On the mere chance of discovering such a passage both vessels had encountered the dangers and terrors of the Arctic desolations. Dunbar located the chasm in latitude 78.6 N., longitude 125 W., and thither we sailed.

"As for the expeditions sent out by the other governments of Europe, jealous of American prowess, we have not seen or heard of any of them. Their vessels followed the direction of the Gulf Stream, and the instructions given their commanders were to first make Spitzbergen, and thence proceed due north, and if possible find there a passage to the pole. For ourselves, I will let Captain Adams tell how we got through the ice barrier."

"That," said Captain Adams, "is a simple enough story, but the actual experiences were not so simple as the recital of them. We found that Dunbar's estimate of the location of the passage was within fifty miles of the exact spot. We found the passage after some days' searching, about fifty miles beyond Dunbar's location on the chart. The veritable passage was there, but, as was expected, instead of open water there was a mass of solid ice of unknown thickness, but fortunately having a smooth surface.

"There was but one thing to do to overcome such an obstacle, and that was to haul the ships on runners on top of the ice, right through the gap formed by nature in the icy barrier. Our labours in making such a passage were simply superhuman. Both crews were employed for more than a week in sloping the ice-foot up which the vessels were to be dragged. Then an enormous cradle had to be constructed of massive beams of wood securely bolted together, large and strong enough to carry either vessel. There was fortunately lumber enough for this purpose, as among the stores of both ships timbers for building Arctic huts had been included. The cradle was first secured to the hull of the *Mercury*, and the crews of both vessels took hold of the ropes made fast to her decks. She was drawn close to the ice, but utterly refused to leave the water. We tried fixing anchors in the ice ahead, to which were attached a system of blocks and ropes. These supplemented the strength of the men by the hoisting engine, but even this was of no avail. We next rigged up a large drum, vertically over the shaft of the propeller, and connected it therewith by means of right-angled cog-wheels. To this was fastened an immense cable, to the other end of which were attached the ropes rove through blocks held firmly a quarter-of a mile ahead by thirty anchors imbedded in the ice. We started the engines, and, sure enough, the bows of the vessel began to rise out of the water. The *Mercury* would have been lifted high and dry on the ice were it not that at that moment several of the smaller cables in the blocks snapped asunder, and thus our third effort failed. At this juncture, Sir John Forbes proposed to plant a few more anchors in the ice, and through the additional blocks work a cable leading from the bows of the *Mercury* to the stern of the *Aurora Borealis*. This being done, he would steam ahead off the ice and add the power of his ship to that of the *Mercury*'s engine, and thus relieve the strain on the *Mercury*'s cables. It was a capital idea, and we immediately put it into execution. The result was a perfect success. The combined energies of the English ship and her crew, together with those of our own vessel and men, drew the *Mercury* up the slide of ice, and placed her erect and dry upon the level surface of the lead. It was now comparatively easy work to draw the ship along the ice. Her own engines were equal to the task; but it was impossible for the *Mercury* to go ahead, as, without her assistance, the *Aurora Borealis* would be unable to leave the water. Then, again, there was only the material for but one cradle for both ships. The difficulty was solved by cutting away one-fourth of the cradle from beneath both bow and stern of the *Mercury*, and, joining these parts, we furnished the *Aurora Borealis* with a sledge as large as that of our own ship, and strong enough to keep her in an upright position while being dragged over the ice. After infinite trouble, and in obedience to the aggregated energies of the engines of both ships and the hauling of the combined crews, the English ship was drawn up upon the ice beside the American vessel. This double feat of skill and determination was duly saluted by a roar of guns and the cheers of the sailors.

"The ice proved so smooth and hard that the crews of each ship, assisted by the engines, were able to work their respective vessels in good order through the entire chasm, a distance of seventy miles. Arriving at the open floe beyond the northern ice-foot, we bevelled off the ice as before, and the ships were finally launched upon the polar sea."

I congratulated Sir John Forbes and Captain Adams on their successful manoeuvre, which resulted in getting their ships across the ice. It was a feat of engineering skill rarely possible of accomplishment, and in their case nature had seconded their efforts by providing a smooth and solid floor to operate upon, otherwise all human endeavour would have been fruitless.

"And now, gentlemen," I said, "what do you say surprised you most in your voyage hither from the ice barrier?"

"I think, admiral," said Captain Adams, "that the grandest sight on earth is the full view of the Polar Gulf, with its suspended abyss of waters surrounding the ship. The colossal flux and reflux of waters produces a feeling of terrible sublimity. It is an awful scene."

"But that scene," said Sir John Forbes, "belongs to the outer world. This aspect of the interior world of Plutusia is ten thousand times more magnificent. What grander glory ever fell on human eyes than this Colosseum of oceans, continents, kingdoms, islands and seas spread upon the vast interior vault surrounding us, and all lit up by the internal sun! The human imagination never conceived anything equal to this. Here nature surpasses the wildest dreams of fancy. We are astounded with the splendour of such a world!"

"You are right, Sir John," said Captain Adams; "this interior sphere surpasses anything hitherto discovered in heaven or earth. And then to think of its enormous riches! The royal fleet of Atvatabar, plated with solid gold, proves the extraordinary profusion of the precious metal."

CHAPTER 46

The Arrest of Lyone

While the entertainment was at its height, we were surprised by one of the guards informing us that a messenger had arrived at the fortress from Egyplosis, bearing for me a despatch of the utmost importance from the high priest Hushnoly.

We were all excitement at the news, and on opening the despatch, I read as follows:

To His Excellency Lexington White, Lord Admiral of Atvatabar,
Greeting:
Your glorious victory over the royal fleet has awakened popular excitement in favour of deposing His Majesty King Aldemegry Bhoolmakar, and establishing our late beloved goddess Lyone on the throne, as queen of Atvatabar. Egyplosis has openly espoused the cause of Lyone, and the sacred college of priests and priestesses have taken up arms in favour of the goddess. His majesty, being resolved to stamp out rebellion at any cost, has caused the arrest of Lyone at her palace, Tanje, and has confined her in the fortress Calnogor as hostage for the good behaviour of the people. He has threatened to put Lyone to death in case her followers attempt any hostile demonstrations against the king's authority. We of Egyplosis are committed to the cause of Her Majesty Lyone, Queen of Atvatabar!
Hushnoly

This was most alarming news! While we had been feasting in inglorious ease our queen had been arrested and imprisoned! The time for action had come.

Ere we could deliberate on the best course to pursue, a second message from Hushnoly arrived, stating that the king, hearing of the outbreak in Egyplosis, had ordered Coltonobory, the commander-in-chief, to proceed with his *wayleals* to Egyplosis, to capture Hushnoly and disband his followers. This being an open declaration of war, had precipitated a civil struggle, and the armies both of the king and queen were being recruited with great excitement on both sides. As for Kioram, that city had declared for our cause, and the governor was overjoyed to know that the victory of the *Polar King* had resulted in the entire fleet espousing the cause of Lyone.

I questioned Governor Lapalme on the strength and equipment of both the king's forces and those willing to support Lyone, and the probabilities of our cause being successful.

He informed me that the king already commanded an army of half a million men, composed two-thirds of *wayleals* and one-third *bockhockids*, or flying cavalry, armed with swords, shields and spears of deadly power. The adherents of Lyone numbered already one hundred thousand men, who had also proclaimed her queen of Atvatabar, including five thousand amazons from Egyplosis, who would fight for their late goddess to the death, all similarly armed.

"The future is doubtful," said the governor; "but with your aid we may well hope for success. I congratulate you on your splendid victory, which is already known throughout the kingdom, and will increase our forces to two hundred and fifty thousand men. It will cheer the heart of our late goddess to know that she also already possesses a powerful fleet."

"Do you consider the queen in any immediate danger at the hands of the king or government?" I inquired.

"Well," said the governor, "at the present stage of affairs it is difficult to think that either king or Borodemy would dare to execute her majesty, even although it might be according to law. Yet, if alarmed at the partial destruction and defection of the fleet and the growing power of the queen's followers, the bloodthirsty king and frightened government might possibly execute her, especially if they saw no hope for themselves in the coming struggle."

"Then," said I, "whether we fight or not, our queen is in very serious danger of death?"

"That is what I most fear," said the governor. "As soon as I heard of the imprisonment of her majesty I called a review of my garrison of *wayleals* and *bockhockids*, and asked them if they would espouse the cause of the queen, and to a man they swore allegiance thereto. I conceive the only way to secure respect for the queen is to make her followers as formidable as possible."

"Action," I added, "is imperative. We must strike the king's army a fearful blow, to impress his majesty with respect for our power. The queen must either be released by the king or we will release her ourselves. There must be an immediate mobilization of the queen's army, and preceding that, a council of war in the fortress of Kioram to appoint a commander-in-chief and generals of division. Governor Lapalme," I continued, "I thank you in the name of Lyone for your allegiance. It is very gratifying to the fleet to know that it is spared the necessity of bombarding your beautiful city."

"We have pledged ourselves to support our queen, to whom be freedom and victory!" said the governor.

"Ay, ay!" said the captains, Pra and Nototherboc.

"The fleet, of course, will assist in defending the city," I said; "and in addition to this duty will furnish a brigade of thirty thousand wing-jackets for active service in the interior. Now, in view of this, how many men can you spare from the garrison?"

The governor replied that he could spare ten thousand *wayleals*, under the command of Pra, and five thousand *bockhockids*, under command of Nototherboc.

I ordered Astronomer Starbottle, with Flathootly as escort, to depart at once for Egyplosis, and summon to Kioram High Priest Hushnoly and the high priestess, Grand Sorcerer Charka and the grand sorceress, together with such a retinue of trusty officers as would be worthy of being made commanders in the coming struggle. After summoning Egyplosis, they were both to go to Gnaphisthasia and summon Yermoul, lord of art, and his trusty captains, also to Kioram, and return hither without delay. "Choose each of you," I said, "a pair of the strongest wings, and arm yourselves with revolvers. You must at all hazards evade the enemy and carry out your mission with the greatest possible speed."

Astronomer Starbottle and Flathootly were enthusiastic at be-

ing allowed to undertake so adventurous a journey. They immediately began to prepare for, an early departure.

"Might I inquire," said the governor, "what you mean by
revolvers?"

We showed him the weapons by which we had resisted the
onslaught of myriads of wing-jackets, to the fatal force of which
thousands had succumbed. He was astonished at the invention, and
said if the army of the queen were equipped with so formidable a
weapon, King Aldemegry Bhoolmakar would very easily be driven
from his throne, and Lyone would be truly Queen of Atvatabar.

It was decided that the fortress of Kioram should be immediately turned into an arsenal for the manufacture of spears and
revolvers, for the use of the *wayleals* and *bockhockids* of Lyone's army.
The mines where the metal *terrelium* was worked and the factories
where *aquelium* was elaborated from the water of the ocean were to
be seized, and vast quantities of these metals sent to Kioram for the
use of the entire army, to furnish a current for the deadly spears, to
be made under the superintendence of Professor Rackiron.

Astronomer Starbottle and the redoubtable Flathootly were
equipped with splendid sets of wings worked by cells of double power. Their magnetic spears were far-reaching and carried
a current of tremendous intensity, contact with which was immediate death.

"Be jabers," said Flathootly, "the fellow that touches us will
foind us hornets of the first magnitude. We'll give him a touch of
the *cholera morbus*."

"I entrust the despatches in your hand, astronomer," said I, "and
with Flathootly as escort and body-guard, I hope you will both
execute your mission and return safe to Kioram."

"Caution and despatch will be our watchwords," said the astronomer, "and you are already assured of our fidelity."

"In addition to your duty as couriers to Egyplosis and Gnaphisthasia I desire you," I said, "to explore the upper atmosphere,
with a view of discovering at what height centrifugal gravity ceases
to operate on bodies, and, if possible, where gravity toward Swang
begins to exert its force. I wish to choose an aerial battle-field,
where there is no gravity, so that our *wayleals* may have absolute
freedom of action."

"We have discovered a perceptible movement toward the sun at a height of fifty miles," said the governor; "at that height our *wayleals* cease to revolve with the earth, and therefore have no weight—but your astronomer can easily verify this fact by his own experience."

"Do you think our couriers will receive opposition from the king's *wayleals*?" I inquired.

"I would suggest their being disguised as the king's *wayleals* as a means of safety. If they travel as *wayleals* of her majesty they are liable to be captured."

The astronomer and Flathootly made the necessary disguise in their attire as a measure of safety, each donning a leathern cuirass, highly decorated with white-metal helmet and boots, and packing a sufficient quantity of food in a portable trunk to supply them during the journey. They bade us goodbye, soaring from the deck into the gulfs of air above Atvatabar, and directed their flight to Egyplosis.

CHAPTER 47

The Council of War in Kioram

The sensation produced by the defeat of the royal fleet, the destruction of forty of the ships, and the defection of the remaining sixty vessels to the cause of Queen Lyone, shook the nation from its centre to circumference. It appeared incredible that one ship could destroy so many well-armed vessels. Our *terrorite* guns were considered demon powers, and such was the consternation produced by their terrible energy that, were it possible for us to use such weapons in aerial battle, their appearance would alone cause the royal army to surrender.

Coltonobory was confident he could soon suppress the insurrection by virtue of his superior force.

As for his majesty, he was beside himself with rage at the loss of his fleet. Had Admiral Jolar been alive he would have answered for his defeat with his life. The following royal proclamation testified to the implacable wrath of the king:

His Majesty King Aldemegry Bhoolmakar of Atvatabar
to his faithful people:
Know ye, my people of Atvatabar, that the desperate barbarian who commands the alien ship, the *Polar King*, has not only alienated the affections of the Goddess Lyone, thereby insulting our holy religion and our laws, but has destroyed forty of our ships of war, and induced the remainder of our fleet to follow his fortunes, thereby giving him power to destroy our commerce, blockade our harbours, and burn our cities. His success has encouraged many who have hitherto been our faithful subjects to flock to his standard, and the terrors of treason and insurrection devastate our beloved country.

What will be thought of Lyone, who was lately our be-loved and adored goddess, who has treasonably allowed her-self to be proclaimed Queen of Atvatabar, and who is the prime cause of all this deluge of crime, treason and apostasy by encouraging a heretical affection for a desperate criminal, and who dares to abuse her holy office by seeking matrimo-ny with a murderer? It would be impossible for this cowardly and desperate assassin to visit our country with such destruc-tion were it not that she who was our goddess sympathizes with his inhuman and infernal work. She has only to speak the word that she has no sympathy with such a monster, and his power will be paralyzed in a moment, and peace restored to our unhappy country. Will it be believed that she abso-lutely refuses to disown such a viper, and even boasts of his work, and that he will shortly set her free?

Our prisoner, she has disregarded our clemency in hold-ing back the sword of justice that hangs over her head. Her life is already forfeited by her own actions. The monster of insurrection and apostasy must be struck in its most vital part. Orders have been given for a full conclave of the Boro-demy, to put our fallen goddess on trial forthwith, and if found guilty to be immediately executed.

The commander-in-chief of the army, Coltonobory, has orders to attack, pursue and put to death without mercy all rebels in arms, and arrest all sympathizers with the rebel cause.

Given in our palace at Calnogor in the twenty-sixth year of our reign.

Aldemegry Bhoolmakar
King of Atvatabar

This proclamation revealed the desperate crisis matters had reached. The bloodthirsty king had Lyone in his power, and unless a miracle happened nothing could save her. The fact that the flag of the queen floated above Kioram must have added enormously to the wrath of the king, and the supreme question with us then was how to save our queen from a cruel fate.

While discussing this important subject with Governor Lapalme and my own retinue, we were agreeably surprised to learn of the arrival of the high priest and priestess and the grand sorcerer and sorceress from Egyplosis. Astronomer Starbottle and Flathootly had so far evidently succeeded in their mission.

Hushnoly reported that all Egyplosis was up in arms for the cause of the queen. The priestesses had formed an Amazonian legion of five thousand *wayleals*. These would be commanded by the high priestess Zooly-Soase and the grand sorceress Thoubool in equal divisions. The sacred phalanx of priests of the spiritual palace would be under the command of the grand sorcerer, while Hushnoly would hold himself in readiness for a special command.

While praising the devotion of the twin-souls, a message by telegraph was received from Gnaphisthasia, stating that the lord of art, Yermoul, was on his way to Kioram. He would travel on the wing by a circuitous route, to avoid contact with any of the king's *wayleals*. Yermoul would be accompanied by the chief priests of poetry, painting, sculpture, music, decoration, architecture, and dancing.

No messenger had been sent to Grasnagallipas, high priest of the palace of inventions in Calnogor, as tidings had been received from that quarter that the priests of invention, owing to their close connection with the seat of government, had become *bockhockids* of the king. The defection of Grasnagallipas was a severe blow to our cause, as he was the greatest inventor in the kingdom, and master of ten thousand magnetic *bockhockids*, that machine being his own invention.

Governor Lapalme said the crisis upon which we were to deliberate demanded immediate action, and the first step to be taken was to appoint a commander-in-chief for the army of the queen. The victory achieved by the commander of the *Polar King* in fighting the royal navy single-handed, and his personal sympathy with her majesty, pointed out His Excellency, Lexington White, already lord admiral of the fleet, as the man of all others fit to assume the supreme command of all operations directed against the royal army to secure the liberation of Lyone and the reformation of the religion of Atvatabar. "I therefore," said he, "nominate His Excellency, Lexington White, commander-in-chief of the army of the queen."

The governor's proposition was received with the wildest enthusiasm, and I gracefully accepted the high honour conferred upon me.

Hushnoly was appointed my assistant, under the title of supreme general of the army, and the list of generals included the grand sorcerer Charka, the grand sorceress Thoubool, the high priestess Zooly-Soase, the lord of art Yermoul, Governor Lapalme, Generals Pra and Nototherboc. The chief priests of poetry, painting, music, architecture and decoration, and Professors Rackiron, Goldrock and Starbottle, Dr. Merryferry and Flathootly were also created generals of the army, being at the same time relieved from service in the fleet.

Rear-Admiral Wallace was promoted to full command of the fleet during my absence therefrom, with the title of admiral.

As president of the council, I spoke as follows:

"Supreme General Hushnoly and generals of the army of Her Majesty Lyone, Queen of Atvatabar, you are aware of the nature of the crisis that calls us together and the cause to which we devote our lives and fortunes. Our beloved queen, for whom we fight, is in the hands and at the mercy of a cruel tyrant. We may hear of her death at any moment. Such an event would crush our hopes and blast our cause beyond hope of recovery. We must be both bold and prudent. We must concentrate our forces to withstand the onset of the enemy. A proclamation must be issued making Kioram, which is under the protection of the fleet, the headquarters of the army and the rallying-ground for volunteers. Our arsenal in the fortress will begin at once to make revolvers, under the superintendence of General Rackiron, for the use of our *wayleals*. Armed with these, one hundred thousand *wayleals* will be equal to half a million men without such weapons.

"We must strike a mighty blow as soon as possible for the sake of Lyone, our queen. Once break the power of the king, and he will be glad to sue for peace by liberating our adored idol, the pride of Atvatabar."

These sentiments were applauded with impetuous excitement.

Hushnoly caused telegraphic despatches as to the proceedings of the council to be sent to Egyplosis, Gnaphisthasia, and to sympathizers in Calnogor, calling on volunteers for the army of the queen to report themselves at Kioram without delay.

Admiral Wallace was instructed to send vessels to various points on the coast of Atvatabar, to receive volunteers and supplies and transmit them to Kioram with all possible speed.

The mines of precious metals of the queen, situated on the northern coast of the kingdom, and the materials for making guns, gunpowder and *terrorite*, were to be accumulated at Kioram without delay.

Professor Rackiron agreed, if furnished with men and materials, to turn out sufficient hand *mitrailleuses* to arm one hundred thousand *wayleals* in less than a month. He also proposed to furnish our *wayleals* with *magnic* spears, and to arm the legs of the *bockhockids* with *magnic* toes, so that a company of the strange animals could rout a legion of *wayleals*. We discovered that the materials for the manufacture of *terrorite* existed in abundance in Atvatabar, and as the secret of this substance was still ours, we were in a position to work fearful havoc on the enemy.

Before the council broke up the most encouraging news was received from our agents throughout the kingdom that the enrolment of volunteers for our cause was proceeding with great rapidity, and a hundred thousand men would arrive in Kioram within a week from the date of our proclamation. Hushnoly was appointed general of volunteers, in addition to his rank as supreme general of the army. General Yermoul and his colleagues would command the contingent from Gnaphisthasia, consisting of fourteen thousand *wayleals*.

While thus discussing the details of our army organization, Astronomer Starbottle and his body-guard, Flathootly, arrived at the fortress, having safely escaped all perils in making a very hazardous journey.

CHAPTER 48

The Report of Astronomer Starbottle

I congratulated our couriers upon their safe return from a successful expedition. The astronomer made the following report of his journey:

Following our instructions to bear despatches to Egyplosis and Gnaphisthasia, and at the same time make such astronomical and meteorological observations as might be valuable to military operations in Atvatabar, we rose to a considerable height in the air after leaving the *Polar King*. We were still under the influence of the earth's revolution, moving with Atvatabar two hundred and fifty miles an hour from east to west. We found the atmosphere of equal density, no matter how high we ascended, showing it to be a continuation of the denser strata of the outer air pressing into the earth by way of the open poles. It fills the hollow shell of the earth as an elastic ball, pressing equally on every part of the interior surface. Notwithstanding its mobility, it partakes of the revolution of the earth, hence the particularly serene climate of *Bilbimtesirol* and the absence of trade-winds in the region of greatest motion, which corresponds to the torrid zone of the outer sphere. The only winds are local disturbances, sometimes excessively violent, caused by the irregularities of the earth's surface and the consequent unequal distribution of heat and cold. Besides the general serenity of the air there are other reasons why the interior planet is really the only true world where human flight is a complete success.

We found that at a height of fifty miles the gravity caused

by centrifugal motion is exactly counterbalanced by the attraction of the central sun overhead. At a height of sixty miles, if the wings remain motionless, we perceptibly ascend with a slowly increasing motion toward the sun, while the centrifugal gravity slowly lessens, owing to the lesser circle of space traversed, the attraction of Swang as gradually increases, and nothing but the strength of our wings prevented our falling into the fires of the sun.

Our chief discovery was the fact that there exists a belt of air at a distance of between fifty and sixty miles above the earth, extremely cold, in which there is no weight, and all objects therein float, indifferent to the presence of the sun above or earth beneath. We saw a distant globe hanging in this region of very small size, and through the glass we could see mountains, rivers and seas thereon, but no traces of cities or human life.

During our stay in this imponderable region Flathootly expressed his satisfaction by grotesque evolutions. He would fly, moving his legs as if he were skating on ice, and again plunging as though he were diving into the sea. Then he would fly upward feet foremost, as though he were falling toward the sun.

'Shure it's foine fun,' he said, 'to shtand upside down, flyin' an' laughin' at the same toime.'

'Take care,' I said, 'and don't fall upward.'

'How can I fall upward when the ground's below me?' he inquired.

'The earth below you has no attraction at this height,' I said; 'but the sun is exerting its influence upon us. If we go any higher up we'll be drawn into the fires of the sun and roasted alive.'

'Be jabers, if that's so, I'll get down an' walk, an' you can fly around as much as you loike,' said Flathootly.

'If you descend you'll be arrested and executed as a spy. Remember, we're in an enemy's country,' said I.

'I'll tell you what I'll do then,' said he; 'now that I've got me siven-leagued boots on, I'll jist go down an' jump from wan mountain top to another.'

Time would not permit us to stay longer in our high altitude, consequently we stretched ourselves on the abyss of air and swept downward to Egyplosis.

'Our flight was exultant and swift. We soared over mighty ranges of mountains and swept into wide valleys with the ecstasy of birds. What a splendid fact to communicate to the outer world—that man, denied for untold ages the power of flight, may now inhabit a world of incomparable beauty, where it is easier to fly than to walk and a thousand times more enjoyable! The powers of the body and the raptures of the soul are not in themselves limited. It is simply a question of environment. No sooner do we inhabit a new environment than both body and soul expand themselves and fill the greater amplitude as easily as that more restricted one. Give the world, weary with ennui, a fresh joy, and see how eager its enjoyment thereof, how voraciously it feasts on the newly-found delight.

We descended to the level of the mountain peaks, and, sure enough, Flathootly, taking his stand on a lofty crag, would flap his wings and sail to the next mountain like an albatross. When alighting on one of the peaks he frightened an immense bird from its nest on a cliff. It was the *seemorgh*, a bird of prey, as large as six eagles, with wings measuring twenty feet from tip to tip. It ferociously flew at Flathootly as he tried to escape it, and caught him with its claws, fastening its strong beak in the back of his neck.

It was a perilous position for my companion.

I flew to his rescue. He was badly frightened, and kept shouting, 'Kill the baste!' The bird being on Flathootly's back, rendered him powerless to cope with it. Suddenly the bird let go its grip of his neck and took hold of his head in its claws, with the idea of carrying him off to its eyrie. Coming behind the monster unseen, I managed by a well-directed blow to transfix him with my *magnic* spear. The *seemorgh*, with wide-distended wings and head falling limp on its breast, slowly revolving, descended to the earth, the first enemy to fall on land at the hands of the invader.

Flathootly now avoided the mountains. He had a narrow

escape, but, excepting an ugly wound in his neck, was otherwise unscathed.

We continued our flight to Egyplosis, dimly visible in the vault before us. We continued to traverse the inner curve of the planet, Atvatabar surrounding us on all sides except that part of the sphere above us which was concealed by the brilliancy of Swang.

Owing to the uniform heat and density of the lower strata of air, every mountain top was covered with foliage. We saw many mansions of the Atvatabarese sculptured out of the solid rock and surrounded with noble forests of tropical vegetation. We flapped our wings thirty miles above Atvatabar, which lay, with its mountains, forests, lakes, cities, temples and dwellings, beneath us like a map.

We had flown for six or eight hours when a feeling of hunger admonished us to partake of food. The tin trunk, which was our commissariat department, had been towed behind us by means of a rope during the entire journey.

'Flathootly,' said I, 'let us call a halt for refreshments.'

'With all my heart,' said he; 'but how are we to howld the trunk up?'

'Let us rise to the height of fifty miles again,' I replied, 'and then it will stand on the air alone, like ourselves.'

'You're a wise man, sorr,' said he. 'It's an illigant idea that we'll adopt immediately.'

Accordingly, we were soon once more in the region of no weight, where we stood in the air as on land, Flathootly on one side of the trunk and I on the other, to dine on its contents.

Flathootly, opening the lid, brought forth some cold venison, which he coolly laid on the air beside us, saying, 'Shtand there now till you're wanted.' The venison quietly floated up against the side of the trunk, that being the only force of gravity acting upon it. In like manner he tossed around us a cold roast fowl, several varieties of cooked vegetables, and some rich puddings. He also produced several bottles of *squang*, the tokay of Atvatabar. These he flung downward, but every bottle, after falling half a mile or so, slowly ascended,

I MOUNTED THE TRUNK AND PROPOSED THE HEALTH OF
HER MAJESTY, LYONE, QUEEN OF ATVATABAR.

and the entire bottles came back to us in a close cluster, as though unwilling to leave us.

It was a novel feast. We closed the lid of the trunk and spread a napkin thereon, and at once began our repast. Flathootly rapidly secured the floating dishes, and the food was demolished as easily as though we stood on *terra firma*. I pulled a pudding off my back, and Flathootly took from his neck the knives and forks that had clustered there.

The wine proved excellent. I mounted the trunk and proposed the health of Her Majesty Lyone, Queen of Atvatabar, and the empyrean rang with the enthusiasm invoked by the toast.

Flathootly proposed the health of our noble master, His Excellency Lexington White, the conqueror of the fleet. The air once more echoed its response to our hurrahs.

We might have rested, and even slept, on the impalpable air, but duty forbade us any such luxury. We repacked our trunk and proceeded straight to Egyplosis, then but two hundred miles away. We arrived safe, and, handing the high priest, Hushnoly, your despatch, hastened on to the palace of art at Gnaphisthasia. We again succeeded in eluding the vigilance of the king's *wayleals*, thanks to our speed and disguise, and delivering your despatch to the grand priest of art Yermoul, in Gnaphisthasia, returned forthwith to Kioram.

CHAPTER 49

Preparation for War

In less than a week, as measured by the time bells of Kioram, the ships began to arrive with troops from various parts of the coast of Atvatabar, bringing volunteers for either branch of the service of her majesty. In ten days one hundred thousand volunteers had arrived, and these were quartered in the city, pending their equipment as *wayleals* and *bockhockids*. As might be expected, a great many were deserters from the royal army, and these were of great assistance in organizing the troops, being already skilled in the tactics of aerial warfare.

General Rackiron had turned the entire fortress into an arsenal of war. Fires blazed everywhere for forging guns and *magnic* spears, and a thousand hammers were shaping the limbs of *bockhockids*. The department for making ammunition was busiest of all, furnishing the elements on whose efficiency depended success or defeat.

A vast quantity of hand *mitrailleuses*, or gigantic revolvers, were made, and being of but little weight, these blew showers of bullets from magazines attached to the tubes. Each *wayleal* carried a thousand cartridges.

The cell in the case of the *wayleals* had to furnish a double current, viz., the current that moved the wings and the death-dealing current of the spear. For each *bockhockid* two powerful cells were necessary, one for the rider and the other to work the *bockhockid* he rode or flew upon. The strongest cell was contained in the body of the mechanical bird, which moved both its wings and legs, and also furnished its claws with a deadly current, so that when a detachment of *bockhockids* dashed into a mass of *wayleals*, legs foremost, the greatest possible havoc could be made with the least possible risk to the mounted riders.

The object of having each cell separate in the case of the *bock-hockids* was apparent. In case a mounted *wayleal* got unhorsed he was able to join the *wayleals*, or infantry, having the same equipment as they.

Our superiority in arms when compared with the royal army, which possessed only *magnic* spears and shields, was apparent.

Of course, the enemy also made the legs and claws of the *bock-hockids magnic* spears in themselves.

It seemed remarkable that a people so inventive, and who possessed the best of all means for manufacturing firearms, should not have thought of a better device than their naval air guns. It was but a further illustration of the fact that the keenest minds are constantly colour-blind to the simplest combinations visible to lookers-on while they are pursuing their elaborate researches.

But the royal army, if inferior in arms, possessed the superiority of numbers. It outnumbered us three to one.

Our total forces consisted of 175,000 *wayleals* and 42,000 *bockhockids*, making a total of 217,000 troops, which included 5,000 Amazons.

We at first expected a much larger army, believing the priests of invention, under Grasnagallipas, would certainly espouse the cause of the queen, but it was a terrible blow to our enthusiasm when we learned that the priests of invention, making a total of 50,000 *wayleals*, had joined the royal army and would fight against their late goddess.

Calnogor being the headquarters of the royal army, it would have been particularly dangerous for the priests of invention to have espoused our cause, surrounded as they were by the enormously more powerful enemy. To our loss, they had chosen to continue part of the army of the king, which at the lowest computation numbered half a million men.

The king seemed strangely reluctant to begin the attack, although he knew the extent of our forces in Kioram. It was evident the protection given the city by the fleet allowed us to complete the arming and drilling of our forces without molestation.

Supreme General Hushnoly reported that, thanks to the indefatigable energy of General Rackiron and his colleagues, Generals Starbottle, Goldrock and Flathootly, assisted by Generals Charka,

Yermoul, Pra and Nototherboc, he had been able to fully equip the *wayleals* with *mitrailleuses*, wings, electric spears and uniforms. The *bockhockids*, in addition, were mounted on mechanical birds that could either fly, trot or walk with tremendous speed.

I instructed Hushnoly to make his appointment of officers without delay, as we might take the field any moment.

General Rackiron informed us that he was hard at work on a portable *terrorite* gun for aerial warfare. He hoped to have a battery of these guns ready in time to decide the war in our favour. I thanked the general for his extraordinary exertions, and informed him I felt sure of his success. With *terrorite* guns we would be invincible.

Our spies, who had been despatched in all directions, informed us that the royal army was in a state of activity not inferior to our own. A daily review was being held in the air above Calnogor, and it was discovered that Coltonobory was about to make a descent on our ships, particularly to seize the *Polar King*, and by thus si-lencing her guns, have Kioram and the army of the queen at his mercy. The plan was approved of by the king, and might be put in operation at any moment. This was most important news, and we decided to take the initiative at once.

"We will attack the enemy even if he is a million strong," I said.

"Everything calls for an immediate advance," said Hushnoly.

We also learned from trusty couriers that Lyone had been brought before the Borodemy, and the legislative assembly in full conclave, after hearing the evidence, had found her guilty of trea-son, impiety and sacrilege to her faith, of treason to the king, and had, by encouraging insurrection, caused her adherents to take up arms against both king and law, thereby endangering the lives and property of the inhabitants of the kingdom. There was no one to recommend Lyone to mercy, and she was condemned to death. The king had already signed her death-warrant.

She might be executed any moment!

It was a dreadful crisis to contemplate. Our first duty was to save the life of our queen at any sacrifice. I at once called a council of war to consider this all-important question. We had only assembled when a royal courier arrived at the fortress with an important des-patch addressed, *To His Excellency Lexington White, Commander-in-Chief of the Insurrectionary Army at Kioram.*

CHAPTER 50

I Visit Lyone in Calnogor

I hastily opened the despatch, which read as follows:

His Majesty King Aldemegry Bhoolmakar of Atvatabar wishes to inform His Excellency Lexington White, commander-in-chief of the insurrectionary army mobilized in Kioram, that Her Holiness Lyone, late Goddess of Atvatabar, has been tried before a full conclave of the Borodemy on the charge of sacrilege, apostasy, and insurrection. Her holiness has been found guilty and is now under sentence of death. His majesty, of merciful intent, wishes it to be known that he will pardon her holiness on this condition, *viz.*: That the insurrectionary army lays down its arms forthwith, and the *wayleals* separate and depart to their respective abodes; that His Excellency, the commander-in-chief, and his generals surrender themselves to his majesty as prisoners of war, to be tried and punished as military law dictates. This surrender to include that of the admiral of the fleet and the ships under his command.

On no other condition whatever will mercy be extended to her holiness, and should this offer be temporized with or rejected nothing can save the late goddess from the sword of justice.

Dictated at the palace in Calnogor, in the twenty-fifth year of his majesty's reign.
Aldemegry Bhoolmakar

The king's communication was received with a sensation of contempt and dismay. The thought of surrender was in itself preposterous, but when we thought that our rebellion would drive a sword into the heart of Lyone, the awful idea struck us dumb with horror!

The king possessed our proudest and most precious soul as hostage, and he was cowardly enough to sacrifice her as his most deadly blow to the insurrection.

The crisis was appalling.

"Shall we," I cried, "continue the fight, now that we know it is our queen we fight against, that it is our arms that will murder her?"

"We certainly do not murder her," said Hushnoly; "and yet this unexpected crisis paralyzes me."

"The king will not dare to murder the queen," said the grand sorcerer; "and if he does—"

The sorcerer suddenly checked himself; the mere contemplation of such an event was overpowering, yet he seemed, of all others, the most composed. His eyes shone with a strange fire that I had not hitherto noticed.

"I am satisfied," said Governor Lapalme, "that unless we lay down our arms and submit ourselves to his mercy, which means death to every one here, the fate of the queen is sealed."

"I think," said the high priestess Zooly-Soase, "that His Excellency, the commander-in-chief, should, if possible, obtain an order from the king permitting him to visit her majesty, and advise her of the entire facts of the situation, and then act as she commands. If she asks us to lay down our arms and surrender ourselves as the price of her liberty, there is none, I think, who would be so faithless as to refuse."

"And I," said the grand sorceress, "approve of your proposal. I am willing to surrender myself to save the life of the late goddess."

"We are all willing to sacrifice ourselves if need be!" shouted the entire council with generous and chivalrous enthusiasm.

"I will go," said I, "and see Lyone, as you propose, and upon her decision will depend our future action."

A courier was immediately despatched under a flag of truce to the palace at Calnogor, with the message that before his majesty's communication could be replied to, the commander-in-chief of the army of the late goddess desired to have an interview with her majesty, to decide upon a final answer thereto, and to request a royal passport not only admitting him to the presence of Lyone in the fortress at Calnogor, but also permitting his safe return to Kioram.

"I fear," said Hushnoly, "the queen herself may be so confident in the success of her cause that she will overlook any danger to herself. It would be a signal success to save her without our own surrender, but that is impossible until we defeat the royal army."

"What say you, grand sorcerer?" said I. "Do you think my mission will be successful as regards the life of Lyone?"

"I have already foreseen this crisis," said he; "but I believe the end will be triumphant."

His majesty, in reply to my despatch, sent me a royal passport that admitted me to the fortress to converse with Lyone, and which would protect me until my return to Kioram.

"Tell her majesty," said the grand sorcerer, "not to fear the king; that we will save her, even should she nobly disdain to accept our surrender for her life."

"How do you propose to save her life in case she forfeits it?" I eagerly inquired.

"I cannot tell you," he replied, "for occult knowledge can only be apprehended by the initiated. Every great reform requires its martyr, and it may be that the queen will be our martyr, no matter what we do."

An audible groan escaped from the lips of all. Was it possible that even should we surrender we could not save the life of our adorable leader, and that to surrender would involve all in a common ruin? Was there ever in human history so great a crisis? I began to doubt the sorcerer's knowledge of the future. At the same time I felt that he alone could guide us in that hour of peril.

"Sorcerer," I cried, "for the love of Lyone, for the glory of our cause, tell me what to do! What shall I say to the queen? How shall I advise her to act for her own safety as well as ours?"

"Do not advise at all," said he. "Let the queen act for herself, and that will be the best solution of the difficulty."

"But should she insist on sacrificing herself, where would be our triumph?"

"The triumph will be assured," said he, "although to win our cause will require the greatest sacrifice to be made."

I began to think that Lyone and the sorcerer understood each other, and that her life would in any case be saved from the violence of death; and, taking this hopeful view of the situation, I departed for Calnogor, escorted by Flathootly and the astronomer.

As we swept toward the metropolis of Atvatabar I wondered if I would be permitted to make the journey in safety. Was the passport of the king but a *ruse de guerre* to entrap me?

I noticed here and there, as we neared the city, detachments of the royal *wayleals*, some suspended in the air, and others being drilled in globular masses in anticipation of the coming struggle.

When within ten miles of Calnogor a party of scouts intercepted us, who demanded to see our passports. The leader examined the royal decree with great minuteness, and only allowed us to proceed with apparent reluctance. I had reason to fear treachery, as I had but lately fought my way out of the country.

At length arriving above the royal fortress, we rapidly descended to the court-yard and inquired for the governor.

With what feelings of excitement I awaited my interview with Lyone! In what state would I find her, and how would she solve the riddle, a destiny that seemed impossible of solution?

The governor, accompanied by his armed staff, approached me, declaring how glad he was to be able to permit an interview with Lyone. His manner was altogether too suspiciously cheerful, and his body-guard surrounded us closely.

I hastened to assure the governor that my visit was made under the protection of the king, and showed him the royal decree. "I have come," I said, "to have an interview with her majesty upon the crisis, and that being accomplished, the royal mandate will secure me a free departure to Kioram."

"You can certainly see the ex-goddess," said the governor, "but you have no right to address her as her majesty, for such a title is high treason to their majesties, the king and queen of Atvatabar. As to your being free to leave the fortress again, I must confer with his majesty in that matter, as you are my prisoner until the king commands your release."

Was this a plot to capture me?

I was too anxious to see Lyone to think of my own safety just then, and requested the governor to lead me at once to her apartments.

"Follow me," said the governor, leading the way into the fortress. We passed along corridor after corridor until we arrived at a heavy gate of bronze, which the governor himself unlocked. We thereupon entered a spacious antechamber, severely furnished with large oaken benches on the marble floor.

I requested Flathootly and the astronomer to remain in the antechamber while I passed through another door unlocked for me by the governor.

I found myself alone in a spacious and finely decorated apartment, the gilded cage of Lyone. There were luxurious couches, and receptacles for books, and painted tapestries on the walls, and in the centre of the floor stood an aquarium, the home of strange animals and plants, from which rose a vase of gold that held a bouquet of the rarest flowers. The floor was covered with a semi-metallic carpet resembling linoleum. I sat down to await the coming of Lyone.

Presently the embroidered tapestry concealing the entrance to another chamber was moved aside, and the pale and breathless figure of Lyone stood before me. She came toward me, robed in a loose white silk gown. Her arms were outstretched, and her face wore an air of indescribable nobility and tenderness. I rushed forward and caught the glorious figure in my arms. It was fitting that our holiest emotions should at first find expression in a mutual deluge of kisses and tears.

CHAPTER 51

The Death of Lyone

When the ecstasy of our meeting had somewhat subsided I informed Lyone of the dreadful crisis in our affairs. I pointed out that to save her life the king required her army to disband itself, and her leaders to deliver themselves up as rebels and insurrectionists, to receive punishment for their so-called offences.

"Now," said I, "notwithstanding the fact that we can defeat the royal army in pitched battle, yet to save your precious life we are willing to surrender ourselves to his majesty."

"And what do you think would life be worth to me," said Lyone, her eyes flashing fire, "with my dearest friends slain, my cause ruined, and my soul covered with the shame of remorse, defeat and the disgrace of having purchased my miserable life by the death of the noblest of souls? I will go to the scaffold alone. You will conquer, and will avenge my death."

"Sweet goddess!" I cried, "you will not thus sacrifice yourself. What will victory be worth if you, for whom we fight, are not our proudest trophy? What avails the triumph of our cause if there remains no queen to possess the triumph? Your life is our life, your death our destruction. With you to fight for, any company of leaders will be successful. Let us surrender ourselves to make you free."

"It can never be," replied Lyone, "that you must suffer, one hundred souls for but one. I am that one, and the cause can more easily suffer the loss of one soul than the loss of all. That the soul may again possess freedom is worthy many a martyr. I only regret I have but one life to give for this blessed cause. I counsel you to depart and carry on the war you have so bravely begun, and in your hour of triumph remember Lyone."

"There is no cause if there is no Lyone," I pleaded. "Do not be your own enemy; accept the condition of freedom so freely offered you, and perhaps even we may still find some means of escape."

"The king, I know," said Lyone, "would much prefer your death to mine. He is exasperated at the loss of the fleet, and that, too, at the hands of strangers. Nothing would give him greater joy, and nothing such fame in the eyes of the nation, than to put yourself and your sailors to death. My capture and your present visit are but the fulfilment of his plot to destroy you. He thinks you will never allow me to be sacrificed, and so hopes for your annihilation. But in this he will be disappointed. In this terrible trial I have eaten my heart out. Without you, and without our faithful comrades, life would be less than worthless. This crisis can only be solved by heroic measures. I have decided for you all. Go!—go and avenge my death!"

I saw that Lyone had firmly steeled her soul for the sacrifice, tremendous at it was, and in the presence of such heroism it seemed sacrilege to again offer our less worthy lives for a life such as hers.

But a resolve so unsupportable agonized me. I clasped the divine girl in my arms in a transport of love and horror, and implored her again and again to accept life while it was offered her.

We stood beside the aquarium in the centre of the apartment, close to the vase of gold filled with flowers. Lyone, in a dazed state, reached for a flower, and in doing so touched the vase, and in a moment fell dead upon the floor!

I cannot dwell upon the horror of the scene. I rushed to the door of the apartment, and stood in the outer chamber, where waited my companions.

The governor of the fortress came forward to explain that I was his prisoner until he had heard from the king whether or not I should be permitted to leave the prison. I raised my spear, and with one blow transfixed the dog at my feet. He never spoke again!

The taking off of the governor was accomplished with so little disturbance that we passed through the body-guard, which was assembled in the outer corridor, without interference.

The situation was war!

Was it really true that our hope was dead, that our jewel, the glory of our cause, was lying cold and lifeless in her prison?

Lyone reached for a flower and in doing so touched the
vase and immediately fell dead upon the floor!

I was stunned with the first shock of the scene. I could only cry out, as though she were still alive, for her radiant soul to come and share our mutual bliss.

But when it clearly dawned upon me that the being for whose freedom I had resolutely laboured had become the victim of her murderers, that I could never again enfold her beauty with my love, however ardent or tender, I was petrified with horror.

My immediate comrades, to whom I communicated the tidings, grew white with the appalling news.

The one cry was, "Could Lyone, the idol of her army, the goddess of her people, be indeed dead? Was the voice that could conjure such love and devotion hushed forever?"

Leaving a guard to watch over the body of the goddess, I set out for Kioram. Barely escaping arrest at the hands of several *wayleals*, we arrived safely at the fortress. It was our wings and spears, and not the passport of the king, that saved us.

The council in Kioram, on hearing of the death of the queen, grew excited. The one desire in the hearts of all had been to save Lyone's life—but, alas!

I despatched a messenger to the king, charging him with the murder of the queen, and stating that I should exact retribution at his hands for the foul deed. I warned him not to do any injury to the person of her majesty, but deliver her dead body to the guard we would send, who would convey it to Egyplosis.

"This is a wound that infuriates me," said the grand sorcerer.

"It is the work of the jealous Koshnili and the murderous Bhoolmakar," said I; "and dearly will they answer for it! I must return at once to Calnogor, and take charge of the body for honourable sepulture."

"I think it better for Your Excellency to remain at the head of the army," said the grand sorcerer, "and allow me to undertake the removal of the body of the queen to Egyplosis. By keeping her death a secret from the army you will be able to defeat Coltonobory, and bring the king and Koshnili to justice. I shall delay the obsequies of the queen until victory is assured."

I agreed to this proposition, being anxious to bring the king to justice, and thereupon relieved General Charka of his command of the 21,000 *bockhockids*, giving him a guard of 100 *wayleals*, and requested him to proceed at once to the fortress of Calnogor, and, demanding the body of Lyone, bear it to Egyplosis for honourable sepulture.

The grand sorcerer, who had anticipated the refusal of Lyone to accept liberty at the price demanded, but did not apprehend her sudden death, had, during my absence, assisted at completing the organization of the army. I gave his command of the right wing of the army to Sir John Forbes, Captain Adams accepting a subordinate command.

Supreme General Hushnoly had fully armed the various battalions with *mitrailleuses* and electric spears, and had furnished all with electric wings.

I instructed Hushnoly to mobilize the army at once and order an immediate advance on Calnogor. All Kioram was alive with warlike preparations. The various generals and captains, accompanied by their *aides-de-camp*, flew over the city, calling their troops to arms. Both *wayleals* and *bockhockids*, soaring into the air, formed themselves into immense living globes, and in the hollow centre of each flew the commanding general and his subordinate officers. In less than an hour the entire army lay marshalled in the air, and Supreme General Hushnoly called me to review our forces.

It was a magnificent sight. High over Kioram stretched a line of enormous spheres composed of *wayleals* and *bockhockids* arranged in the following order:

The Army of Her Majesty Queen Lyone
His Excellency Lexington White, Commander-in-Chief

**General Sir John Forbes, commanding the right wing
of 21,000 bockhockids, as follows:
The Legion of Art commanded by General Yermoul
commander**

Phalanx of Poetry	Vice-General Ahornus	2,000
Phalanx of Painting	Vice-General Rhemegron	2,000
Phalanx of Architecture	Vice-General Vanablis	2,000
Phalanx of Sculpture	Vice-General Hitturkey	2,000
The Kioram Legion	General Nototherboc	5,000
Phalanx of Music	Vice-General Arnondar	2,000
Phalanx of Dancing	Vice-General Osornon	2,000
Phalanx of Drama	Vice-General Clamavappy	2,000
Phalanx of Decoration	Vice-General Drapasius	2,000

Supreme General Hushnoly, commanding the centre of the army, comprising 175,000 wayleals

	commander	
The Phalanx of Egyplosis	General Gerolio	5,000
Second Amazonian Phalanx	General Thoubool	2,500
First Fletyeming Brigade	General Starbottle	10,000
Third Fletyeming Brigade	General Goldrock	10,000
Second Volunteer Army	General Akerbole	25,000
First Volunteer Legion	General Swilkar	10,000
Third Volunteer Legion	General Karramby	10,000
Fifth Volunteer Legion	General Heralion	5,000
First Amazonian Phalanx	General Zooly-Soase	2,500
The Kioram Phalanx	General Pra	10,000
Second Fletyeming Brigade	General Flathootly	10,000
First Volunteer Army	General Jolgos	25,000
Third Volunteer Army	General Tarabesq	25,000
Second Volunteer Legion	General Garreoc	10,000
Fourth Volunteer Legion	General Botarnic	10,000
Sixth Volunteer Legion	General Nosofrassy	5,000

General Lapalme, commanding the left wing of 21,000 bockhockids, as follows:

	commander	
First Volunteer Legion *Bockhockids*	Vice-General Adams	5,000
Third Volunteer Legion *Bockhockids*	Vice-General Madneaf	2,000
Fifth Volunteer Legion *Bockhockids*	Vice-General Roumix	2,000
Seventh Volunteer Legion *Bockhockids*	Vice-General Dnublis	2,000
Ninth Volunteer Legion *Bockhockids*	Vice-General Dumargo	2,000
Second Volunteer Legion *Bockhockids*	Vice-General Doroccy	2,000
Fourth Volunteer Legion *Bockhockids*	Vice-General Darjiltis	2,000
Sixth Volunteer Legion *Bockhockids*	Vice-General Hieralto	2,000
Eighth Volunteer Legion *Bockhockids*	Vice-Gen. Napasacco	2,000

The army in all consisted of 182,000 men and 5,000 amazons. The amazons were dressed similar to the priests of Egyplosis—that is, in pale brown soft-leather tights, high boots emblazoned with scales of white metal, heavy spider-silk tunics, ornamented with beautiful embroidery and held close to the figure by a belt. The knapsack held the *magnic* cell, dynamo and wings, and also furnished the current for their spears.

As each *wayleal* required ample space for the movement of his or her wings, it will be seen that each living globe was of immense size, and the entire army became of enormous proportions as it lay stretched upon the air. I assumed supreme command as commander-in-chief, with Flathootly as special *aide-de-camp*, and gave orders for each globe to double up its *wayleals*, so that in each case there would be two globes, the outer or fighting force and the interior or reserve force. In the centre of each living shell was placed the commissariat department and the medical, musical and commanding staffs.

The death of Lyone had been kept a secret. The bands of each army began to play the "March of Lyone," and at the word of command the vast-flying mass of armed men moved grandly forward to Calnogor.

CHAPTER 52

The Battle of Calnogor

Long ere we reached Calnogor we discovered the royal army already marshalled to meet us. It lay above the city in globes of *wayleals* and *bockhockids* still more prodigious than ours. It was composed of three armies, ranged one above the other, and each army being equal in numbers to our own. Thus, forming a solid parallelogram of amazing magnificence, the royal army awaited our onset. Its *bockhockids*, formed in ten globes of ten thousand in each, and led by Grasnagallipas, the lord of invention, were the flower of the army, and occupied a central position, where possibly they would do the greatest damage to us. High overhead in a chair of state, supported by twenty *wayleals*, sat Coltonobory, commander-in-chief of those immense legions that were ready to do battle for the defeat of the cause of their late goddess and the honour of their king.

The sight of two such armies of winged gladiators sweeping toward each other in revolving globes was one of breathless interest. The approaching fight was a question of life or death to both combatants. Defeat to Aldemegry Bhoolmakar meant possibly the loss of crown and kingdom, and our defeat meant the annihilation of the party of reform and the cause of Lyone. We were eager to begin the fight without delay.

To obtain greater freedom of action, I led the army up into the region where there was no gravity. The movement was followed by a similar movement on the part of the royal armies, who rose like a swarm of locusts to meet us. The noise of so many wings in motion was like that of a roaring storm, and formed an inspiring accompaniment to the music that rang upon the sunlit air.

Here, fifty miles above the white city beneath, both armies closed upon each other. There was a fearful yell of "Bhoolmakar!" answered by as loud a shout of "Lyone!"

Our army was literally buried in the centre of the enemy. The impetuous priests of Egyplosis and the no less eager priestesses performed prodigies of valour.

Our *mitrailleuses* were a complete surprise to the enemy. Thousands of their *wayleals* were killed ere they could deliver a blow with their spears.

There was considerable slaughter on both sides, but the enemy depended largely on their *magnic* spears and shields, while we handled our guns with terrible effect.

The volunteer army under Hushnoly suffered greatly by the demoralization caused by the enemy's *bockhockids* under Grasnagallipas. The terrible legs of those machines destroyed the military formation of our *wayleals*, producing a continuous panic, and permitting the enemy's *wayleals* to work a ghastly slaughter in their broken ranks. In revenge our *bockhockids* with their more deadly weapons literally tore their globes to pieces. Notwithstanding our superior arms, the greater numbers of the enemy made them a match for us.

The rushing of wings, the explosions of the machine guns, the clashing of spears and the yells of the combatants made a scene of infernal horror. As the focus of battle swayed hither and thither, it left behind a trail of blood, dead and wounded bodies, broken wings, spears and revolvers. The debris of the battle simply floated out on the air, veritable clouds of disaster. Irregular masses of dead and wounded *wayleals* and broken *bockhockids* floated in heaps amid pools of blood.

The enemy could only succeed by stabbing, whereas our *wayleals* were scorpions whose guns were fatal. With the points of their spears they made great havoc in our battalions. But as long as our ammunition lasted their formations were immediately shrivelled up.

Coltonobory began to mass his army in the form of an immense outspreading hemisphere of the form of an open umbrella. His intention was to enclose us on all sides, and so if possible devour us. I at once ordered the army to take the form of a cone, each legion being a segment thereof, whose apex was formed of *bockhockids*, and whose base was wide circles of *wayleals*. With a blast of the trumpet I drove the entire army like an enormous javelin right through the heart of the foe, tearing a yawning chasm, half a mile in diameter, in his ranks!

We lost fully two thousand men in this movement, and the foe over ten thousand in killed and wounded.

The enemy, paralyzed by the onset, became consolidated into three or four immense globes. In front of these they placed their *bockhockids*, whose monstrous limbs alone could keep our spears at a safe distance. It was the intention of Coltonobory to ram us with the cohorts led by Grasnagallipas and his *bockhockids*.

Hastily re-forming our broken ranks as before, I ordered a flank movement, rapid and decisive. Our *bockhockids* plunged into a tremendous mass of *wayleals*. Into the chasm thus made in the ranks of the enemy General Zooly-Soase threw her amazons, protected on either side by the legion of priests of Egyplosis under Gerolio. The priestesses, whose spears were particularly long and powerful, did terrible execution. The enemy was for a time panic-stricken as the glorious girls made their successful onset. Their dramatic beauty and the flash of their spears made a scene of imposing grandeur. Coltonobory, recovering from his surprise, ordered his *bockhockids* to the centre of the fight. To prevent the sacrifice of the priestesses by overwhelming odds I sent the *bockhockids* of art to their assistance. These swept to the rescue like a flight of eagles, and the empyrean echoed to the roar of the combat.

The fighting now became general. The sunlit heavens seemed filled with the ferocity of war. The discharge of guns, the yells of *wayleals*, the trumpet signals of the commanders, the crash of swords and spears, the ceaseless motion of wings, and the long trail of dead and wounded combatants that followed the fight like the debris of a comet, was a sight but rarely beheld by human eyes.

Each army seemed so equally balanced—the king's army had the advantage in numbers and our own the advantage in weapons—that neither party could yet claim a victory. Further fighting seemed useless until some new tactics were employed; therefore I gave orders for a cessation of the battle, and caused flags of truce to be hoisted.

Both armies indeed required food and repose, and the wounded required immediate attention. The enemy was no less anxious for a truce than ourselves, consequently all fighting ceased and both armies withdrew. Several miles apart sentinels were placed on guard on outposts in the atmosphere, and our *wayleals* threw themselves upon the air in various attitudes of repose.

In company with Generals Hushnoly, Lapalme, Gerolio, Zooly-Soase, Thoubool, Charka, Yermoul, Starbottle and Goldrock, I visited the scene of the battle.

How ghastly the realities of war! There floated irregular piles of dead and wounded bodies, from which poured many a trickling stream of ruddy life, which formed immense cloud-pools of blood surrounding each ghastly pile. The heaped-up masses of the dead would vibrate, as some poor suffocating wretch struggled in his last agonies. Dr. Merryferry and his assistants hastily took possession of the wounded, and ministered to their necessities. Water was supplied them from the leathern bags of water that formed part of the commissariat supplies.

I ordered a detachment of *wayleals* to separate the living from the dead, and bear the wounded to Kioram for immediate attention.

The saddest sight of all was a cluster of fifty beautiful priestesses, embracing one another in the long caress of death. They had been slain with the *magnic* spears, so happily there were no gaping wounds from which the life-blood flowed. Ardsolus and Merga lay dead where the fight was hottest, both slain at once.

The dead and wounded twin-souls were sent to Egyplosis as quickly as possible, and the process of clearing the air of the havoc of war was carried out both by the enemy and ourselves with the greatest despatch.

The losses of the enemy were four times greater than ours, owing to the tremendous execution done by our gigantic pistols. The royal troops presented in ghastly groups every possible posture of the human body that could be created by rage, pain, fear or madness.

How I wished some eloquent historian could have floated through that abyss of horror on distended wings, and, pen in hand, describe its dramatic desolation and terror. Clouds of vultures and the *seemorgh* were devouring the dead bodies, and, as they fought for choice morsels, flapped their wings in pools of gore. Many of the combatants, including some of my own sailors, were drowned in globes of blood.

CHAPTER 53

Victory

The *wayleals* rested and slept outstretched upon the air close
to the scene of battle. Not having any weight as regarded external
objects, they mutually attracted each other, and to obtain freedom
and rest without being crushed together into suffocating masses
of men, they were formed into companies of one hundred each,
with their feet pressing against solid cylinders of spears. Mutual
gravity was sufficient to hold them together, and each *wayleal*
spread himself upon the air, as upon a bed of down, enjoying
luxurious repose.

I had slept I know not how long, in company with the leaders
of our army, when I was awakened by Flathootly, who informed
me that a trusty messenger from Grasnagallipas, lord of invention
and general of the king's *bockhockids*, desired to see me as bearer of
an important despatch from his master.

The messenger, saluting, handed me the following document:

*To His Excellency Lexington White, Commander-in-Chief of the
Army of Queen Lyone, from Grasnagallipas, General of the Royal
Bockhockids, Greeting:*

General Grasnagallipas begs to report that he and his
bockhockids have ever been in sympathy with the late goddess,
but were prevented from espousing her cause by the overwhelming presence of the royal army in Calnogor. To show
his detestation of the horrible act of criminal cowardice on
the part of his majesty, he offers his sword and command
of *bockhockids* to the cause of the late adorable goddess and
queen of Atvatabar, and on the acceptance of such assistance
by Your Excellency will at once leave the ranks of the royal

army and enter that of her late majesty, to fight for the sacred cause and assist in punishing a perfidious king.

Grasnagallipas

The loss attending the withdrawal of the priests and priestesses to form a guard of honour to the illustrious dead was more than compensated for by the re-enforcements under Grasnagallipas, to whom I sent a message of gracious acceptance of his services.

The army being fully aroused for conflict, had the satisfaction of welcoming re-enforcements from two opposite directions, *viz.*, the fifty thousand *bockhockids* under Grasnagallipas and the *terrorite* battery under command of General Rackiron.

As was expected, the departure of the bravest general in the royal army was the signal for a renewal of hostilities, and Coltonobory, mad at the serious defection of his troops, at once assumed the offensive. He had received a large recruitment of *wayleals*, and felt as formidable as ever. His army swept down upon us with warlike music rolling like thunder, and cries of "Bhoolmakar!" The king himself, having dealt us his most terrible blow, was a witness to the onset of his hosts. He sat aloft in a golden palanquin, borne on the shoulders of his followers, with a body-guard on either side.

The advance guard of the enemy consisted of several regiments, armed with our own hand *mitrailleuses*, taken from prisoners. These did a terrible execution among our *wayleals*.

Grasnagallipas, anxious to undo the injury he inflicted on us during the first battle, and emulous of the prowess of our own forty thousand *bockhockids*, plunged headlong amid the foe, creating a panic wherever his gigantic birds descended. He fought like a demon, neither asking nor giving quarter.

General Rackiron, having got his *terrorite* battery in position, was eager to check the advance of the enemy by saluting him with a few aerial torpedoes. There was some delay incidental to the first actual operations of a hastily-constructed battery, but the daring ingenuity of the professor overcame every obstacle. Each gun, supported by fifty men, possessed a solid foundation from which to direct its operations.

The enemy, though harassed by our *bockhockids*, had worked into the centre of our army by sheer weight of numbers. Our *wayleals*, having exhausted their ammunition, had to fall back on their electric spears, and at times were obliged to retire in confusion. At this juncture a shell of *terrorite* exploded among the foe with thrilling effect, destroying at least two hundred *bockhockids*.

Coltonobory, who evidently attributed the disaster to an explosion of gunpowder in his own ranks, closed up the broken columns and renewed the attack.

Three explosions in rapid succession, right in the centre of the enemy, caused the greatest consternation, and produced a frightful gap, where but a moment before the air was thick with an armed host.

Generals Yermoul, Gerolio, Lapalme and Grasnagallipas plunged with their *bockhockids* into the living cavern produced by the torpedoes, and with their spears mowed down thousands of the panic-stricken *wayleals*.

Another *terrorite* shell, thrown in the direction of the king, destroyed a few hundred of his protectors and induced his majesty to seek safety in immediate flight.

Not wishing to lose so important an enemy, I ordered General Flathootly and the second legion of *fletyemings* to start in hot pursuit of the royal party and bring me back the king, dead or alive. Flathootly, delighted with his mission, started off at once in pursuit of Bhoolmakar.

The *terrorite* battery proved our most effective weapon in castigating the enemy. I could not thank Professor Rackiron sufficiently for his great genius and mechanical skill in so rapidly perfecting his weapons, which were modelled on the plan of the guns belonging to the *Polar King*. Every discharge proved a blast of destruction to the foe.

The deadly missiles wrought a fearful slaughter, steadily decimating the ranks of the royal army, which had no similar weapons with which to retaliate upon us.

The frightened hosts, constantly changing their focus, left behind them vast heaps of the dead and wounded and globes of floating blood.

On one occasion the first brigade of *fletyemings*, led by General Starbottle, in eagerly pursuing the enemy dashed through a pool of blood three feet in thickness, and every *wayleal* emerged dripping with gore.

AT THIS JUNCTURE, A SHELL OF TERRORITE EXPLODED AMONG THE FOE WITH THRILLING EFFECT, ESTROYING AT LEAST TWO HUNDRED BOCKHOCKIDS.

Coltonobory, finding further resistance useless, at once surrendered himself and his army to our mercy.

My brave *wayleals*, flushed with victory, saluted me with cries of "Long live Lexington White, King of Atvatabar!"

But what was success now without the one priceless soul to share my triumph?

Did ever glory so grand and defeat so terrible so mingle themselves in human experience?

My *wayleals*, now for the first time hearing of the death of their queen, would have torn Coltonobory to pieces had I not protected him.

I knew he was personally innocent, and my *wayleals* were already in pursuit of the king.

We entered Calnogor in triumph. I heard on all sides a wail of lamentation for Lyone, mingled with applause for the conqueror.

It was a scene in which conquest and misery, rapture and failure, life and death, were indissolubly united.

Chapter 54

Reincarnation

The grand sorcerer Charka and his guard had with reverend flight borne the body of their goddess Lyone to the palace of souls, mourning the death of their adored, who had been so precious, so beautiful, so holy.

The high priestess and the grand sorceress, together with the priests and priestesses of Egyplosis, on hearing of the death of Lyone, departed at once for Egyplosis, to mourn the death of their goddess.

Lyone was dead!

Ah me! what was triumph then, without my soul of souls to share its delights? The blessed cup of joy, quivering to the brim, was about to touch my yearning lips when it was dashed aside by a treacherous hand. Well might the crownless Bhoolmakar laugh in whatever damnable retreat he had retired to! His revenge was complete.

Oh, the pity of it! The young, the adorable, the divine soul who was just about to remount her throne to receive a purer adoration from her people; she who was to be queen of Atvatabar, slain treacherously, within sight of the Bormidophia, wherein she had so long been worshipped.

It was impossible for me to remain longer on the field of battle. I wanted to fling myself on that once happy form and kiss her death-cold lips!

I left Coltonobory and his surrendered army in the hands of the supreme general Hushnoly, and started at once for Egyplosis. As my wings devoured the leagues of air I thought, was this the climax for which I fought? I flew along with none to share my torture. My heart was rent wide open, and in my agony I rolled upon the air as I flew, for brain and soul seemed an ocean of fire.

I arrived at Egyplosis full of anguish. With quivering lips and burning tears I staggered into the portal that led to the subterranean palace where I knew my loved one was laid. I silently entered the magnificent abode of the sorcerer, horror-stricken with despair.

Suddenly, beyond the labyrinth I heard a golden sound, the sound of that blessed bell that once before rolled its waves of delight over my spirit. I stood leaning against a pillar, dissolved in its bewitching moans, luxuriating in the Agapamone of music breathed from the delirious bronze. I heard wafted from the mysterious temple the refrain of thousands of voices chanting a ritual of love and peace. The multitudinous sound seemed so soft and so thrilling, so powerful and so holy, that I was eager to know if such burden of love was the sorrowing passion of the twin-souls in honour of their dead goddess.

I saw through the open doors of the temple a moving throng of twin-souls, swaying in masses hither and thither, with naked feet on the *aquelium* floor. On every forehead burned an electric star, giving a spectral flush to the scene. That was the singing multitude I had heard, the *hierophants* of the holy soul.

As my eyes grew accustomed to the objects before me, I saw the interior of the temple, on whose sculptured walls and roof roses woven of smouldering electric fires revealed their burning bloom. Wires of platinum, *terrelium*, and *aquelium* had been woven into a filigree of roses, with leaves and stems made red hot by the electric current. High above the sculptured dado rose strange windows of illuminated glass, in colours sad and brilliant, made visible by thousands of electric lights hidden in the sculptured recesses behind each window. The subject of each jewelled pane was a tableau of reincarnation, in which the figures of sorcerers and magicians, robed in splendid attire, gave life to beings that had died.

The frieze was one continual blaze of colour, formed also of enamelled glass emblazoned with life-sized processional figures and illuminated with incandescent lights.

In a distant part of the temple, on a *terrelium* pedestal, I again saw a monster of gold, with a terrible head and outstretched wings.

As I surveyed this stupendous figure, I discovered that it held in its fore paws an immense helix of *terrelium* wire, ten feet in length and nine feet in diameter. One end of the wire was joined to ten thousand wires, whose extremities, terminating in *terrelium* wands, were held by the twin-souls. Each priest held a wand in his right hand, and each priestess a wand in her left, and their disengaged arms were wound around one another's waists.

The other end of the voluminous wire forming the helix terminated in the rivet of an enormous spring that held a circular *rheotome* close to the circular mouth of the helix.

On a pedestal level with the upheld battery, reached by a spiral stairway, stood the grand sorcerer Charka, robed in tissues of white silk and golden embroidery. An assistant priest turned a wheel that moved a screw point toward the spring of the *rheotome*. The moment the screw point touched the spring, the circular plate over the heart of the helix began to vibrate audibly. Another turn of the screw, and a vital thrill filled the temple with its sonorous music.

I then knew that all that mysterious structure with its *terrelium* wires was an immense spiritual battery, charged with the life and love of ten thousand souls. The vital fluid, generated in the yearnings of ideal love, flooded the helix with its vitality and induced a magnetism of life that made the *rheotome* vibrate with emotion, until the whole temple shook with the thrilling sound.

The priests and priestesses sang their *ritournels* of passion and love, and the grand sorcerer waved his wand over the monster's head. It was then the thought of Lyone filled my soul with a terrible yearning.

Where was her hapless body? Was this feast of passion that I beheld her obsequies, or could it be some occult incantation to raise her from the dead?

The thought fired my brain with madness! Oh, that it might be possible for her to live again, if only for one hour, that she might hear of victory! All at once I seemed to know that Lyone was laid in the heart of the helix held by the *hehorrent*. I knew, oh, I knew that the spectacle I beheld was the ceremony of reincarnation. I knew that the goddess was being swathed with currents of life from her votaries. How I blessed those living batteries, so faithful in their glorious work! How I blessed the adorable sorcerer who conducted this precious ministry of life, who focussed the love of thrilling souls upon the person of their goddess!

I stood transfixed to the floor, watching with straining eyes those flamens of life perform their ritual of reincarnation. The air of the temple grew warm as blood, and infinitely holy. Soft and piercing music rose from unseen chambers of the temple, which, mingling with the blessed storm of life that beat upon the mouth of the helix, seemed to whirl away my senses.

The first circle of souls around the dragon comprised the votaries of Bishano, or Sorcery; Hielano, or Magic; Nidialano, or Astrology; Padamano, or Soothsaying.

The second circle embraced the adepts of Niano, or Witchcraft; Redohano, or Wizardry; Biccano, or the Oracle; Kielano, or Augury; Tocderano, or Prophecy; Jiracano, or Geomancy; Jocdilano, or Necromancy.

The third circle embraced the *hierophants* of Orphitano, or Conjuration; Orielano, or Divination; Pridano, or Clairvoyance; Ecthyano, or Mesmerism; Cideshano, or Electro-Biology; Omdolophano, or Theosophy; Bishanamano, or Spiritualism.

How shall I describe the spell of that hour? Glimmering figures, clad in robes of finest gossamer of the rarest colours, powderings and embroiderings, sang the songs of pained and enraptured sensibility.

They loved, they wept, they supplicated Harikar!

I saw twin-souls embrace in infinite tenderness, and again with ecstatic enthusiasm. It was a sea of supernatural emotion. It was an abyss of affection, filled with a whirlwind of bold, delicate, enormous love.

A *religieuse* of Tocderano shouted, "She will live again!"

A priest of Biccano sang, "She will be born again of mystical, chivalrous love!"

As the enraptured host sang of life and love, I felt a million exaggerations of the delicacies of emotion. I felt as though fanned with warm winds blowing over wildernesses of flowers. I heard the multiplied splendour of bells, roaring like the soft vociferations of far-off tropic seas. I heard music ineffably tender and sublime, wailing its intoxicating melodies. I saw strange illuminations dissolve in never-ceasing explosions of colour on the glorified windows. I saw upon the floor endless arabesques of twin-souls, fantastically entangled and unrolled.

Suddenly the temple shook with an explosion of sound that seemed the concentrated madness of drums and organs and bells; the roaring of the *rheotome* grew deafeningly louder, mingling with a strange shivering sound, such as is produced by the suddenly transfixed wheels of a flying locomotive, tearing the metals into a hissing blaze. From the mouth of the *hehorrent* streamed a blaze of fire. I looked where the sorcerer stood—

Heavens and earth! He was holding Lyone in his arms, alive from the living battery! Lyone, the peerless soul of souls, alive once more and triumphant over death!

The temple whirled around me rapid as fire, and I fell to the ground insensible with joy!

CHAPTER 55

Lexington and Lyone Hailed King and Queen of Atvatabar

The extraordinary scenes attending the reincarnation of Lyone had left me, when I returned to my senses, exhausted with emotion. It was gloriously true that she who was the Supreme Goddess, she who had suffered death in the fortress of Calnogor, had been restored to life by the powerful necromancy of the sorcerer and his college of twin-souls.

I rushed forward in presence of the entire congregation and embraced in turn the radiant Lyone and the beloved Charka.

I took her living figure in my arms. She was in a limp, tranquil condition, yet happily alive. The happy priests and priestesses shouted with enthusiasm: "Long live Lexington and Lyone, King and Queen of Atvatabar!"

It was a blissful moment to us both. The future, that had lain under the terrors of death, now smiled again. I gazed upon my beloved's face with unspeakable tenderness. I saw that she smiled at me sweetly.

Her apostasy was victorious, but who could have supposed that martyrdom and reincarnation were the path to glory? She had exchanged the crown of the goddess for that of a queen.

Handing my precious burden back to Charka again, I addressed the congregation as follows:

"Priests and priestesses of Egyplosis, *wayleals* and amazons of the sacred and victorious army, I thank you from the depths of my heart for your loyal salutation, but I particularly thank the grand sorcerer Charka, and you his *hierophants*, for your glorious restoration of her majesty to life, king and crown, thus defeating the cow-

Heavens and earth! He was holding Lyone in his arms, alive from the living battery! Lyone, the peerless soul of souls, alive once more and triumphant over death.

ardly crime of the ex-king. By reason of our victory, their majesties King Bhoolmakar and Queen Toplissy of Atvatabar are deposed from the throne, and his ex-majesty, by reason of his great crime, is condemned to death.

"The causes that led to this revolution are already known to you. The time was ripe for a reform in Egyplosis. Regulation and not suppression will be our aim, and they who have helped us to this great conquest will not go unrewarded.

"After her tremendous experiences, the queen will require a season of absolute rest to restore her to perfect health. I will entrust the task of establishing a reform of Egyplosis in competent hands, assisted by a council of your own representatives. The present crisis is too overwhelmingly happy to permit me to say more to you. On another occasion I will thank you more effectively."

This speech was received with enthusiastic applause.

On a litter, supported by six twin-souls, Lyone was tenderly borne out of the temple. We departed amid joyful paeans of music, our pathway being strewn with flowers. We reached the supernal palace, and saw from every roof floating the flag of Lyone, in token of our victory.

In her palace, on a couch of pale green velvet, lay the reincarnated form of Lyone, filled with a sense of luxurious rest. The experiences of the past few days demanded a period of profound repose. Her face wore a blessed and triumphant smile. She had paid with suffering for that Nirvana of joy. With reincarnation, or rather resurrection, had come a holier transfiguration of form and face. She was still too weak physically to discuss at length the great changes that had come to her or to the history of Atvatabar.

She was the symbol of the more sensitive souls of humanity, who, capable of intense suffering and delirious rapture, must needs purchase all their joys with heart-rending experiences. The culture that comes from agony is our most priceless possession, and brings the soul to every feast, as well as the body. The body, daily slain by suffering, is resurrected with a purer flesh, and receives a reincarnated soul fitted for ideal delights. It has attained a measure of Nirvana. It anticipates immortality by reason of suffering and love. Lyone had more than all achieved an ideal existence. Before she would be able to return again to the realities of the world, it was necessary that time should be given her for physical and spiritual invigoration.

"I feel neither pain nor fatigue," said Lyone; "my senses seemed drowned in a delicious rest. You tell me that I have been dead and brought to life again, and although I have no sense of having passed through the agony, I must believe you. I remember touching a golden vase of flowers in my prison, and then all became a blank until I stood with the grand sorcerer in the temple of reincarnation."

"That vase you touched," said I, "was connected with a powerful *magnic* battery, which was placed in your apartment by the king's order, to kill you. Grasnagallipas, leader of the king's *bockhockids*, on learning of his royal master's treachery, immediately transferred his allegiance and important command to our army, and was mainly instrumental in securing the victory."

"So our cause has triumphed," said Lyone; "and what has become of the king?"

"The king," I replied, "is king no more. I am King of Atvatabar and you are my beloved queen."

Lyone turned aside her face and wept tears of joy.

"Our marriage," I added, "will inaugurate the reign of a religion of wedded love, and you will sit with me as queen on the throne of Atvatabar."

"That will be glorious," said Lyone, "but I fear our marriage will also end ideal love and sorcery, and the Nirvana of a hundred years, the fairest products of Egyplosis."

"Do you see now," I said, "that ideal joys in the world can only be built on more extensive miseries? It would be a glorious thing to build houses of jewels, but so long as real jewels are so rare, we must be content with rocks. Still, there are jewels, and in Atvatabar I learn they are much more abundant than on the outer planet; therefore it might be proper for twin-souls to walk on love's enchanted ground for a brief though definite period."

Lyone had undergone transfiguration. Beautiful as a spirit, her figure seemed plastic porcelain. Death had made more luminous the splendid sculpture of her face. As she spoke, it seemed to me that we had closed the door on the infelicitous experiences of actual life, and were opening the gates of a more glorious day.

I informed Lyone of the arrival of the two vessels from the outer world, and of the great services of Captain Adams and Sir John Forbes in turning the tide of battle by sea in our favour. She was delighted at the prospect of meeting fresh visitors from the outer world, and in due time Captain Adams and Sir John Forbes and their entire ships' companies stood before her who was delighted with the fuller acquaintance thus made with the people of the outer world. Both the captains and their officers realized her ideal of exotic manhood, which combined stalwart proportions with intellectual benignity of face.

Sir John Forbes was very complimentary in his praise of the grace and beauty of Lyone and her associates among the priestesses of Egyplosis. He considered Lyone to possess spiritual beauty to an extraordinary degree. The wonderful pale-gold of her complexion was in marked contrast to the old-gold complexion of the women of Atvatabar. He also praised the splendid beauty of Zooly-Soase and Thoubool, who were indeed magnificent women.

My success encouraged the strangers to consider that conquest in other realms of Plutusia would be an easy accomplishment, especially if armed with such weapons as those possessed by the sailors of the *Polar King*. But even admitting superiority of weapons, they thought it a marvellous thing that one small vessel with but eighty men could conquer fifty millions of people.

In my own mind I thought it possible that the *Polar King* might conquer still greater kingdoms, and that in time I might be Plutarch of Plutusia. But in such business one realm at a time is enough. I suggested to our visitors that there were at least twenty realms, each as large as Atvatabar, in this interior planet, that would give them opportunity for adventure.

"We also wish," said I, "both the United States and England to know that our ports are open for commerce, and foreign trade is welcome to seek our shores. We have gold enough to enrich all comers from the outer world."

The eyes of our visitors and their officers glistened at this intelligence. And well they might, for Atvatabar was worth a thousand realms like Golconda or Peru. We had wealth for literature and science, art and commerce, which rightly used would make Atvatabar the wonder of the ages, a realm of palaces and temples, the fountain of wisdom, the mother of art, and its commerce would make both the earths rich beyond the dreams of fortune. I was determined that the royal magnificence of the thrones of all time on either surface of the earth should be outrivaled by the supreme glory of that of Atvatabar. I knew there was an inspiration to human endeavour that magnificence alone can give, and would use my wealth to advance the happiness of humanity.

Lyone being at last fully restored to health, we determined to delay no longer the important ceremonies of our royal marriage and coronation, not only to complete our happiness, but to really establish the government on a personal basis so agreeable to the wishes and customs of the people.

Lyone's aerial yacht was made ready for the journey to Calnogor. It was large enough to carry the captains, officers, and men of the *Mercury* and *Aurora Borealis*, the captain, officers, and men of the *Polar King*, as well as Lyone and myself and the great officers of state and retinue. All being safely on board, I gave the signal for flight, and in a moment we were launched on the air with tremendous speed.

CHAPTER 56

Our Reception in Calnogor

The royal city of Calnogor never contained such splendour, such importance of historic event, nor such a multitude of people, as on the occasion of the triple event of our marriage, our coronation, and the reception of the distinguished strangers from beyond the Polar Gulf. How shall the glory of that day be described? What occult power must animate the pen that must be at once the stylus of a poet, the brush of a painter, and the wand of a magician, to do justice to the splendid theme?

The entire army, composed of half a million *wayleals*, had come from Calnogor to Kioram to escort the aerial ship containing myself, Lyone, and the distinguished strangers, together with our retinue and the sailors from America and Great Britain. On either side of the ship the army was massed in two equal hosts, waving a million of wings. Either army was led by a phalanx of flying *bockhockids*, led by Yermoul and Grasnagallipas. A body-guard of *wayleals* bore fifty gigantic golden sceptres, being the ensigns of sovereignty over the fifty provinces of the kingdom.

All the way to Calnogor, five hundred miles distant, the army performed the most incredible evolutions to the measured thunders of music. Its legions massed themselves in ever-whirling globes, undulating all along the line of flight like monstrous serpents.

Again, mighty cones of *wayleals* would stream from our yacht on both sides, upward and backward, like a blaze of comet splendour.

Then, suddenly, globes of *wayleals* would surround us, globe within globe flying alternately in different directions; and we seemed to move on the centre of another earth.

To describe the endless flight and counter-flight, the concentration and radiation of the *wayleals* in grand review, would be impossible. Captain Adams and Sir John Forbes were astounded at the extraordinary evolutions possible to winged men in a world where there is practically no gravity. The army moved in Daedalian march; it was at times sinuous with labyrinthic movement to the sound of drums and the roar of bugles. The *wayleals* formed arches and crowns, conchoidal convolutions, zones and wheels, hemispheres and globes, cones and pyramids. The yacht was clothed with sublime torsions, peristaltic splendours, and immense radiations of living bodies. It was the grandest movement of men ever seen on earth.

We were again completely surrounded by a single globe of *wayleals*, in the centre of which moved the yacht with fearful speed. The globe moved as fast as we, and the living shell obliterated both earth and sun from, sight. Then, with a roar of artillery, the globe exploded, and lo! before us the infinite golden dome of the Bormidophia, the marble city of Calnogor, and dense multitudes of excited people!

The city was decorated with the conquering flag of Lyone and with flowers; and the inscriptions on the triumphal arches were: "Long live Lexington and Lyone, King and Queen of Atvatabar!"

The entire army, augmented by the allegiance of the defeated king's troops, headed by the supreme general Hushnoly, received us at the entrance to the city.

Pending the reconstruction of the government, law and order were being administered by Hushnoly, assisted by a military council consisting of all the victorious leaders.

The festivities incidental to our entry into Calnogor and the public rejoicings over the reincarnation of Lyone lasted several days. I took occasion at a reception at the royal palace to confer suitable honours and rewards on my victorious generals. I created the supreme general Hushnoly a noble of the first rank under the title of *goiloor*, or Duke of Calnogor, and confirmed his authority as commander-in-chief of the army, and Zooly-Soase was also created Goiloose of Calnogor. General Gerolio was created *boiroon* of Swerga, an inland city, and appointed vice-commander to Hushnoly. General Rackiron was made *goiloor* of Swondab, and his appointment as general of the royal artillery was confirmed. General Lapalme was made *goiloor* of Kioram and commandant of the fortress. General Yermoul, who retired from the army, was made *goiloor* of Gnaphisthasia. The grand sorcerer Charka was made *goiloor*, and the grand sorceress Goiloose of Egyplosis, while Grasnagallipas was created *boiroon* of Invention and General of the Royal *Bockhockids*.

General Starbottle was made *goiloor* of Savasse, a province of the kingdom, and Prime Minister of the government. General Goldrock, who was now fully recovered from his wounded leg, was made Royal Treasurer and *goiloor* of Blindis, a distant city. Dr. Merryferry was made Minister of Foreign Affairs; General Nototherboc, Minister of Naval Affairs; General Pra, Chief of Police; and General Flathootly, Minister of War.

I assumed the title of "His Majesty Lexington, King of Atvatabar," and Lyone that of "Her Majesty Lyone, Queen of Atvatabar," of equal authority and dignity to myself.

I issued a decree confirming all titles and dignities for the life of the recipient only. As a man cannot transfer his character or abilities to his children, more especially the virtues that made him famous, so neither could he transfer his titles or dignities to posterity; and a man who had no other claims to greatness than the plumes he had borrowed from his father, should be despised for strutting in artificial glory.

The Borodemy was maintained, and no restriction of popular or constitutional liberty already enjoyed by the people was permitted. All titles given to men who were simply fortunate enough to receive a majority of votes, making them representatives of the people in the Borodemy, were abolished, and men only were honoured by virtue of great services accomplished. All members of the Borodemy were paid liberal salaries, on the principle that a prince had no more right to an appropriation from the public purse than a legislator. All public measures adopted by the Borodemy were subject to the veto of the Royal Council, composed of the king, queen, and actual members of the government.

I need not say that the victory of Lyone over death and the fact of our army having conquered in battle gave us unlimited power. I was the supreme lord of Atvatabar; but, nevertheless, in the hour of triumph I determined to use my power for the good of the people. The sensation caused by the return of Lyone to life had stirred all Atvatabar with feelings of the profoundest awe and loyalty. Vast crowds of people came as pilgrims to see their queen and offer congratulations.

Had the old creed, with its worship of Lyone and Harikar, not fallen with the success of our arms, Lyone would undoubtedly have been worshipped anew as goddess more devotedly than ever; but the revolution being founded on antagonism of the old faith to social welfare and the laws of nature, a new creed must necessarily take its place.

The new creed of one body and one soul was based on order, truth, justice, benevolence and temperance. This I styled the Remeliora, or better thing to that which had gone before. The new creed gave the soul mastery of its feelings, and love was measured by a regular throb. Souls becoming stronger and more masculine were the better able to bear the pulsations of joy and despair. They could sustain their emotions with a cordial enthusiasm, and passion, no longer a frantic flame, became a soft and abiding fire.

I appointed the grand sorcerer Pontiff of Remeliorism, giving him authority to formulate a code of ethics that all could adhere to. With such a code as a solid foundation, I hoped in time to establish a purer faith than that possessing only the human soul for its deity.

Not many days after our coming to Calnogor, and while still engaged in settling the government of the kingdom, we received a visit from Hushnoly and Zooly-Soase. It was with feelings of pain that we heard the object of the supreme general's visit.

With a voice softened with emotion Hushnoly told his story. In carrying out the reforms at Egyplosis made necessary by the success of the army of the late goddess, a great difficulty presented itself. It was found that, notwithstanding the fact that all of the priests and priestesses had fought for Lyone and the new faith, as against the old order of things, nearly one-half of the twin-souls were still at heart as great devotees of Harikar and hopeless love as ever, while the remaining half had renounced the practices of Egyplosis in common with their queen. It was found impossible to change the faith of the entire priesthood in a moment, so to speak, and many still believed that the old faith possessed fruits of self-sacrifice, culture, spirit-power, and the ideal life, such as the new state of things would utterly destroy. Hushnoly and the high priestess were in sympathy with the adherents of the ancient faith, and they too believed in sacrificing marital rights for the sake of the ideal existence.

The revelation of such a spiritual revolt in Egyplosis, headed, too, by the man and woman who had sacrificed so much for the cause of Lyone and myself, revealed human nature in a new light, while it astounded us. I had foolishly supposed the supremacy of the sword could carry dominion into spiritual things, and that Egyplosis was wholly converted to the new faith, to Remeliorism.

The situation was extremely painful.

"Supreme general and high priestess," I said, "both her majesty Lyone and myself are greatly indebted to your courage and support in the late struggle; a support heroically given us in spite of your own secret faith. Is there no way by which you might be reconciled, both of you, to the new order of things?"

"We fear not, your majesty," said Hushnoly.

"Will riches, will honours not tempt you?"

"Your majesty, we cannot be tempted," replied he.

"You are doubtless aware," I continued, "that it would be impossible for the government to recognize, much less give support to, a system of faith for the destruction of which the war was carried on. Much as we love you, much as we love the priests and priestesses, we cannot give allegiance to the old faith, We cannot, we dare not countenance your creed. It will be therefore impossible for yourselves or your people to remain at Egyplosis, which will be the chief shrine of the new faith hereafter."

"We have already anticipated all this," said Hushnoly, "and do not propose even to remain in Atvatabar."

"And where do you go to?" said Lyone, in astonishment.

"Well, your majesty," replied he, "we have determined to take possession of the sphere Hilar, one of the untenanted spheres above us, and there create an ideal world. Thus we will relieve your majesty of all embarrassment and remove any obstacle in the way of religious or political reform."

I was bewildered by the reply of Hushnoly, as I had never before heard of any one desiring to dwell on the wandering sphere Hilar, and begged an explanation.

"Hilar, as your majesty is probably aware," said Hushnoly, "is a sphere twenty-five miles in diameter that floats in space at a distance of fifty miles from the surface of Atvatabar. It revolves on its own axis at the rate of a mile an hour, making a complete revolution in seventy-five hours. It also revolves around Swang once during a hundred aerial revolutions, or in one hundred of its days. It has tropic, temperate, and frigid zones, with perpetual ice capping its poles. It contains one ocean of irregular outline and has one continent. The areas of land and water are about equal. There are two mountain ranges, turning from a given centre of upheaval and determining the configuration of the land. There are one hundred islands in the sea and a dozen rivers on the land. In fact, it seems to be a facsimile in climate, geologic, and physiographical conditions to the outer world you have come from; and on such a sphere we propose to build a new throne for Harikar, and seat thereon another goddess like the virtuous and glorious Lyone."

"Ah," said Lyone, "I know who that other goddess will be—she will be the fair Zooly-Soase."

The high priestess blushed in her robe of crimson silk, making her golden beauty superb and precious. As for Hushnoly, it was evident the destiny of his counterpart soul was already fully anticipated. Her ascension to the throne of a goddess would virtually make him ruler of Hilar.

"We desire, your majesty," said he, "to resign our titles and offices of high priest and priestess of Egyplosis and supreme general and general of the amazons of the royal army of Atvatabar. Our only request is that we be allowed to depart to Hilar, together with such of the priests and priestesses of Harikar as are willing to follow us thither. Also, that all new converts to Harikar desirous of emigrating to our spiritual kingdom will be secured freedom of departure from Atvatabar for all time hereafter."

I willingly granted Hushnoly and Zooly-Soase their request, and added: "You both shall be promptly and liberally rewarded for the great services rendered your king and queen in time of war, as well as recompensed for past services to the country in Egyplosis and for loss of estate in Atvatabar."

I promised to issue a royal decree embodying all of the aforesaid liberties and bounties in favour of Hushnoly and his fair consort and their followers. The late high priest and high priestess, with grateful, cordial adieus, departed from the audience-chamber.

I thereupon appointed General Rackiron the commander-in-chief of the army in place of Hushnoly, with General Gerolio the vice-commander.

CHAPTER 57

The Combined Ceremony
of Marriage and Coronation

The day of our marriage and coronation as king and queen of Atvatabar at length arrived. The scene in the Bormidophia was of surpassing magnificence. For the first time in history Lyone sat before the throne of the gods not as goddess, but as queen; and I, her compeer, as king sat beside her. Lyone was attired in a loosely-fitting robe of old-ivory silk, over which was an outer network of lace formed of thread of gold, the design being a golden sun on the breast, which, with its long streaming rays, was held together by a golden cobweb that covered the entire figure of the queen. She also wore her belt of jewels. Beside her stood a page bearing her crown as Queen of Atvatabar. For myself I had caused to be made a knightly suit of golden armour that shone mightily as I wore it on that eventful occasion.

The priestesses of Egyplosis, taught by a priest of decorative art from Gnaphisthasia, had been for some time engaged in creating a tapestry of lace, wrought with a thread of heavy bullion gold, as a bridal gift to their queen. The design took the form of a winged twin-soul in loving converse, in the centre, surrounded by Atvatabarese arabesque—all held together by a most poetic fancy of floral scrolls and formed of gold thread lace work. This enormous piece of work was twelve feet in width, seventy-five feet in length, and four inches in thickness. The gold used in its marvellous intricacies weighed five tons. Such was the glorious piece of tapestry that was hung over the side of the throne, and which, reaching downward three-fourths of its height, concealed a considerable part of the august structure.

Around us swept the amphitheatre, filled with the leaders of the army and navy, the great officers of government, and the people of Atvatabar. Surrounding the base of the throne, sat those priests and priestesses of Egyplosis who had embraced the new faith of "one body and one soul."

The pontiff Charka performed the marriage ceremony when the roar of guns had subsided. He performed his august duties sustained by the splendours of music and the adoration of the people.

"Wilt thou have this woman, Lyone, Queen of Atvatabar, to be thy wife until death, according to the customs of our people and not according to the customs of Egyplosis?"

"I will."

"Wilt thou have this man, Lexington, King of Atvatabar, to be thy husband until death, according to the new faith of 'one body and one soul?'"

"I will."

The deed was done. Around the throne swept a cyclone of twin-souls resolved on matrimony. In their bewildering flight they became radiant with strange transformations of feeling and gesture, and their songs symbolized the intensity of the great crisis that had arrived in the history of the nation.

All around the amphitheatre rose the enormous multitude, as one soul, shouting their joy. The guns of the fortress volleyed their thunders, and the first act of the great drama ended amid the shouting of armed hosts, the singing of twin-souls, and the hosannas of the multitude.

The second scene was perhaps still more impressive. The grand chamberlain of the palace Cleperelyum had put into his phonograph beside us a coil containing the charter of coronation. Fitting a megaphone to the phonograph, there issued the following proclamation from the instrument, like a blast of music:

Charter of Coronation of Their Majesties Lexington and Lyone, King and Queen of Atvatabar.

The crown and throne of the realm of Atvatabar, heretofore possessed in the persons of their ex-majesties King Aldemegry Bhoolmakar and Queen Toplissy, being now declared vacant by reason of the desertion, flight, deposition, and defeat of said ex-majesties, and said crown and throne of Atvatabar being now possessed, both by conquest and by will of the people, in the persons of their majesties Lexington and Lyone, King and Queen of Atvatabar, now, therefore, we, the priests, nobles, statesmen, and commanders of army and navy, as representatives of the people, do hereby confirm said possession of the crown and throne of this realm, by placing upon the head of Lexington and upon the head of Lyone their respective crowns as King and Queen of Atvatabar, and do hereby render both king and queen equal loyalty, fealty, and homage, as the true and rightful sovereigns of Atvatabar.

(Signed)

Starbottle, Goiloor of Calnogor
   First Minister of the Government
Charka, Pontiff of Remeliorism, Goiloor of Egyplosis
Thoubool, Goiloose of Egyplosis
Rackiron, Goiloor of Swondab
   Commander-in-Chief of the Army
Wallace, Admiral of the Fleet
Yermoul, Lord of Art, Goiloor of Gnaphisthasia
Grasnagallipas, Commander-in-Chief of Bockhockids
Lapalme, Goiloor of Kioram
Pra, Minister of Police
Nototherboc, Minister of Naval Affairs
Goldrock, Royal Treasurer
Dr Merryferry, Minister of Foreign Affairs
Flathootly, Minister of War
Gerolio, Vice-Commander of the Army
Coltonobory, Vice-Commander of Bockhockids

During the declamation of the megaphone the pontiff Charka raised the crown to my head, while his consort Thoubool raised the crown of the queen to Lyone's head. We sat thus crowned amid the tremendous excitement. The guns of the fortress shook the Bormidophia with their explosions. The people shouted: "Life, health, and prosperity to our sovereign lord and lady, Lexington and Lyone, King and Queen of Atvatabar!" Men heard no sweeter music than the coronation march executed by a thousand instruments. I realized as I sat with Lyone beneath the throne of the gods a portion of that immeasurable feeling of being universally exalted,

WE SAT THUS CROWNED AMID THE TREMENDOUS EXCITEMENT. THE PEOPLE
SHOUTED "LIFE, HEALTH, AND PROSPERITY, TO OUR SOVEREIGN LORD
AND LADY, LEXINGTON AND LYONE, KING AND QUEEN OF ATVATABAR."

universally loved, universally adored. It is true, the fervour of idolatry for Lyone had largely subsided, but in its stead came a more perfect loyalty of soul and body on the part of priest and priestess. Souls that had balanced themselves, as it were, on the edge of a sword, once more stood on the solid earth.

The magnificence of royalty, which kings born to the purple but rarely feel, was ours. Our sudden good fortune unveiled to us the splendours of power, and riches, and honour. The people themselves, enchanted with the product of their own abnegation, made their obeisance to us as to gods.

Lyone grew perceptibly paler with the intensity of her excitement; her breast rose and fell more rapidly, as the soarings of song told her that her supreme realization of life and fortune as goddess had not wholly died with her apostasy, but that a new life no less glorious had begun.

As for myself, seated on the focus of human endeavour, it thrilled me to think what power of realization I possessed for things I had considered impossible and unattainable. I determined that art should sound the abysses of the inexpressible and bring from thence radiant symbols of all things, clothed with imagination and emotion. Invention would still further extend man's empire over matter. Soul-culture and spirit-power would be cultivated in a reformed Egyplosis. Lyone, mystical and divine, would ever rule queen of hearts with the sorcery of her beauty.

CHAPTER 58

The Death of Bhoolmakar

General Flathootly, with his command of 10,000 *fletyemings*, who was ordered to pursue and capture the ex-king Bhoolmakar, returned to Calnogor after a month's absence to report the death of King Bhoolmakar and Koshnili, together with several hundred of their followers, and the capture of several thousand *wayleals* as prisoners.

At a special interview with the general I requested him to report the story of his defeat of the king's troops and the death of the king.

"Well, yer majesty," said Flathootly, "Oi must first of all congratulate you on ascendin' the throne of the inimy. It was the shmartest bit of work Oi've seen iver since Oi lift the other wurruld."

"The troops behaved nobly," I said, "but I am all anxiety to hear how you captured the king."

"Well, thin, yer majesty, Oi kim up to him at a place called Gapthis, about 1,500 miles from here, away beyant on the wild say-shore."

"Had he a large force with him?" I asked.

"Bedad an' he had. He had a body-guard of about 5,000 *wayleals*, but shure, we made short work of the flyin' sojers."

"Well, tell me exactly what happened," I said.

"Troth, an' Oi will, yer majesty; shure our flyin' sailors are darlin' fellows! We skirmished up to the inimy until we got him between us an' the say an' thin we fell to. The bloody rascals tried to spear us, an' did kill about a dozen or two of the bhoys, but we touched thim up lively wid our pitchforks, an' begorra they didn't loike that at all, at all.

"A wee red-faced captain called out that they were goin' to fight for their king to the last.'How long are ye goin' to last yerself, sonny?' says Oi, an' afore the words were out of me mouth somebody laid the wee fellow out as nate as a funeral. Well, we fell upon thim front an' rear, as the sayin' is, an' be jabers, Oi killed a man wid the first blow.

"''Walk right into thim!' Oi shouted, an' there we wor, fightin' an' slashin' an' killin' wan another as if it wor a mere matther of business. If the king's sojers flew up, why, we flew up too, an' chased thim down ag'in. It was loike a pandemonium of fightin' cocks.

"There was a big fellow who made a slash at me wid his sword, but Oi lifted him on me fork, an' he very nicely showed me the whites of his eyes. The best part of the performance was ould Bhooly, who had himself in the middle of his body-guard, an', waving a toy sword, asked his kind friends to kill us.

"Well, to make a long shtory short, the inimy being very badly beaten, threw up their arms, an' we captured the entire lot, excipt about five hundred *wayleals* who flew away as fast as their heels cud carry thim."

"How did the king conduct himself when captured?" I inquired.

"He came up to me, an' bowin' very nicely, offered me his sword. He said he was glad to surrender to a brave giniral an' hoped Oi would give him the honours of war.

"''Be jabers, Oi will that,' said Oi;'but that'll be afther we thry ye by coort-martial. But where's Mrs. Bhooly?' says Oi.

"''Does Your Excellency mean her late majesty?' said Bhooly; 'if so, Oi regret to say the unhappy fate which has overtaken both myself and my counthry prostrated her so much that she died.'

"''Well, thin,' said Oi, 'where's that other conspirator, Koshnili?'

"''Oi am here, Your Excellency,' said he, steppin' forward an' han-din' me his sword, 'an' Oi also surrender.'

"''You do well,' said Oi, 'to give up yer sword, for it saves me the throuble of takin' it from you.

"''An' now, me rascals,' Oi said, 'we're goin' to save the throuble of lookin' afther you by thryin' you by coort-martial. Let the coort be formed,' said Oi, 'an' bring forth the prisoners.' The king's sojers were disarmed, an' their wings taken off, an' were assimbled in a circle undher guard. Bhooly an' Koshnili, undher a special guard, stood in the middle of the ring.

311

"'Now, bhoys,' said Oi, 'fair play an' no favour. Who has got a charge agin' the prisoners?' Wid that, wan of me min stepped forward an' said that Bhooly an' Koshnili had organized resistance to a change of government an' religion, thereby blockin' the wheels of reform, an' furthermore had conspired to murdher, an', be jabers, did murdher, her holiness the goddess, of blessed memory, who, although alive ag'in, was undoubtedly kilt.

"When Bhooly an' Koshnili heard that the goddess was alive ag'in their knees knocked together wid fear.

"'This is a terrible charge agin' ye both,' said Oi. 'Oi don't know which offince is the greatest—killin' a dacent goddess or blockin' the wheels of reform; annyhow, the wan crime is as bad as the other. Who supports this charge?' Oi added in thunderin' tones.

"Well, ivery sojer on the spot volunteered to give evidence as to the blockin' of the wheels of reform, but nobody saw the murdher committed.

"'Now,' said Oi, addressin' the prisoners, 'did yez murdher the goddess or did yez not? By yer sowls, tell the truth. Guilty or not guilty?'

"'Guilty,' said both prisoners.

"'Thin, by yer own mouths be ye condimned,' said Oi. 'The sintince of this coort is that ye both be beheaded on the mortal spot.'"

"I think, Flathootly," said I, "that you rather exceeded your duty in so hastily condemning the prisoners. You should have brought them to Calnogor for proper trial and execution."

"Shure, Oi knew that, but, to tell yer majesty the truth, it wudn't have added to yer credit to have ordhered the execution of Bhooly, an' so Oi took the responsibility of the whole thing on meself. Oi made Bhooly an' Koshnili kneel down, an' a sojer tied their hands behind their backs. Then Oi ordhered a *wayleal* to behead thim wid their own swords. Afther some hot work the heads av both murdherers rolled on the ground."

"Why didn't you shoot them or kill them at once with your spears?"

"Oi considered it too aisy a death for thim. Oi didn't want thim to die widout knowin' they were gittin' hurt."

I forgave Flathootly his too hasty execution of the ex-king, as he had undoubtedly saved me a very disagreeable duty, and the hasty taking off of his ex-majesty prevented any demonstration in his favour.

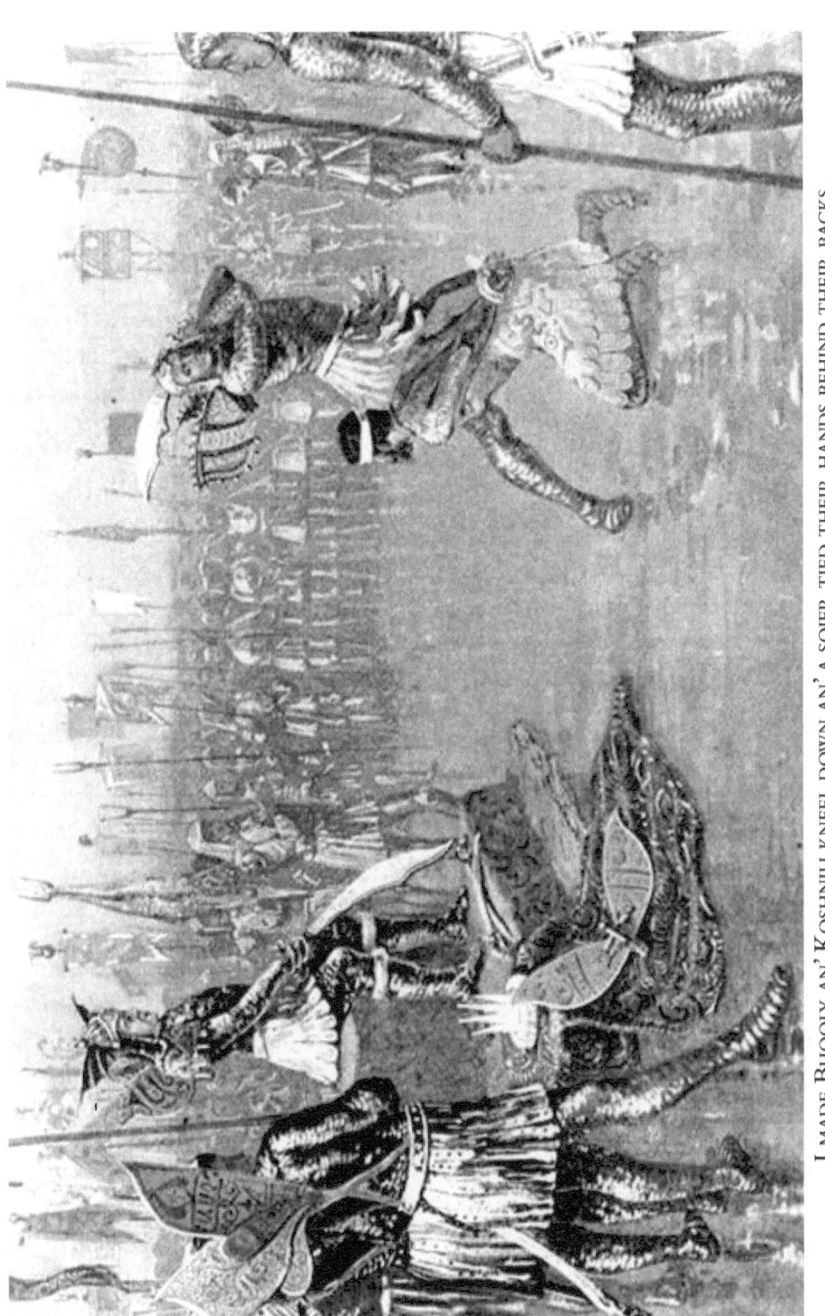

I made Bhooly an' Koshnili kneel down an' a sojer tied their hands behind their backs. Then I ordhered a wayleal to behead them wid their own swords.

To assure the people of my anxiety for a popular government, I issued a proclamation ordering a general election, to create a new Borodemy in place of the assembly whose members had disappeared, or were made prisoners of war, or were dead. In thus providing for a constitutional government, I granted the nation not only all its ancient privileges, but added new and more important measures of political liberty.

As the revenues of Atvatabar amounted to $8,000,000,000 per annum, there was no danger of myself or comrades of the *Polar King* falling short of handsome revenues.

The re-establishment of the government, the reorganization of the army, navy, and police, together with the care of the palaces of Calnogor and Tanje and the new ritual for the Bormidophia and Egyplosis, occupied my attention for a longer period than I at first contemplated. While these things were being accomplished I gave a grand public reception and royal banquet to Captain Adams and Sir John Forbes and the officers and seamen of the ships *Mercury* and *Aurora Borealis*, in acknowledgment of their great services to our cause. At the same time I did not forget to give our friends a more solid proof of my gratitude in the shape of a large bounty in gold.

CHAPTER 59

The History Concluded

I think it is right that I should conclude the history of the conquest of Atvatabar with my being crowned king of the realm.

I at once assumed my functions as ruler of Atvatabar. I was supreme commander of the army and grand admiral of the fleet. In
council with the ministers of the government appointed by the
Borodemy, I caused the adoption of many beneficent laws, calculated to make my people prosperous and happy.

Hushnoly soon departed, with his retinue of twin-souls, to
found a new Egyplosis on the sphere of Hilar, with Zooly-Soase
as goddess. It was with great grief that I parted with these beloved friends. Hushnoly and his flock were not to be persuaded that
nature herself was hostile to their esoteric practices; so, to avoid
antagonism, it was best that we should part. I promised Hushnoly
that, together with Lyone, I would visit his globe some time in the
future and see how his colony progressed. He was an enthusiast
who required a great many defeats from fortune before he could
see the fatal defects of his social and religious system.

The grand sorcerer, as the pontiff of Remeliorism, or the ethics
of nature, achieved a triumph in restoring Egyplosis to the reign of
order, truth, justice, benevolence, and temperance. In time I hoped
to see the Christian faith rule the souls of those who had so recent-
ly worshipped themselves under the guise of Harikar, the universal
human soul. I was anxious to see men and women possessing that
serene poise of passion that alone can sustain virile action. Lyone
herself was the first to be convinced that the human soul, with its
limitations, its narrowness, its impatience, its selfishness, its arro-
gance, its cruelty, was a very inferior deity. It was true that rare ideal

315

joys might be purchased for a brief time under the old regime, but they were only purchased at an immense price, out of all proportion to the value received, and their possession produced a sickly sublimity totally unfitting the soul for the practical duties of life.

Captain Adams and Sir John Forbes, excited at my good fortune, declared themselves anxious, with my consent, to explore the further hemisphere of the interior planet, in the interests of science, discovery, commerce, and possibly conquest. They were anxious to discover the continents that lie above and beyond Atvatabar, surrounded by unknown Plutusian seas, and bear to their respective countries some signal trophies of their daring and prowess in the internal world.

It was arranged that on their return to Kioram, the *Polar King*, with myself and Lyone on board, should sail with the *Mercury* and *Aurora Borealis* for the United States. The sailing of the three vessels up New York Bay would be a historic event, and great would be the curiosity of the American people to see the Goddess of Atvatabar and our retinue of *wayleals* as proof of the existence of *Bilbimtesirol*, the interior world.

And now, my dear reader, we must part for the present. By a change of plans on the part of Captain Adams, the *Mercury*, the vessel that will bear the manuscript of my adventures in the interior world, is already waiting to start on her voyage. I regret that many strange things have been left unsaid. Many extraordinary experiences have been omitted, because I am desirous that this brief history of the happiness that befell me and my devoted sailors in Atvatabar should be published without delay, to allay the natural curiosity excited in the outer world by the story of our discovery of Plutusia.

You may possibly feel a desire to know the future fortunes of Queen Lyone and myself in a part of the world hitherto undreamed of, and when I again address you I hope to describe our future experiences on the throne of Atvatabar. We purpose to apply a liberal portion of the vast wealth of our kingdom to the pursuit of invention, art, and spirituality, preserving and enlarging the existing palaces of invention and art and the palaces of Egyplosis as institutions for the development of the soul and its attributes of spirit power. It will be our purpose to extend to the utmost limits the empire of

"The love letter."

mind over matter in developing invention. In art, we will, by means of its manifold radiant symbols, reproduce every idea of the soul shaped by sentiment and imagination, and in sounding the abysses of the heart express what is considered the inexpressible.

In spirituality, the science and art of soul and its manifestations in the body, and after the temporary or complete severance therefrom, will be investigated on a much wider basis than ever before, and spirit power, apart from the worship of soul as deity, will be developed and elaborated into an enduring force, possessing creative energy. What boundless empire of life will not such ideas realize, and how entrancing the story of such discoveries in the interior world of the soul!

I may also, dear reader, request you to accompany me to other undiscovered realms of Plutusia, where, according to report, exist fairy-lands, peopled with strange, fantastic races of men and women, as well as fabulous animals, with characteristics surpassing the wildest dreams of fancy.

As shown on the map of the interior world, which forms the frontispiece of this volume, many more continents remain yet unknown to me, to explore which will be my ambition. If the rumours I have heard of semi-spiritual men and semi-human monsters that dwell in tropical environments, where mountains rise so high that there is no weight on their summits, and where torrents of water roll upward, sweeping away villages in their path; of rocks of gold suspended in the air; of tribes dwelling on floating islands of jewels in the empyrean, and of a thousand still stranger places and peoples, where every fantasy of the imagination can be produced in reality by spirit power, then, indeed, the story of my adventures will develop the soul of the age with a profound delight.

I therefore bid *adieu* to you, dear reader, in the hope of meeting you again, to feast you with these wonders. I hope to have you accompany me on the *Polar King*, which, after a season of repair and refitment, will most assuredly be launched for a still more adventurous voyage on the waters of the interior sea. How many books have been written on the discovery of the western hemisphere by Columbus, while, as yet, but one has been written about the interior sphere, a region not less important than the outer earth, whose geographical features are now for the first time revealed to human eyes! What a wonder it would be if one could travel to the moon or the planet Mars and return to the earth to tell of all that he had seen or heard on those distant spheres! Here indeed is no less a miracle that for ages two vast planets have existed each unknown to the other, although only a thousand miles apart, with the means of communication possessing but few difficulties to be overcome. The mutual discovery of two such worlds has opened up a future for the human race that may well strike one dumb with its splendour. It has conferred on the meanest individual a glory, a birthright of the spirit, as vast as the proportions of the twin-planet. I will not further anticipate the future, and for the present will ask you to accept from Lyone and myself a courteous farewell.

LEONAUR

ALSO FROM LEONAUR
AVAILABLE IN SOFTCOVER OR HARDCOVER WITH DUST JACKET

THE EMPIRE OF THE AIR: 1 *by George Griffiths*—*The Angel of the Revolution*—a rich brew that calls to mind Verne's tales of futuristic wars while being original, visionary, exciting and technologically prescient.

THE EMPIRE OF THE AIR: 2 *by George Griffiths*—*Olga Romanoff or, The Syren of the Skies*—the sequel to *The Angel of the Revolution*—a future Earth in which nation states are given full self determination when the Aerians, the descendants of 'The Brotherhood of Freedom,' who have policed world peace for more than a century, decide they are mature enough to have outgrown war.

THE INTERPLANETARY ADVENTURES OF DR KINNEY *by Homer Eon Flint*—*The Lord of Death, The Queen of Life, The Devolutionist & The Emancipatrix.*

ARCOT, MOREY & WADE *by John W. Campbell, Jr.*—The Complete, Classic Space Opera Series—*The Black Star Passes, Islands of Space, Invaders from the Infinite.*

CHALLENGER & COMPANY *by Arthur Conan Doyle*—The Complete Adventures of Professor Challenger and His Intrepid Team-*The Lost World, The Poison Belt, The Land of Mists, The Disintegration Machine* and *When the World Screamed.*

GARRETT P. SERVISS' SCIENCE FICTION *by Garrett P. Serviss*—Three Interplanetary Adventures including the unauthorised sequel to H. G. Wells' *War of the Worlds-Edison's Conquest of Mars, A Columbus of Space, The Moon Metal.*

JUNK DAY *by Arthur Sellings*—". . . . his finest novel was his last, Junk Day, a post-holocaust tale set in the ruins of his native London and peopled with engrossing character types . . . . perhaps grimmer than his previous work but pointedly more energetic." *The Encyclopedia of Science Fiction*

KIPLING'S SCIENCE FICTION *by Rudyard Kipling*—Science Fiction & Fantasy stories by a Master Storyteller including 'As East As A,B,C' 'With The Night Mail'.

DARKNESS AND DAWN 1—THE VACANT WORLD *by George Allen England*—A Novel of a future New York.

DARKNESS AND DAWN 2—BEYOND THE GREAT OBLIVION *by George Allen England*—The last vestiges of humanity set out across America's devastated landscape in search of their dream.

DARKNESS AND DAWN 3—THE AFTER GLOW *by George Allen England*—Somewhere near the Great Lakes, 1000 years from now. Beneath our planet's surface tribes of near human albino warriors eke out an existence in a hostile environment.

LEONAUR

ALSO FROM LEONAUR
AVAILABLE IN SOFTCOVER OR HARDCOVER WITH DUST JACKET

THE COLLECTED SCIENCE FICTION AND FANTASY OF STANLEY G. WEINBAUM 1—INTERPLANETARY ODYSSEYS *by Stanley G. Weinbaum*—Classic Tales of Interplanetary Adventure Including: A Martian Odyssey, its Sequel Valley of Dreams, the Complete 'Ham' Hammond Stories and Others.

THE COLLECTED SCIENCE FICTION AND FANTASY OF STANLEY G. WEINBAUM 2—OTHER EARTHS *by Stanley G. Weinbaum*—Classic Futuristic Tales Including: *Dawn of Flame* & its Sequel The Black Flame, plus The Revolution of 1960 & Others.

THE COLLECTED SCIENCE FICTION AND FANTASY OF STANLEY G. WEINBAUM 3—STRANGE GENIUS *by Stanley G. Weinbaum*—Classic Tales of the Human Mind at Work Including the Complete Novel The New Adam, the 'van Manderpootz' Stories and Others.

THE COLLECTED SCIENCE FICTION AND FANTASY OF STANLEY G. WEINBAUM 4—THE BLACK HEART *by Stanley G. Weinbaum*—Classic Strange Tales Including: the Complete Novel The Dark Other, Plus Proteus Island and Others.

THE COLLECTED SCIENCE FICTION & FANTASY OF JACK LONDON 1—BEFORE ADAM & OTHER STORIES *by Jack London*—included in this Volume Before Adam The Scarlet Plague A Relic of the Pliocene When the World Was Young The Red One Planchette A Thousand Deaths Goliah A Curious Fragment The Rejuvenation of Major Rathbone.

THE COLLECTED SCIENCE FICTION & FANTASY OF JACK LONDON 2—THE IRON HEEL & OTHER STORIES *by Jack London*—included in this Volume The Iron Heel The Enemy of All the World The Shadow and the Flash The Strength of the Strong The Unparalleled Invasion The Dream of Debs.

THE COLLECTED SCIENCE FICTION & FANTASY OF JACK LONDON 3—THE STAR ROVER & OTHER STORIES *by Jack London*—included in this Volume The Star Rover The Minions of Midas The Eternity of Forms The Man With the Gash.

THE CRETAN TEAT *by Brian Aldiss*—The Cretan Teat is a wry and comic novel that interweaves its own fiction with an inner fiction about the discovery of a Byzantine painting of the Mother of the Blessed Virgin Mary suckling the infant Jesus and a fake ikon that becomes an instrument of Nemesis.

LEONAUR

ALSO FROM LEONAUR
AVAILABLE IN SOFTCOVER OR HARDCOVER WITH DUST JACKET

THE CIVIL WAR NOVELS: 1 *by Joseph A. Altsheler*—*The Guns of Bull Run &* *The Guns of Shiloh*—the first and second novels of a series of eight adventures which follow the momentous events, campaigns and battles of the great American Civil War between the Northern and Southern states.

THE CIVIL WAR NOVELS: 2 *by Joseph A. Altsheler*—*The Scouts of Stonewall* & *The Sword of Antietam*—the third and fourth novels of a series of nine adventures which follow the momentous events, campaigns and battles of the great American Civil War between the Northern and Southern states.

THE CIVIL WAR NOVELS: 3 *by Joseph A. Altsheler*—*The Star of Gettysburg* & *The Rock of Chickamauga*—the fifth and sixth novels of a series of nine adventures which follow the momentous events, campaigns and battles of the great American Civil War between the Northern and Southern states.

THE CIVIL WAR NOVELS: 4 *by Joseph A. Altsheler*—*The Shades of the Wilderness* & *The Tree of Appomattox*—the seventh and eighth novels of a series of nine adventures which follow the momentous events, campaigns and battles of the great American Civil War between the Northern and Southern states.

THE CIVIL WAR NOVELS: 5 *by Joseph A. Altsheler*—*Before the Dawn: a Story* *of the Fall of Richmond*—the last of a series of nine adventures which follow the momentous events, campaigns and battles of the great American Civil War between the Northern and Southern states.

THE FRENCH & INDIAN WAR NOVELS: 1 *by Joseph A. Altsheler*—*The Hunters of the Hills* & *The Shadow of the North*—In this three volume, six novel set the story of the war, with many of its real life characters, is told through the adventures of its principal characters, Robert Lennox, the hunter Willet and his Indian companion Tayoga.

THE FRENCH & INDIAN WAR NOVELS: 2 *by Joseph A. Altsheler*—*The Rulers of the Lakes* & *The Masters of the Peaks*—In this three volume, six novel set the story of the war, with many of its real life characters, is told through the adventures of its principal characters, Robert Lennox, the hunter Willet and his Indian companion Tayoga.

THE FRENCH & INDIAN WAR NOVELS: 1 *by Joseph A. Altsheler*—*The Lords* *of the Wild & The Sun of Quebec*—In this three volume, six novel set the story of the war, with many of its real life characters, is told through the adventures of its principal characters, Robert Lennox, the hunter Willet and his Indian companion Tayoga.

LEONAUR

ALSO FROM LEONAUR
AVAILABLE IN SOFTCOVER OR HARDCOVER WITH DUST JACKET

THE LONG PATROL *by George Berrie*—A Novel of Light Horsemen from Gallipoli to the Palestine campaign of the First World War.

NAPOLEONIC WAR STORIES *by Arthur Quiller-Couch*—Tales of soldiers, spies, battles & sieges from the Peninsular & Waterloo campaingns.

THE FIRST DETECTIVE *by Edgar Allan Poe*—The Complete Auguste Dupin Stories—The Murders in the Rue Morgue, The Mystery of Marie Rogêt & The Purloined Letter.

THE COMPLETE DR NIKOLA—MAN OF MYSTERY: 1 *by Guy Boothby*—*A Bid for Fortune & Dr Nikola Returns*—Guy Boothby's Dr.Nikola adventures continue to fascinate readers and enthusiasts of crime and mystery fiction because—in the manner of Raffles, the gentleman cracksman—here is character far removed from the uncompromising goodness of Holmes and Watson or the uncompromising evil of Professor Moriarty.

THE COMPLETE DR NIKOLA—MAN OF MYSTERY: 2 *by Guy Boothby*—*The Lust of Hate, Dr Nikola's Experiment & Farewell, Nikola*—Guy Boothby's Dr.Nikola adventures continue to fascinate readers and enthusiasts of crime and mystery fiction because—in the manner of Raffles, the gentleman cracksman—here is character far removed from the uncompromising goodness of Holmes and Watson or the uncompromising evil of Professor Moriarty.

THE CASEBOOKS OF MR J. G. REEDER: BOOK 1 *by Edgar Wallace*—*Room 13, The Mind of Mr J. G. Reeder* and *Terror Keep*—Edgar Wallace's sleuth—whose territory is the London of the 1920s—is an unlikely figure, more bank clerk than detective in appearance, ever wearing his square topped bowler, frock coat, cravat and muffler, Mr Reeder is usually inseparable from his umbrella.

THE CASEBOOKS OF MR J. G. REEDER: BOOK 2 *by Edgar Wallace*—*Red Aces, Mr J. G. Reeder Returns, The Guv'nor* and *The Man Who Passed*—Edgar Wallace's sleuth—whose territory is the London of the 1920s—is an unlikely figure, more bank clerk than detective in appearance, ever wearing his square topped bowler, frock coat, cravat and muffler, Mr Reeder is usually inseparable from his umbrella.

THE COMPLETE FOUR JUST MEN: VOLUME 1 *by Edgar Wallace*—*The Four Just Men, The Council of Justice & The Just Men of Cordova*—disillusioned with a world where the wicked and the abusers of power perpetually go unpunished, the Just Men set about to rectify matters according to their own standards, and retribution is dispensed on swift and deadly wings.